Emotional Roulette

Also by Margaret Burt

Sweet Dreams Are Made of This

Emotional Roulette

MARGARET BURT

FLAME
Hodder & Stoughton

First published in 2001 by Hodder and Stoughton
A division of Hodder Headline
A Flame Book

10 9 8 7 6 5 4 3 2 1

A CIP catalogue record for this book is available
from the British Library.

ISBN 0 340 76664 6

Typeset by Palimpsest Book Production Limited,
Polmont, Stirlingshire
Printed and bound in Great Britain by
Mackays of Chatham plc, Chatham, Kent

Hodder and Stoughton
A division of Hodder Headline
338 Euston Road
London NW1 3BH

To Geoff Yates, with my love

Acknowledgements

Thank you, Geoff, for never letting me down and for sharing my own visions so generously. Thank you, Dad, and Ann. Thank you, Rosemarie, Tony, Jim, Chris, Derek and Peter. I could never forget you – the funniest and the strangest casino training school ever. Now you see that I wasn't trying to deny my past! Thanks, Newcastle, for providing the perfect, sparkling, night-time atmosphere I needed for this book. Thank you so much Edwards Fuglewicz literary agency – Ros, Helenka, Jo and Julia – for providing inspiration, support and entirely appropriate demands, as and when needed. I really value your advice. Thank you, Sue Fletcher at Hodder, and Swati, Karen and Lucy, for all of your very hard work and patience. Thank you Stephen Mellor, for reading this novel, and for being incisive, enthusiastic and kind when giving me feedback. Good luck with your own novel! So many thanks to Dave, Jane, Roger, Susan, Sheena and others, for on-going friendship, encouragement and support. Diane Kaylor, thanks for the exchange of thousands of ideas (at thousands of terrible parties) over the years. Thank you, my lovely village neighbours, for being my home and such a crucial part of my life. Thanks Enid, for all of your help, and Andrew, Linda and Diane, and many other staff, and students, at Northumberland College for your enthusiasm about, and interest in, my writing. Thanks Nick and Barry, for the bike info. (I would have been totally lost without it!). Thanks to everyone who wrote to tell me they liked my first novel, I really do appreciate it, and thank you to everyone who has bought this one.

I hope you like it!

Contents

In a Lonely Place

1. The Street

'Angelo, touched by the angels.'
'Sit down here with me, look into Angelo Paulillo's
eyes, and you will fall in love from your armchair.'

This is a story of the night and it is night now, brightened only by my lamp, my torch, and the words inside the petrol-soaked square of paper that I turn over with the matches in my hand. Midnight. Flakes of blood-red rust fall down on to my skin while the wind sings like a siren through the cracks in the walls, then spits rain on to my hair and howls. The stench of petrol has seeped into my clothes.

I *miss* her. I miss them both. And I really want to tell you about it.

I roll my story back like a Turkish rug at my feet. Pictures of my life, my loves, of my converted church, the casino, Christina, me and Mic, are hand-knotted into it and I stare at the figures in the half-light, forming words to tell my tale to you. My dark red love story. I see the rug so clearly in my mind. I touch it and its redness touches me – the redness of fire, women, blood, and blooms and heat.

Its redness touches me like Christina touches . . . touched me.

Please, let me tell you about it. I don't know what else to do.

Well, when you hear about some of the experiences that we had, some of the dreams we shared, I know you'll think it was strange. Weird, then. But you weren't with him. You didn't see his eyes and you didn't see through his eyes. Sit down here with me, look into Angelo Paulillo's eyes, and you will fall in love from your armchair. Because Angelo was bitter chocolate dipped in cream. Rich. You will not want to move from your armchair, once you've felt what I felt. Hot! But at the same time, he was as cool as iced Coke to a woman finishing a power-walk. And this to a girl who'd just run a sticky marathon!

I was more than thirsty for him. You get the message?

But from the start, there were so many things I couldn't be certain about. Why did he step in on that first day like that, when nobody else dared to, for a start? Did he even see me then? I didn't know at first.

I only knew that I'd seen him, for sure.

That first time I saw her, I didn't actually *see* her. Not properly, I mean. But she saw me. Let me make out those first few patterns on the rug for you. The meeting.

I was just walking through the Town on my way to work. (Newcastle is a city, but everybody calls it 'the Town' or 'the Toon'.) I was on an early that day and I had a couple of shirts to buy from the shops before my shift. The Town was fairly buzzing: pubs, shops, people, noises and jostling everywhere. Then I stopped short. I had to. There was a solid circle of backs blocking my way, wind swirling around. Intrigue. Scuffling noises and jagged, raw breathing were at its centre. Evil.

His voice came first, between laboured breaths. 'Bitch! Fucking bitch!' Male, metallic and angry. Half mad. I peered over a ginger-haired girl's head so that I could see what they were all standing watching. Or who.

He was wellying her, kicking down into her, hard, a young bloke and a dark girl. 'My cross . . . you've lost my cross . . .' His breath was going; he was wearing himself out on her ribs. 'My fucking cross!' She was curled up like a bean, like a baby, on the pavement, with her arms up over her head and some straight brown hair sticking out. All the others were just standing in this great circle, watching like it was some sort of sick wrestling match. *'You could do nothing to help?'* Her voice came first. *'You could do nothing?'*

And then Mic switched into my mind. Mic. I could never, *never* let it happen again.

I pushed through the audience and wrenched boot boy's arm back, but hard. Really hard and sudden. That was my first glimpse of his face, close to mine, of his great eyes, glaring, his greasy hair and the slaver all around his mouth. A chemical smell was coming off him, rising off his clothes, his breath. Dangerous. Quick.

'I'm a copper, mate,' I said quietly, but I was gripping his wrist tight as a mastiff's jaws. 'Off duty.' His head kind of twitched towards me. His eyes sussed out mine, timing the exchange of stares, then narrowing. I spoke again. 'Just leave the girl alone.' I sounded like a macho character from some corny 1940s 'Get out of the city!'-type gangster film, but it did the trick. My glance held steady. Five seconds passed and his eyes just edged away.

Still gripping his wrist, I noticed that a girl from the crowd – I just got a shot of blonde hair and a trace of CK One – had shown some guts at last and was pulling the curled up, beaten dog of a girl off the pavement, tugging her away from the man (if man's the right word) with the big boots, away from the crowd. The bloke's wrist dropped and some of his energy went. Listen, I swear I could see it coming off him in waves. The shoulders went down, the head went back and the beaten girl was gone. I dropped the hard man's arm.

The audience split to let him through and he was off,

giving out, 'Bastard, bastard,' over his shoulder as he swaggered off. I breathed as if for the first time, and headed off towards work. From far away I could still hear him shouting, his voice full of dirt and tin. 'Fucking probation! Fucking bastard could have fucking ruined my probation, man.' Then, 'Bastard,' but harder now that the distance was wider. 'Fucking bastard.' I turned around to give him the stare.

The popcorn crowd had left the ring and I saw him standing there with the dark girl; she was right next to him, waiting for him to finish, glaring at *me*, shaking. Puce face, trying not to cry. Jesus. I just walked away. What else could I do? Some hero. Some hope. Film noir, I thought. *In a Lonely Place.*

It's funny, but when I was younger, I'd always thought that it was women who were more closely connected to the harshest things in life: birth and madness, blood and death. Mess. I'd always thought that it was women who led men into the darker, uncharted places, like Eurydice tempting Orpheus down into Hades to find her. It often is. But that wasn't the way it was between us, between her and me. Because that was just the first time that I led her into a dark place, a *dangerous* place, though I didn't mean to.

I was shaking as well, but not because of boot boy. All I could think about was Mic, and what happened to Mic. Why there was no one there for him that day.

Where was my big heroic act then?

I was shrivelled with nerves that day, absolutely shrivelled. Dead scared. So I spent the whole morning on my make-up mask. I hardly dared leave my flat for the Town. Wimp City! My interview at the casino was for half-one, but I made sure that I was heading for the Town before half-twelve, dressed like I guessed a dealer in a casino should be dressed. The last thing I wanted was to be late.

I was stamping out my 17 times table as I made my way through the Bigg Market: 1x17=17, 2x17=34, 3x17=51. Just in case they asked me, like. 4x17=68. And then I stepped out of the Market and in to a circle of onlookers, watching with the crowd like I was at a baseball game or in one of those gigantic Roman arenas from Michael's dad's Spartacus, *you know, the ones you draw diagrams of at school. The Colosseum. The lion's den. Gusts of wind pushed me to my place in the ring. I'll spare you the description – I'm sure you know the sort of scene – and just before this, I'd found myself alone with a pretty big-mouthed lion myself. Some Geordie men really know how to make a show, but it's not often that a* real *hero steps in to help. Spectacular. It made me braver than I knew I could be as well. I thought of Rose, going back down into the bowels of the Titanic to rescue Jack, before that choppy bit with the axe when he risks his wrists. But wouldn't you risk the water, the depths, for lovely Leonardo or corseted Kate? One look at Angelo's face was enough to make up* my *mind.*

And he even sounded like the hero out of a really classy old black and white film. Dead strong. 'I'm a copper, mate,' he said. Deep. 'Just leave the girl alone.' Seemed more like a fire fighter to me, all cool and collected in the face of emergency, not to mention the sooty-black little waves of hair. But his eyes were the first things I noticed. Magnetic, totally magnetic. What with the jet-black hair and the dark, dark eyes, he didn't look like he belonged in Newcastle at all – Italian was my first thought. La Vita E Bella! *He hardly spoke, action was more his thing, but when he did speak the accent was Geordie but soft, like. For a lad, that is. Have you ever noticed, their accents are usually worse than ours? Well, his was softer than mine. And his voice was sort of still and cool. But you knew not to cross him and you knew he meant what he said, straightaway.*

That's why I was so surprised by what, or who, *I found when I finally got to the casino for my interview. I was sitting in the reception area, waiting, my head back into my tables. (Jonty's top tip, the tables – he'd joined the last training school. Said the interview was a 'piece of piss' naturally, for a genius like him.) Doing the splits, bets covering two numbers. 5x17=85. Doing the splits, like the dancers at Sun City. Then black eyes appears all of a sudden, cool as anything, walks right down the massive* Gone with the Wind *staircase they've got there, right past me and over to the receptionist. Dead casual. I couldn't believe it. And I couldn't stop looking at him.*

This might sound stupid to you, or it might even sound familiar, I don't know, but right from the start, he seemed to have this edge of light all around his head and body and a darker edge inside that. My eyes were fixed on his face and my breath went. Why wasn't everybody in reception staring at him the way I was?

He looked right through me and walked over to the reception desk. 'Message from above, Paula?' he asked, looking up at the ceiling and doing a tiny, a really *slow half grin. The girl was all polished up – sports-car red lips, smooth white face, and jet black hair and eyebrows that looked like they'd been painted on. Dead professional she looked, at first – until she spoke to him that is, then she couldn't resist a dig.*

'Mr Andreas wants a tray of ham sandwiches and some home-made shortbread taken up to the office now, Angelo.' Then she turned and whispered in his ear, so quietly that I had to strain my head towards them to hear. 'As if the miserable old pig isn't well *porky enough to start with.' She laughed and flickered her eyes across reception towards me, all mischief. His eyes, Angelo's eyes, were dead steady; they always were. Only the minutest twitch of the lips on the left-hand side of his face showed me that he thought this was funny at all, which made old Porsche Lips laugh even more, poking his arm and flashing her shiny eyes into his face, all flirty.*

One nod in her direction and he was back off to the kitchen.

Angelo, touched by the angels, I thought, followed by 6x17=102, 7x17=119. I felt dizzy, disorientated. Vertigo. I felt like I was staring down at him from this endless Jacob's ladder of lust. Is that why they call it falling *in love, then? Then a stuffed-looking old suit showed up at the desk, so I stood up to shake his hand, walked through to his office and concentrated on my numbers, smiling and leg swivelling for the next thirty minutes. I really hate interviews, don't you?*

Not a policeman at all but a waiter. Always did look like an Italian waiter, only taller. Much taller. I thought about him all the way home, racking my brains for everything I knew about Italy. The Old World. Milan, Turin, Florence, beautiful Venice resting in its salty, salty lagoon, the Bridge of Sighs. Big beautiful Angelo Paulillo, dead salty, and little ordinary me, Christina Rae, all sighs. Four hundred bridges in Venice meant four hundred chances to connect island to land, him to me, man to woman. I did a massive *sigh* – *practically blowing some poor old woman off the pavement with the draught* – *a sigh for him, for Angelo and Italy. Brilliant. Of course I fancied him, more than that, right from the start, Jonty or no Jonty. But you've already worked that one out for yourself, haven't you?*

I'll only say this to you once, I can only stand *to say this once to anybody, but it's a really big part of Angelo's story and mine: Angelo is better looking for a man than I am for a woman. Definitely. No point in dwelling on things you can't change, but it has to be said. It's important. And I knew from the start that he would hurt me. Did that put me off? Not for one single second. Do you think it should have done?*

Angelo. Touched by the angels.

Looked right through me.

Maybe if I'd had someone to talk to when I got home, it would have been easier. If I could even have rung someone up, sent out a message, instead of receiving them all the time, on my own. I'd turned a tarot card over that morning and found the Six of Cups staring at me. 'Don't let the past detract from the present' was the message – one I know now, sitting here, I should definitely have listened to.

Still, the old church didn't seem as lonely that night as it could do. At least I had the notebook.

And I knew I'd be hearing from Mic in a few days' time.

*   *   *

I went straight back to my flat after my interview, couldn't afford any more time in town, with all those shop windows blinking at me, bars of silver-wrapped chocolate twinkling at me from every till and me with no money in my pocket. Typical. So I curled up at home with a coffee, wondering whether there'd been enough leg swivelling, fake smiling and number spinning to win me a contract at the Casino Club. I'd know soon enough: they were going to give me a ring at the weekend, after they'd finished all the other interviews. Jonty was on a late, so I knew there'd be no sight of him to disturb me; he got fed at the casino. Time for some peace.

Except there never was any peace in that flat. I know that in London, the West End of the city is where it's at. Swish and smart. Newcastle's West End is a bit different. Dangerous dump. My flat was near to Benwell: try typing 'Benwell' into a computer and it won't understand you, keeps turning it into 'Bengal'. Pretty perceptive, I'd say.

Loads of developers had bought the flats around mine as investments: you could buy one of them for four or five grand, it was that rough an area, but it was right by the city centre. So these developers had bought the flats at auction, boarded them up and had a bet with themselves that house prices would go up in the end. Losers. The whole area was dead. Dead depressing. At least you could have some fun, spending your money in a casino, I thought. (I thought then.) *I mean, that night was typical. At one point, just about the only light on in the block was mine, one lit window, reminding me of the last rotten tooth that poked out from my great-auntie's gums for twenty years until she died. A pickle stabber, my mam used to call it, neither use nor ornament. Only got in the way.*

I got up to stir some more sugar into my mug. At least you were never lonely in the flats, what with the voices from every side, when they were in, and the buzz of the traffic from down below. And the views out over the town were fantastic, as good as the views from the Quayside flats or St Peter's Basin any day. (Five grand would barely buy you a bog seat down there.)

What I liked best of all about the flats (apart from the rent, like) was being right up high in the sky with the stars. The gods. If you stuck your head out far enough, you could see all the people rushing around down below, like they were in a tiny world of their own. While you were right up there in the blackness, on your own, like a bird. High. You saw the wind pushing the clouds past, the seasons change, and then at night you saw all the stars and the ins and outs of the moon. You felt *like a star, watching the Milky Way and the Plough, the Big Dipper, and dreaming of what your own path right into the skies, or across the seas, might have to offer.*

I stuck the telly on. Dead Calm. *Dead Boring! Best not to think about the casino job, I decided. Jonty'd said they'd had loads of applications and I was hardly your prime candidate, was I, one of the notorious Raes, with my two good GCSEs, my crappy work history and my scraggy hair that hadn't quite grown out of its perm? That had been the last thing Jonty had said to me before the interview. 'For God's sake, Teen, get your hair sorted before you go. Other girls'd be seein' a counsellor over hair like yours.' Well, I'd had a trim. I wondered if he'd put in a good word for me.*

I filled in my diary, but I wasn't holding out great hopes that night.

SMALL DREAMS
Get a hairstyle that suits
Get the job at the Casino Club
If not, get more hours at the Dunston Club and look around for other jobs

BIG DREAMS
Casinos, America, Las Vegas, New York, Los Angeles and Chicago, Angelo, stretch limousines, white wine, chocolate, lots of money and heaven in general

---

Those first ones are pretty inspiring, eh? Bet you're seething *with jealousy there. And the second ones are ridiculous. Bette Midler chunked pineapples, you know, and Sean Connery polished coffins! But Bette could sing; Sean could act. What exactly could I do? Things like being a dealer in a casino, exciting things, never happen to people like me: that was my last thought, before the telly did its usual anaesthetic bit.*

I had no idea then just how exciting things were going to get.

It was pretty hard to get through those next days at the casino when I was waiting to hear from Mic the whole time, waiting while getting Mr Andreas' sandwiches ready or watching the other waiters spitting in the most miserable punters' coffee and stirring it in. Only three months before, I'd been at university. Some people would have said I was letting myself down – people who didn't understand me, that is, which was most people. I just kept my head down, my brain clear and myself busy. Felt like I was between things, that I needed to get my energy back. Renew myself. After that I could do all the things I'd planned before. In the meantime, I was glad of the peace, the normality, after everything I'd been through before.

And all that I was about to go through with her, if I had but known it then.

Well, just how wrong can you be? Christina Rae, the Queen of Chance. The phone woke me up a few days later.

'Miss Rae?' he said. I nearly squealed. I knew who it was the second I heard his voice. Dead formal, he sounded.

'Speaking,' I said. I made my voice all posh and calm.

'Mike Turner speaking. I'm happy to say that we've decided to offer you a position, Miss Rae. You were very impressive at interview.'

Impressive? Me? I wondered which bits had impressed him? Brilliant! But I kept my voice dead cool, tried to pretend I wasn't a Geordie (because Mr Turner wasn't, more your Las Vegas, or your Cockney, type). 'Thank you, Mr Turner. How kind of you to say so.'

There was a bit more of the same, some information about when the training school would start, and expenses, contracts and so on. You didn't get paid until the six-week training school was finished, but I knew that already from Jonty. Six more weeks of doing pensioners' discos part-time and singing along to Going Loco, Down in Acapulco with people pretty much like me, who'd barely been across the Tyne Bridge. Six more weeks of beer-sticky shoes, pulling pints for men with hair cream and appetites like Elvis (grease is the word) before listening to that woman in the long dress who pretended to be all different birds, doing her turn. Or was that having a turn? Fantastic! Six more weeks with nothing to look forward to but the Dunston dawn chorus singing their hearts out in the Dunston, not-so-many-of-them-are-working-now, Working Men's Club.

But it would soon be different. Because now I had a ticket into a brand new world. And which part of Disneyland are you most interested in seeing, Miss Rae? Whose autograph are you going to sign first? It was a massive leap. I could choose my future now: a little casino in Newcastle at first and then maybe one of the bigger ones in London or Birmingham. After that I might try the liners, cruising the Caribbean or the Mediterranean or the Scandinavian fjords even. Next stop, Los Angeles, City of Angels.

Who knows where it could lead? I'll let you in on a bit of one of my very favourite (and very private) scenarios. Dream on, vision one. Hello!

Christina Rae's Pismo Beach Home

Halfway between San Francisco and Los Angeles lies the beautiful Pismo Beach, a classic Californian beach town. It was here that Rudolph Valentino filmed The Sheikh and Cecil B. De Mille is reported

---

to have buried the set of *The Ten Commandments*. This is one of the only beaches in the States on which cars can be driven.

Christina Rae walks between her enormous beachside house, with its works of art and its walls of glass overlooking the coastline, and sea, laughing. She glances over her shoulder and smiles at the startlingly attractive, dark-haired man who is waving to her from the house.

Christina looks remarkably like the young Julia Roberts in her *Sleeping with the Enemy* heyday ...

... only happier. Because my version was Sleeping with the Lover, *a wonderful, glossy love story, rather than some horrible, gloomy thriller where you get all your make-up washed off and there's a load of battering and boring fuss about a few old towels. Wide-screen vision. Miramax, megavision, megavoice. Forget about* Little Voice, *LV, altogether, I said to myself. Start thinking* huge.

I'd have to get some contacts and grow my hair.

It would be like stepping inside a film.

2. Irene's

'He sez y' not t' blame y'self.'
'Stepping inside a film?'

A lot of people think these places are glamorous, somehow. Special. But there's nothing glamorous about Irene, or her house, though 'special' might be closer to the mark. Clean would've been nice. I always made sure I gave my hands a good wash after I got out and I'd never have eaten there. Sitting at that dismal table was bad enough. I pressed my elbows down into the tea cup-ringed, sticky grit, and refused Irene's offer of tea, like I always did.

'Aye, Ango, Mic sez t' tell y' y've always been a right snob,' said Irene. 'But divvn't worry y' heed, son. I never tek offence. I've never been the *Homes and Gardens* type – I knaa that well enough. Just mek yourself comfy. I've got a canny bit t' tell y', the day.'

So I did make myself 'comfy', and I breathed in the germs from her house, family and lungs, because she always did have a 'canny bit' to tell me. And because we both knew this was the only way I could get to my brother, to Mic, now. Through Irene.

Maybe when I know you better, I'll be able to tell you what Irene and Mic had to say.

*   *   *

Stepping inside a film? Glossy? Story of my life! Stepping inside a roll of cellulose, more like. Sticky, sticky, sticky! Just that first day put me right. The reception area was like something out of a film; the managers' meals were like something out of a film; the gaming tables were like something out of a film. The staff quarters were like the back rooms of the Rover's Return, thirty years ago. Christina Rae, the Queen of Coronation Street. *All the dealers who'd been there a while had these great big red lumps on their legs and ankles from the fleabites. And the punters were more flea-bitten still. (Not that I saw them for a bit, thank God. Trainees usually do early shifts, when the casino's shut.)*

For weeks I'd been imagining them all: the gorgeous women dealers in their smart long dresses, the bloke dealers in their sharp suits, the inspectors stalking around, looking all important. And the customers would be the most spectacular of all. Oh, I know that they'd spelled it out dead clear at the interview: no sex with the punters, not so much as a bit of hand holding, at any cost. But still, I could dream and I did! Dream on.

Christina Rae and the Casino Club

Christina Rae walked in through the glacial doors of Newcastle upon Tyne's Casino Club, stood in the glitter of the chandeliers and took in the scene around her. Tall, good-looking men with straight spines and black shining hair, reeking of money, dynamism and success, were crowded around the gaming tables. Women with dramatic, swept-up hairstyles stood at an adjoining table, wearing designer clothing, sipping drinks and watching the men gamble. In one corner of the casino was the whole of the Newcastle United football team, playing roulette with several well-known musicians. To Christina's left were many of Tyneside's best-known actors and a whole skyful of other stars as well. Sparkling. In between were the Casino Club's dealers, classy, unreal, floating through this glittering world of the night as if they were on roller blades.

At the very centre of this scene stood Christina, in her elegant dress and strappy sandals, gliding glamorously around her roulette

---

table, laughing at the customers' comments and pushing piles of chips
out before making well-timed and witty responses to her audience.

*Get the picture? Shiny. Who'd have guessed that I'd end up
playing 'Animal, Mineral or Vegetable?' with half the punters?
Tacky.*

*The casino was more or less empty when I walked in. The
first shiny person I saw as I walked through to the staffroom
with Mr Turner was a dealer, in a long dress – a massively
pregnant dealer with a five-foot waist (that she was scratching)
and three-inch roots. A right badger head! Gliding wasn't quite
the right word. All the money in the Casino Club obviously didn't
stretch to decent maternity pay and you don't glide in cheap,
well-stretched red jersey anyway – crackle, more like. There was
a faint sheen over her bum, where the chairs had been polishing
her dress up nicely over the months. Years.*

*'Just come in a bit early to get on with me cross stitch, Mr
Turner,' she said, over her shoulder, 'if that's all right?' I could
see some nicotine stains on the one hand and a filthy-looking novel
and a carrier bag in the other.*

*The next room I saw was the staffroom, with its burst, greasy-
looking chairs, its coffee-ringed table and its gigantic 1970s
teak-bound telly. Silver screen? And the next people were my
fellow trainees, my fellow croupiers – or 'croups' some of the girls
called themselves I found out later, like an awful sort of annoying
cough. Every one of those croupiers is a story in themself.*

Anyway, you'll hear a bit more about them in just a minute.

There were only generally two messages that came from
Mic through Irene, although she had about a thousand
different ways of saying them. That day was no different.

'Eeh, Ango, but y've had a bad week, mind y' have.
But don't y' always bring it on y'sel', son, an' that's the
truth? Watch y' jumper in that bit o' milk there, bonny
lad.'

Anybody south of Sunderland would've needed a translator: it was a struggle for me when she spoke too fast. Only Mic kept me going back there and the fact that she'd been a friend of my grandmother's. 'Mic sez t' tell y' that them heroics there the other day was bloody good telly, Ango, better than them *Gladiators*.' She squinted up her pouchy eyes, as if she was listening to him. 'Aye, an' he sez he wasn't the only one watching. Sez y've been charming th' lasses, or one lass. "Not before time, Ango," he sez. "Glued t' the box, she was." By, he's a filthy bugger! Laughing his heed off.' Mic generally was. Irene laughed away to herself, like she always did. Mic was one of her favourites, one of everybody's favourites. Thank God I hadn't lost him.

'Wait on. There's summat important t' say t' y'.' Her head tilted and she waited. 'He sez y' not t' blame y'self. An' y' not t' brood on all that stuff, in yer own heed, like. Why, he always sez that, doesn't he, Ango, but y' never listen, bonny lad, d' y'? Even after I telt y' about th' Duke – even after that – y' never listen.'

The Duke. Why did she have to bring up the Duke? I turned my head away from her.

There were more instructions, punctuated by Irene's dry cackles and fruity, germ-ridden coughs, and then she started to draw the conversation to a close. 'Time t' go then, Ango. Just one last thing.

'He sez that y' not t' forget that there's other people tryin' t' keep in touch with y'. Sez y've got t' keep y' mind open t' them.' She thought again, for a second, and then nodded. 'Aye, and y' heart, bonny lad. Y' heart an' all. Eeh, what a soft lad he is, with ye, tho' but. Anyway son, that's what he sez.'

Irene sighed. 'By, I'm parchin' fer a cup of *nice* tea.'

This was her favourite way of closing our conversation, and she always did look tired, shrunken almost, at the end of our talks, so I thanked her and left. I breathed in hard when I got into the clean air outside her rancid little house.

Irene was right, I thought, as I set off down the cigarette box-strewn path. I always did ignore a lot of what Mic said. Not exactly ignore – I wish that Mic was easier to ignore sometimes – more like couldn't take it in. Take it 'to heart', to use his words.

But I did wonder about the girl.

Well, now I bet I've got you wondering! Wondering about my exciting life at the casino, and all the glitzy people I was meeting. Not to mention old black eyes.

We'll start off with some of my new friends. Because that's what they were, right from the start. Well, to be honest, they were more like enemies right at the start, come to think of it, but that stage didn't last for long.

The first thing I noticed was that two of them were university students. Yes, I did say 'notice', because in Newcastle, and Durham's worse again, you can spot the students a mile off and you can hear the difference from ten miles off, unless they're Geordie students, as soon as one of them opens their big mouth. (Which they always do before long, gobshites – must be part of what they teach them.) The first thing I thought when I walked into that staffroom was, They're a load of snotty gets, and the second thing was, And they've all come straight out of university. They'll all have dead rich mummies and daddies. So I just sat down, on my own, twiddled my bracelet, and kept myself to myself until the manager who was going to be training us turned up.

It got a bit better then. For a load of university students, they were pretty thick. For one thing, I was the only one who'd had the sense to learn my 17 and 35 times tables before the training school started. (The only time in my life I'd done my homework!) And when it came to cutting down the chips they were total coneheads, with their brains getting in the way more than anything, carrying on like it was some kind of a scientific experiment, instead of just getting on and having a go at it. Pity there were no degrees in common sense, as my mam used to say. Maybe they were trying to look good, with all their questions and carry on, but Gerry, the manageress, didn't look that taken with them either. She rolled her eyes once when one of the lads, the one with a big nose, stuck right up in the air, asked if there was 'any other method' for cutting down his chips.

Still, I was dead excited. Me, Christina Rae, with my two GCSEs, in training school with all these smart arses who had been to university. If only the local blabbermouths could have seen me! ('Who do they think they are, those Raes, with their fancy names? And hardly a qualification between the lot of them!') *I'd spent the first half of my time at school trying to see over the lads' heads, while they carried on all the time, struggling to pick up something through the din, and the second half totally ignoring the teachers and looking at nothing* but *the lads' heads. Dreaming was much more interesting to me than actually learning anything. (Not to mention I couldn't see a thing; wouldn't wear my glasses at all after I was about eleven. Too vain. I looked great in soft focus and so did everybody else.) There was only English, all people and words, and geography, all people and places, that'd interested me much at all. And drama, of course.*

So now I was dead excited and then dead worried. All right, the university types hadn't been exactly impressive so far, but surely the differences between our brains would tell in the end? Surely sooner or later my spectacular lack of success to date would show itself? Not *to be looked forward to.*

You know, despite the tat behind the scenes, I loved it there every bit as much as I'd dreamed I would. The roulette tables were very James Bond; the wood of the wheels dead smooth and expensive-looking. And I loved the feeling of the chips, clicking away in my fingers, all cool and classy, not to mention a damned sight easier than picking out the black crisps from the good ones from a turbo-charged conveyor belt in a factory all day, until your clothes and hair (net!) were all covered in grease, like my mam. (Only time my dad dirtied his hands was when he spilled his pint!) I had a bit of a problem seeing the ball in the wheel at first, swivelling my head around the whole time, but the electronics helped. I loved feeling for twenty, stretching my fingers like a piano player to take in the piles of chips. And I loved the clicking sound that got smoother and smoother, and quicker and quicker, as I broke down the chips into all those croupy little patterns they gradually show you how to make up. My favourite one was the pyramid pattern: made you feel like an Egyptian princess when you passed that one out.

And did I tell you about the chandeliers they've got in there? In the casino itself there are these two amazing *chandeliers, one on each side of the room. Double wide-screen! It's like having the front of your face taken off when you look up at them: the light comes into your brain and floods right through to your soul, filling you up with all this brightness and power. My version of stained glass windows, I suppose. And best of all, in just six weeks it would be, 'Lights, cameras and action. Miss Christina Rae, please,' and I would be on, right under those cinema-style chandeliers, performing my heart out. I couldn't wait.*

Then the coffee break arrived, and the university types all started comparing degrees, and hometowns and future careers and that. Out of the seven of us, two were graduates; one girl, Susie, all dark and sallow, had just moved up from Middlesborough; and only four of us were resident Geordies, like. Two of them were already mates from school, Iain and Ben. Those first days, the Geordies were the quietest, even Peter who turned out to have the biggest mouth of the lot of us, but it wasn't long before we came into our own. One of the university types, Alex, the big-nosed one, was from Hertfordshire, and the other one, Shelley, was from Hull. (Not that I'd been to either of those places.) So I decided to say that my parents were from 'around' Jesmond (dead posh) and not Gateshead (dead rough) and just told them, 'I live in the West End at the moment, in an apartment,' which was true, but I've always thought it sounded a bit Cockney, 'apartment', a bit classy. Well, you know the truth at least, or some of it, don't you?

Just my luck, so did one of them, which was my first clue that they didn't all have posh parents. 'I've just moved into a flat in

Elswick. Is it near there?' this Shelley asked. She looked sideways at me and her eyes reminded me of two bitter little almonds.

'Not really,' I said and left it at that. Nobody *admits to living in, or anywhere near, Elswick in company; it's practically been torched to a crisp more times than enough. I wished she would shut up, Shelley.*

'Near where the Tyne Theatre is?' This was Alex, the one with all the questions and the nose again, sticking it right into my business now. I nodded. It was much nearer to Elswick than to the Tyne Theatre, but that wasn't the point. That Shelley looked a bit depressed then, so I changed the subject and started chattering on about the training course and Jonty and what had gone on in his training school. The atmosphere got quite friendly, really, and we all started to relax with each other a bit more.

Which was just as well because we were going to have to get pretty close to each other over the next few months, what with the shifts, and other, more important, things.

One of which was old black eyes.

September's training school is always a bit of a mixed bunch, or that's what the dealers had all said to me. The season can't decide whether it's summer or autumn and the graduates can't decide whether they're tomorrow's high-flying professionals or today's unemployable losers. (I'd had to face that one myself back in August.) And casinos attract a load of weirdos anyway, staff and punters, period. This lot was no exception.

They were an odd collection. One of them, the strong and silent type, looked like a bouncer in a night-club, all shoulders and chin. Two of them were graduates, swapping university stories (I recognised the bloke from my hall of residence) and two of them looked like old mates. There were two youngish blonde girls there as well, the graduate and another one. Quite pretty.

I showed them where to get their free coffee and soft drinks and brought through a few sandwiches. One of the blonde girls was fiddling with her hair and looking at me all the time I was explaining how to use the coffee machine, frowning, as if it was really important. Very pretty. Although, like Mic said, women weren't exactly my forte just then.

And still I didn't recognise her.

So much for feeling sorry for that Shelley: I soon hoped she would live and die in her flat in Elswick and finish up her days as human toast (or 'Melba toast' as they called it at the Casino Club). Shit! Only showed herself up the whole time by making eyes at Angelo, the first time I could have actually got to speak to him. 'I've just finished with my boyfriend from university,' she said in the break. 'Angelo's nice, isn't he?' Double shit!

He looked gorgeous, as well. Angelo, that is. His bum was dead neat and tidy in his black clothes and his chest was dead proud as he walked around the machine, showing us how it worked. How can explaining how a coffee machine works be so totally sexy? Except he was explaining it to her, *while she was giggling up into his face. Didn't recognise me at all. It was that concentration, that dark depth, in his eyes that did it, I decided, and the way he always listened so hard. I obviously wasn't the only one who thought so. Bloody Shelley. That had spoiled the whole of the first day, I thought, as I was walking home on my own. Things like being a croupier never happened to me; things like being a croup* always *did.*

And I still had mardy-faced old Jonty to face later on.

Some days, when I'd be doing something totally unconnected, it was as if I could hear her voice, whispering through to me, just whispering through. So quiet. There was no way she could speak to me, yet I felt I was getting the sense of her feelings anyway.

But I never could let myself listen to her, however much I wanted to hear. And every time I ignored her, I pushed her one step further away.

*   *   *

I was knackered that night: there'd been a lot of false smiling, even by my standards. Exhausting. And like I say, I knew Jonty would be coming round later, at around half-nine, after his early. I was sort of looking forward to that, in a way. Maybe I need to explain a bit.

Nothing much wrong with Jonty, that's the first thing to tell you, nothing much wrong at all. Tall, blond, nice-looking, good talker, all that; he was dead sweet at the beginning. It was me that was the problem. Never satisfied, my mam used to say. No, Jonty was a nice enough bloke in most ways, or could be; it was just that he wasn't very, well . . . constant, really. And he wasn't that kind, especially when he'd had a drink. He wasn't *kind. But he wasn't bad either. Best not to expect too much from people in general: that's what my mam always said. And best not to expect* anything *much from blokes. Getting there?*

I'll try again. Take that night. Please take that night! Take it right out of my memory.

Like I said, Jonty was on an early, so he'd said that he would come around afterwards some time, which with Jonty could mean any *time – any time after a bit of banter with 'the lads', after a few drinks in the pub, after the night-clubs had shut. After he'd finished with another girl. Starting to get the picture? That night, I was lucky: 'after' meant just after ten and he was still the reasonable side of sober. The only trouble was I'd been starting to give up on him and I'd decided to go for a bath. And* nobody *gives up on Jonty. Jonty can give up on himself, and on you, and on his life, and his work and the whole hard awkward bastard of a world, but* nobody *gives up on Jonty. And* nobody *goes in the bath when he's said he's coming round to see them. Not a cracking start.*

Soon as I heard the knock, that 'Why aren't you waiting behind this door when I knock for you?' knock some men have, I hauled myself out of the bath and into my towel, then dressing gown, Radox bubbles everywhere, and headed for the door. There were only two rooms in my flat, really, a big living room-cum-bedroom, with a tiny kitchen in the corner, and a square bathroom, so it wasn't exactly a long walk to the door, but there was a pretty long face behind it when I got there – more long than pretty, it has to be said, at that exact point.

'Charmin'. Fuckin' charmin'.' At least there was only a hint of beer on his breath. 'Don't fuckin' put yourself out, Teen. I've got all night.'

Jonty! Fucking charming, as usual. 'Well, I've been waiting for you half the night!' I said. I wasn't a complete *door mat. Jonty cocked his head at me, as if to say, 'Just open the door, will you?' 'Come in, then,' I said. Wipe your feet on me, why don't you? I always did get tired of the bickering before the blokes did – just one of my problems.*

So in he stalked, like he was doing me a great big, fat favour, scuffing my door with his boot, dumping his jacket on the chair and grabbing a biscuit as he went. 'Any sign of some food here, Teen? There was nowt at Richie's, fucking hunger-striker.' Richie was one of Jonty's new mates from his training school. So I fixed him some cheese, crackers, crisps, salad and pâté, didn't mention the fact that he had a proper wage coming in now and I'd had to cut the Elvis hours to the scalp, settled him down in a chair and got him a coffee (hoping to dilute however much beer he'd had). I smiled *at him. No sign of spirits anyway, alcoholic ones, I mean. Bit on the unpredictable side though, Jonty – even after just a few beers you had to be pretty careful. He was talking away as usual, mouth full of bullshit, slaver and biscuit crumbs, all the time I was fixing his food. 'Casino was packed when I left, Teen. Old Mordue was in there, doin' his brains in, fucking loser. Took two grand off him, easy – biggest game going in the place. Fucking wiped him out, man. Made a* definite *mark on Andreas: he came down from his meal, 'specially to watch my game.' And more of the same heroics until he remembered, just for a minute, that he was with another human being who could also feel, speak and think. 'What about you, Teen? How was your first day?'*

I told him a couple of the funniest bits about the other trainees: Peter the Pit Bull (because of his strong neck and his attitude), Alex the Nose, Shelley, Susie Stuffer (ex-taxidermist's assistant), and asked him a couple of questions about different odds, bets and rules. I told him nothing *about Angelo. Then, because he'd finished his food and drink, we got down to what he'd really come to see me for. Sex, as per. A shag, as Jonty would have put it. Fucking charming. We'd been seeing each other for a few months by then and we'd slipped into having sex after about a month or so, I suppose. Not that I minded that much, really.*

It all starts when he grabs me on to his knee on the chair and slips his hand inside my dressing gown, all clumsy with the drink. 'You could have got yourself a bit dressed up for me, Teen.' This is Jonty's idea of a chat-up line. 'Still.' His hands are on my boobs, no bra to get in the way, dead convenient, like those shops that are open half the night to anybody walking in off the street and fancying something. Convenience store. He hadn't been like that when I'd first started going out with him, no way. If anything, I thought, he'd been keener than me at the start. Still, the rubbing was pleasant enough, less rough now. He was a man of the world, Jonty, knew his erogenous zones from his traffic zones, which was more than some *of the lads I'd gone out with, so I snuggled up a bit closer.*

The boobs took about two minutes, from boob to nipple and back again, while Jonty nuzzled my neck, and then it was a little feel of the bum, through the material of my dressing gown, a nice stroke. I was just feeling a bit warmer when it was straight on to the clitoris for a second before he slipped it (in its plastic jacket, thank God) straight in for some friction. Not that I was complaining and not that I was spending much longer on him either: I knew I didn't need to. So it was in, out, in, out, shake it all about, and then it was finished. Jonty never said a word to me the whole time, he never did, and I only knew he'd come when he slipped it out with a small sort of grunt. The silence was the worst. He never knew whether I'd come or not, certainly never asked me, but to do him justice, I think he just took it for granted that I had. Which I hadn't.

Mind you, it was quick. Ten minutes later, with a 'See you at the roulette tables then, Teen!', a big grin and a bigger swagger, he'd slipped out of the door as well, grabbing another biscuit on his way — typical — back to his mam's. She didn't really like him to stay out all night, God knows why. The one and only time he had stayed at mine, he'd woken me up trying to slip it inside me while I was fast asleep! Mind you, I don't think even Jonty had tried that one at home. Don't think. Another one of my problems.

It was gone eleven o'clock by then, bedtime. At least I didn't need the telly to anaesthetise me after that. I filled in my diary.

Small Dreams

Dump Jonty, whatever it takes, before he gets even worse

Big Dreams

Trap Angelo, with force, imagination or sheer hard work, whatever that takes

---

My mam had always said to me that sex was nothing more than five minutes of fun — no way was it worth the lifetime of hassle afterwards (meaning clearing up after men and babies, which she'd spent her life doing one way and another, between crisps, I suppose), so I wasn't expecting much. And I got even less. I sighed, stretched, stashed my diary away and headed for my bed.

Angelo, touched by the angels.

I was thinking of him as I drifted off into sleep.

3. The Venetian Dagger and the Church

'The glass blade broke inside her flesh, her back.'
'And you could do nothing to help?'

One bit of luck I have had is the church where I live. Mic and I inherited it from our Italian grandmother. She, as you'll have worked out from her friendship with Irene, I suppose, was fairly eccentric and lived on her own there for about fifteen years, doing nothing much to it except for adding the odd coat of paint. My mother had done bits to it for us, seen to the wet rot at the windows and that kind of thing, but it was still less than a palace.

It was a mixed blessing. First of all, I wasn't really used to living on my own; don't know if I ever will get used to it completely. And the church had been sold to my grandmother because the local people had no more need for it. I know some really solid people who never go to church, but you think about it, in general, I mean. Are people who don't need their church very likely to need each other or to care much about each other either? Well, that's what people around here are like: you're very much on your own. Mostly, that suits me fine. Mostly.

It's a bit on the basic side as well, and a bit on the bleak side in late October, so it was just as well I hadn't had much company for a while, female or otherwise. But I had started thinking about that young dealer at the casino, the one with the blonde hair and the smile. Like I said, my grandmother never bothered much about how the church looked, and my mum hadn't had time to do much with it, so it was a bit on the rough and ready side. It was cleaner than Irene's, of course, always clean. And I'd added one or two touches of my own to the place, just candles and prints and so on, prints that meant something to me: like *Noli me Tangere*, do not touch me, Jesus warning Mary Magdalene away after the Resurrection. Me, warning the world away after everything that had happened. Everything that I'd done. And Bosch's *The Garden of Earthly Delights* shone out, mocking me from its corner.

The main thing was that the church was mine, completely mine. Nobody could criticise me in there, or tell me what to do, or hurt me. *Noli me Tangere*. Nobody could touch me. Safe.

Or that's what I thought until I met her.

Wait *until you hear this bit. If you thought that my first meeting with Angelo was dramatic, well, this one was an Oscar winner.* Titanic. *Remember the really famous bit when Leonardo goes right to the front of the ship and sort of turns into the figurehead? My head thought it was a bit on the macho side, but you shouldn't always listen to your head, should you? Not if you want some fun out of life. And definitely not if you want to be Kate Winslet, only thinner, poorer and Geordier, from time to time. (Or Kate Moss, only fatter, healthier and smilier.)*

By this time we were all really looking forward to getting out on to the tables properly, not to mention earning a wage. We even knew some of the customers' names by then, through conversations with the other dealers, mainly. There were The Glums (a right pair of old miseries who spent about £5 a night between them and slit their wrists when they lost), and The Grungies (local musos, useful only for providing a scruffy sort of contrast to the sequins, nylon and shiny suits of the rest of the punters). Mr Fawcett was a regular, Fatty Foreskin to his friends, and everybody watched what he ate and exactly how it returned to haunt him later. Prostitute spotting was another big part of our training, not that we dealers had to do much when we did recognise one, the pit bosses had to deal with that, but it was excellent spectator sport. The Red Jersey was ready for me to race in – another dealer of around *my size, give or take a stone or two, had just left, or died, or something, the glamour! – and I couldn't wait to get on down to that roulette wheel. By this time I could get the ball spinning around the wheel about ten times at least; I could spread the cards and even do that funny little trick that shows you're a real pro where you shuffle the chips together between the fingers of one hand. Dead hard. The training course was trailing to its end.*

Also trailing to its end was my so-called relationship with Jonty.

It all started, or ended, when Gerry shouted me into the loos to try on my new (to me) Red Jersey and get into the race. Well, really, nineteen-year-olds and red jersey just don't mix. You'd have thought even double-breasted, triple-gutted old Mr Andreas would have worked that *one out! And if the dress had been new, maybe it wouldn't have been quite as bad – sometimes it seemed like I never got anything really nice, just to myself, like. (I'm a second child, 'another girl', yawn, yawn. Not quite as pretty as the first sprog, not quite as bad as the last.) Anyway, I dragged the old nylonny sack on and walked out of the loos to meet Gerry and the others, sort of keen to see what they thought. Cat walk. I was still in pre-lens, soft-focus mode, but even I could tell through the mists that I didn't look great. Luckily, the casino was pretty empty; it was just about to open to the punters.*

'Christina. Brilliant! Do you feel really glam?' Shelley was the first to say anything and I almost forgave her that Angelo business and forgot I was wearing the twenty-first-century equivalent of Crimplene. Then she tilted her head and squinted those almondy eyes at me. 'Maybe you should try a couple of those chicken breast-type implant things inside your bra? Argos have got an

offer on them!' Almost *forgave her. Old Big Nose, my mate Alex by then, knew better than to snigger and he kept his mouth well shut. Stuck a little smile on it, even. Iain and Ben just looked at each other and grinned. So far, so bearable. I never had much of a cleavage to start with and the Red Jersey wasn't exactly strong on shape, so I was looking bony on the boob front and saggy around the bum.*

'Not too *bad,' said Gerry, who was fairly honest, I'd found. She walked around and looked at the rear view. 'Maybe it needs a bit of a tuck around the back.' I swivelled my head around for a quick look and that's when I heard Jonty. Heard him laugh.*

'Christ, Teen! Been a visit down the Oxfam shop, have you? You were done.' The usual Jonty combination of cruelty and cliché: a total pain in the ass.

'All right, Jonty. Have your laugh and get it over with,' I said, but I felt even worse in the thing than I had done before, not to mention everybody *was looking at me now. God's judgement, I said to myself, for my first thoughts when I saw the pregnant badger in hers.*

'Get what over with? If you think I'll be getting my leg over with you after seeing you in that, *you've got another think coming!' Jonty was shouting, looking around at his audience to see if he was getting a reaction, 'a good laugh'. Maybe this audience was more polite than he was used to because a nervous pause came in where he'd expected some applause. His eyes lost their glint and then they creased up at the corners. Peeved. Even Jonty's head, Jonty's stone of bone, could work out that he'd slipped up. He looked pretty annoyed, with* me, *of course, and then he thought he'd better plug the gap. Plug it with double humiliation. He kind of whispered into the side of my face, but just loud enough for the other dealers to hear: 'Don't think of becoming one of the casino tarts, Teen! There is a limit, even for the wanker punters around here.' For once, a suitably sarky comment deserted me. Shit.*

That is *when I saw Angelo coming over, as if my silence had set off the fire bells.*

*   *   *

If it hadn't have been for those awful dresses that they made them wear, I might never have noticed her properly at all. But this time I spotted *her* first. Couldn't miss her really. She was small anyway, tiny, but that awful baggy dress made her look tinier still. Her skin looked really white and thin against that cheap red stuff, and you could see all the bones below her throat. Her eyes were all over the place. She felt absolutely stupid in it: anybody could see that. Anybody with half a brain that is, which didn't include Jonty, as I'd noticed way before this point.

I didn't catch the last nugget of wisdom, but I heard the bit about getting his leg over clearly enough. (In his dreams, I thought, with a lovely, bright-looking girl like that.) And I saw her drop her head. He whispered something else into her ear then, slipping the Venetian dagger in slyly. Her face fell, the glass blade broke inside her flesh, her back, she was stuck for words and Jonty actually smiled. There was a crawling, uncomfortable silence. I dumped the plate of sandwiches I was carrying and walked straight across to them.

That seemed to make it worse. Even before I could get right up to her, I could see her eyes were full of tears and that stupid red dress made her look like a dressed-up child who'd been told off. What a shit, I thought. I could see her swallow, right down her throat, and then swallow again. Jonty's turn to swallow something now, preferably his tongue. He was a big bloke, as tall as me, but square with it. His size worried me, but there was no way, after Mic, that I was going to let myself shrink away.

'That's enough bullshit, Jonty,' I said to him. 'She looks fine to me.' He took a few seconds to process these complicated words and then his thick neck, with his thick head on the top of it, stiffened.

'Fine by me, Ango,' he said, with a very unfunny smile. 'Fine by me. Yours for the asking. Or for the shagging if that's what you're after.' He smiled again and went to put his hand on her backside, but her head jerked up and her body moved automatically away from him. And she looked *straight* at me, met my eyes, then looked away again. I couldn't take my eyes away from her after that.

And as I looked at her my back went hard with anger, with hatred for him, Jonty, for talking about her like that. I turned to him and glared out my contempt, my threat. It was important to keep my job, so when I spoke, I hissed out the words.

'Shut your mouth, Jonty,' I said. 'Unless you're planning to apologise.'

Well, what Angelo didn't realise was that Jonty had a very short fuse, a very nasty side to him altogether. And I could have looked after myself: I'd seen Jonty off more than once already, after much worse mouthfuls than that. After much worse incidents than that. That stupid dress. Feminism is one thing, but standing up to men who do such realistic animal impersonations can be exhausting. Nice to be rescued, I thought, and nicer still to be noticed. By Angelo, I mean. He was talking to Jonty, but he'd looked right into my eyes. At last.

What would happen next? I held my breath.

Words were no use after that. Action. Fine by me.

Jonty tried to take me by surprise, to knock me off my feet with his first push. Then his mouth was in my face. 'What's it to do with you, Ango? Fancy her, do you? It's true then. You're not right in the head, are you? Get out of my fuckin' business, man.'

You couldn't even call it a fight. One hard slam against the wall winded Jonty. Better still, shut him up. I stepped back and Gerry's bellowing finished it off altogether. 'Pack it in, the pair of you, or you're both sacked!' That wouldn't have stopped me, not then, whatever I'd thought before, but it stopped that moron in his tracks.

He spat on the floor, hard man that he was, and swaggered away, all hips, muscles and mouth.

Straight off into the staffroom to tell his carefully edited version of events: the world according to Jonty – the one where he'd beaten Angelo to a pulp with his bare fists, scooped up the flesh from the carpet, made a few burgers with it, gone into business, opened up a chain of shops and won a big award. Microphone mouth! I shivered a bit though, and watched Jonty's spit sink into the red casino carpet.

That was exactly how long it took me to get over Jonty.

'All right, Christina?' Gerry put her hand on my arm. 'Angelo, make yourself scarce and save the Mike Tyson impersonations for home, before I do what I should do now and call Mr Andreas down here.' That saw Angelo off, sadly. 'And the rest of you, get on with your practice game.' Big Nose and Co. went back to their tables and Gerry steered me over towards the loos again. 'I think we'll try that dress on somebody else, Christina, don't you?' She looked dead stern and I thought I was going to get told off as well, but as soon as we were out of sight, she added, 'If that's the effect it has on men, I daren't risk you wearing it in the pit. Who needs chicken tits when you can get a reaction like that? Go for it, Christina!' And she just about laughed her head off.

But I didn't laugh. The only one I wanted to go for it with had gone.

4. The Red Notebook

'The terrible night that Angelo was born.'

The church finally fixed up the meeting for us.

It was my day off, Tuesday, a standard day off for those fairly new to the casino, for obvious reasons, so I was relaxing in the church – reading, listening to music and so on.

It's important for you to know what I was reading.

Mic and his comments had started it off, the point about other people trying to get in touch. I'd been, as my mother would have said, brooding about it for a few days. After my grandma died, my mum had only ever had time to stay there occasionally while she was trying to do it up. (I was at Newcastle University by then, living away.) Did she know back then, my mother, I wonder, that I would find the little old candle box with its big old store of secrets? The red notebook? She'd had no idea I would be living in the church so soon.

We'd had an awful row. It had ended with my mother pushing the keys to the church across the table and into my hands. 'If you can't stand to live with me, then perhaps it would be better if you tried living on your own again,' she'd said. I'd rushed off to the church, let myself in and locked the door behind me. And although I'd had no idea of it at the time, that was the last time I spoke to my mother. A week or so later, when I was clearing up in the church, I'd come across the wooden box hidden in the back of a cupboard underneath some old sheets and tins of paint. It was like a tiny coffin, or a treasure chest. The box itself smelled of sawdust, white spirit and secrets, and as I pulled open the sliding lid, I saw the red notebook for the first time, nestled in with lace and pictures and handkerchiefs. The bits and pieces were my grandmother's, stuffed in at various times, not meant to be a coffin at all: her focus was very much on life. And the notebook was my last connection with my mother: she had written it, and that was why I rationed my reading of it so carefully. (Not to mention, some of it could be pretty traumatic to read.) Altogether, it was a real Pandora's box, packed with its books, Bible, Burano lace and rings, its postcards and ribbons. Hopes, secrets and scars.

Anyway, I was reading the red notebook that day. The cover had shredded apart, bending the red layer on the front away from the brown layers beneath, like leaves lifting from the branches of a tree. Like a child pulling away from its family. '*My special son.*' My mother's voice was whispering in my ear and my fingers felt heavy, sad.

I was reading a section from near the start, a section that went right back to Mic – he's older than me – and his birth. I'd read it before often enough, it was the first part of the notebook that I did read, but have a look at it with me now and see what it means to you.

Out of it all, the blood, the energy, the redness and the hot pain, came Michael, right from the boiling centre of me, like a miracle. The centre of a woman, the most intimate centre, the hardness of a woman's belly, the strength of a woman's body, pushing, as only a woman can push, the softness of my body, split by him, the softness of my love for him and yet the hardness of it all, the redness of it. Raw pain. Raw love. Raw life.

> Beautiful Michael came out of that, hot and red and noisy and pained.
> He was full of life from the start and his little eyes were full of light.
>   I never thought I'd see anything so beautiful again, and I never did,
> not until the terrible night that Angelo was born.

I'd read that part over and over again: I never could read
it enough. That's the only time that I envy women, think
they've got something men can't touch. Birth and love.
The red, red tenderness at the centre of a woman – it's just
miraculous. I mean, sex, love, intimacy, those things can be
a miracle for a man or a woman, can be a miracle for a man
like me, but the redness, the life, the energy at the centre is
purely woman. Ripeness and tenderness everywhere. The
part about the *'terrible night'* I was born always made me
stop and think because from what my mother had told me,
my birth was brutal for her, which always made me feel
like a complete shit when I thought about it.

I walked over to the door and made for the step, planning
to get some air and drink my tea. I opened the door, sat
down, and looked up.

A miracle. A birth. *La Vita Nuova.*

*I'll have to come clean with you on this one, there was nothing
miraculous about it. Or rather, it was one of your more everyday,
pre-planned, very* female *sort of miracles.*

*You see, Angelo always seemed to be in such a world of his own,
a totally separate world from mine. I'd noticed that right from the
off. Every now and then, you could even see him tilt his head as if
he was listening to secrets, murmurings, that only he could hear.
Dark secrets. He fascinated me, more and more. But what with the
combination of the shifts, the fact that he was a waiter and I was
a dealer, not to mention the way he didn't even seem to notice I
existed, I only ever saw him from a distance. And I wanted to be
close. So I'd asked around, I'd got his address (roughly, he didn't
seem to invite many visitors home, exactly) and I'd rehearsed a*

scenario. Twice I'd seen him in handsome prince mode, rescuing a woman, so I'd made up a third little drama of my own – a bit more subtle than the first two, though not much.

I suppose it was warm for November, but I was still frozen to death as I sat on the wall of his church, coughing like a TB victim from time to time in the hope of drawing him out. November in Newcastle. I was dying of cold. When I'd read his address, I'd got all excited with ideas of a lovely little stone church, hanging baskets and everything cheering it up. But it didn't look like anybody lived there at all: the windows, lovely pointy ones, were covered up and the roof was missing some slates. But Angelo was so smart. I was sure he'd have done the whole laminated floor and chic furniture thing inside. There was a little porchway there, but I didn't like to go inside that. I'd been there half an hour without a sign of him. Maybe I had the wrong address? I doublechecked Gerry's scrap of paper. I was dying of boredom. And I was really *dying for a wee. Typical!*

At last the door opened, in more ways than one.

She was just sitting there. 'Christina!' I couldn't believe it. I'd thought about her so often in the last few days that it felt like I'd conjured her right into life. The wind caught in her hair, making her look like Venus rising out of the sea, the foam, in Botticelli's *The Birth of Venus*. A real birth. A real miracle. Magic.

'What's going on?'

'Angelo!' I said, all surprised. 'I'm lost,' I went on, waving my A to Z helplessly, shaking my head and widening my eyes for maximum impact. 'I've been wandering around for ages, trying to find my friend's house. I was hoping to surprise her. Looks like I've surprised you instead.' I eyed up his steaming china cup with totally genuine desire. Who would have thought that a tiny, old lady's cup could look so sexy in a big young bloke's hands? Plus his drink was hot!

'Honestly, Angelo, I'm turning into a block of ice out here.' I

lifted my eyes to his face like the little match girl looking up at the Christmas tree. Practically dribbled. I should have got an Oscar. 'Is this where you live?'

And then (dead cool), 'I couldn't use your toilet, could I?'

It was the smallest thing she could have asked me for and yet the biggest: it was so intimate somehow, personal, and she looked so embarrassed. And it gave me the chance to ask her inside the church. I don't think I'd have asked her in under any other circumstances at all. Like I said before, it was a bit of a mess, really.

I had never seen anything like it in my life and I hope I never will again, especially now that I understand the situation properly. But I didn't understand the situation properly then. I felt something from the state of the place, though. Felt plenty.

My mouth was open but for once in my life there wasn't a sound coming out of it.

I always know how other people are feeling anyway, and with Christina, it seemed to have something to do with her fairness – her fairness and my darkness. I could see right through her skin. That day, I knew as soon as she crossed the threshold into the church that she was frightened.

First there was the mess and then there were all the paintings and everything. I half wished that I'd painted out those words, the words that I'd scribbled around the windows that night. I half wished I wasn't so different, that some of the things that had happened to me had never happened. Half.

It all looked so much worse through her eyes. So I took her through to the cubby-hole where I have my kitchen, because it was much saner in there. More 'normal' as my mother used to say. 'Cheerful.'

And it worked – Christina definitely settled down. A minute later she went up to the bathroom and then she came back down the stairs and into the kitchen corner, with her hair combed, looking calmer. Started to chat to me after another minute, drank the coffee that I'd made her and when we came to wander back into the main living space, she soon decided not to look at it all, much. She decided to concentrate on me instead.

That suited me fine.

The darkness he held in his eyes had been the first thing I had ever noticed about Angelo, and the first thing I noticed about his home was the darkness that it held inside.

The windows were covered in black sheets, and I could see bits of words and sentences leaking out of the plaster around them. I didn't dare walk across to read them or try to work out what they said. Not to mention, I was pretending, hard, that everything was perfectly ordinary. Did you know, casinos have no clocks in them and no windows either? A funny, claustrophobic little world. Angelo's church was much the same.

Then there were these pictures everywhere. Some of them were really old-fashioned religious ones and there were loads of red and black ones around as well. I recognised one of them, you see it everywhere, that one of the skeletal bloke running across a bridge and hoying a wobbler, with his mouth wide open. The one that went missing for a bit. It's called The Scream. *Knew how he felt now, old skull face. I'd even seen a blow-up version of him once in a shop with a sandbag at the bottom that you were supposed to use like a punch bag. Tempting. One of the others was of a woman, with all these dead, black babies wound into its frame, all in red, bloody colours everywhere else; it could only have been done by the same bloke who did* The Scream, *same sort of Technicolor moodiness.* Madonna. *It made me shiver, that one. Horrible. Jesus was there in another picture, with thorns all round his head. A totally depressing little display it was! No wonder poor Angelo looked so thoughtful and moody all of the time, I thought. The last one I noticed was obviously God – old face, long beard, the lot – zapping some very laidback bloke into life with his finger.*

There were iron candelabra all over the place that Angelo must have lit at night: the wax was all dripping down the sides. Never had him down as an Eco Warrior, but he obviously wasn't keen on the old electricity bills: the room was lit by just the one light, not much to fight against the blackout curtains with. It was all messy too, chairs lying on their backs and boxes spread about. And there he was, Angelo, sitting right in the middle of all this, loose as a goose, drinking coffee and chatting on like he was in the Metro Centre!

Something Jonty had said about Angelo that day in the casino, 'It's true, then. You're not right in the head', *came back to me and I felt all cold. Looking around, it was practically as if Angelo* wanted *to push himself over the edge. I shrugged off my doubts. Traitor, I thought. If* Jonty *was right in the head, then the whole world was round the bend. I'd seen nothing but kindness from Angelo so far, and courage. I'd seen little enough of those qualities elsewhere, God knows, Jonty very much included. Apart from the ten-screen, two-dimensional versions of manhood I'd seen at the Warner, that is.*

Angelo's not the only bloke in the North East who's a bit lacking in the interior design department, I thought, and it is his house after all, not yours. Thank God. At least my cup was clean, I noticed. Quite good for a bloke, I suppose. Angelo did look like he could do with a bit of a hand, though, because there was all this awful-coloured, old-fashioned blue paint behind the pictures and it smelled vaguely of damp. Poor thing obviously lived on his own, like me. But his place had a really *lonely feel to it.*

Just as I thought that, a double bed peeped over the edge of the galleried bedroom at me, cheering me up. Excellent. *Then I noticed that the screaming bloke on the bridge was staring straight into the poor bed's eyes. God knows how Angelo ever got any sleep. Shit.*

I started to feel better, though, as soon as the big bed came into sight. It couldn't be as weird as it looked, could it? Surely? Concentrate on him, I said to myself, try believing in him – seems like he needs that the most. We can always do a bit of decorating later on.

'What've you been up to then, Angelo?' I asked him. 'Day off today, is it?' (Thank you, Gerry, thank you.)

Angelo nodded. 'Nothing much,' he said. 'A bit of reading, bit of listening to music, that sort of thing.'

'No television?' (Notice I'd dropped the 'telly'. I told you his accent was better than mine, so I had to catch up.)

'No,' he said, and his eyes flicked over to a corner of the room. I noticed for the first time that there was what looked like a telly there, but it was covered in this green material. He always had this half sort of 'fuck off' expression on his face; he was wearing it right then. Why was that so attractive to me? A worry. I carried on anyway.

'What have you been reading, then?' I asked, trying to warm him up a bit, like.

'Nothing much.'

Small talk obviously wasn't Angelo's speciality – I'd already spotted that. Maybe I was putting him off. So I shut up for a bit.

Words can only do certain jobs for you and I know more about words than most. What I'd wanted to do for Christina, right since that episode with Jonty and the red dress, was to make her feel happier, make her feel better about herself. I'd had something in mind since that day, something I wanted to give her, something that probably seemed small. Yet it was a big sacrifice for me. I broke the silence.

'That day you tried your dress on for the first time,' I said. 'I thought of something that would help.'

'Shutting Jonty up helped,' I said, catching his eye for the first time in ages, and it was true. 'He was being a complete pain in the neck.' I sounded dead cool, dead classy. I'd dropped my more usual way of putting it, 'pain in the arse'. But I did want Angelo to know that I was grateful to him. Very.

'Jonty had no right to speak to you like that,' Angelo said, shaking his head on the 'no' and looking quite annoyed. 'It's

obvious a girl like you wouldn't go anywhere near a bloke like that.' I liked that bit well enough, but you could tell he didn't talk much to the other blokes in the kitchen, or to the dealers. 'A girl like you'. He obviously didn't know what kind of girl I was and what kind of family I was from, and he seemed completely oblivious to the fact that Jonty and I had ever been an item. To be honest, that seemed pretty dim and distant to me as well, by then. It was such a relief to be free of Jonty at last. Still, I felt a bit guilty about not putting Angelo right. 'Anyway,' he was saying, shaking his head, casting Jonty right out of his hair, 'I'll show you what I meant.' And he heads off towards this spindly black iron staircase that goes up to his bedroom.

I was so busy watching his bum as he walked up the stairs – it looked gorgeous, believe me, very touchable – that I didn't start to wonder what he was looking for up there.

I needed a message. I turned to the tarot pack beside my bed, cut it four times and picked out a card. The High Priestess stared at me – one of the major arcana, the profound secrets. I looked in my book: 'Trust your intuition. To win, don't withdraw. Trust yourself.' Trust myself. Mic's arms around my waist. Corners. Still, it was a good message and I eased her back inside the pack and looked around me for the candle box.

It took me a minute to unearth it and to breathe in its scent of wood and wax, which was useful thinking time. Funny coincidence that Christina should get lost outside my house, right outside my house, on her day off and mine. And then there were her eyes, searching mine out every time; when she dared to, that is. The sacrifice, the important sacrifice of the hair clasp, would be worth it, I told myself, delving down into the permanent Christmas of my grandmother's box, sifting through the various treasures blind until I felt it out. I held it in my hand for the last time. Then I remembered what my grandmother always used to say about loving people, rather than things, and receiving more by giving away rather than trying to grasp. I fingered the little diamanté bumps of the tortoiseshell clasp, seeing my grandmother's face as I did so, then I walked back down the stairs.

Christina's blue eyes, raised straight up to mine, told me for certain that I'd got it right. I sat down beside her on the settee this time, leaving my old armchair on its own, in its corner. Her eyes were fixed on me.

'Here,' I said, opening my palm with the hair clasp inside it. Christina held her head at an angle so that most of her hair fell to one side, like a waterfall dropping down to a pool, a waterfall of molten glass. And her face was as pretty as cut crystal beneath her hair. I pulled her black hairband off backwards through her hair. 'It was my grandmother's,' I told her. I secured the clasp on the left-hand side, so that the dark tortoiseshell and the diamanté stones were shiny against her soft, blonde hair.

Who would have dreamed that an old woman's fifty-year-old clasp could look so beautiful in a young woman's hair? It was like a spell.

Thank God I got the last of that perm cut out, I thought, and thank God for natural blonde hair and conditioner. He'd never have got that slide through old badger's roots. And thank God for Angelo, more than anything. To think that I'd thought he was slow! He was certainly zapped right *into life by God's finger now. To think that I'd thought I was getting nowhere!*

Then I looked into his eyes, his deep, deep eyes.

He blinked those spectacular eyelashes, tilted his head to one side slightly to look at my hair, to look into my eyes, and I knew I was getting everywhere with him, all at once.

I left my hand in her soft hair, I looked into her blue eyes (she was younger than I was), I drew her head towards me and I kissed her. Her eyelids came down as I got nearer her and her lips parted. I kissed her. I kissed her as if she was crystal. She was crystal. Light shone through her, always, and threw out colours from her everywhere.

I kissed her really, really gently. Glass girl.

He was really gentle, at first, but I definitely knew I'd been kissed, that's for sure. I felt like I was on virgin territory, for the first time in about a lifetime.

Seriously, that kiss from Angelo, just that first kiss, meant more to me than every single slippery sexual encounter I'd ever had with Jonty; meant more than every sexual encounter I'd ever had altogether until then. It just wasn't the same experience at all. It was still something to do with sex, still everything to do with sex, but it was so much more as well: magic, for one thing. Serious magic.

Angelo, touched by the angels.

And now that Angelo had touched me, nothing would ever be the same again.

5. The Italian Restaurant

*'I kissed the thin skin on the top of her ear and the
taxi pulled up outside the church.'*

Mic, as usual, had plenty to say about it.

'"Back in dry fuck drive again, Ango?" he sez.' Bursts of
smoky breath were coughed up from Irene's sticky lungs as
she laughed with him, until she just about couldn't breathe.
'Eeh, Michael Paulillo, the language coming out of ye! And
out of my mouth as weel.' The smoky blasts wheezed on. 'I
de *not* enjoy it, y' cheeky young bugger.' Irene calmed down
at last, settling her saggy backside into the hard wooden
chair. 'This'll nivver buy the bairn a new coat. Let's get on
with it, then.' I gritted my teeth, waiting. Privacy was the
one thing that eluded me now, one way and another, and
I sorely missed it when I was with Irene. 'He sez that the
red book is a start, a good start. D' y' follow him, Ango?
And the girl's another plus. "Definite progress," he sez. But
he sez he's telt y' before, get on with your own life. "Leave
the past behind," he sez. "But don't forget the people that
love y'." That's what he's sayin'.'

Mic was always telling me what to do, acting the big
brother, the big shot. Still, better hear the rest of what Irene
had to say. 'He sez the sparks'll fly between you and this girl,
Ango, the sparks'll fly. "Pity asbestos's gone out o' fashion,"

he sez. "Just watch y'sel'." Sez she's a cracker!' Nosiness ruptured the skin of Irene's professionalism. 'Got y'self a nice bit of a lass then, have y', Ango? Not before time, I must say, nice bit of arm candy like ye.' Her vocabulary was a funny mixture of the Durham pits, nineteenth century, and, because of her granddaughters, the Bigg Market, twenty-first century. I couldn't picture her wearing the tortoiseshell clasp, either at twenty or the two hundred years old she looked as if she was nearing then. Yet she and my grandmother had been so close. There were photographs of them in the candle box. I knew that they'd danced together as girls, laughed together after the war, victorious and full of fight, with their boxy little suits and their boxy little attitudes, and cackled together over rivers of tea at family dos and grandchildren's birthday parties. This made me smile at Irene, rather than pretending as usual that I hadn't heard her. Luckily, she was absorbed in Mic's words again. 'Aye, "Use it or lose it, Ango," that's what your brother's sayin' t' y'. And for what it's worth, bonny lad, I agree with him.

'Eeh, it's hot in here, though but, don't y' think, Ango?' She broke away, wiped her parchment map of a face on a sticky-looking hanky and closed our meeting. 'That's it for the day, pet. Some people takes it out of y' worse than others and by the time I've passed on all the devilment Mic's got, I'm about ready for me beed.' She yawned. 'Mind you remember what y' brother says to y', Ango. Don't go mekkin' y'sel' lonely.' I grimaced a smile at her and left.

I wonder if he ever talks to her when I'm not there? I thought as I walked down old Irene's crazily crazy-paved path. I hoped not. Just as I thought that, I heard her voice, croaking down the street after my back. 'Ango! Ango! Ha'd on a minute.' I had to turn around. 'One last thing from Mic. He sez good luck the neet.' Irene stuck one bony old claw up in the air and a neighbour coming in the opposite

direction grinned at me, watching. Shit. ''E sez 'e hopes y'
see some action!' she said, her head wagging in time for
emphasis. '"But don't forget," he sez, "what we all know
about the *Female of the Species*." Eeh, what a voice he's got,
your brother. Bit rough on th' high notes, tho' but. Sings
his little heed off, he does!'

Her words pecked into my back as I hurried away from
her down the street.

*It was as bad as getting ready for the interview – worse, even.
I scented, groomed and smoothed myself down until I was as
smelly and as sweet as a freesia. But even with my best dress
on and my sister's smart shoes (like* boats *on my feet, but mine
needed heeling and I was skint), I was worried that I wouldn't
look smart enough or smooth enough for Angelo. If I'm honest
with you, with myself even, I was worried that I wasn't smart
enough for Angelo altogether.*

*And I was worried about where we would go and what we
would talk about. He'd mentioned a restaurant, that afternoon
in the church. What would we eat? I wondered. What would he
be wearing and would we go together OK clothes-wise? Would I
want to stay the night? Would* he *want me to stay the night? The
questions got worse and worse.*

*Ready or not, I just had to go for it in the end. Casanova
had piles, you know, I said to myself. So what are you worrying
about? By the time it was time to leave the flat, I reckoned I'd
rehearsed every possible disaster in my head and I was just about
prepared.*

I'd thought forever about her. Every time I looked in a
window, or I looked in a mirror, I imagined her face there,
waiting for me. And I'd thought forever about where to
take her. It had to be special, really special. It also had
to be somewhere with an intimate atmosphere: I needed
to find out about her, all about her. And nowhere cheap,
obviously. Because there was something hungry about her,

I'd decided on a meal. I'd have to go carefully with her, a gentle girl like that. I was really looking forward to talking to her, learning about her, touching her. Really touching her.

After that kiss, what I was really *looking forward to was ripping his kit off, naturally. Mind you, the build up to the event was just as exciting.*

Not to mention, I was glad of the square meal. I was out on the tables by then, but I'd only been earning for a couple of weeks, the pay was fairly pathetic anyway at first, and I owed my mam some money from when I'd been at the training school. Starvation School! (Jonty had never been too hot on the wining and dining front, as you'll have guessed. His idea of a meal out was a trip to Netto for a frozen Bird's Eye chicken tikka. For one. Guess who'd be carrying the wire basket and the purse?) One way and another, it was going to be a real treat.

I met Angelo in town, didn't want him to find out where I lived, even though his own house was a bit on the wild side, so we met in a pub on Percy Street. He was standing right beside the door, watching out for me, so I didn't have to squint around the bar looking for him, which was great.

He just appeared.

'Gin and tonic?' I said, and pushed it into her fingers. Her head came up and her eyebrows, surprised. 'I had to guess. I can easily get you something else if you don't like it.' No point telling her it was a Slimline tonic: I've never met a girl yet who would waste calories, but they don't want to talk to you about it on a first night out, do they?

Not that Christina needed to diet. The second she walked into the pub, men's heads were turning to look her up and down. I wanted to put my arm around her, to show them that she was with me and to shield her from them at the same time, but it was too soon for that. She was looking at me anyway, not them, tugging her dress down and not quite sure of where to stand. She looked a bit nervous.

She looked gorgeous. Very gorgeous.

'Thanks.' Angelo looked amazing, *and he was very welcome, not to mention the gin. It was my favourite, with ice and lemon and everything. Dead sophisticated. I took a massive swig to calm the nerves. Less sophisticated. If it'd been with a Slimline, it would've been perfect (but at least he didn't seem to think I had a bum like Ben Nevis). It was spooky enough as it was, the way he sort of knew what I liked.*

'Let's sit down,' he said, and he led me – he was quite tall when he was beside me, maybe a foot taller than me – over to a table beside one of those squashy sofas that they've got in pubs, with a little table for our drinks at either side of it. With Jonty, it'd have been a barstool job, I thought, for him *of course, carpet cushion for me. Angelo sat down right beside me. He had on black trousers and a midnight blue shirt, so clean and so well-ironed that it puffed out around his body a bit, but in a crispy kind of a way. He even smelled nice. Expensive. Expensive and male. Expensive and male and very,* very *sexy. I settled down into the lovely blue sofa. I settled down into the lovely, dark Angelo. I sank right down into the night. Gorgeous.*

Again, I thought, things like this just don't happen to girls like me. Life'd taught me, bit by bit, to forget about pots of gold at the end of rainbows, the buried pirate's treasure in the sea, or the coin beneath my pillow when I'd lost a tooth. (The tooth fairy couldn't fly as far as Gateshead – never made it across the Tyne.) Just being there with Angelo was teaching me I should always walk the extra mile to the rainbow. Even after everything that's happened, I'll never forget that now.

Angelo wanted to know all *about me, so I gave him the strictly edited version, the RP version, if you like: told him all about my family, 'mother', 'father' and 'sister', and left my little brother right out of the conversation, where he belonged. None of it was lies, exactly, but all the material was pretty carefully selected. I was soon starting to run dry, though, so I was glad when Angelo looked down at his watch and said, 'We'd better head off to the restaurant.'*

Restaurants, gin and tonic (with calories and without paying), Angelo and me. Black eyes and the blonde, I thought, Bogie and Bacall. What a combination. What a future.

I had to stop thinking about the past. I looked down and saw that Christina had this funny little handbag, like a square silver safe, only soft, and with a New York address written on the front of it. I wondered what exactly was inside it. I could tell she was still feeling nervous – those blue eyes were all over the place, even when she was just talking about her sister and school – so I put my arm around her when we got out of the pub. It felt great. She had bones like a bird.

That arm was so warm, so big and so welcome the first time I felt it around my shoulders, that I laughed. I smiled up at Angelo's face, about to say something, and then got stuck at the black, black eyes. Lost my thread altogether. He could see right inside you, anybody could tell that, and he was really *special, anybody could also tell that.*

And I was starting to hope that he might just, maybe later on some time, be mine.

Mine, I thought, walking down the street, looking down into her tilted, oval, open little face. Mine, as I sat down opposite her in the restaurant, and helped her to order some wine and food. Mine, I thought, especially when I touched her hand, her knee, her thigh.

Mine.

It was embarrassing: I was wired to him. Every time Angelo touched me, I jumped; when he went to the loo, my eyes were glued to his hips, shoulders, legs – and obviously his bum (though that's not news to you, now). Slight touch of Jude Law to the walk.

It was one treat after another. 'Make sure you get enough to eat,' he says. 'And don't worry about ordering the right kind of wine or anything: have exactly what you like best.' I had been going to ask for half a lager. And he looked after my coat, found out where the loo was for me, told me what some of the sauces were. 'You'll like the Pollo alla Fiorentina,*' he says. His voice sounded even more gorgeous than ever, and there was this little half moon of light lying along his eyelashes. 'Or the fillet steak in brandy.' Well, both of those sounded lush, but the pasta price alone would've just about emptied my pay packet! Just as I thought that, he says, 'Don't worry about the bill, Christina. Have whatever you like.' Like I said, as smooth and as dark as chocolate. It was like being in a different century, a really civilised one.*

The restaurant had these great high ceilings; you could look up and really breathe out. Angel air. The whole place was done out in different creams and whites. Dead cool. And there were these really posh people all around us: their voices were floating up to the ceiling on their own. Totally effortless. I would never sound like that, I thought, even in my Cockney/Las Vegas voice. Especially in my Las Vegas voice. (Totally laboured.)

I settled for the Pollo alla Fiorentina *in the end: chicken in a smooth sauce, on a spinachy green little mattress, with loads of other vegetables as well. The green beans were squeaky clean on my teeth, reminding me of my hair when I tested whether it was clean enough after I'd washed it. (If only the rest of me, inside and out, were as clean as that.) The salad had artichoke hearts and petals in it. Swallowing hearts and flowers, I thought. Any time.*

*I nearly passed out when Angelo ordered the wine. '*Vernaccia di San Gimignano.*' Superb, they were – the wine, the voice and the accent. I was dreaming about Angelo and Italy the whole time I was eating the meal: Angelo, Italy and Florence – all palaces, Ponte Vecchio and paintings. My mouth was all creamy and warm, and quiet, for once, as I ate pieces of chicken – tiny,* *closed mouth, nodding little head. All this time, the candlelight was flickering away: Angelo, with the light making shadows on his beautiful bones; Angelo, with that little quirk on the one side of his face, and me, sat right opposite him, with his grandma's clasp in my hair. Angelo, with his great black eyes concentrating on* me. *What I couldn't understand was why every woman in the restaurant wasn't winging her way over to my table to dribble over my dish! Then we had these special cakes,* panforte *and* ricciarelli: *one was a triangle of cake, dry and dusty and solid, made me cough (all spicy!), and the other one was like a boat, full of honey (all smooth!). A boat that took me to Italy. And he could talk, and rarer still for a bloke, listen. By the time that meal was over, Angelo could have written my biography. A very cleaned up version of it, that is.*

It's funny, though I asked him loads of questions as well, I hardly remember finding out anything about him that night. He'd been to university, no surprise there: he was obviously dead intelligent, not like me. He came from Gosforth, dead posh, also not like me. He quite liked working at the casino, but not as much as I did, I reckoned.

There was some mention of a brother and that was about all I got out of him.

I'd worked out a while before that Christina had had some sort of a fling with Jonty (I tried very hard not to think about that one) and it was also obvious that I wasn't getting the whole truth about every aspect of her life. Each time there was a bit of the story that didn't quite fit, she changed her voice and looked away from me. I put it down to wanting to impress me and left it at that. Tried to leave it at that, tried not to let it nag at me. And she talked so quickly, her words kind of cancelling one another out, as if she never expected anyone to listen to her at all.

A band of white light lay across her wrist, laid there by the candlelit glass lamp at her side. The candlelight kept catching on my grandmother's clasp, and I wondered who was looking over or across to our table that night, one way and another.

The second I thought that, there was one of the blacker moments. A hint. The waiter was coming across to hand over the bill and a few chocolates, I could see the dish in his hand, and he was just saying, 'Would you like me to get you anything else?' meaning our coats, or whatever, when Mic's laugh rang out across the restaurant, as if the waiter had said something obscene. *'And is there nothing wrong with you at all?'* My eyes were all around the room, looking for the dark head thrown back, laughing, searching for Mic, sitting at a table, carrying on with his girlfriend or a group of friends, and as the laughter carried on, several dark heads turned and everything went bright. Staring faces were reflected in mirrors and laughter bounced around the walls. Echoes. It's starting, I thought, it's starting again. Some tinny voices, staring faces and dark brown hair. *'Come with me, Ango!'* It was Mic's voice, but it was just in my head. *'Come with me!'* My conscience. *'Raw pain.'* Cornered. Christina looked at me, everything darkened slightly, and then it all clicked back into place. *'Raw love.'* The laughter died down, Mic was nowhere in sight and nothing had really happened. *'Raw life.'*

Thank God, I thought. Really, thank you God. Not that I didn't want to see Mic.

But now I could concentrate on Christina.

All of a sudden there, Angelo was gone. (He'd hardly drunk anything all night either, gave most of the wine to me.) I thought he was going to do a runner and leave me with the bill, then I said, 'Traitor!' to myself, for the second time. By that time he was back to me, organising coats and credit cards and insisting I had the chocolates that had come with the bill. I was worried about him, really worried. His pupils were massive and his face was full of panic. And after the panic, waiting, waiting and what else? I tried to describe it properly to myself.

Waiting and despair. What was it that was hurting him so much?

Just about managed to get away with that, I thought, as I slipped her coat over her shoulders for her and breathed in, but it still took me a minute to settle down. *'You didn't even try to look after him?'* What am I doing? I thought. Out on the Town, out in Newcastle having a good time, while my brother, my brother . . . Mic, my brother.

Then, when we walked past the Haymarket Metro station, I saw a giant advertisement on the wall in there, a poster of a baby. Sounds ordinary, but it wasn't. You see, the front of the baby's brow had been torn off, so that underneath it, you could see an older advert. So that inside the baby's white skin, the baby's head, were all these mechanical things, CDs and tapes and stuff, spilling out all over. Out of control. Frightening.

That's exactly how I felt, sometimes. Exactly how I'd started to feel that night.

Shit. All of a sudden my thoughts flipped back to Christina. We hadn't even discussed where we were going; I'd just been walking along the street without a word about her place or mine, let alone taxis, another drink, or whatever.

I looked down at her face and saw the same questions in her eyes.

Does Angelo want me to go back with him? I was thinking. He'd been funny ever since leaving the restaurant; before leaving, even. Distant. Should I have offered to pay my half of the bill, even though he'd implied that he would pay? I wanted to take that terrible expression off his face, wanted to make him smile. No chance. And then there was a poster of a baby staring at me that just gave me the creeps. It was as if it could see into me. It was all going wrong! I glanced up at Angelo's profile.

Then the hardness went, he looked down at me and into my

eyes for ages. Dead steady. His head tilted down and he said right into my ear, 'Christina, you look great. Please come back to the church with me.' He grabbed my hand and squeezed it, tight. His face was still serious, but he was totally concentrating on me now. Much better. 'It will change everything between us.'

I looked back at him. Only thing some blokes were interested in changing when they asked you back home with them was the sheets, and not always those. But Angelo was completely different: he was waiting for my reply as if I was the most important woman in the world to him. I think I was the most important woman in the world to him. He was all eyes and bones, and eyes and bones last forever. So I smiled right into those eyes, and I nodded, slowly.

So I steered her over in the direction of the taxi rank. We could have walked, but there were moments when she looked like she'd been walking everywhere her whole life.

I would have carried her there in my arms, if that had been what Christina wanted.

And then we got a taxi home. I mean, we could've walked, it was only five minutes. The guilt was starting to kick in about how much he was spending that night, because obviously he was just on a waiter's pay. (Though I was glad I hadn't far to walk in those shoes: it was a struggle to stay on my feet, let alone look elegant.) Taxis are so New York, don't you think? Arthur Miller's city. Big yellow cabs. As we drove out of the Haymarket, it was just like all of Newcastle's Georgian buildings had turned into the Empire State building. And the statue in front of the Civic Centre of the bloke diving down, with his head and his fingers leading the way, was the Statue of Liberty (all that feeling) and Newcastle University was Harvard University (all those men). Fantastic.

Inside the taxi it was weird: Angelo's presence was so big, and the taxi was so small. You know when your eyes are greedy for someone? Mine were practically feasting on his flesh. I couldn't breathe and I still couldn't believe Angelo was actually with me. He gripped my hand really tightly again, like Keanu Reeves in Speed, *just before they crash – you know, when Sandra's tied to the metal post, jiggling away like mad, and Keanu clings on anyway? Dead brave. Then Angelo put one hand on the top of my thigh, underneath my dress, and some of his magnetism went right inside me. Dead sexy. I couldn't even chat: just breathing was getting to be a struggle! He moved his hand.*

I didn't dare *look into his eyes.*

Christina looked stunning in that dress, stunning. It was dark and satiny, like a slip, and when I glided my hand inside the hem to touch her, I could feel sheer material, lace and then satiny, warm skin, so touchable. And touching. My fingers caught very slightly on the web of fabric as I stroked her thigh, and she jumped. She'd worn stockings for me, for me and her. Us. I hoped that nobody sitting in the restaurant had seen her stockings, had seen her thighs. Mine.

I kissed the thin skin on the top of her ear and the taxi pulled up outside the church.

Eyes Wide Shut

6. The Black Iron Staircase

'Churches are for lovers everywhere and she belonged in mine.'

I felt dead shaky then; felt like I was walking right inside a film of a Stephen King novel, with Jack Nicholson holding the one hand and Kathy Bates the other. Shining? *Shocking! And there was old big gob, still screaming and running across his bridge, hands over his ears, right over my head. Angelo had definitely tidied up, though: the place looked less chaotic altogether. Good for both my ego and his own, I reckoned.*

'Angelo,' I said, 'can't you do something about that picture?' I waved my hand up at the screamer. 'Honestly, it terrifies the life out of me.'

He looked up at it, smiled slowly, and laughed out a 'Really?' making me realise for the first time that he never *laughed normally. Really rare, for him. Then he went over to a corner, came back with some step-ladders, climbed right up there, making this great Italian-type show of the whole affair, and threw a massive towel over old big gob's head, until the picture looked like the Elephant Man on a bad hair day.*

'Better?' I asked, and Christina actually breathed out, nodding and smiling, then she turned from me and sat down on the settee. I sat down close beside her, really close, so that I could breathe in her skin, which smelled of pollen and creams. I held her in my arms and kissed her nose, and when she shut her eyes and put her arms around my neck, I kissed her lips and touched her tongue with mine, fingering the tops of her thighs with both of my hands. Christina shuddered and pulled back from me, all at once.

'Can I have a drink?' she said, her hands down on her hem, exactly as if she was posing for a middle-school class photo.

Cool down, she meant. Too late, I thought. Much too late.

Suddenly I wasn't so sure of myself; I wasn't quite so sure of Angelo. Why *had I put those hold-ups on? He would think I was a* complete *slapper, that's if he didn't already. How well did I really know him, anyway?* Eyes Wide Shut, *as always.*

Thank God he went off, fixing me with those eyes first, but I wasn't sure what the eyes were saying to me this time. Then he shouted over from his kitchen corner, 'Do you want some orange juice or coffee? Or should I open a bottle of wine? I've got one in the fridge.'

Jesus Christ, was he trying to anaesthetise me or what? I'd already had four glasses of wine and a gin. Fear brought my backbone snapping back! 'Just a very *small glass please, Angelo,' I yelled through, for my* very *short stay, I meant, wriggling my spine right back up into its place. 'Orange juice will be fine.' Definitely.*

Definitely nervous. And my whole body was going for it. Back off, I said to myself. Gently, remember? Softly, softly. Back right off.

But I had to touch her.

The glass, practically pint-sized, of course, was in my hand, and then my legs were on the settee: Angelo lifted them right

*up in one movement, so that my back was on the arm now,
my juice was nearly on the floor and my feet were smack in
his lap. I sucked my spinachy stomach well in and stuck my
'not-scared-for-one-second' smile on my face.*

At least he'd put a few more lamps on. The church wasn't
quite *so* Nostradamus.

Christina's hands were tiny when she reached out to take
the glass from my fingers; I'd never seen such small hands.
And her shoes were wrong; they were at least a size too big.
I smiled as I pulled them off, as they fell off, almost, some
tissue tipping out of the toe of one of them on the way,
and I tried to catch Christina's eye to share the joke, but
she looked away and her mouth drooped a bit. She's got
no money, I thought. Shit. My smile faded and for once in
my life, I stopped thinking about my erection.

Christina's feet weren't much bigger than my hands, so I
held them between my palms, stroking the bony little webs
at the top while she drank her juice; she forgot about her
worrying and started to soften up. Her sips grew smaller and
smaller while my hold grew stronger and stronger. Minutes
passed as she finally began to let go. At last.

'Are you tired?' I asked, when the sips had stopped
almost completely. 'You *must* be tired.'

'I must not,' she said, flashing her eyes at me. 'Not really!'
But then she put down her glass on the floor. And she made
no move to leave.

'I know you are,' I told her. 'Just relax for a few minutes.'

'What if I want to go home?' She sounded about twelve.

'If you want to go home, we'll sort it out,' I said. But I'd
make sure that she didn't ask that again. Then, 'Relax.'

'Just for a minute, then.'

Christina moved her body down the settee, so that her
head was tilted back against the arm and her feet and her
calves were on my lap now. A tiny toe touched my groin

for one electric second, but I don't think she even noticed. She turned on her side, with one forearm supporting her head, reminding me of Titian's *Venus of Urbino*, almost.

The little curves of her calves were like the longer curves of her thighs and the arch of her foot in my hand was like a narrowing waist in my palm. I felt the lines of her feet, holding them tightly together in one hand while stroking them with the other, then I followed the lines of her feet up to her calves and back again.

Churches are for lovers everywhere and she belonged in mine. Her legs began to warm; her blood began to warm. Women are all liquid, I thought, young women, that is. Soft. Deep. Down, down into the water to find Eurydice. I traced the lines of her legs with my fingers, the curves. The curves that were like blood and milk to me.

Blood, milk, tears and feelings, I thought. And babies. My babies. Young women.

There were some shudders again, but I wasn't frightened now, not really. Deeply passive was how I felt, deeply relaxed. Almost hypnotised. It was so intimate, the way that Angelo cradled my feet in his hands, and it was lovely having my legs stroked and my feet touched. I felt wanted. Completely wanted. Really rare, for me.

I closed my eyes and edged my way down the settee a few inches, arranged the old prayerbones to look their least Moss-like, and when my dress edged up over my thighs by a few inches too, I just let it, feeling his eyes on me. I really enjoyed the thrill of the thought that Angelo was looking at my legs, right up to the stocking tops.

Almost up to my knickers.

If Christina changes her mind now, I will *explode*, I thought. But I knew she wouldn't, not lying the way she was on the settee. I hated the thought that Jonty had seen her body before me, that anybody had seen her body before me, but I made myself concentrate on the present.

She looked gorgeous. I could have painted her: I'll never forget it.

Her legs were slim, but there was a slight roundness to them at the calves and the thighs. (I needed to feel, know, the exact curves of her backside and cunt.) Her legs were bent slightly at the knees and twisted, so that I got a strategically arranged view of the tops of her thighs and the tiny, secret v-shape of the front of her knickers. You could see the top of one milky little breast, just coming out of the neckline of her dress as well.

Very, very soft.

I hadn't been out with a woman for more than six months, not since university, and the size of my erection proved it. Even the skin round there felt tight and my balls felt heavy and full, impossible to ignore.

My hand moved very slowly up her leg and I edged myself alongside her on the settee. Her hair smelled of lime and coconut and grass, but the traces of oil at the roots of her hair smelled warmer and woodier, like pine resin. She moved slightly and pressed both warm breasts against my chest, just rubbing them against me as she put her arms around my shoulders.

'Your breasts are lovely,' I said, fingering the tops of them where they slightly spilled out of her dress. 'I love feeling them against my chest.' My arms went around her back and I held her tight, I couldn't hold back, and I pressed myself hard against that private, secret black v-shape that I'd just been focussing on before. Her knickers were so flimsy – silky soft and slippery. I had to touch them with one hand, while I carried on holding her tight and safe against me with the other. 'You feel lovely and warm there,' I told her. Actually, she felt hot – hot and soft. I got to know her back, which was narrow and bony inside the dark satin, and she even shivered when I touched her shoulders. My chest moved forward a bit, forcing her nipples to rub against it more, and my hands slipped down towards her bum. I savoured the feeling of pressing her padded arse into my hip bones, moving my hands firmly over the satin of her dress which was tight against her curves now, tucked up. She actually gasped, once.

My cock felt bigger than the whole of her body at that second.

'Your body is gorgeous, Christina,' I said, rubbing my face into her scented neck as she stretched her spine. 'All night, you've just looked so slim, so smart.' I gave her bum a little squeeze, slipping my hands inside the dress now so that both of my hands were pressed to her knickers. 'Your arse is spectacular,' I whispered into her neck, massaging her behind with the palms of my hands. You have to be so careful what you say to girls, because they all hate their bodies and worry about looking fat all the time, but I wouldn't have moved my hands for the world. 'Is that nice?'

I wanted Christina to know that she was beautiful to me. I wanted her to feel confident, sexy – to *be* confident and sexy.

Nice*? As if Angelo wasn't enough in himself, he was making me feel like Naomi Campbell, only white, poor and short, just when I was worrying in case he found a bit of cellulite. (Not that I had any: I'm a bit on the spelky side actually, but that didn't stop me worrying about it at moments like that.) It was really hard not to make a moaning noise.*

But the best thing of all was that he was talking with me, and thinking about me, all the time. He spoke quite slowly. Every word counted. My eyes filled up with tears: it was such a contrast to Jonty and his wordless sweating and slavering. Angelo even had the voice of an angel, a voice that connected his body to his soul. It sort of hummed, underneath. He was lovely; I felt lovely. Dead sexy.

I moved my nipples against his chest and I liked their hardness, their sensitivity. I hoped he would too and pushed Shelley's, Argos's, chicken breasts right to the back of my mind where they belonged. My hands started on the buttons of his shirt, one at a time, teasing him (although from what I could feel against the front of my undies and what I could hear in his voice, he was more than worked up enough already).

Christina undid my shirt buttons, then I ripped my shirt and trousers and socks off. Her dress came next and she looked lighter than ever in nothing but her knickers, bra and stockings. She had a big yellowing bruise on the back of her shoulder that'd been hidden by her dress and there was a fading grey bruise on her arm as well that I'd noticed before. I'll ask her about them later, I thought, wondering. I took her bra off and touched the tips of her nipples over and over again. My fingers barely grazed them yet she shut her eyes at once and bit her lip. Her bum squirmed, so that her sex was pushing against mine, and I held her really tight and felt like I could come there and then, up against her pants. I ran my hands along her thighs up to her knickers and touched her at the front, at one of the reddest, the most sensitive parts of her. 'Does that feel nice?' I asked again, more to reassure her that I cared about her feelings than because I needed an answer. Bodies speak louder than words and Christina's closed eyes and concentrated expression told me she was blissful, physically.

But women need you to talk to them, don't they?

Pec paradise! His body was amazing. *I mean, I'd hoped it would be good, but it was* gorgeous. *Does he work out? I wondered. And his fingers were pretty amazing too. By the time he finally touched my clitoris, I was shaking, which had never happened to me before. Angelo moved his hands then and put them on either side of my face. 'It's great that you're here with me, Christina. And I'm glad you trust me,' he said. He looked right into my eyes. 'Are you all right?' Those wonderful eyelashes. I butterfly touched them.*

Until he said that, I'd actually been feeling a bit dodgy on the trust front, as you know, but he'd sort of reassured me. Sneaky. 'Brilliant,' I said. Then I thought, Don't boost his ego any more: it's not really good for blokes, is it? And I knew I was really falling for him. His chest was so muscular, like a row of little cushions. His arms were the same. And for somebody who'd been so buttoned up all night, he certainly had a lot to say in bed. Then he let his fingers do the work. One hand was rhythmically rubbing my clitoris, in small circular movements, and the other arm was holding me to him really tightly, and that hand kept stroking my stocking tops and pushing at the curves of my bum, forcefully, so that I was right up against his massive hard-on.

Forcefully? I loved it. Every second.

I pulled her knickers off in one hard yank and she unclasped her bra. She went to pull down the stockings, but I said, 'No. Leave them on, Christina. Leave them on for me.' Her little hand went down to my big cock and she fingered it, then held it in her hand, smiling up into my eyes. I had to move her hand away. 'I want to be inside you,' I told her.

Her eyes moved towards the staircase and I nodded.

'Upstairs,' I said. And because I knew I had no cellulite, and because I knew Angelo liked my bum, I walked slowly up the staircase ahead of him. Every movement was a luxury. A total luxury.

How we got as far as the bedroom, I'll never know.

Christina walked so slowly up those black iron steps and my eyes started at the bottom and moved up. First of all, I saw her dainty stockinged feet on the lower rungs, then those sculpted, shapely calves rotated up the steps. When the thighs were at my eye level, the tops of the stockings were just biting into her white, milky flesh, indenting her skin, nipping her slightly, temptingly. Black, white and black. Ripe. She even smelled warm, warm and milky. I reached up and adjusted the lacy black fabric at her thighs a little on each side, slowly (the skin on her legs smelled like musk rose, a mixture of creams that she must have put on and her own body's scent), and then she moved up one more rung, with my hands still on her legs. Her bare white arse was right in my face, soft, round and split, and the instinct to penetrate, hard, strong and swift, was almost overwhelming, but I held back. I pressed one palm firmly on to each cheek, though, feeling her, and she finally moaned, bent forward slightly with her head against the cool steps, her lips open, and pressed her breasts into the cold, black iron in front of her. Very ripe. Her behind pouted out at me, curved like a question mark.

I opened the rose of her backside with my palms, and I kissed its peppery centre.

Well, no one had ever done that *to me before! I didn't know I had feelings like that in that bit. Best get into bed quick, I thought: I wasn't quite sure what he was thinking.*

It was funny, but all the time Angelo was looking at me on the stairs, I wanted to cover myself up, yet that was the biggest part of the excitement. Shame. Shame, nakedness and sex. Sex is weird, isn't it?

The bed was clean, The Scream *was masked, and I snuggled into Angelo's dark embrace, we were side by side on his bed, wound my arms tight around his neck and held on for my life: DiCaprio and Kate, coming up to the very tip of the* Titanic! *'Trust me?' DiCaprio. 'We're flying!' Kate. I couldn't wait.*

I fingered Christina around her clitoris, to make sure she was hot and happy and ready: touching her lightly told me she definitely was. Her eyes were shut and she was holding on really tight, as though we were going to fly, almost.

I kissed her shut eyelids. 'Can I put my hand inside you, Christina?' She gave a tiny nod and bit her lip. The closed eyes made it look like she was praying, praying for me. She looked exactly like Rossetti's *Beata Beatrix*, with her face tilted up and her eyes closed. Mystical. The skin of her breasts was like the skin of milk when it warms – creamy, thin and soft-scented.

I pushed my middle finger inside her, and when her backside jerked back instinctively from the pain, I forced her body back towards me with my arm, so that her clitoris was still stimulated against my hardness; her little breasts were still shaking against my chest.

It was the nearest thing, the very nearest thing, to the red notebook for me. I held her hot, red intimacy in my hand, touched the centre of her, the life of her, the vulnerability, the death of her. I moved my hand, hard, and she jerked again, crying out, but the liquid flow increased, slightly. Her arms were so tight around my neck that she was hurting me.

I pulled my hand out, pulled a condom on, waited for her blind nod, and drove myself, hard, four inches into her raw, red, tight body.

Despite the condom, it was her womb I was aiming at.

I didn't let myself go until Christina cried, once, shaking and jerking. Then I pushed harder still into the friction and life and redness and tenderness, and Christina cried out again, louder this time.

I was pushed by my own need as much as Angelo's. He was so intense: he put his whole life into it, his whole life into my body. Then he made an awful noise, he felt heavy in my arms, and our senses seemed joined. I think I'd made a noise as well. A big noise, then. Noises. I didn't dare open my eyes and look at him.

I was really *embarrassed.*

I knew Christina would be shy, she was shy about everything, despite all the talking and the jokes.

I pulled out straightaway and got rid of the condom. Her arms were still around my neck and her head was down. I just hugged her to me so that she didn't have to look at me until she felt more confident, more like herself. And I held her until the raw, red tenderness of her skin, of her feelings, began to fade, because I wanted the tenderness to fade without a mark, without a single insecure memory. When she eventually rocked back slightly against me, I whispered into her ear, 'You're a beautiful lover, Christina, a beautiful girl,' and I held the back of her head in my hand. But she bent her head down, which took her face right away from me, and I could only see the crown of her head, the small swirl of blonde hair. She was silent.

I started to worry myself, then. Did she regret what had happened between us? She hadn't been faking, had she? She hadn't been comparing me with anybody else?

I needed to look into her eyes.

I could feel Angelo looking at me, so I lifted my head up and met those eyes, which was, as you know by now, meeting the whole of Angelo, body and soul. He smiled the most beautiful, crooked smile, and the lids of his black, black eyes creased. His teeth were actually quite small and white. 'Okay?' he said. 'You did come, didn't you?' Well, if I didn't, I'm wasting my talents as a croupier, I thought: I could be an internationally renowned porno actress after a performance like that.

But I didn't want to be crude with Angelo; with Angelo who cared so much about whether I came or not, and talked to me, and made love to me like a man and not an animal, so I just nodded and smiled at him.

And then I snuggled her in and said, 'You will stay the night, won't you?' and she snuggled back and said yes, that would be great. And I smoothed her creamy, cooling skin all calm again, and I kissed her, and teased her, and she smiled and started to relax, and she touched my eyes and my face and began to chat to me and be a bit more ordinary again, but also more intimate in a different kind of way. And it was lovely, really lovely.

But there was just one thing that had to be said before I could sleep.

There was just one thing that worried me, afterwards, a few minutes later, when we were wrapped up all close and sleepy and chatty together in bed, the screaming man nicely masked and every one of my defences down. It started with a little, tiny cough – a little cough I grew to really, really hate.

I cleared my throat and leaned up over her on one elbow. 'One point, Christina,' I said. It was eating into me. I looked down towards her open, lovely, question-marked face, which was resting on the pillow. I touched her curved cheek. 'There's just one thing that's bothering me, Christina.

'I know that you had some sort of a thing going with Jonty. I don't like him and I don't like it, I don't like it at all. I can't stand to think about it, to talk about it. I never want to have to mention it to you again.' I couldn't quite read the expression on her face, so I shook her hand.

'Do you understand?'

I just nodded. That worried me too.

7. Coincidences?

'I often dream it's my father who's dead.'

And that, I thought, as I nestled down against Angelo's lovely olivey skin to sleep, was that. I really reckoned I had Angelo well and truly sussed. Angelo Paulillo, strong, silent until stirred, passionate, both a bottom and a breast man, a bit on the possessive side, a bit intense, maybe. He seemed perfect for me. Christina Rae, the Queen of Innocence. I couldn't believe my luck.

What I can't believe now is how I felt Angelo drift down into sleep beside me, felt his happiness murmuring away alongside my own, yet was totally unaware of all the other feelings that must have been going on in his head at the same time. I was totally unaware of all the other feelings that must have been building up in him for days. Months.

Because the first I knew about all that was the shouting.

'Michael, Michael.' The noise of the voice, shouting, woke me up seconds before I heard Christina's voice. 'Michael. Michael!' Was that Mic shouting or me? And why Michael? I hadn't called him Michael since I was about six and him seven, since we'd both started to get fed up of that whole, stupid 'Michelangelo' thing, when the other kids at school started to take the piss. But it wasn't the seven-year-old Mic that I'd just seen. It was the adult Mic. *'He was full of life from the start.'* The whispers never left me. *'You could do nothing to help him?' 'You could do nothing to help?'*

The adult Mic, curled up like a bean, like a baby, on a pavement in a street near Newcastle, with his straight brown hair sticking out. Mic, in my dream (or was he?), lifting his head up from the pavement and laughing straight into my eyes, his face evil and changed. Frighteningly alive, as always. My chest ached. And my throat.

Mic. Michael.

'Michael. Michael.'

Angelo was completely gone. Didn't seem to know where he was, or who he was with. Terrible. He was sitting up in bed, rigid, staring, awake, but his head was somewhere else, like a kid, sitting up in the middle of a totally real nightmare. I reached over him and clicked on the lamp.

'You were dreaming,' I said. 'Who's Michael?' I asked. 'Who is he?'

'Michael,' Angelo said again, quieter now, not seeming to hear me at all, and I searched for the words to describe the look on his face and the sound of his voice in the new light. Waiting, I thought. Waiting and despair. Again. What was *hurting him? And how could I help?*

'What were you dreaming about?' I asked, keeping my voice quite hushed.

'Michael.' Angelo's voice was broken, then he shut up altogether. I thought he was going to cry. I think he *thought he was going to cry.*

It's sometimes worse in the night because when you dream of them, they're alive. They *are* alive. I often dream it's my dad who's dead: my dad who left when I was three; my dad who's never really lived, for me. Of course, Mic is always alive in the dreams, very much alive.

Waking is terrible.

That night, Christina was there, there for me, and I knew

I had a world worth coming back to. I felt her arm on my back, stroking me, and her voice was in my ear.

'Angelo?' He heard me that time; he knew I was there at last. My big-screen movie star, my satyr of the night before, had melted into the darkness, had joined the darkness, and his eyes looked all young and old at once when he finally turned around to me. Lost. All of the dominance, strength and intensity of the night before had been turned into the most domineering, strongest, most intense suffering in the night. Totally unforgiving.

'What happened then, Angelo?' I put my arm around him and rubbed his back. 'Just tell me what happened.'

I knew that I could help.

It was weird. I obviously wasn't going to go into detail or anything, wasn't going to mention Mic at all, but I had to say something, so I just talked about a dream and a street near Newcastle and a person all curled up on the pavement. 'It was terrible,' I said to her. 'It was so terrible, I can't tell you.'

And then Christina began to talk.

I'd thought of that day often, the day of my interview. I was always aware that I could have been the girl on the ground, and that Jonty could have been the bloke with the cross: God knows, he was violent enough when he had a drink in him. Of course, I hadn't talked about any of that Jonty-King-of-Clubs side at all with Angelo (and I couldn't now, after what he'd said the night before).

But I'd been dying to tell Angelo about how gorgeous and strong I'd thought he was that day. I carried on from where he left off, from the person curled up on the pavement.

'You were a hero,' I said. 'Brilliant. Then I dragged the girl out of the way, and you left, and then she went back to the bloke in the end, after all that. And then I saw you at the casino just a few minutes later. What a coincidence! Do you remember?'

*   *   *

I remembered that, the smell of CK One, the blonde hair and more. 'I remember,' I said, 'but I don't believe in coincidence, Christina. It wasn't a coincidence at all.'

The fact that she had been there for that scene, that much smaller scene, made it feel as though I could trust her. Made it feel as though she was connected to what had happened to Mic as well. And because I was separated from Mic and just about everybody who knew him (apart from old Irene), that made Christina very special to me, as if she wasn't special enough to start with.

And she could soothe me. The luxury of being soothed.

That calmed Angelo down, for some reason, and we lay back down together again on the bed. Not a coincidence, I thought. What did it mean, then? Something more significant altogether, I hoped. And what had happened in the street that day was maybe connected to something else, I thought to myself, he'd got that upset about it all.

I lay on my back, pulled Angelo down the bed until he was half lying on top of me, and rested his head against my boobs, stroking his black, black hair with my fingers and murmuring nothingness into him, feeding it into him to starve the awful feelings away. His breathing turned regular, then sleepy after a while, but I stroked and murmured on. I wanted to make sure there was no repetition of the horrors and I wanted Angelo to know that whatever awful thing had happened in the darkness, he could rest now. I wanted to rescue him this time. Galileo had trouble sleeping, you know. Special people obviously do. (I sleep like a log.) But eventually I calmed Angelo down and he went back to sleep.

Then I lay there in the darkness alone, thinking about Angelo, and thinking about Michael. Who was he, for a start? Why was he so important to Angelo?

And what on earth had happened to them both?

8. Black-Red Roses and Glass

'Christina, wrapped around my iron steps, wrapped around my body.'
'He could be such hard work. Difficult. Moody.'

After nights like that, I sometimes found that the red notebook could help, that it held coded answers, messages, especially for me. So after Christina had gone the next day, I couldn't wait to look inside it and read what it had to tell me.

Everybody looks for the lost children. How many kids get lost, in supermarkets, on caravan sites and beaches, on the way home from school? And so many children are lost before they're even born, through abortions, miscarriages. (I hate abortion, hate it. The waste of it.) Think about Mary Shelley, sifting through the water and the words for her dead babies. But what about the lost children, the adult lost children, looking for their mothers? You can call and call all you like, but you can't make a lost mother come back to you. The only time you have sight of them is when you're doing something they would hate, like having sex, or drinking too much, or something. Then you get the sense of them clearly enough, right at the end of your bed, like my screaming man.

Anyway, the only way of getting any help from my

mother now was the notebook, so I headed for the candle box again. I opened the book at random, after some forceful concentration and a request for help. Instead I got accusations. Criticisms.

> *Sometimes, it felt like everything I ever did for Angelo was wrong, from losing his father to naming him and Michael. Because he always felt like he was the second half of the name and Michael was the first, and Angelo definitely didn't like being the second half of anything, not even as a toddler. He could be such hard work. Difficult. Moody. But that wasn't what I'd meant by the name at all, he must have known that, and Michelangelo himself was the second son.*
>
> *I'd just always thought it was a beautiful name, felt that I'd found unique, special names for my two unique, special sons. I still do. Angelo, touched by the angels. (Maybe even that was partly my fault: I've read that it might be partly a genetic thing, or a family problem.)*
>
> *Except it turned out that it was my poor, brilliant Michael who had the worst problems. The very worst. A nightmare. Michael.*

A nightmare. *'A genetic thing.' 'A family problem.'* Like a mutation. *'Difficult.'* Like an abortion, not a birth. *'Brilliant Michael.'*

There were two fat, unopened packages in there as well, splashed with stamps and postmarks. I put the red notebook on top, pushed them even further beneath the other debris and shoved the box away.

I tried to forget it all, and I sent Christina some flowers.

A spectacular *bouquet of roses arrived at my flat before my day shift, size of a fuchsia hedge. Angelo had sent them, of course, the blackness in the deep red told me that. 'See you soon, darling' was written on the card. (We'd arranged to meet in a few days' time.) I suppose if I'd managed to get his address and shifts from people at work, then my own address wasn't altogether a mystery, however hard I'd tried to make up a more important-sounding one. Just so long as he didn't decide to pay me a visit.*

When the middle-aged, middle management at the casino call you 'darling', or the punters, it just about turns your stomach. But from Angelo, all black eyes and bones, when Angelo called you 'darling', it was like seeing a shooting star flash across the sky. And the roses were so Miller and Monroe, so San Francisco, the Sunshine State, cheering up the West End winter, transforming it into California, Marilyn and Walt's state – Hollywood, Universal Studios, Sunset Strip, huge houses in Malibu and Palm Beach. The New World. I felt as if Angelo and his roses had actually taken me there. It was the first time anyone had ever sent me flowers. Spectacular.

Except Angelo's life wasn't exactly Hollywood, was it? I kept thinking of his face when he'd woken up from his dream: Brad Pitt, at the end of Seven, *in the desert, bending over that box with (probably) his wife's head in it. Burning. Michael Douglas, just after he thinks he's killed his brother, Sean Penn, and just before he jumps off the roof and into all that glass at the end of* The Game. *Hard. Too hard. Terrible.*

But, 'darling'! I used every one of them, every single rose. I left them in their rustly cellophane wrapper in a bucket until after my shift, then I thought of Angelo for ages when I came home to them that night, crinkling the cellophane, running my fingers through the dark, shiny, curly ribbons again and again, thinking of his dark, shiny, semi-curly hair. 'Darling.' I arranged them in a vase, like a display. 'Darling.' Then I left some in the vase and spread the rest around my rooms. One rose lay on my pillow, to speak to me as I slept. One wound itself into my hair, like the diamanté clasp. One shredded itself into petals and pollen in my bath, to scent my skin. One sat on the table, near my food, to feed my feelings. 'Darling.'

I laid the petals of the last one on my tongue, feeling them in my mouth, tasting the dry papery perfume, breathing it right down inside me. Almost tasting Angelo, it felt like. Breathing him in. I wanted the blackness, the nightness *of him then.*

It irritated me, my gratefulness. I was like a slave to him, always. But I knew even then that Angelo would have loved it, if he could have seen: the roses in my bath, my skin, my food, my hair. My mouth. Angelo, in my skin, my hair and my mouth. My redness, his darkness, right inside of me, running right through me, even then.

That was one of the points when I should have been more afraid.

I wasn't at work until nine that night, so I had plenty of time to remember her, to dream of her.

I dreamed of her tender white skin, wound around with my roses, wound around in ribbons, wound around with my desires, my needs. Wound. And the fantasies built up around her, around beautiful Christina, with her blonde, glassy, daytime frailty and her woman's strength in the night. Her white, white skin. Beautiful Christina, wrapped around my iron steps, wrapped around my body.

It would be a few days, because of our shifts, before I would be able to see her alone again. A few days, because of Jonty's shifts, when she would see quite a lot of him. But I had decided not to think about that one.

Angelo might not have wanted to talk about Jonty, but Jonty certainly wanted to talk about Angelo. And I'd thought he had a nasty streak before. He went from nibbling, irritating goldfish to snapping, savage piranha overnight when he heard – from Shelley – that I was seeing Angelo.

The first time I got a break from the tables with him, the day after Angelo's roses had arrived, he started straight in.

'How's life with the Italian Stallion then, Teen?' he said. I'd progressed to contact lenses by then, and there was something about Jonty's expression, somewhere around the eyes, that made me wonder how much contact with the rest of the world I needed. I stared him full in the face though and brazened it out.

'A damn' sight better than life with the Wallsend Wanker

ever was, Jonty,' I snapped. 'Sent me a massive *bunch of roses yesterday, size of a Cadillac. Filled the whole flat up, they did.' I couldn't resist it, but it was asking for trouble. 'Any more questions?'*

Jonty's face froze and his fist twitched. The staffroom, with Alex and Peter the Pit Bull from Cowgate there, felt pretty safe, though. So I just prepared to sit Jonty and his mood out. But he couldn't leave it at that, of course. 'Hung like a horse, is he, Teen?' He spat the words out before stalking back, early, to the tables, throwing over his shoulder, 'That the big attraction, is it? I suppose it helps you to forget he's two sandwiches short of a picnic!' I blushed blood red, mortified. What was he on about? Then he 'accidentally' caught the side of my leg with his great foot as he left. All the other dealers looked away, which was a relief, as quickly as my own thoughts turned away. As quickly as my thoughts turned back to Angelo, trying to bury what Jonty had said about him and, worse, the fact that the other dealers had heard what he'd said.

Alex came and sat with me two minutes later. 'Take no notice of Jonty, Christina,' he said. 'He was just trying to get at you. I knew Ango at university, you know.'

I hadn't known. 'What was he like then?' I asked. 'How did you know him?'

'Well, he always seemed pretty clued up, I know that much.' Alex rolled his eyes at Jonty's comment. 'I was surprised to see him working here, but Newcastle's not exactly full of jobs for graduates, is it?'

'He never finished his course,' I said. 'Left at the end of the second year.'

'Of course.'

Gerry came in just then. 'Alex, I need you on AR6. They're doing their brains on there.' Alex nodded and stood up, throwing a few last sentences over his shoulder to me as he left. 'Ango was in my halls in his first year, then he left to go and live on a farm with a group of friends. He knows how to enjoy himself, and he's pretty bright as well. Forget what Jonty said – he doesn't know what he's talking about.' I was glad to follow Alex's advice.

And five minutes later, when I went out to get a coffee, Peter, lovely Peter, came with me. 'Is Jonty hassling ye, Chrissie?' he asked, then carried on, without waiting for an answer. ''Cos ye tell me if he is and I'll chin him for y'. I'll fuckin' chin him.' His jabbing chin joined in with his words. Subtlety was never Peter's strong point, but loyalty was, and I was really glad of his concern. I played it down, though. Didn't want to set up a whole new notoriety of my own in the casino.

'Bit on the bad-tempered side, Peter,' I said, shaking my head. 'That's all. Nothing to worry about. He'll get over it.' So one way and another, I stopped worrying about Jonty for a while.

Anyway, I couldn't think of anyone else but Angelo just then.

I'd been thinking of Christina more or less constantly, and mulling over a few other issues, but I didn't actually see her again for three days, and then she appeared out of the blue on my doorstep again, knocking this time.

'Just popped around to say thanks for the roses,' she said. 'Have you got a minute?'

Somehow, it all went wrong.

My first mistake, I realised straightaway, was that I hadn't checked up on Angelo's shifts: I'd been so keen to see him that I'd just turned up, and he was on an early. That left him with about twenty seconds to speak to me. But I'd been dying to see him. That was my second mistake, I reckon now. 'I thought we could sort out when we're going to see each other again,' I said, all keen, all confident, because of the roses and the memory of his mega-lust for me.

Angelo gave me that 'fuck off' look that could be so deadly attractive, and that was so painful now. I wished that I could swallow back my words, walk back my visit.

Too keen. Too confident. Too obvious altogether.

Couldn't she see that I was in a real hurry? I kissed her cheek, but my mind was full of other things, things I couldn't just send away. Not to mention, I had to get ready for work.

'Nice to see you,' I said. 'I've been thinking about you.' Amongst other things. 'Listen, I'm sorry about this, but could you just wait for me for a minute? I've got to get changed for work.' I headed upstairs.

My next mistake: temptation. Angelo went up to change his shirt and two seconds later, I dashed across to the windows to lift those old sheets up.

I'd been dying to find out what all that writing was and I'd finally plucked up the courage to look. It was all in ink, and he'd had one go, at least, at rubbing it off at some point. I began to read the words.

Once, the word was love
But the love grew pale
And so the word was lost.
And once . . .

What? I asked myself. Is he on drugs, or what? But it was getting through to me on one level at least that Angelo was having a hard time of it. It didn't sound like something he would normally write or say, obviously. He worked on being pretty cool, on a day-to-day basis. So was it a joke? It wasn't particularly funny. Worse, it reminded me of a loss of my own, a big loss, that I wouldn't be telling Angelo or anybody else about. Ever. It reminded me of a voice that I pushed away over and over again.

Just as I was thinking that, feeling like a spy and moving the sheets back over the writing, Angelo appeared at the top of the stairs, staring right down at me. He sucked in his stomach and his cheekbones, sharp as anything. Not a joke, I thought. Not funny at all. What exactly was going on then? It was so difficult to make it all out.

*   *   *

'Difficult.' 'A genetic thing.' 'A family problem.' How many times had I thought about those words?

That was what I was thinking when I felt a flash of interest about what Christina was up to, rushed down the stairs again, and found her trying to decipher the words around the windows, concentrating, frowning, tracing one nosy finger around the writing at a time.

'Difficult.' 'Moody.'

Shit. His face told me more than the writing had. Black *angry.*

'Just wondering about your drapery,' I said, switching the sheet properly back into place. Nervous. Then I straightened up. 'Bit on the unusual side, isn't it?' I said to him. Silence. He stared right through me. Double shit. 'Sorry,' I tried. Silence and more staring. 'Angelo?' I touched his arm, looked into his face. 'Sorry?'

But that didn't do it either.

I couldn't even look at her. As if it wasn't going to be hard enough to tell her anyway – if I told her – without all this snooping around.

'I've got to go to work,' I said. 'Don't mind if I lock up, do you? Don't want anybody prowling around the place when I'm not in it, do I, Christina?'

It wasn't Christina's business. It really wasn't her business and I had to punish her for that. But I'll never forgive myself for what happened over the next few days.

So that was it. Iceberg. Certainly there was no mention of another date. Titanic iceberg. Not to mention, I'd just worked out that Shelley was on his shift. Somehow, I knew better than to quiz him about her. I wanted to, though, very much. I can't have blown it that *easily, I thought, as I slunk back home to worry, depressed.*

Can I?

Those next days, the mood that I was in, I was pretty easy prey for Jonty. You couldn't let down your guard with him for a minute and I was definitely on his shit list.

But all I could think about was Angelo, and how miserable he was making me feel, and worst of all, how worried I was that I'd never get back with him again. No more 'darling', no more roses. It had been two full days since the window-watching episode and still he hadn't spoken to me.

'Put a drop of rat poison in there, have you, Angelo?' I said, smiling up at him as he walked through the casino with Mr Andreas' cup of consolation tea. (One of the big games was going badly.) Nothing. Or, 'How's it going today then, Angelo?' as he came across to my blackjack table with a round of sandwiches for Mr Gold, the jeweller (honestly!). Nothing. Mr Gold gave me a sympathetic wink. He was about thirty, older even, but there was a definite glint in his eye. Typical punter.

But from Angelo, nothing.

The third time I tried, bloody Jonty was the star witness. I was in the kitchen waiting for my tea on the second day. (Meals are free for casino staff and dear at the price.) 'Food's nice today, Angelo,' I lied, pointing at the slop of left-over-from-the-buffet-lasagne. 'Had any of this yourself?' Nothing. He looked right over my head. 'Had time for your tea yet, have you?' Nothing, nothing, nothing. My face dropped by about a mile, and when I turned around to walk back to the staffroom with my meal, Jonty was standing behind me in the queue, grinning hideously in my face, his crooked, fishy little teeth grimacing at me.

'Not looking very cheerful today, are we, Teen?' He grabbed the top of my arm, right where he knew I had the remnants of a big bruise from before. 'Love life going well for you, I hope? Any more roses appeared?' A red-hot splash of his sauce fell on to my collar bone, marking my dress strap and stinging my skin, and my eyes burned with tears which I blinked right away. If I let Jonty know that he was getting to me, he would only step it up. So when he followed me into the staffroom to 'entertain' me with his comments, thoughtfully, as I ate my lasagne and chips,

I just gritted my teeth, rubbed at my dress, snarled him a smile, shut up and put up with it.

I could have cheerfully pierced Jonty's lips with my teeth.

If I'd seen Jonty there, gloating, I'd have softened up a bit, I know I would. One of the other waiters told me what Jonty had said to Christina after she'd spoken to me, later on, and I felt pretty low when I thought about it. By the time I left my shift to go home, I was thinking I'd overdone it a bit. But I still couldn't bring myself to try and get in touch with her that night. I really wish now that I had.

Knowing full well that it would be a mistake, I went to my mam's house that night, partly to pay off some of the money that I owed her and partly to offload about Angelo and Jonty.

Except, of course, that my mam had really liked Jonty. She hadn't met him (I'd made quite sure of that) but she'd heard all about him, and she didn't like a good man to go to waste, as she always said. (Or a bad one. She had married my dad, after all.) But there was nothing else to do that night, so I went round there straight from the casino, with my money in my fist and my tale of tragedy ready to spill from my mouth.

I should have known the conversation was doomed from the second I saw the Angel of the North looming up against the black sky over my mam's house, the biggest, most often seen angel in the world (and probably the North East's biggest construction contract in decades). It looked even more scary than usual, its blind face pointing right at me, and when I knocked on the door and let myself into the living room, I could still see it through the window, its massive wings looking as if they were lifting in the black breeze. Typical bloke, I thought, casting his own body, that size, over and over again. What an ego that took! It makes a better skyline sculpture than an ornament – hardly goes with the décor in my mam's house. I tried to shrug the doomy feeling off.

'It's only me, Mam,' I shouted up the stairs as I walked in,

because she always thought I was a burglar. 'I've just brought your money round.'

'Chris?' she shouted down. Then I heard her slippered feet start down the stairs. 'That's a relief. Our Carol's out and I didn't know who it was.' Her blonde hair bobbed along with her words, for emphasis, like.

'Have you got time for a chat, Mam?' I asked. 'I've just finished work.'

'Yes. And I know what it is that you'll be wantin' to chat about,' she said, the blonde rinse doing its usual punctuation job. 'Finishin' with a canny lad like Jonty.' She'd already heard some of the details over the phone. 'I thought you were keen on him? It was him that got you into that casino, wasn't it? A lad that's always had a job and never been in any real trouble. Oh, that reminds me, Chris, your brother . . .' And she was off, with a few choice details about visiting Jamie, and what she'd seen that she shouldn't have in his flat, and my sister Carolina's boyfriend's probation, and then all her own diseases and depressions.

I jumped in, between the pile cream and the prospect of prison, to try and get some advice from her about the Angelo situation. 'He sent me some roses, Mam. Really nice ones.' I thought she'd be impressed. 'I mean, Jonty never did anything like that, did he?'

'Oh, Angelo this and Angelo that. You've only known him five minutes – bloody Eyetie! You lose your sense of humour with poor Jonty over that dress business, some other bloke sends you a bunch of flowers, and you're off.

'Christina Rae, you don't know as you're born. Same when you moved out of here into that flat you're so determined to keep. What's wrong with your room here, I don't know. You can't always have . . .'

And so it continued, until the Angel of the North looked like a really nice version of a Christmassy Gabriel, and the bus ride home in the dark, fighting off the brainless Geordie piss heads with my tongue, seemed like a taxi ride to Alton Towers. I had to get out. She always made me feel like that. My mam is the sort of person who gives you your own Christmas presents back eighteen months later. 'Here, have this cheap thing. I've never liked it.' Funny, though, she always likes my sister's presents.

I dropped that idea, dropped the conversation, dumped Carol's shoes and then left. The Northern Star guided me home, as always, while I tried to make sense of what she'd said. What was wrong with my room at home?

Sometimes, if the parents you've got aren't quite up to scratch every time (and who could be?), you've got to be your own parents. What was wrong with my room at home was that it was inside my parents' house. And right *inside my parents' marriage. All right, the West End was grottier than Gateshead even, and living on my own had taken a lot more getting used to at first than my mam would ever know, but at least I got some peace there. Peace to dream my dreams and make some plans, without their arguments, their dirt and their miserable example of a life staring me in the face, and without the poisonous gossip of the neighbours to bring me down. (*'The youngest lassie couldn't wait t' get away, you know! Left when she was just sixteen.'*) I mean, you don't inherit your* future *from your parents, do you? Not if you don't want to. I didn't want to. 'Couldn't wait to get away' was right.*

And Jonty had been in trouble, plenty of it, it was just that he'd been lucky enough never to be charged. Maybe if I'd given my mother a bit more than the edited highlights of my life, she might have understood me better. Might have. There'd been one especially foul story involving five pints of Stella lager, three treble vodkas, an awful row and his mother's eye socket. I didn't want *to believe that one, but I kept thinking about it anyway. Seemed like there was always some drama going on in Jonty's family and he'd kind of got used to that level of action. 'Families don't press charges,' he'd said, like it was a line in a play. 'Ever.' And he wasn't a bad lad, he'd said, not at all. Just drunk. He'd been drunk when he'd bragged to me about that one, come to think of it, drunk and stroppy and bad. That was the point when I knew he would have to go: 'Families don't press charges.' Sons don't damage eye sockets, was my version of the story. So I was glad that*

Angelo had given me a hand with getting rid of Jonty, whatever was about to happen next. I was actually looking forward to work the next day. Foresight has never exactly been my strength.

Because all of a sudden, the Jonty situation got totally out of hand.

9. The *Gone with the Wind* Staircase

'I felt like I was carrying a woman made of glass.'

The next day, what do you know? We were all three on the same shift. Christina Rae, the Queen of Fortune. The Fortune Cookie! *And Jonty started nibbling into me from just about the second the shift began. Biting.*

*I mean, it's not even as if he was that keen on me when he had the chance, was he? Anybody could see that. So what exactly was it that was making him so pissed off now? Hurt pride because of the scene over the dress with Angelo? Or the shame of losing face (and girlfriend) in front of the other dealers? The last was probably closer to the truth: Jonty and his precious mates. Whatever the reason, the piranha's teeth were definitely sharp that night. Not that I was thinking of Jonty, or his teeth, as I walked in. I was thinking of angel eyes. Black eyes and the blonde. Kidman and Cruise. (*Eyes Wide Shut: *that's me all over.) I was even wearing the lovely old hair clasp that he'd given me, as part of a last-ditch attempt to melt his cast-iron heart. See how well that worked!*

We were all on a late: nine at night until four in the morning, plus the count. (That's where the inspectors, dealers and cashiers count the drop – the takings – at the end of the night. No one at the Casino Club was allowed to leave until they'd finished.) It would be a long shift for me if Angelo's cold-shoulder treatment carried on, I thought. Endless. So although I flashed my usual croupy smile at old Porsche Lips as I walked through reception, my legs were so heavy at first that they were pulling my mouth down as I made my way up the dramatic, swirly staircase to the changing room to put the Red Jersey on. I didn't even bother imagining that I was Scarlett O'Hara, like I usually did when I walked up the stairs. What was the point without Rhett? Then I noticed there were fairy lights and Chrissie deccies all over the place; it looked lovely, all sparkly. Even in my mood I couldn't ignore it all. My legs lightened. Surely Angelo would break his silence with me tonight?

'Cheer up, Christina,' Paula, old Car Lips, said. I turned around to look at her. 'The lovely Angelo's just gone through for his shift as well.' That made it worse. Me and my mega-gob, I thought. Why had I told them all I was seeing him? I scowled at her and continued on my way up the red-carpeted path. Carpet of blood, I thought. Maybe some of Angelo's intuition was starting to rub off on me. Didn't feel very intuitive though, as I plodded my way through to the back to don the Red Jersey (this one was just about the right width, but it was way too long for me) and paint a Ferrari red number of my own on my lips.

One glance around the casino as I walked through told me the wanker punters were out in force that night – the usual dead heads, definite 'Animal, Mineral or Vegetable?' material. They'd match my mood perfectly, I thought. Dismal. Thank God Peter and Shelley were both on my shift. That cheered me up a bit as I got changed.

They were both there in the staffroom as I came out in all my nylon glory, electrocuting a few thousand fleas with the train of my dress as I swept (stumbled) along the carpet.

'Aal reet, Chrissie?' asked Peter as I walked into the staffroom, without even seeming to take his eyes off the telly. 'How y' dein'?'

'Great, Peter,' I replied, even feeling it for a second because I'd seen him. Peter always cheered me up. 'And you?'

He turned his full attention on me, like a light bulb. 'Fuckin' crackin' neet, last neet, Chrissie,' he replied. 'Y' should've been there. Drank the fuckin' Quayside dry.' I caught Shelley's eye and we grinned. This was a totally typical Peter conversation and it meant we could relax in silence for twenty minutes at least. 'Fuckin' crackin' lasses. Linin' up for me and the lads.' He did a quick Tiger Woods impersonation, one of his specialities. 'Clubbin' them oot of the way we were with the empty bottles, t' get t' th' fuckin' bar for th' beer. Tits oot, the lot, man.'

'That's funny, I must have missed those bits then, Pete,' said Shelley. 'Because by the time I got down there to meet you, there were only a few sad-looking old piss heads talking about football and telly programmes, and a load of empty Beck's bottles lined up like skittles in a bowling alley.' She grinned at Peter and he grinned back, showing both his good teeth and his good nature. He never got away with his bullshit for long, like, and I don't think he really expected to. 'Not a woman in sight,' Shelley finished off. 'Tits right in. And no wonder!'

'Fuckin' lasses, man!' Peter shook his head at Shelley, shook extra feeling into his words. 'Fuckin' knaa nowt. Tekkin' the piss oot of me.' Camping it up for his audience's sake. 'Lasses. Shouldn't let them on the tables, havin' the lads' jobs. I'm tellin' ye, Chrissie, before Shelley here turned up and scared them aal reet off with her student-type patter and her fuckin' ugly, student-type hand-grenade hair do – ne wonder she canna get hersel' a bloke – these lasses were queuin' up for th' lads, tits oot, the lot . . .' I didn't want reminding that Shelley was between men! And Peter couldn't resist the chance to wind her up about it. Then it was my turn.

'How's it goin' with Ango these days then, Chrissie?' he asked, always one to home in on a weakness of any sort. 'Sent y' any more funeral parlours full of flowers, has he?'

'Lucky if he speaks to me just now, Pete,' I said. Might as well tell him, I thought, he always manages to winkle the truth out of you anyway. 'He's in a right strop with me.'

Peter was always more than well tuned into the casino gossip. 'Aye, well, I've heard from the lads in th' kitchen that 'e's a bit *on th' moody side, like. Divvn't let him get y' doon, Chrissie. And divvn't take any shite! Tell him life's too short, man. When I'm oot with th' lads and some lass has a strop, I aalways . . .'*

More of Peter's half-baked banter gave me the chance to relax, switch off and think of you-know-who. I fingered the diamanté clasp in my hair – diamonds, Montana, Gary Cooper's state. The silver screen flicked on. Angelo and I were there together, riding chestnut thoroughbred horses right up to our spectacular house overlooking this vast desert. Just the two of us. I smiled across at him, a bit breathless from all the riding, and he gave me his slow, dazzling half grin in return. The dust rose from the horses' hooves and the sun was starting to set, the redness of the night touching the yellow of the desert. It was fantastic!

Meanwhile, back in Flea City UK, all the other dealers on the shift had drifted into the staffroom one by one, including Jonty, who had the pleasures of a coal-black scowl from Peter, to his face, and a dramatic two-fingered salute behind his back. Great. My new, clear sight was turning out to be a pain. Everybody looked clearer, smaller and wrinklier, now that I could actually see them properly. See Angelo stick his head around the staffroom door for a second and smile at Shelley, *for example. Wish I hadn't seen that!*

And see that Jonty was the smallest of the lot of them, really. Somehow, as we left the staffroom, the old, red-barred electric heater got knocked smack against my red dress and Jonty's arm banged against my old bruises as he swayed out of the room, barging into me and laughing to his mates, his mouth hanging right open. 'Sorry, Teen,' he said. 'Looks like you've hurt yourself, there. Want me to have a word with that Ango for you?' Bastard, I thought, he's pissed. One sniff confirmed it, as I pushed past him on my way to the door. Vodka and orange, trebles. Really great.

There was no time to think, only to get on out and glam our way over to the roulette tables.

The staffroom was packed when I looked around the door, not to mention that Jonty and Co. were there, looking a bit shaky, come to think of it. Drinking before your shift was definitely frowned on, but they looked like they'd been to the pub.

One way and another, it was not a good time to have a word with Christina. Or that's what I thought. I could always find a moment with her later.

But everything was different later.

It started the minute we were on the tables.

Mike Turner put me straight on to one of the biggest games and told Jonty to stand by to help me with the chips, picking them out of the machine and piling them up. Well, because Jonty had come off the training school before mine, it would have been more usual to have done it the other way around, which Jonty cottoned on to straightaway, trebles or no trebles. Not pleased. So all the time I was doing the automatic stuff, 'Place your bets, please' and 'No more bets', Jonty was beside me, needling me, muttering 'little breasts' when I said 'Place your bets' and other such crap. Get the picture? Pathetic. So pathetic that I remembered my mam's advice about losing my sense of humour and I laughed in his face. Big mistake. (Remember my mam's advice about sex?) And after his next dig, I really let him have it.

'Piss off and grow up, Jonty,' I hissed at him, not even caring about the security cameras or my job. 'Let me get on with my game.' Foreskin snorted a laugh back into his coffee, alongside a burp, and Jonty bent down towards my ear.

'Nobody tells me to piss off and lives, Teen,' he said.

'Well, I just did!' I cleared my hands of my game and left the pit.

That was the third time I'd noticed that Christina was bruised. I was just taking a coffee across to old Mr Fawcett, who was doing his brains at her table, when I looked up at her, hoping to catch her eye, and caught the diamanté on her hair clasp instead. Was that her way of trying to get through to me? But she was really involved in her game: there were enormous piles of chips and punters everywhere, and she only had Jonty to help her, chipping. He was even more fingers and thumbs than usual. I watched her carefully with the punters, I always did. I could tell that some of them fancied her and I knew which ones by then.

I noticed a faded bruise on her upper arm as she left for her break, and I looked at Jonty's face, smirking spitefully over her shoulder, saying something I couldn't quite hear at the same time. Venetian daggers. *'And you could do nothing to help?'* After a minute, he followed her.

Shit, I thought. Why didn't I ask her about those bruises the other night?

Peter was on the same break as me, which was great news, his chunk of a body taking up most of the settee, arms resting along the whole back of it. 'Where's Jonty, Chrissie? Have they left him on?' He laughed his massive laugh. 'I hope the bastard never gets a break aal *neet!'*

I flopped down on to the one square foot of flea-breeder available underneath his arm and punched his side affectionately out of the way with my fist. 'Honestly, Peter, he's doing my head in tonight. He's a complete pain in the arse. Why *did I go out with him?' I rolled my head along the top of the settee, towards Peter's arm. 'Shit. Not to mention, he picks up the chips like something out of a PG Tips tea advert.'*

Peter's second roar of laughter masked Jonty's entry into the staffroom, complete with a jug full of fresh coffee to get rid of his vodka haze. I looked at his face as he walked across the room and I recognised that expression.

To get rid of me.

The first scream was Christina's, I knew it.

If Jonty's hurt her, I'll kill him, I thought. Mic's voice was in my head. *'Why didn't you look after her better? Why? Can't you ever forgive anybody anything?'*

I dropped what I was doing in the kitchen and ran towards the staffroom.

Boiling hot coffee, all over my arms, burning into my arms and shoulders. I just ran out of the staffroom; I didn't know what else to do. I was heading towards reception, away from Jonty and all the customers, to Paula and her lovely, red, capable smile.

I was too late. By the time I got to the staffroom, I could see Christina running towards the staircase, heading out of the place. Then I saw Jonty go after her.

I ran as fast as I could.

There was no one at the top of the staircase and I stopped, leaned over the side and tried to get my breath back. I was still gasping from the pain of the scald and the shock of it all.

Then a new pain hit me right in the centre of my back, hard, knocking all the breath straight out of me.

Jonty thumped her, right in the back of the spine, hard. I couldn't believe it. 'Christina!' I shouted and she turned her head and saw me.

I saw Angelo's face, his eyes, that stupid dress caught around my feet, he moved towards me and I spun straight across the banister down the stairs. Flying, I thought, flying.

Like that night at the church with Angelo, with my arms around his neck and my eyes closed.

She fell down a whole flight of stairs. It was really violent, because she was all caught up in her dress, and it kind of speeded the fall right up. By the time I got to the top of the staircase, she was lying below it, all twisted up, on the first landing, with one arm underneath her and everything looking wrong. Her dress was up over her thighs and one arm was flung above her head. I couldn't see the other arm.

Peter had reached Jonty by then and it was looking pretty ugly there.

I just wanted to get to Christina.

There were these voices everywhere, like I was in a half doze. I wasn't sure which ones were real. There were men shouting, dealers calling out bets, people talking everywhere.

And my arm was hurting me. It was really hurting me.

Nothing else hurt, just then.

Jonty's voice was in my head. 'She just fell. I never meant to hurt her. Get off me!' Pathetic now. 'She just fell.'

I was the first to touch her. 'Christina,' I said. 'Christina?' Her eyes were shut and her hair was all over her face. I pushed it back over her temples with both of my hands and my fingers caught in the clasp. Her eyes were still closed. I felt the arm that I could see, very carefully, until I'd made certain that it wasn't broken. Those old bruises. And there were pink marks, too, and some wetness. I touched her face again. Nothing. Then her eyes opened.

'Tell me what's hurting you,' I said.

'My arm,' she said. 'My wrist.'

Mike Turner made his appearance: somebody must have eventually told him what was going on. 'How is she?' he asked. 'Do you think we need an ambulance, Angelo?'

'She seems a bit . . . vague,' I said. 'Maybe she's concussed.'

'No ambulance,' I said. I was sure enough about that. The embarrassment. ('They're trouble, the lot of them. Nothing but trouble. Couldn't keep out of it if they tried!') Wouldn't they all just shut up? 'I'm feeling fine.'

But when I tried to sit myself up, my head was thumping.

*　　　*　　　*

And she tried to lever herself up, pushing with her elbows. 'Rest,' I said. 'Stay there.' And I eased her back down by the shoulders. I checked her quickly to see if anything was broken. She screwed up her face and I noticed those red marks again.

'Jonty,' explained Peter, his eyes following the track of mine. 'Fucking psycho threw hot coffee all over her.' He pushed his sleeve, which was soaked through with coffee as well, underneath my face. 'He used to beat her up, y' know?'

Jesus Christ.

Mike Turner decided, probably worried about the scene we were causing in front of the punters as much as anything else. 'Sure there are no broken bones, Angelo?' I nodded, glad that, after what happened to Mic, I'd done a first aid course, about the only thing I'd been able to stick at. 'Well, if you can get her down the stairs, I'll organise a taxi to wait for you outside and you can take her into casualty, have her checked over properly. All right?' I nodded.

When Paula gave me the signal for the taxi, I turned my back on Peter, put one arm underneath Christina's legs and the other around her back and lifted her up with me, as carefully as I possibly could. I walked right down the stairs with her in my arms, past all the lights, the tinsel and the staring faces. I didn't want their eyes to touch her.

She was so fair and light and fragile that I felt like I was carrying a woman made of glass.

Angelo smelled of soap. I curled my face right into his chest and held on to him, rubbing his crisp shirt with my cheek and closing my eyes, and I didn't look up from there until we were beside the main door. The cold outside air hit my shoulders. Paula had opened the door for us, and then I felt Angelo bend down, so I opened my eyes and edged myself into the back of the taxicab.

We were at the General in seconds: it's just around the

corner from the casino. I filled in the forms, and explained what had happened, and fended off the ten o'clock drunks who couldn't believe their luck that a lovely blonde girl with a cleavage and a long dress had turned up in casualty to complete the night's live entertainment for them. I made sure that they didn't get *near* her. I hate hospitals, always have done, I even avoid doctors in general. *'A family problem.' 'A genetic thing.'* But I stayed there with Christina for what felt like hours. Stayed until there were violet marks along her wrist and violet smudges underneath her eyes.

And at last, at long last, I apologised, apologised for hurting her first with my words and then with my silences, and she just nodded, almost as if she hadn't heard, and we waited for a doctor to see her. We waited forever and I thought, This is the end of it for me. I'm never going to ruin another relationship with my hardness and my bitterness and my anger and my stupid, stupid pride.

Maybe I'll even tell her about the walls and everything, I thought.

In the end, they said that the headache was shock and the wrist was sprained but not broken. They just strapped it up. If she had someone to keep an eye open for concussion, they said, and gave me a sheet about it, she could leave the hospital and go home there and then. The casino's taxi was still waiting outside.

That wasn't the way I wanted to come back into Angelo's house at all.

When we got back inside the privacy of the church, I couldn't keep it all in any longer. I just curled up in a corner of the settee, covered my head and cried my eyes out. I kept my back turned to Angelo and I cried until the tears were running down into my mouth and the back of my throat was hot and sore.

Christina was absolutely heartbroken. It was terrible to see her like that, all hunched up against me, ignoring me, probably hating me. And I knew she didn't want me to watch, but I also knew she had to get it off her chest somehow.

I sat on the settee and put my arm around her. She tried to push me away at first, but then hurt things always do, so I held on and soon she melted into me. 'I know,' I said. 'I know.' And I did know. Grief was making her cry, grief at losing the glossy version of herself that she presented to the world, at having it removed like a thick layer of make-up, the protective take-the-world-on-and-win-every-time mask of Christina she had to wear all the time. But I understood her, trusted her, better without it. I thought again of glass, delicate, transparent, Venetian glass, from the tiny island of Murano. Glass and islands. Venice. *Santa Maria della Salute's* rounded beauty. Women.

I had to build a bridge.

Words weren't much use, so I just kept saying, 'All right. You'll be all right. Just cry until it's all gone. I'm sorry, I'm so sorry.' Sorry because Jonty had hurt her and I had hurt her and life had hurt her, and way before this time as well, which was the only reason that a smart girl with Christina's personality and looks would go out with something resembling Jonty in the first place. Pity I hadn't got my head around that one a few days earlier.

I was very quiet with her, so quiet, so soft. It's like an animal thing. You have to go into new places, dark places, on tiptoe, almost. I knew I had to feel my way into this redness, this sore redness, very carefully, very slowly. I know how hard it is to trust, to believe in other people, yourself, even, and it felt like everybody had just let Christina down, including me. Especially me.

When she was calming down at last, and her breath was going through the jagged stages, and her hands were fists, turned in towards me, I asked her about the bruises, which I should have done days earlier, and she said that it had only happened the once, when he was drunk and she was building up to finishing with him, so that after that she just hoped he would get sick of her and go away. But he wouldn't. He wouldn't. She'd never told anybody about it, never would, so Jonty must have told people at work himself, which was how Peter must have found out. Maybe Jonty had even bragged about it.

This might sound sick, but actually it was nice to be involved in somebody else's problems, in Christina's problems especially, instead of just thinking about myself all the time. And I knew I could help with some of hers.

She suddenly looked really tired.

'Are you feeling better?' Angelo asked, when I was finally in bed beside him, wearing one of his sweatshirts. I nodded. 'Sure?' he said. I mean, I had been annoyed with him, making me suffer like that. But that lasted for about the three minutes it took before I said to myself, Well, haven't you ever done anything you were ashamed of, then? And he was sorry. Very sorry.

Soon, I started to feel a whole lot more human about myself. Stronger. Started to feel stupid about everything that had happened and even to have a bit of a go at Angelo.

'I would have managed, you know,' I said. 'Jonty, I mean. And everything else. I've got rid of him on my own before now, and he really did only push me around that once. Apart from tonight.'

'He should never have pushed you around at all, tonight or any other night,' Angelo snapped, and his face went all tight. 'You're about half his size.'

'And the fall on the stairs, that was just an accident,' I said, ignoring him. 'I'd been managing him fine until then. There's no need for a fuss.'

Angelo scowled, and his eyes looked even blacker and more 'fuck off' than usual, his pupils taking over his big brown irises. 'You don't get it, do you?' he half shouted at me and then his face went a bit softer, because he could see that I was still a bit upset. 'Why the hell are you sticking up for him? Telling him you didn't want to see him should have "got rid" of him. And you don't have to just "manage".' His voice dropped, trying to get through to me. 'That's not what life is about at all. You mustn't try to "manage" situations like that again, Christina, or imply that they don't matter, that Jonty only hurt you the once, or the fall was just an accident. It's like . . . it's like saying that what's happened to you tonight doesn't count, doesn't matter, or even that you don't matter.' He stroked my sore shoulders. 'It matters a lot,' he said, looking at me hard. 'It matters to me, Christina. And you have to admit that it matters to you, and you have to try to make sure that no one else hurts you like you were hurt tonight. Make sure that you don't have friends, or whatever, who treat you like that.'

Well, it was the direct opposite to the 'put up and shut up' advice that I'd always got from my mam about lads, but what Angelo said did make sense. And he looked gorgeous when he was talking to me, honestly, I wish I'd had a video camera. He was all intense and you could tell he was really starting to care for me. It was lovely. Then I noticed that the windows had lost their funny coverings, and some more awful, almost-matching, blue paint had been put on to cover up the words. It was all starting to look a bit more civilised and a lot less terrifying than before. More normal. Thank God.

And then, of all the things to do, Angelo started to tell me a story.

10. The Skeleton Woman

*'I rested there, just a broken tangle of bones and hair
on the seabed.'*

It was the old Skeleton Woman story – I'd come across it
at university in some trendy, reclaiming-the-oral-traditions
seminar. I adapted it for Christina.

'Once upon a time,' I started, and she actually snuggled
into my shoulder when I said that, 'there was a girl
called Christina who lived in the ancient kingdom of
Northumbria, in Newcastle, high above the ground in a
black and magical tower. All around her in the sky were
bats and stars and deep, deep loneliness . . .'

*He's seen the flat, I thought, but I don't think he had. It was weird.
Then I thought about his name, Angelo, Angel, the shoulder
muscles of a man and the story muscles of a woman. The best
of both worlds. Fantastic.*

'. . . and all below her was the swirling turquoise sea. So the
lovely Christina was trapped in the swaying tower, between
the blueness of the sea and the blackness of the sky. And
between the sky and the sea, keeping Christina trapped in
that unhappy flat, was . . .'

*   *   *

. . . a total villain. Jonty, of course. And so it went on, until one day there was a terrible accident in the tower, and I fell down, down into the sea. I rested there, just a broken tangle of bones and hair on the seabed, with lobsters and oysters and mussels crawling between my ribs and my toes to keep their tiny, shelly little selves warm and safe.

'That sounds a bit cold,' I interrupted Angelo, shivering. I'd been in bits at the bottom of the sea more than once already, and I knew exactly how much time and energy it took to get yourself back together again afterwards. Had done since I was sixteen. He laughed and cheered it up a bit. Apparently, I soon found this rusting, golden casket at the bottom of the sea, and when I looked inside it, there was an ancient map (ancient though laminated, I guess) that showed me all the best places to go around there. I swam around then, having this just incredible journey and getting to know all the starfish and sea urchins and sea horses and so on, surviving by eating magical chocolate sea shells, imported from Italy, out of the casket.

Well, that sounded great, and I was hoping I'd soon be bobbing back up to the surface again for a breath of air, as usual, but then apparently I got trapped in the sea for a long time. And I started to think about all the countries that I hadn't seen, the wonderful journeys I'd never make to all the places between the sky and the sea. And I started to get all hungry and lonely.

Depression was starting to bite: it was too much like real life now.

I hoped Angelo had something good up his sleeve.

And that's where I came into the story. 'Angelo, a fisherman. And I hooked you up into my net by accident, when I was fishing for lobsters and king prawns for Mr Andreas' tea, setting down pots for them and everything, but you were just shiny bones by then, with pearly eyes and polished ivory ribs and piano key fingers and toes, all covered in sea creatures, with long strings of diamonds holding your whole body together. But still I had to have you.' Christina liked that part: she gave me a little smile as a reward.

'I picked you up and took you jangling back to my stone cottage with me anyway, all tangled up in my net, because I could see from your pearly, pearly eyes and your bony, opened up little fingers, how hungry and lonely you were. And I always knew how beautiful you were underneath.'

Underneath the bruises, I thought, drawing my hand away from his, and the things that had happened to me in the past? Would he see how beautiful I was underneath all that? But I put that out of my mind and got back into the story, the present, where I belonged.

And how did I repay the fisherman, Angelo, for his act of selfless charity? (Apparently, untangling me alone took hours.) *Only waited until he was fast asleep and then crept into bed with him to get warm, and drank up this* massive *teardrop out of his eye, until I was all fat and happy and solid again, with a lovely padded body like an old settee and a stomach fuller than a woman pregnant with twins. 'Slurp, slurp, slurp,' Angelo went, showing me how the teardrop was drunk, acting my part, less bony now altogether, patting his belly, all satisfied afterwards. 'Aaah!' He sounded exactly like old Foreskin after too many free sandwiches. He was quite good at the sound effects!*

So far so good, I thought, but what about the poor fisherman, poor Angelo? Did he develop dehydration, or anorexia, or what?

No, I explained to her. That was the whole point of the story. She could take just everything she needed from him, make herself all fat and happy and satisfied and warm, and he would be fine too. That was what most people didn't realise about being in love.

'And are we in love?' Christina said, and her voice was as tired and as tiny and as distant as it had been when she'd finally spoken on the stairs.

Deep breath. 'Well, I am,' I said.

My breath locked for a minute, waiting, and I hoped I hadn't picked a bad time to say it. It was pretty early, but I was sure about my feelings for her.

That woke me up well enough! What on earth should I say? I felt plenty for Angelo, that was certain, but I was just too nervous to commit myself to him, especially after everything that had happened over the previous days. I felt ecstatic, though; I couldn't believe it, that something so good had come out of the whole Jonty drama after all. Something more than good. Brilliant. And I kissed him and kissed him and laughed and kissed some more, and he laughed and kissed back, and I felt so glad and fat and happy that I would even have licked up his big old, salty old tears, and listened to some more of his funny stories forever if he'd have wanted me to.

But I still couldn't tell him what he needed to hear from me most.

11. The Old Monastery

'The shrine to the gods.'

I don't think they were expecting Christina at work the next day at all, because of the wrist and everything, but I rang Gerry anyway and let her know Christina would be taking a few days off. 'I'm not surprised, Ango,' said Gerry. 'Tell her to take her time. Mr Andreas sacked Jonty on the spot. Showed some sense, for once!' I hoped that meant Christina would never have to see Jonty's face again.

I was off work anyway that day, so I decided it would be a good idea for Christina and me to spend the day together, to help her start to get over what she had just been through. She was still asleep upstairs. I'd hardly slept at all myself the previous night; there was so much to mull over and to think about, what with Jonty and the damage he had inflicted one way and another, not to mention my own part.

The last words we'd said to each other the night before felt unreal somehow; the last words I'd said. The whole previous day's events felt pretty strange altogether. And surely Christina must be feeling strangest of all? I was hurt by her silence, but I could wait for her, wait for her feelings and her confidence to catch up with mine. One thing I wasn't going to do was to argue with her again; I wasn't going to risk losing her. I'll let her dictate the pace emotionally, I decided. She's already been through so much.

When I went back up to the bedroom, Christina was just getting around to sitting up: a fog of sleep surrounded her body and she started to stretch it away.

'How are you feeling today, then?' I asked. 'Or is that a stupid question?'

'I feel great within myself,' she told me. 'I'm just glad that the whole thing has come to an end. With Jonty, I mean. Rid of him at last.' She tried to keep the smile up, but even saying his name had made her face droop. She rubbed her wrist and then shut her eyes for seconds.

I sat down on the edge of the bed. Something to take Christina's mind off the whole nightmare, take her mind off Jonty forever, that was what I needed. And maybe something to lighten the whole situation between us, until she could cope with it. But what should I do? What should we do?

Christina's toes wriggled up towards me like a reminder as she pulled her legs up towards her chest: white calves, white thighs, fair hair, and then the curled up, bare white feet. Totally vulnerable. Pale. She was so naked, even in my sweatshirt, but she didn't know how naked she was, thought that her tongue protected her from everything. Yet other people's tongues seemed to have done her more damage than anything.

Then I remembered those big shoes that first night and I knew what to do.

He took me shopping – shopping for shoes. Smart shoes.

'I've got loads of shoes,' I said, 'loads. Dead smart ones.' Christina Rae, the Queen of Couture. 'Honestly.' Not honestly. ('They haven't got two pennies t' rub together.') 'It's just I really liked those ones of my sister's.' I wasn't having Angelo think I was some kind of a charity case.

He looked straight into my eyes and then he said, in the coolest of cool voices, 'Well, we'll see if we can get you some exactly like those, then.' He saw right through me, always. Glass girl.

I had never realised that shopping for shoes could be so sexy, could be even a bit sexy. But first of all, Angelo took me back to the flat, just to pick some clothes up. (I could hardly go out into town in the Red Jersey could I?) He didn't even raise his eyes when he dropped me off outside the block, but there was a hard expression on his face by the time I got back into my seat beside him with a bagful of clothes to change into, and he didn't look at me properly once before dropping the handbrake and starting the growly old Fiat up again.

He was really pissed off with me. 'Theatre village?' he said, with his lip all curled up. What would he have said if he had seen my mam's house?

Theatre village! It was nowhere near there. That was the second time I'd seen that flat, I'd gone round to suss it out before I'd sent the roses, but it looked even worse in the daylight, if that was possible. It was in one of the roughest parts of Newcastle. One of Mic's friends used to live around there. There was a Cyrenians' house for homeless men, just around the corner from it, and the back streets were full of drunks, masturbating and muttering through the bins, and kids selling Tac and Es, or worse.

Christina wasn't going to stay there. No filthy bastard was ever going to touch her, or wank himself off, or whatever, watching her as she walked past him in the street. No way. This was one problem that I could definitely solve.

Then we headed into town: 'To see the Christmas lights,' Angelo said, smiling, losing his bad temper then, thank God. Even the way he drove was so sexy, with his elbow resting against the door of the car and his head leaning towards his elbow, as if he didn't think about, care about, how he manoeuvred the car. As if he didn't care if he lived or died. Why was that so sexy? It's life that's supposed to be sexy, isn't it? Not death.

Anyway, it was the afternoon by the time we got into town, and first of all we had to go into every single *shoe shop, until the most perfect pair of shoes in Newcastle, or the world, had been tracked down for me. Honestly, Angelo made me try so many of them on, holding my ankle in his hand every time. He didn't even notice the young sales girls were giggling at us: he was so serious and intent.*

We finally settled on some slim, sleek ones, with two-inch, tapered heels and long, pointy toes, all sharp, shiny, black and hard. Public protection. I didn't want other people, strange people, to see her whiteness, her softness. Extreme softness. And I wanted her to get the message that she had to have perfect shoes, a perfect life, chosen especially for her.

Those shoes made Christina's feet look so elegant and finely shaped. The new leather scented the skin of her feet beautifully and the low fronts made her legs look much longer. Really classy. They were worth at least the two days' wages they'd cost me, I was sure. And they fitted perfectly.

Then he took me to this old monastery place, the Friary, that had been turned into shops and a café, for coffee and cakes, and we talked there for at least two hours. Angelo was looser, more human somehow, than he had been in the restaurant before. And we talked about things that I'd never talked to anybody about before.

We started off with the small stuff, like what we would do if we won a million pounds.

'Go to America to work!' Christina corrected herself and laughed. 'To live, I mean. Work would be the last thing on my mind.' She answered so quickly that this was obviously one of her favourite dreams.

'What would you see there then, Christina? What are

the seven wonders of your world? The seven sights you've promised yourself you'll see before you die?'

Much more difficult! I didn't know what half the original *wonders were for a start, not that I would be telling Angelo that. Give me a clue.*

'Start me off, then,' I said.

'Well, there was the Colossus at Rhodes. There was a huge – ' *he practically turned into a Colossus, showing me 'huge' with his arms ' – statue of Apollo there, the god of sun, music, poetry, medicine, prophecy, male beauty.' He did his half smile. 'Who's your Apollo?'*

Guess who? Angelo had just described my vision of himself perfectly, not that I'd risk swelling his head by letting him know that.

'Still working that one out,' *I said, shaking my head at him, teasing.* 'Who's your Apollo, then, Angelo?' *I asked, turning the tables on him.*

'The statue of David.' *He looked quite excited; his eyes were all bright, and his arms were on the go.* 'It's colossal as well, carved from a huge block of Carrara marble.' *He questioned me again.* 'The pyramids then, the shrine to the gods. What do you think?'

Much easier. 'The Luxor Hotel! It's on The Strip in the middle of Las Vegas. I want to go and work there. Now's the time to see Las Vegas. It's like a monument to prove what you can do if you've got enough imagination and money, and it's right at its peak now.' *I was really starting to get into his game.* 'I mean, I suppose the Luxor's a shrine to money, but it's a load of fun at the same time. There's this gigantic sphinx in the grounds. Gerry reckons it's got a laser show in its eyes. It's my favourite one out of all of them.

'There's another casino based on a just* huge *circus – ' I showed him 'huge' with my hands ' – and then there's one with a Pirates' Walk, where there's a battle between pirates staged every hour for the tourists.' I pictured myself walking down the gangway*

to Treasure Island, on my way to work, like, all dressed up. 'They've got their own shops and everything. I'd love to see that.' Dream on.
  This was one of my very favourite ones.

Christina Rae and the Luxor Hotel

The super extravagant Luxor Hotel is based on an Egyptian theme and has a thirty-storey high pyramid shape and a ten-storey copy of the Sphinx of Giza at its entrance.

This is also the hotel that saw the start of the career of the world-renowned Christina Rae when she first made the journey across from the United Kingdom to America ...

Better not get too deeply into that: I still wasn't exactly sure what I was going to be world renowned for, *for a start.*
  Anyway, Angelo was still talking.

'A laser show in its eyes?' I said, and shivered. Christina knew the strangest things. But it didn't matter that our dreams and visions were so different: it mattered that we both had them. And actually, I'd been to the States already. 'I've not been to Vegas,' I said to her, 'but I worked in a summer camp in America for a while, in between school and university. I saw Kentucky, the Carolinas, the Smokeys – all around that area.'

'Vegas'? 'The Carolinas'? Dead familiar. 'The Smokeys'? Dead impressive. Could Tom Cruise interest Nicole Kidman in a few days in North Carolina? Dead Calm. Days of Thunder more like. Because a part of me – all right, most of me, then – was really jealous. It sounded like Angelo had got to America practically by accident. People like him, from richer backgrounds, just know they can go anywhere in the world they choose. I was only just working that one out for myself; hadn't thought beyond Newcastle until Jonty had got the job at the casino and started telling me the

stories. The world popped open for me then like a pomegranate. Whereas Angelo sounded like he'd been a citizen of the world since birth!

He hadn't noticed my expression and he'd started up the conversation again. I tuned back in to what he was saying.

'Hanging gardens of Babylon?' I said. 'Where are your hanging gardens, then?'

'Opryland Hotel in Nashville. It's got its own river and a massive glass dome, sky-high, full of trees and plants.' She was quite quick now. 'What about you?'

'The gardens in the Vatican. They're full of orange trees. The smell clings to everyone who walks through them. It's amazing.' I thought again. 'Or what about the Temple of Artemis, goddess of the moon, chastity? The hunt.' I smiled at her as she thought about it. Apollo's sister. It was getting dark outside and she looked like a young goddess of the moon herself. Then I thought again of Rossetti's *Beata Beatrix* with her fuzz of red-gold hair, her open, petal palm, and the Ponte Vecchio melting into the pinking sun behind her like a dream. Beautiful.

'Marilyn Monroe . . .' Christina blurted it out then stopped herself. 'Too many abortions, though.' She looked depressed. She screwed her eyes up then, trying to find a better Artemis, and failing. 'Is that all of them?'

'I can't remember the rest.' I had to laugh at her: she was really funny when she got involved in something. 'They're the best ones. Is that all of your Wonders?' She was still thinking, so I jumped in with another one of my own. 'The whole of Venice is one of mine.' I paused for a few seconds, as I imagined myself stepping on to a *vaporetto* with Christina, and floating along the Grand Canal with her, or wandering from the Rialto to the Piazza San Marco and then losing ourselves in the back streets until the magic took us over completely. Venice, alive but dying. Alive and dying.

Christina's stare jolted me back into the conversation and I carried on talking, smiling at her. 'Over one hundred islands, all connected. Only one bridge to the mainland . . .'

'. . . out of more than four hundred,' I finished for him. 'Venice is the only city where you can't drive.' He looked that surprised, I couldn't help laughing at him. 'I know all about Venice,' I said, feeling dead pleased with myself, not half as thick as usual. Geography, English and drama: places, people, dressing up and dreams, always my specialities. 'I'd really like to go there. And then there's Las Vegas, Vegas,' my voice took the piss out of his, 'then Manhattan, and the whole of the New York skyline,' I continued. The whole of Angelo Paulillo, I thought. 'Riding through the streets of Chicago in a stretch limousine with a beautiful man, some soft leather seats and a well-stocked mini-bar: that's my last wonder. Nothing much.' Angelo was really smiling at me.

Then I remembered his silence – how long it had lasted. And how it had ended.

Her face fell. Up until that moment she'd been full of life, almost back to her normal self.

'What's the matter?' I asked, and Christina looked down at the table, seeming to need to think hard before she could put whatever it was into words and then she just said, 'Nothing.' But she looked worried sick.

Really worrying. 'Tell me.'

'It's the writing,' I explained, in the end. I forced myself to look at him directly. 'The writing around the windows, I mean, I don't understand it,' I told him at last. 'And I still don't understand why you were so angry with me.'

Angelo looked down at his mug and sighed. He began by telling me about university, the good bits at first, meeting all sorts of different people, getting into ideas he'd never known about, doing things he'd never dreamed about before. There *were quite a few stories about a friend called Brett that made him smile.*

Then the smile fell and he breathed in.

I didn't want to frighten Christina off and I didn't want to block her out any more either. I'd learnt that much. It was so difficult to explain. Impossible. I tried.

'There were some problems with my family.' Christina's fine eyebrows questioned me further. 'When you looked at the writing, it was like me finding out about Jonty, in a way that you didn't like.' Her eyebrows rose slightly. I tried harder. 'I felt betrayed, exposed.' Still she looked on, looked right into my eyes. Right from that first day in the Bigg Market, I'd known that Christina had more guts than most blokes I knew. I saw it again now. She made me answer her.

'Mic,' I said, at last. 'My brother. Messages.' I looked away. 'Then the writing.'

That really was it. I thought I had really blown it with her.

The way that Angelo breathed out marked the end of the discussion with a definite full stop. It was a start, but what had happened to Mic, whom I still hadn't met, and what the writing was all about, wasn't much clearer to me even so. It was clear that something pretty bad had happened to him and that the writing probably expressed that. Messages. I thought suddenly of a voice that tried to speak to me, a voice I had always pushed away. A voice without words, almost without a shape. Totally without power. Angelo was staring out of the window of the old monastery. His eyes were miles away.

Funny though, I felt as if I was touching Angelo, touching the black and tarry barrel of his soul, even though I was as far away from the ordinary facts about him as ever. I even loved the fact that he was so hard to get through to, but I, ordinary little, very ordinary, very little, Christina Rae was starting to get there.

Hard work. But it was the strength of his feelings I was pulled towards: it was as if I could sense, I could smell, honestly, the strength of them. What exactly was that smell? Sulphur. Heat. That was why he couldn't talk easily, couldn't stand me to touch the sticky, scarring heat of all those feelings. Burning alive.

I fingered my shoulder through my thin blouse. Angelo was the complete opposite of Jonty, who was fuelled by coldness, spite, drink and not much else.

But was it my whiteness, my coolness, my smallness, that drew Angelo to me?

Talking like that always wears me out and I had to get outside for some fresh air.

The night had come down in the time that we'd been at the Friary and Christina's coat was thin. Still I welcomed it, the dark. Privacy. I breathed in the night, the air, the outside, just for a few seconds.

Then we headed back down into the town to see the Christmas lights, just like I'd promised her.

All of a sudden it was black dark and the sky was full of sparkle. It really reminded me of nights in my flat, the stars, but I didn't mention that to Angelo; I'd seen the look on his face, not impressed, when I'd got back into the car earlier, and I was starting to know what that type of black concentration meant. But the stars along Northumberland Street were red and green and blue as well as white, and there were sleighs and Santas and angels and stockings and gifts and bells, spangling all around us in the night. There was even, definitely, a touch of Vegas to it. There were people and noises everywhere, and loads of laughing, calling and music. Jangling. It was fantastic. Some of the lights' sparkle went through me like a shot, even at an ancient-feeling nineteen years old.

Angelo put his arm around me and looked right down into my face, looked right inside me, like a taller, stronger River Phoenix, but alive, and he really laughed, with his head thrown back and everything, doing an angel trumpeting impersonation, staring at the lights, dead loud, dead embarrassing. It was as if the lights were on inside of him. He looked brilliant.

'Do you want to go for something to eat?' he asked. It was about seven o'clock.

'No,' I said, snuggling into his shoulder. 'I'm hungry, but I'd rather go back to yours.' And I tried to look seductive, hiding my nagging, violet-streaked, wrist behind my back and looking up sideways into his face. Bogie and Bacall, Kidman and Cruise. Black eyes and the blonde.

Take me home.

Christina was always trying to hide the intimate, personal things from me, not realising that it was the vulnerability of her, her openness to wounding, that attracted me to her, partly. I pulled out her damaged wrist from behind her back and I held both of her hands in mine, the wrapped and the bare, the twisted and the strong. Then I asked her my question with my eyes.

Was she ready to be close to me again, after everything that had happened over the last few days?

Before we'd even got to the church, the tension was thick. You could touch it, almost. I didn't know how to sit in the car beside him, how to arrange my body, my face. My thighs were warm inside the thin material of my trousers.

As soon as we were inside, the first star I saw flashing in the darkness was the light on his ancient answering machine. Without looking at me, Angelo rewound it and moved his fingers to the reset button.

'You'll lose your message,' I said, before I could think about it, 'doing that. If anybody else rings, that is.' The click of the button marked the end of that *one-way dialogue clearly enough. Then Angelo put all the lamps on and I was glad to see that* The Scream *was still fully screened. I nipped into the loo to take out the contacts for a bit of soft focus.*

As I walked back downstairs, Angelo was just looking at me.
I felt nervous. I felt cold.

I wanted to be intimate with her, uniquely intimate, more intimate with her bruising and her pain and herself than Jonty, or anybody else, ever had been or ever could be. I wanted her stripped. I rested one hand on her leg and my one hand spanned the whole of her thigh in those filmy black trousers. Her hands were tiny. Her leg was tiny.

Mine, mine, mine.

I unbuttoned her tissue of a blouse and edged it down over her thin shoulders. She hadn't washed her hair, for once, what with all the recent upset, and the warm roots smelled sharp when I moved my face closer to hers. I wondered how, exactly how, the warming, pinking pockets of skin between her legs would smell? The bra came off next. A shiver went down her breastbone, and her nipples were high, nervous and cold, but I pressed her shoulders back. I ran my fingers along her neck and shoulders, outlining her upper body with my hands, holding her attention with my eyes. The redness of the scalding had died down. I was glad, and kissed the tops of her shoulders.

I just wanted to know her.

Then Angelo moved on to my bottom half. He unzipped my trousers and gestured with his eyebrows that I should lift my body slightly, then he pulled them down on to the floor and discarded them. My knickers followed.

Angelo laid me down on the settee. I was totally still, waiting, and he looked at my back and my shoulders and my hips and my spine. He felt every bone, one by one, limb by limb, arms, legs, torso, and touched every curve, felt every line of flesh and every inch of skin. His face shifted and shadowed with every change that he found with his gaze, every feeling that he felt with his hands. The attention was brilliant. Gold screen.

Suddenly, Angelo breathed in, like he was diving way down

into a new place. Deep. His face came close to mine and he looked into my eyes. I held my own breath at once.

Because then he got intimate.

I'd noticed before that Christina had the breasts and the bum of a young girl, which she was, of course. Playing with her nipples made her squirm, really squirm. The skin on her nipples was so delicate – more delicate than the skin on her face, or her lips, even. It was similar to the skin on her lips, but it was skin made more for a baby's lips. Just the thinnest web of skin. That night, I also noticed that she had the beginnings of the belly of a woman, which she also was, of course. It was a wonderful, *bellying* belly, but the bellying was so slight and new below the wishbone ribs that it was touching. I put both hands on it heavily, watching her peaceful face, and thought about my red notebook.

When I turned her over, the great, swelling bruise on her back was in complete contrast to the rest of her skin. Shocking. The mark of Jonty and his fist, I thought, as clumsy and ugly as he was himself, dark against the pale, girlish skin.

My fingers tingled with the deep, natural need to take away the heat, the swelling, the damage, from her skin, her tissues, her memories.

My hips actually twisted slightly, embarrassingly, and my boobs felt extra alive. Alert. I turned right around towards him, and I wrapped my arms tight around his neck and my legs around his back, drawing his dark, his alive face close to mine, fusing my boobs to his chest.

'I really want you, Angelo,' I said.

Christina might, or might not, love me; she might, or might not, be ready to *admit* that she loved me, but she definitely wanted me. Blonde hair fell back on to the dark settee as her neck arched, her breasts tilted and her body hung from mine like a fruit from the branch of a tree. My back ached where her legs wrapped round me, but the pressure of her need, the weight of her body, was so welcome to me that I touched her face. I ached to tell her I loved her, but I wouldn't rush it again.

Slipping my hands beneath her, I supported Christina's spine, holding her weight in my arms and forcing her sex up against mine. She hung more slackly then, waiting, wanting, her eyes closed, and I pushed my face, my mouth, into her white neck, her soft hair. As she moved her arms up slightly there was a sharp, clean smell, almost as if I had clenched a fistful of fresh earth and a few emerald green mint leaves in my fist, and then released my fingers. Crushed and released. Loose. Warm. Gorgeous. I could have done anything I wanted to her.

There was a lot I wanted to do.

Christina opened her legs as I laid her on her back on the settee and went in search of a condom. She lifted her arms above her head when I returned, and then she raised her fairness to my face and widened her thighs to take my body inside her. She was ready. Her lips were pink and parted and her body was warm when I took her in my arms and asked her with my eyes what she wanted.

Strength, tenderness, softness? Which part of me was best for her?

All of the feelings running through me made me relax in Angelo's arms, with his will as mine, his needs as mine. I gripped his neck in my hands and I bit my lip, but when I drew Angelo's head down to mine, I kissed him as tenderly as I possibly could.

Strength. Strength and tenderness, I asked, with my body. Please. Now.

It was very quick, very quick and very strong.

One arm was around the back of her shoulders, holding Christina and her face close to mine, and the other was beneath her hips while I pushed myself inside her. I would have loved to have left the condom off, but there were some battles that I had with my conscience and won.

Christina cried, then tightened and tightened and tightened against me, before falling back on to the settee with her face averted and her breaths slowing. Only then did I give in to the force of a powerful orgasm, shouting at the ceiling, touching her hair, as the strongest feelings of protectiveness, power and pleasure took over me.

Not telling her that I loved her was like not breathing.

Minutes passed and the living room started to look more like it normally did to me, grey, still and shadowy. I pulled myself up and headed for the bedroom, drawing Christina after me by the hand. We lay down together in bed. I warmed her cooling body against mine, then she turned, grabbing her nightie and knickers from beside the bed, before snuggling back into me again.

The next time I looked down towards my chest, I saw Christina's face looking up at mine, full of questions.

It was then that she spoke.

12. Certaldo and the River Elsa

'And where's your mother now?'

Angelo was so relaxed, lying close beside me in the bed, that I thought I might manage to get away with a few questions. I started with an easy one, my voice all innocent. 'Are you actually Italian then, Angelo? Everybody at the casino has got a different version of how Italian you are.' It was true.

'People at the casino should mind their own business,' he said, giving me a bit of a hint, a slight but definite touch of the 'fuck off' to the eyebrows. Brow beaten. I thought I'd blown it again, but then he seemed to change his mind. He tried again. 'Partly,' he explained. 'But it feels like the bigger part. My mother's family was English, my father's Tuscan. My dad's dad came across here from Tuscany. He grew up near Florence, in a farm close to a walled town called Certaldo – not far from where the marble came from that Michelangelo used to make the David statue. On the River Elsa.'

His mind was back in Tuscany – I could see it in his eyes.

The River Elsa, feeding Tuscany's farms, like a woman feeding her children with her milk. Mic and I, winding our way around the roads of Tuscany, feeling Tuscan and tall, leaning into the speed, hearing the guttural growl of the bike and feeling the life of it, the danger of it. Feeling the bike bucking like a horse as Mic squeezed and heeled its powerful brakes into touch. But Christina was waiting for the rest of the story.

'My grandfather moved to England to work in a friend's café on Percy Street and that's where he met my grandmother. She was Italian, too, by birth, pure Geordie in every other way. My Tuscan grandfather died before I was born. I did know my grandmother, though.'

Angelo waved his arm around the church, smiling. 'She was lovely. She left the church to me and Mic, because she reckoned my dad had enough money, anyway. She sided with my mother when my parents split up, hoped for ages they'd get back together – Catholic, of course.

'And I went to Italy four or five times with my mother and Mic when I was younger, to meet great-aunts and other family. See some of the country.' He laughed. 'We even saw the Sistine Chapel, which Mic and I reckoned had a lot to answer for.'

'What about your dad?'

'I hardly remember him. My parents split up when I was a toddler and he didn't keep in touch with us much. We saw him a few times when we were little, but it soon ended up that we only heard from him at Christmas time or birthdays. Just cards. My Italian grandmother used to help to keep us in touch with what he was doing. Then he remarried and we never saw him – or not that I can remember. Mic didn't see him then either – not that it seemed to bother him much.' Angelo's fingers drummed on the quilt, then gripped it and twisted. 'Most of the time, that is. We kept his name, though, but my mother went back to using her maiden name, Logan.

'Anyway, my mother always said my dad had a Catholic conscience; he paid money into her bank account right until Mic and I both left university, quite recently.'

I nodded. A direct-debit sort of a relationship. I'd come across a few of those before. I'd wished my own dad had a more 'Catholic' conscience at times. Anyway, I looked at Angelo. 'Aren't you curious about your dad at all, then?'

'Not really. While we were growing up, Mic and I always reckoned my mother was more than enough to keep both of us going. And we didn't want to hurt her feelings by contacting him. She never seemed very keen on the idea.' His eyelids dropped, giving me a hint that this was a definite understatement. 'Not to mention, he'd made no effort to contact us all the time we were growing up.'

'And where's your mother now?'

'Dead, too,' he said. It was so final, the way that he said it: his voice sounded dead as well. 'That's all you need to know, Christina. She's dead.' His head turned away from mine on the pillow, and he spoke as if his mouth felt dry and stiff.

How awful for him – losing his mother. At least I knew the situation with his family now, I thought, except for what had happened to Mic. Still, enough was enough. It looked like Angelo had done enough talking for one night: his silence told me that.

'I'm sorry, Angelo. I'm really sorry. Try to sleep now,' I said, turning him back to face me and wrapping him in my arms, trying to blot the blackness out. 'Try to sleep.' I nuzzled into the side of his tensed up face, soothing him.

And I tried to stay awake, but I was starting to feel pretty sleepy myself.

But my mind was full of worms, coiling their way through my conscience. Gradually, as I lay there with Christina, I let go, bit by bit, and the worms slid into my pillow, one by one. I knew, though, from experience that they would re-emerge in my dreams and in my waking dreams, crawling across the pillow towards my face. Within ten minutes, Christina was asleep. I felt like I would never sleep again.

But eventually, just when I was feeling cooler, feeling for once that there was so much to look forward to, my mind racing and racing with the possibilities, it happened again.

Looking at the moon through glass started it off. I was in the bathroom, which was just off the bedroom gallery upstairs. The window was a skylight, so it was as if you were actually in the sky when you looked through it. Everything was very bald and very surreal, the way that it always is when you're exhausted, and you have to remember that I'd hardly slept the night before and it was quite late at night too. Everything was unreal.

I saw the moon first, a new moon, in the mirror. Then I looked up over my shoulder to the window in the darkness and froze. The moon was like a silver sickle beyond the glass, its blade glinting down at me. Evil. And when I looked up at the moon that night, looked at it properly, I thought that it started to grow. Glow. I didn't want to believe it but I was fascinated, and stared at it with eyes that mirrored its shape. It grew bigger then, feeding on my imagination, on my power as well as its own. It grew bigger and bigger, and fuller and fuller, and it moved nearer to me. It moved nearer to the glass. Unreal.

Really. It passed through the glass like a whisper and was in the room with me, right in my face. Imagine it. Six feet across, white, shining. Alive. Vibrating. Yet the rest of the room was unchanged, the soap sticky and damp. The whiteness was so bright, so powerful, that it was like a noise. It *was* a noise, a droning, regular, resonant hum, at first. A hum that grew louder and louder until it formed a word. It was a word that was especially for me, a word I would have to work with to understand. One word.

'Split,' it said to me, in a voice that vibrated with power. 'Split.' It emphasised the last part of the word, as if it was an extra syllable. Its round whiteness was in my face, I felt exalted, close to embracing it completely, and one word was all I was going to get out of it. Split. I knew it was important to understand, vital.

I stared, awed, at the whiteness of it, the purity of it, and the humming continued. Mounted. At last I reached out to touch it, leaning towards it, and it receded. It backed away from me slowly, shrinking, shrinking back into the window, until it was just a normal moon in a normal sky – that's if there is ever anything normal about the moon. Isn't it supposed to be a symbol of woman and of the spirit? I thought again of Artemis, the goddess of the moon and the hunt, Apollo's twin sister.

But what was split? I had had just about the most decisively bonding experience with Christina possible. Surely it couldn't be warning me that this too could be split? Split by me? Not now.

At night, I often ask myself, or my God, I'm never sure where one starts and the other ends, for solutions to all kinds of problems. Somehow, I always get an answer, but not always the one that I expect. And sometimes, I get a whole new set of problems.

I padded down the stairs and drew my mother's notebook out from its hiding place. Because I knew these were the last words I would ever hear from her, I usually read the pages randomly. This meant that I had read several passages several times and some passages not at all, and it also ensured that I still had some passages to look forward to reading. What would I do when I had read it all? Reading the notebook was my only way of talking to my mother now, of asking her for her advice.

I opened it up. It was a familiar part, a part that I loved. I could breathe again. Her honeymoon.

> *Michelangelo's Sistine Chapel inspired and created me. And it created my now family too.*
>
> *Tony and I had 'done' most of the sights by then – the Galleria D' Arte, the palazzos, most of the Vatican buildings – and I'd progressed from excited to awed, through overawed, until I'd worked my way right back to jaded. Beauty fatigue. Until I finally got through the maze of the Vatican into the Sistine Chapel and looked upwards to the frescoes, that is.*

It was a huge, huge shock to me. Because the ceiling of the Sistine Chapel is where man meets God, earth meets heaven and genius becomes divine. Strong words, but I'm not exaggerating. Fantastic. And right at the centre of it all, is the creation, the beautiful creation, of Adam. I'll never forget it, never, and I never want to. The sky of the chapel was just boiling over with golden, gleaming magnificence: the creation of Adam, the creation of Eve, the creation of the sun, the moon and the stars. The touching of the fingers.

And I put one hand in Tony's fingers, and one hand on to my empty belly, and I thought, When I have children, when I have sons, they're going to be connected to this, connected to Michelangelo and to this ceiling and to this larger glory. Gold. Divine and driven. The Delphic Sybil looked down at me, two boys behind her, her lips open and a sheet of paper in her hand. A message for me. Two boys. And they'd also be connected to Italy, like my husband.

That was the night that my Michael was conceived: Michael, who grew up to have such straight, dark hair, dark, beautiful eyes and strong, carved cheekbones and nose, looking so much like the Adam that God and Michelangelo had created first. Divine. Divine and human. And later, Angelo.

My children would be the golden place where heaven and earth and God and man would meet. I'd decided. They would be as beautiful, inspired and inspirational as Michelangelo, God and I could make them between us. My sons.

And they were, they definitely were. But they were so much more as well.

Honeymoon. The sweetest part of the spirit and body of a woman, my mother, joining the spirit and body of my father to make my brother and myself. Blood. Brothers' warm, warm blood. Mic's arms around my waist. Corners. Brothers. *'My special son.'*

I had felt warm myself until I remembered the message. Split. The split between my parents? A split between Christina and me? God, no. The picture of the Delphic

Sybil's face was in my mind, the divine spirit flooding her eyes. A third possibility was also at the back of my mind, but I left it there to fester, where it belonged. I needed some help.

Sleep for me was impossible. I went into the bathroom to grab an old blanket and made my way downstairs. Then I read, wandered and thought; thought, wandered and read for I don't know how long, until I must have fallen asleep, having made a decision at last about how to let Christina in on some of what had gone on in my family.

I would take her to Irene's with me.

13. The Dirty Ridge Tent

'Just pick up th' phone.'

I woke up the next morning alone. Where on earth was Angelo? 'Angelo?' No reply. I sat up. 'Angelo!' Louder and higher this time. Still no reply.

Thinking of our awful conversation the night before, I headed for the stairs, shivering. The church was icy. And the first thing I saw as my feet hit the freezing cold living room floor was that Angelo lay curled up there, half wrapped up in an old tartan blanket, with one arm and both legs sticking out of it, sleeping like a car crash victim in a coma.

Shit! I said to myself. How's this for a tragedy? I've found the most gorgeous bloke in the world. I fancy him (brilliant); he fancies me (miracle). He's got a brain, a body, feelings, money, muscles, the lot. There's just one problem – he's going round the bend. Typical! I almost laughed.

Then I knelt down on the floor beside him, I touched his bare shoulder, and everything changed. His poor shoulder was freezing! And he didn't even move when I touched him. You could see every separate hair on his face, black against the yellow. Maybe he was ill? Definitely he was ill.

I pulled a bit of blanket over his shoulder. 'What are you doing down here?' I said to him, gentle as I could, and I wasn't putting it on: I really felt for him, he got that upset. I shook his shoulder, but he only moved his head a couple of inches and parted his lips. I shook his shoulder harder then, 'Angelo!' He was frightening me, and then I said, 'You'll freeze to death here,' and shook again. He opened his eyes.

'Hi!' he said, but he stared for seconds and seconds, as if he didn't know who I was. Then his fingers came out to stroke my face and his eyes changed. Warmed. His other hand came out until it was resting against my stomach underneath my nightie. 'I've been thinking about you all night,' he said. 'You were full of questions last night,' he went on, 'and today I'm going to answer some. We're going to meet someone who will answer some.'

'Where are we going, then?'

'Irene's,' he replied. 'Obviously.' But his grin told me that he knew he was being deliberately mysterious, winding me up. 'Get ready, then.'

Later, as we were on our way, he gave me the tiniest clue of what was coming. 'We're going to see Irene so that you can learn something about Mic,' he said, as we climbed into the Fiat. 'She's at a country fair today.' That explained a lot! Was Irene an auntie, then, or the other grandma? Not to mention, what was going down with Mic? All I knew about him was that he'd somehow ended up on a hard, cold street in Newcastle. The only other clue from Angelo on the way there was, 'Don't touch anything around Irene. Her house is scruffy and so will the stuff be in her tent.' Maybe not a grandma then, but you never can tell. (Look at my *parents, for God's sake.)*

We parked the car and walked around the country fair. As I had no idea who I was looking for, I let Angelo steer me around the field like a collie with a lamb. We must have walked past her tent twice, because it was that far below eye level. Third time around the field, Angelo laughed. 'There it is,' he said, pointing. 'Very Irene!' It was a white (grey) kid's ridge tent, about three feet off the ground, and there were about half a dozen people sitting on rickety wooden chairs waiting to go inside it.

When it was our turn at last Angelo went in first, pulling me after him into the darkness. I had to crouch right down to get inside it, and as I stumbled around in the pitch blackness, clinging to his hand, I saw this ancient, huddled body arranged around these gleaming false teeth. Irene? I could smell grass and earth. Old earth. I could smell her: old, old skin and smoke. Her eyes were old as well, and piercing. She didn't look anything like Angelo. I looked over to him for support, but his eyes were fixed on her. If it hadn't been for wanting to impress Angelo the whole time, I'd have run a mile.

As it was, I hovered in the doorway as I dithered over whether or not I should go in. 'Howay in, hinny,' Irene called over from her grubby table, as if she'd heard what I was thinking, just as the urge to run was worst. 'There's plenty of room once y're in.' Maybe she was just a real sweetie underneath, a friend of the family? 'I've got the kettle goin'.' She pointed at the corner where she had this very wobbly campus stove on the go.

The kettle sang, then screeched, as Angelo and I walked towards the table, and as we sat down on the wooden chairs opposite Irene's seat, she was humming and bustling away, organising tea and biscuits. Eventually, everything was done the way she wanted it. When I took a dark-looking drink of tea, in this frighteningly *stained cup, from her hands, her face split into a great grin of triumph, before she turned to fetch the crusty old sugar bowl out of the box of tricks she had in the corner. Angelo was right: everything she had was minging.*

'Is that nice, pet?' she asked, and I nodded through the choking. 'And how are you dein', son?' she said to Angelo. 'Still muddlin' along?'

'I'm fine, Irene, thanks. Just thought I'd come by for an update from Mic,' he said. 'See what he's got to say today.'

'Aye, well, for once in his life he's been quiet lately,' Irene said. 'Barely heard a word from the lad.' Why would Mic want to ring this scruffy old woman? She turned towards me then, with those eyes that seemed to know all about me already. Seemed like only the light in her eyes kept her husk of a body alive. But she smiled when she spoke, the white rows of plastic teeth all shiny. 'Why don't we have a look at what this little lass is up to instead?'

'Me?' My eyes widened. I turned to Angelo and saw my own surprise reflected back from his face.

Irene grinned wider, and I saw a child's smile formed by the bright false teeth. 'Go on, love. It'll only take a few minutes.' I looked at Angelo and he gave me his classic 'fuck right off' face before looking away from me, all nonchalant.

'Go on, then,' I said.

Sheer joy lit up Irene's old face. She scuttled across to the box she had in the corner of the tent, nestling in the soil, and came back with a pack of ordinary playing cards, shuffling the greasy, well-thumbed pack as she settled herself down into her seat beside us. She laid the pack out in front of me. 'Cut them three times, pet, any way you like. Don't think about it too much.' This wasn't turning out how I'd expected at all, or how Angelo had expected, judging from the stiffness of his body at my side, but I did as Irene asked me. Is this, like, a séance? I thought to myself. Weird!

The pack lay in Irene's gnarled, knowing left hand, and she turned the cards over one by one with her right hand before laying them down on the table in front of me. As she put down the cards there was a stream of chatter, her eyes flickering across the flimsy table to meet mine every now and then.

'Eeh, well, it wasn't such a bad start, pet. Not too bad at all.' Loads of red hearts came up, spotted with only the odd spade or club. 'By, your mam's a nice woman. But she will not stand up to your dad, will she? My word, he wants tellin'! By, what a life he's led her. And you, pet. You an' all.' Some sort of a clairvoyant, then. I started to feel even more uncomfortable. There was one voice that spoke to me that I did not want Angelo to know about. And I didn't want him to find out about the notorious Rae family from anybody either, especially not Irene.

Just as I thought that, she looked me right in the eye. ' "He will not grow up!" ' she said. 'That's what I'm hearing about him. Your dad.' Hearing from who? I thought, and then this waft of pipe smoke hit me. Angelo actually sniffed, looking at me sharply. ' "George!" ' she said, like she was explaining. ' "After everything I told him, all those years! He will not grow up." '

The voice was Irene's, but I had heard the words and smelled the smell often enough before. For life-changing seconds, I knew he was in the tent with us. She said it exactly the way he used to. Old *George. My dad's dad died when I was fourteen. He was the only person who had called my dad 'George'! (Dad changed his name to 'Sean' twenty-odd years ago and now even my mam calls him that. Could have been worse, I suppose. Could have changed it to 'Pierce Rae'. 'Roger Rae'. Roger Rabbit, more like.) My dad's dad had tried so hard to wrap my dad up in this straitjacket of normality, like himself, that my dad ended up wanting a different jacket for every night of the week! A different woman, a different job, a different name. A different life. And that was what my granddad had always said to my dad, when I was little. 'You will* not *grow up, will you, George?' He* insisted *on the 'George': just about annoyed my dad to death.*

Now Angelo had heard, for the first time, some of the crap that constituted my family. I did not *want him to hear any more. I put my hand on his leg and shook it, and he turned, smiled at me at once, and squeezed my hand. 'It's OK,' he said. 'You'll get used to it.' Used to him knowing my worst secrets, or used to Irene talking to my dead relatives? I wasn't sure I* wanted *to get used to either of those things. But he was gripping my hand – a message that I had to stay.*

She was carrying on. 'School's not done y' many favours either then, has it? You're not the only one there, though. And there's one sister and a brother.' Pale eyes looked deep into mine. 'Mind, you've got to get over this, pet. It's dein' ye no good at all. I know your sister gets all the attention, what with bein' th' eldest, and she's bonny and all that, and your brother doesn't de s' bad either, because he's the youngest and a lad. Aye, and he's a divil, like your dad. But you're as important as they are. Divvn't ye forget that, pet, mind ye don't, even when other people around y' de.'

Did Irene glance over towards Angelo as she said that, or did I just imagine she did?

I'd never heard Irene doing the business with anybody else

but me. Part of me was annoyed, to be honest. Surely Mic and I were her priority? And the way that Christina was smiling across at her, listening intently and drinking that filthy tea, made me feel a bit strange as well. Evil old woman, winding me up. No wonder she'd been such great friends with my grandmother, I thought. I often felt that her candle box was more like Pandora's box than anything else.

But Irene was obviously hitting the spot with Christina and I was picking up some pretty useful information about her. It all sounded very different from what she'd said about her family in the restaurant the night of our first date, and a lot closer to what I'd started to guess at myself.

Irene's gnarled hand kept on turning over the cards. It seemed that the dark cards showed a dark time, and as she talked her way through my childhood, my teens and up to my present, the number of dark cards began to step up. 'And what hev y' been up to lately, then? Eeh, but ye pick the bad apples out, that y' de, the bad lads, and not only th' once. That's a right bad 'un that y've just got y'sel' rid of, pet. Y're well rid of him, but ye divvn't need me t' tell y' that, do ye? A bonny lass like ye!' She shook her white-grey head at me and sighed. 'What were ye dein'? But things is lookin' better at th' minute for y', what with Ango, here, and with the new job you've got. Much better.' She nodded in Angelo's direction, but her brow was all wrinkled up and worried. 'And they'll be better again before ye're finished. Ye'll be in mink knickers before I will, aye, that y' will, one way and another.' Irene's head snapped closer to mine and she let out her breath. 'But that's another story altogether, pet, and that's all I can tell y' at the minute.'

Angelo stood up to go, without so much as a signal to me. Old Irene's attention was maybe more important to him than he'd admitted even to himself. What sort of help did she give him with his brother? I wondered. Was Mic still alive? It was looking less and less likely. And how would Angelo react if I asked him?

At last Irene spoke to Angelo directly, but I still didn't know whether it was a message or a visitation; they both sounded so normal *the whole time.*

'Just one thing for you, Ango,' she said. Christina and I turned our heads, mid-crouch, as we stooped through the tent flap. 'Mic sez t' pick up th' phone from time t' time. That's all. He sez y' know full well what he means. Sez, "Remember the Duke! Look after y'self and pick up th' phone, Ango!"'

That split. Christina's eyes were full of questions that I closed off with the strongest look I could. So much for Irene's help.

Weirder still. Just who the fuck was the 'Duke'? But Angelo would say nothing when I asked him.

Jacob's Ladder

14. Stained Glass

'Was he . . . special? Gifted? Evil? Dying? All of those?'

One night after work, when Mr Andreas had been feeling generous and the drink (one drink!) was flowing (dripping, then), I managed to pump a bit more information out of Alex about Angelo. In between hearing about Peter's love life, Peter's mega-skill as a croupier and Peter's drinking capacity (all of which I could have told him by this time), I learnt that Iain and Ben had snogged eight girls between them at some croupy party and, at last, that life for Angelo on his farm had been a bit wild. 'One of his friends grew more marijuana there than anything else,' said Alex. Quite sniffy about it, he was. 'Practically set himself up in business. That wasn't all that changed hands there, either. But I never saw Ango the worse for wear, though he was well into the parties, then.' Then Peter jumped back in with another drinking story, Alex went to the loo, the taxis arrived and that was it.

The next night, I went around to the church. I wasn't even supposed to be seeing Angelo that night. My wrist was mending and I was back at work, but they were sticking me on all the smaller games, which was deadly boring when I was used to the bigger ones, like sitting with your back to the direction of travel on a train, so I was feeling a bit down that night. And I missed Angelo; I hadn't seen him for a few days, hadn't properly had a chance to discuss the meeting with Irene, or

*anything. After my day shift, I just dropped around to the church
to see him.*

*Every other time that I'd been to the church, Angelo had been
there on his own. But this time when he came to the door, there
was a young bloke with fair, floppy hair standing just behind
him, the nosiest smile on his face and at* least *a dozen questions
on his lips.*

Not what I had intended. Not at all. I'd had no idea that
Christina was coming that night, and I'd also had no idea
that Brett was on his way.

That first knock on the door was a complete surprise.
When I opened the door and saw that it was Brett, blazing
a broad white smile and a bright red jacket, I smiled until
my face hurt. I hadn't seen him for months.

'Brett!' I banged the top of his arm, hard, with my hand.
That's the nearest a bloke around here can get to touching
another bloke, in case you've never been to the frozen
wastes of the North East. 'Come inside, then. You'll die
out there.'

Brett banged my arm back, and smiled until *his* face
hurt, and then we went inside where we both sat down
together. I was so pleased to see him. I thought of Brett,
in the room next door to mine in halls, shouting through
the door to me, my first day at university; Brett's room,
vibrating with the boom of his CD player and his voice,
making the party wall shake; Brett, rowing a boatful of
girls across a lake and then standing up and howling
at the moon, nearly tipping them, shrieking, into the
water; Brett, sweet-talking the pair of us into party after
party, club after club and girl after girl, at one stage. A
long time ago. A moment ago, it felt like at that second. As soon as he'd walked into the church it was as
if I was inside his room at university again, the clean,
slightly leathery, smell of his skin taking me back there
at once.

'It's great to see you, Brett,' I said. 'Great. How's it going?'

'Oh, the usual, Ango, same as ever – one assignment a month and three women a week. You know how it is!' He cocked his head towards the high ceiling and laughed.

'The usual bullshit, then?' I said.

'Can't deny it.' He laughed. 'Haven't shagged anything without fur on its back for at least three months.' Brett was an agricultural student. 'I've been ringing you, Ango,' he said. 'Something wrong with your answering machine? Or have you gone off me?'

'Got it in one,' I said, giving his arm another thump. 'No, it's just a bit of hassle I've been getting, phone-wise.'

'Hassle of the female sort, is it?' he said. 'Nothing changes much, Ango, does it?'

Everything changes, I thought. Like all my mates from university call me 'Ango'. I'd thought I was finally rid of the 'Michelangelo' crap forever when I'd left school, but the casino, or rather Mr Andreas, had half brought it back: he thought 'Angelo' was more Casino Club, more Mediterranean somehow. Everything changes. But I just grinned and played along with Brett. 'Hassle of the female sort is right, Brett. Never any peace!' It wasn't a lie, really, but I didn't want to pursue that conversation. 'I'll get you a coffee, shall I?' I said, and Brett nodded. He followed me into the kitchen corner, relating stories of his flat, his flatmates, his family (who were based in Durham), and various other people we'd both known at university as well. I interrupted, when I could get a word in, with the odd story from the casino and bits and pieces of news from other people I'd spoken to, and then we sat on the settee facing each other, coffee in hand, and any chance of facing the larger issues gone, I hoped.

'So how have you really been then, Ango? Any sign of all that weird business happening again?' Shit. Just the tone of his voice told me what Brett was on about.

'Minimal, Brett. Minimal.' I kept my voice light. 'Just about behind me now.'

'Any chance of you coming back to university to finish your course, then?' he asked. 'I could easily sort you a room out at the flat.'

'No chance, cheers, Brett. I'm fine at the casino for now.'

He nodded, and was just about to send the conversation down another track when there was a knock at the door. Brett ambled over behind me as I answered it, not wanting to miss any chance to take the piss or to pick up some information, as usual.

'Christina!' It was the second total surprise.

Quite an attractive type he was, if you like them fair, that is (which I don't). I focussed straight back on Angelo. 'Sorry, Angelo – I didn't realise you had company,' I said. 'I just called around on the off-chance. I can catch you later, if you like.' (Roughly translates as, 'Invite me in and introduce me to your friend, then. Now!')

Angelo looked trapped.

Trapped. 'No, not at all. Come in and meet Brett. I've talked to you about him,' I said. Shit. I just hoped that Brett wouldn't say anything too monumentally crass or tactless in front of Christina. The sheer scale of the grin on his face as I opened the door to her was not a good sign. 'Come in.'

Because it was obvious that Angelo wanted me nowhere near his friend, I went in. But when he asked me if I wanted a coffee, I just said, 'Don't worry, I can look after myself,' and headed for the kitchen corner on my own, so that he could carry on talking to Brett.

For ages it was nothing but banter and small talk, university talk. I just settled myself down into the corner of the settee, curled

*up with my granny's cup in my hand and my legs beneath me,
and listened to the pair of them, spinning their stories. You should
have heard them. I mean, Brett was definitely the worst, like, with
his 1001 spotty tales from the harem, but once Angelo had cottoned
on to the fact that I thought it was a good laugh, rather than being
madly jealous, he had a fair bit to add to the discussion as well.
I think he was enjoying the attention. They both were. Nice for
them to have an audience. It was a bit like being in the staffroom
with Peter again, to be honest, having a rest while the blokes got
on with their bullshit.*

*But the stories were making me feel sad. Really sad. You see, this
was a different Angelo they were talking about, not the Angelo I
knew at all. This was an Angelo who'd chopped up his landlord's
tatty old furniture to use as kindling for coal fires; who'd shaved in
his wellies in old farmhouses so he wouldn't get an electric shock;
who'd danced the tango with old ladies at twenty-firsts and made
young ones in night clubs collapse at his feet. Who'd passed exams
with flying colours, after being up all night at parties and hardly
even trying at all. This was not my Angelo. Yet it had been such
a short time ago. And something about Brett's voice let me know
that he missed his Angelo very much. I just let them get on with
it for a while, and eventually I think they forgot that I was there
– anyone could tell they were dead close. For lads, that is. Men.
And that's when it started to get even more interesting again.*

*I'd picked up one of Angelo's books from a shelf and was
flicking through it. It was full of these old, religious paintings.
There were some poems typed out and put inside the middle of
the book, too.*

*He hath awakened from the dream of life,
'Tis we, who lost in stormy visions, keep
With phantoms an unprofitable strife,
And in mad trance, strike with our spirit's knife
Invulnerable nothings . . .
Life, like a dome of many-coloured glass,
Stains the white radiance of eternity.*

Percy Shelley. I liked the words, but I wasn't quite sure what they meant, and I was less sure again of what they meant to Angelo. For some reason, they reminded me of that day when I'd found the frightening little poem underneath the sheet at the window.

The last typed poem was by a different poet: William Blake.

This life's five windows of the soul
Distort the Heavens from pole to pole
And lead you to believe a lie
When you see with, not through, the eye.

Seeing through the eye? Horrible. I love poetry, but I didn't understand this lot. They only added to the feeling I already had that Angelo was really yearning for something the whole time. I flicked through the books, half listening to their conversation, when suddenly it started to get good.

It was Brett who started the ball rolling. 'How's the family situation then, Ango?' he asked. Family? I thought. Not many of them left from what I understood. 'Mic, I mean?' Ah, Mic. 'Are you finding it any easier to . . . to get over what happened to him?'

Angelo's voice was so quiet that I could hardly hear it. 'That's not the point, Brett.' His voice had dropped. He sounded hoarser, older, which could have been partly because his head was turned away from me. 'And I never want to forget what's happened to him.'

I could recognise the end-of-the-conversation-signs there and then, but either Brett was immune to them or he actually knew Angelo better than I did. He carried on with his questions. 'What about the other thing, then? Have you got over that? Was it a one-off, or what?'

I could feel Angelo's eyes on me, though mine were stuck fast to the book, and I could also feel his intense *discomfort. I was listening that hard, I'm sure my ears were turned in their direction. 'Definitely a one-off, Brett,' he said. 'And definitely to be kept between the two of us, if you remember?'*

'No offence, Ango, only checking everything's all right.' Brett actually put his arm on Angelo's. What was he talking about? Words and windows again, was my guess. Brett's voice went up a note. 'Just checking the old sex god's still up to it, eh, Christina? Paulillo the Performer, pulling them in. Nothing's changed. Do you think I should be worrying, or do you think I should be taking notes?' The tilt of Brett's head showed he knew he didn't have to take notes from anyone, but he wanted to please his friend.

So did I. 'Taking notes, Brett, definitely.' I closed the conversation off, and I'm sure I heard Angelo sigh with relief. 'Look, Angelo, I'd better go,' I said. 'Time's getting on and you've obviously got a lot of ground to make up with Brett.'

'Stay where you are, Christina.' Brett was waving me down with his hand. 'Sorry, Ango, it's me who's got to get off,' he said. 'I'm back to the parents tomorrow for Christmas. Just called in to see how you were doing. Keep in touch!' Then he was out and off down the path in a red and white flash, leaving Angelo and me in a new and very uncompanionable silence. Not cosy.

Did he want me to stay?

I was furious about the whole conversation, close to boiling over, but there was no way I was going to let either Christina or Brett know that. Why did people keep letting me down? I hated it that Brett had talked about what had happened to Mic like that, as if it was a trivial accident, that it could be casually 'got over'. My brother. Brett had no brothers which maybe explained it a bit. Still. And he'd stirred up all the old feelings inside me, talking the way that he had.

He was even pushing it with some of his macho stories. If Christina had talked about other blokes like that in front of me, I'd have walked out. She looked more entertained than anything else, though, seemed pretty easygoing about it all. Still, Brett could have stirred up a load of shit for me.

And, of course, I wasn't 'fine' at the casino at all. Fine for now, yes. But not for the rest of my life. All of the

things that I'd done before, travel, education, different jobs,
I wasn't finished with any of that. I might not know what
I wanted the future to hold, after my 'rest' in the casino,
but I did know that there was a future for me. Later. But
Brett's questions had wound me right up.

I did something I'd decided not to do a very long time
before. 'Would you like a drink?' I took some beers and
a bottle of wine out of the fridge and then started telling
Christina some of the early stuff about Mic, all the stuff
I never got to talk to anybody about any more. All the
accidents that we'd had as kids came out, the trouble we'd
got into, the scams, the fights. Plenty of fights always, with
Mic and me. 'You know, Christina, I used to think I could
kill him, used to dream of killing him,' I said. 'It was because
he was always bigger than me when we were younger,
although I'd caught up with him by the time we got into
our teens. He could be a real shit, you know, bossy, full of
it, always messing around, and I would never back down
from him. Half the time, it was verbal, but we'd fight often
enough as well. We used to drive my mother mad.

'I remember one time, when I was finally beating him
in some fight, I hit him over the head with a bottle. He lay
down as if he were dead . . .'

*And Angelo did all the actions, lying down in my lap, eyes shut,
looking fatally wounded and everything: he was pretty good with
stories. His head was in my hands and it felt as heavy as a
boulder.*

'*And I was really bricking it. I was only about twelve; I was
more scared of what my mother would say than the fact that it
looked like I'd just killed my brother.*

'*I got down on the floor beside him and I was just putting
my hands to his eyes, to do some sort of a test, you know.*' *He
changed roles now, playing his own part in the drama, and
demonstrated on my eyes, lifting their lids up slowly with his
fingers and peering inside, staring, until I giggled.* '*Next thing*

you know – POW!' Angelo's head and shoulders shot back as he mimed himself getting a mega-smack off Mic and I squealed.

'He wasn't hurt at all.' Angelo was just about killing himself laughing, with his head thrown back. 'Not even scratched. Until he jumped right up in my face, of course. Nearly knocked each other out cold, then. Then we had to start the fight up all over again.' He smiled, with this distant but happy expression on his face. Then it changed and he turned away and took a huge swig of beer.

When he spoke again, you could hear the drink in his voice. He was obviously upset by Brett's visit, but Brett had seemed really protective of Angelo. I was starting to see why. And that was the first time I heard him talk properly about his mother. 'My mum was happy, despite all the rows and broken ornaments, having her two "boys" to herself and all that.' Angelo smiled. 'Not to mention, we had to do everything her way, then. She was very much the boss.' He filled up my glass of wine again. 'A long time ago.' His eyes went to the floor and then the bottle went to his lips. Again.

The sudden ringing of the phone split the silence. With one hand Angelo signalled towards me to ignore the sound, and so the unknown voice spoke its message to the machine unheard. For some reason, the interruption seemed to make him even more agitated: he finished his bottle of beer in one great swallow and then went into the kitchen to open another. Coming back to the settee, and me, I noticed he rewound the machine again so that whatever the caller had said would be lost forever. I remembered what Irene had said about picking up the phone, but now was not the time to mention that. If it was another girl, then at least I didn't have to be jealous of the treatment Angelo was dishing out to her! This time, I kept my mouth shut. But Angelo didn't.

And this was the pattern of the evening. The memories that Brett had stirred up would not be sent away and so I shared some of them with Christina, courtesy of the beer and the wine. Others lay deep within me, so deep that I was unable, or unwilling, to access them for myself, let alone share them with another person.

Somehow, the beer and wine was helping me to swim down into all of that, to dip into the blackness, ignoring the surface stuff, and see what was there underneath. *'Come with me, Ango!'* Mic's voice. *'You wouldn't let me go on my own, would you?'* And my mother's. *'My special son.'* I drank more and felt further and further away from Christina. I knew what I was risking. The first couple of times that the messages came, I'd been trying stuff at University, stuff I wasn't really used to. It was just spliffs, that's all, and a few other bits and pieces besides, but I'd decided not to do that again. After the anaesthetic came the darkness, the dreams, and I wanted to be strong enough to get through life, and death, without anaesthetic. But I had to forget, and I had to really remember, somehow. So, just for once, I took another drink.

Later, stumbling up the steps to bed with Christina I thought, I am *never* going to do this again. Why do I always push it, push it too far? But in fact, and I've only admitted this to myself and to you, although I'm scared, I'm shit-scared of what happens when I push it too far, I really look forward to it as well. I listen for it. I wait for it. And I didn't have to wait for it long that night.

I slept like a beer-spattered baby in Christina's arms, practically blacked out, but then my dreams grew more and more frantic and less and less dreamy. Urgent. When I finally shrugged them away and forced myself to open my eyes a couple of hours later in the night, any memories of childhood were way out of sight. The darkness was waiting, waiting for me, with something hiding in its shadows, about to emerge. I lay there, waiting, thinking, grabbing at my dreams. My breathing stilled. And then it all came.

The message was first, urgent. 'Jesus. Jesus.' There were bars of gold light in front of my eyes, all at once. The windows are on the same level as my bed in the church, and I hardly dared look at them, but I was dying to look at them at the same time. I was terrified of what I would see, yet I knew that what I would see would be vital, would be rare. Unique. True. They were just windows, normally, but nothing would ever be normal again, not for me. I would never be normal again. I was shit scared, like I said before, but excited more than that.

I lifted my head and then my body, from Christina's sleeping arms and from my pillows, and turned my eyes to the tops of the old, arched windows. Searching. Waiting. I knew I was waiting for God, that I'd always been waiting for God, really, the whole time. We all are underneath, aren't we?

They were streaming down the windows, just streaming down. It was fantastic. Isaiah and Zachariah, and Jeremiah and Jonah, Jesus and Mary, and cherubs and angels – they were just pouring down the windows and dripping over the walls on to the floor. Roses and golds and aquamarines and oranges and ochres and greens were pooling on the floorboards. The prophets and the angels were slipping down the windows, like Jacob's ladder, the divine touching the earth. It was the most fantastic thing I've ever seen. Angels were melting in my house.

And all the time, I could hear this calling, calling, in this deafening metallic tone: 'Jesus. Jesus, Jacob, Jason, Joshua, Joseph, John, James and Jesus. Jesus.' Bright gold bars were still there in front of my eyes and the more I looked at the colours, through the bars, the louder the voice grew. It kind of vibrated. It was human and electronic, woman and man, angel and human, all at once. The colours and the noise and the power and the light boomed, all around me, and I was a part of it. The angels spoke to me, just to me. I was a part of the echo and a part of the sound; I was both behind the mirror and in front of it. I was part of flight and fear, and part of life and death, all at once. Elation, complete elation. I was an angel without wings, just like Rossetti's. Don't you wish that it could happen to you, really? Underneath? It changed my life forever: it showed me heaven. Yet it made me feel like, made me know that, I was very close to death as well. To hell.

I can't send it all away and I don't want to, but nothing ever asks if it can come in anymore. That's one of the biggest changes. And would another person, could another person, possibly understand it, if they hadn't experienced something similar?

'What is the matter with you, Angelo?' That was what she used to say to me. Her whispers joined in with the rest, and Mic's voice, singing as usual, way over the top. Still, the angels were melting in my house. Isn't that what we're all waiting for, underneath, whether people admit it or not?

Jesus.

'Jesus. Jesus.'

It was so loud, so definite. Bad dream again? I'd been having a pretty vivid dream of my own, a dream about dying. Horrible. Rubbing it out of my eyes, I sat up beside Angelo, ready to comfort him, but comfort was the last thing he needed. He was awake, but he was totally out of it. A different kind of horrible. 'Jesus, Jacob, Jason, Joshua, Joseph, John, James and Jesus.' He was sitting up in bed, talking and talking, and waving his arms around, full of life and energy, hyper, but making no sense at all, or so I thought at first – until I listened to him, until I separated then reconnected the words. There was a totally new light switched on inside him. Powerful. 'Jesus. Jesus.' Frightening.

I kept shaking his arm: I really wanted him to come back to me, back to himself, back to where it was safe and familiar. 'Angelo!' I said, shaking him again. 'Angelo. Are you all right? Wake up.' Yet I knew he was awake: that was the worst part. That was the very first time that I thought he might actually be insane. And that was the very first time, for just one second, that I thought I might eventually have to finish with him. One awful, awful second.

All I could do, though, was to sit there on the bed beside him and wait for him to come back to me. And when he eventually realised I was there, he turned towards me and said, 'Do you see, Christina, do you see the lights?' I stared into the darkness, the frightening blackness, with him. 'Harder,' he said. 'Look harder! Don't you see them?' 'No,' was not an option. Or even the answer. Because in the darkness, as soon as I looked, I really looked, spangles of green and gold and white and red appeared around us, I swear they did. And Angelo was rambling the whole time, staring ahead of himself, like he was on drugs, except you couldn't call it rambling; it was too energetic for that, and sort of spiralling rather than circling, and his hands were twisting round the sheets and his voice was rising and panicking, and then dropping and whispering. 'Angels. Angels are where heaven meets earth, God meets man, man meets woman. And windows, stained glass windows, are the sea, the brightly coloured sea between sky and earth, the air and the rocks, God and man, man and woman. John and James, the brothers. The brothers and the glass.' And the glass sending him messages, and the angels, through the glass, just to him, just for him, Angelo. And the golden bars. He was seeing everything through golden bars. 'What does it mean, Christina? You have to see it. You have to understand. What does it mean?' And the lights and the power and the noises, and his voice going on and on and on. Could anybody understand? Was it God, or was it Angelo? And if it was God, what was God playing at? Was he, Angelo, special? Gifted? Evil? Dying? All of those? Could anybody understand it all but him? Including him?

Do you follow his thinking? It was like Angelo was some sort of a missing link, missing medium. It was like he was extraordinary, unearthly, but wasn't that what I'd always sensed about him? What I had always been drawn to? Then again, aren't we all special, gifted, evil and dying? But we don't all get the angel treatment. Or do we?

Because I could see lights, I definitely could, all around us. Not Angelo's solid gold bars, but I did see spangles of light. Honestly. I was really with him and I wanted to be with him in everything.

For hours, it seemed, he went on to me, 'Do you see, Christina, do you see? What does it mean? What does it mean?' as he was describing the colours and the sights and the sounds. I rubbed his back and I tried to soothe him and to talk him down, and I listened to everything he saw and felt and knew, but still it all went on until I had to give up and just hold his hand and let him carry on.

And all the time I was thinking about him, about his intensity, his colour, the colour of rare, bright, beautiful glass. Jewelled. His strangeness. His specialness. And my stains. Not rare, not bright, not beautiful. Not special. Just stains. And thinking of what he would think if he knew about them. How I would never be perfect, or classy, or cool to him again. And how I would never, never tell him, or anybody else.

But I did see some of the lights with him, I really did, saw the lights, felt the feelings, or some of them. I just had no idea what any of it meant.

Do you?

15. One Page from the Bible

'Like real life, only more coloured in?'

The next day, Angelo was like a dead man. Still. The calm after the storm. Angelo and those nightmare experiences worried me, and his darkness, differences, seemed even more extreme in broad daylight. Was it possible that Angelo had been involved in whatever had happened to Mic? Maybe this Duke had been involved too?

Surely not. Surely not?

Instead of dwelling on that, I pottered around downstairs, clearing up after the night before, hoping that when Angelo did wake up, he might have managed to make sense of the night before in a way that I'd not managed to myself.

Christina woke me up as soon as she started down the iron staircase to the kitchen. I was desperate for advice, although it took me a while to get the energy together to get out of bed. I knew exactly where to look for guidance.

With the clinking of cups and the metallic clanking of the toaster in the background to assure me that Christina didn't know what I was doing in the bedroom, I went straight to my grandmother's candle box and lifted its domed lid. The first item that I saw would be the one that could help me most, I decided. A Bible. It was ridiculous, really, because my grandmother had seemed anything but God-fearing in her lifetime: she'd been about as outrageous as Irene was now, in her own way. Still, she knew what she was doing. Who better to advise me after my experiences of the night before? What better to advise me than the Bible? Stick in a pin and pray. I opened it up and the first section I saw gave me my message.

> *Your father wants to give you the Kingdom. Sell what you have and give your money to the poor. Make sure your treasure is safe in Heaven, where thieves cannot steal it and moths cannot destroy it. Your heart will always be where your treasure is.*

That was clear enough. Give. I grabbed my tarot cards from the drawer where I always put them when Christina was coming over, I cut them into the special pattern I had devised and turned over the Wheel of Fortune. It was all beginning to fit together now. The hair clasp had been the first message, in its own way; giving it away had brought Christina and me together. And then look what had happened when I'd ignored Christina while she was wearing it, when I'd failed to give. Give? I could easily give something else away – my car, maybe, or a piece of furniture of my grandmother's that might be worth something.

But what about Christina? How *could* she understand about the messages properly? I would have found it difficult to understand if I hadn't experienced them myself, impossible even. But Christina had to understand it all. Because what was the alternative to connecting the messages to the rest of my life? The alternative was to see the messages as meaningless, random interventions over which I had no control, to see part of my life, my mind, as random and out of control, even. As a sickness. The alternative was what my mother had suggested to me. Suggested once.

I'd have to be very careful how I put the whole situation

across to Christina: that was one lesson I had learned. I knew how weird it all seemed, I did know that. I could imagine it from the outside; I'd tested the response before. There was no way I was going to scare her off. I couldn't face a repetition of what had happened with my mother. No way.

I shouted down to Christina and started to talk as soon as she got up the stairs with the toast and everything, sussing her out. She set the tray down on the bed and I said to her at once, 'Last night must have been pretty weird, for you.' I watched her face.

'And you,' she said, after a second. But then she lifted her worried blue eyes from the food and looked at me, met my eyes. A good sign. 'How often does that happen to you?'

'That's the third time,' I replied (which was about the truth, I didn't want to frighten her off altogether). 'That's how the writing came to be around the windows. It often involves windows, or glass. The writing was one way of expressing it all.'

'I guessed,' she said. 'Half guessed. Do you get any closer to what it might all mean?' she asked.

'Only hints.' I smiled at her. 'That's what makes it bearable. The hints.' Hints that I'm special, I thought, and hints about how to live, really live. Hints that other people, 'normal' people, 'sane' people, might ignore, might not even hear. 'I think the angels being there was a kind of message about being giving. I always have to think about it, to interpret exactly what it means. Look for other messages to make sense of the first one, sometimes. And my grandmother used to say the same sort of thing about giving.'

'Right,' was all Christina said, but it was a start, a much better start than, 'See a doctor'. It encouraged me enough to try out, adapt, a speech I'd given my mother, in fairly similar circumstances. It hadn't worked with her, but I had to hope that I could make my point clearly to Christina. And she was still listening to me, her head inclined.

'It's like a circle,' I said, 'normally, I mean.' The circle of life. I tried to explain without sounding like a complete head case. 'Normally, a dream becomes a plan, which becomes a vision, which you turn into an experience. This becomes a memory, which drives you towards another plan. And then you're off again.' More like a spiral than a circle. I knew Christina had plenty of dreams that she was busy turning into visions of her own. 'Well, with me,' I said, 'I have visions, fantastic visions. A vision is just a dream and an experience combined, but one that you hadn't planned on. A vision comes to you, then you have to make sense of it afterwards.'

Christina thought about that for a bit. 'Like waking up all of a sudden in Los Angeles, wondering which of the thirty thousand fast food places you should try today?'

Even then she could make me smile. 'Very much like that,' I said. 'Only then you have to work out what it means.'

'Sounds good,' she said, and then she thought about it a bit more and half dropped her eyelids. 'Sort of.' She looked up again. 'Is it?' She really wanted to know.

'Sort of.' I tried again. 'It's as real as real: you actually hear the voices and see the sights and everything, you don't imagine them. And it's exciting because they tell you bigger, more important things than ordinary voices do. And you get filled with these feelings of just intense excitement, elation, energy. Life, really. Larger than life. Love, too.' But I had to tell her the other truth. 'It's also a bit frightening.' A bit? And lonely, especially afterwards. Very lonely. I thought of the first time it had happened, thought of Brett's nonplussed, embarrassed face when I'd tried, eventually, to explain. Tried not to think of my mother's face after she'd seen me like Christina just had. Lose a sense and everyone's all sympathy: gain one and the reaction's pretty different.

Christina was still thinking. 'Like real life, only more

coloured in?' she asked, her head tilted, and I nodded and smiled. She thought for a second. 'It's chaos and destiny, isn't it? Exactly like in *Forrest Gump.*' She thought again. 'You have to work out which one is which. Easier said than done.' She was quiet for a minute and looked worried.

'I can always see you,' I said, and touched her arm. 'Even in the middle of it all. I know you didn't see exactly what I saw, but you saw lights as well, didn't you?'

'Yes,' she said, looking more puzzled still. What will I do if she doesn't understand? I thought. Can I carry on living in this loneliness?

No.

I looked at Christina's face. She'd listened to it. She nodded. She smiled. She accepted it. She accepted me. It was the first time since it had been happening that I hadn't been totally alone with it. Can you just imagine the relief of that?

I put my arms around Christina, burying my face in her shoulder, and she cuddled back automatically, like she always did, holding on to my neck like a baby chimpanzee. Then she pulled away, smiling though still thoughtful, and handed me some toast, some coffee. 'And you think it means that you have to give this time? What might you give?'

'Give to you, like the clasp.' I laid back and gestured towards the coffee cup. 'Or like you, making me breakfast. Little things, but important. There's a way that you could give too.'

'Me?'

He got weirder still then, my exceptional Angelo, very weird but very sensible, depending on how you look at things. I was so worried for him, but I swallowed that and listened to what he was telling me.

'The casino,' he said. 'Why does the house – Mr Andreas – always win? I mean, I know it's partly maths, the way that the

bets work, plus who always runs out of money first, and I know it's partly psychology, the way that the punters' minds work. But doesn't the way that you spin the ball have something to do with it as well?'

'Not much,' I said, and laughed. 'Although you wouldn't think so if you were to hear Mr Andreas when one of us is doing our brains on a big game, or if you heard what some of the punters say when they're losing.' I thought about it. 'I mean, they tend to back sections of the wheel: the Tier, usually, or the Orphans, or the Neighbours of Zero, from time to time. Sounds like a band, doesn't it? They back one part of the wheel and so the dealers are supposed to avoid that part, if they can.'

He brought me back to the point. 'Well, maybe the next time that the casino is winning and some poor loser is backing the Tier, you could spin for that section instead of avoiding it? Look at how many people we know whose lives have been ruined by playing roulette, how many people have lost their businesses or their marriages through it. The casino makes enough money anyway, doesn't it?' He laughed. 'Mr Andreas doesn't exactly go short, does he? His business is booming.'

No arguing with that. Angelo did his 'Mr-Andreas-as-Henry-the-Eighth' impression, smiling, inclining his head and lifting his eyebrows, exactly like Mr Andreas did, and putting his hands to either side of his puffed out belly. Mr Andreas had a waistline that could easily have accommodated half the Third World! About time for the Feed the World era to reach him at last, I reckoned. And I wanted so much to go along with Angelo, to be on the same side as he was. The good side. I wanted so much to ignore the tiny voice that had spoken to me, telling me that Angelo was seriously disturbed and that if I wanted to avoid ending up the same, I would have to, at some stage, finish with him.

I shrugged the voice off and considered what he had said, instead. Black eyes and the blonde, a sort of alternative Bonnie and Clyde, or a twenty-first-century Robin Hood couple, robbing the fat to feed the failures. It was a strange logic, but it did make sense in a way. I touched the angles of his face with my fingers. His angel face.

'And roulette is such an unpredictable game that nobody would have a clue what I was doing.' I spoke slowly. 'They'd just think I was on a losing streak, or something. It's only the really small, privately owned casinos that believe dealers can spin in sections anyway, or so I've heard. Although I think you can. We used to practise all the time at training school. I was excellent *at spinning sections – beat Alex every time.' I was full of myself, laughing.*

'Give it a go, then.' Angelo smiled down at me, pulling at my hand, trying dead hard to persuade me. 'For real, this time.' And he grinned.

I tried to grin back. Surely someone so good, I thought, so giving, so sensitive, so lovely, would never hurt me. A little voice inside of me spoke. He would never have hurt his own brother? I knew he wouldn't. Didn't I?

She was the only person that had really trusted me, and she had seen me closest.

I honestly believe she saved my life then.

16. The Wheel of Fortune

'Your heart will always be where your treasure is.'

In fact, it was nearly Christmas by the time I tried our little experiment out, because I had to wait until Angelo was on the same shift as me. I wanted him to actually see that I had been listening, that I understood him and that I was with him.

Not to mention, I needed a bit of a diversion. There was no way that I'd have told Angelo, but Jonty had been making his presence felt, sacking or no sacking. Twice in the last week, I'd walked down the stairs into the parking area outside the flats to see an empty red Peugeot parked right outside the door. Guess whose? If Jonty wants to risk coming back to find his car turned into a skeleton, with its car-cushioned arse kicked out of it, that's his problem, I said to myself. Forget it. But that was my problem. I couldn't forget it. Because it worried me, just like Jonty intended it to. One time, he left the 'Situations Vacant' section of the Evening Chronicle *staring out at me from the dashboard, bastard, just to make his point. Maybe Angelo sensed something, I don't know, but he'd called on me a few times to walk me from the flat to my shift.*

I shrugged thoughts of Jonty off for a minute and looked around me at the casino. In a way, it was a brilliant place to be at Christmas. The clothes some of the punters wore made the Elvis impersonators from my old working men's clubland look tame. Sequin City. The Joan Collins look is alive and kicking in the Casino Club. Then, of course, the punters were totally *going for it*. You can't drink on the tables, but nothing can stop you from getting as pissed as a fart in the bar, then *going on the tables and doing your brains in*. Mr Andreas had even been buying us drinks after the place had shut, to celebrate the winnings and the festive spirit. I was almost starting to like the globey-stomached old devil. Almost. Anyway, I'd promised Angelo, so that was that.

I'd decided a random approach would be the most fun. I looked at the first person who was playing on my table as I started my shift, Mr Todd – The Stiff (mineral, probably coal, not exactly lively). German for death, Todd, Alex had said, hence the nickname. He was a middle-aged bloke, taxi driver, and was busy telling another middle-aged bloke how his business was going as I took Alex off. Typical punter conversation.

'Five taxis I had last year,' he was saying. 'Five. Employing six drivers, I was.' A pile of chips plopped on to one number at a time as he spoke. 'Five taxis', plop, 'one wife', plop, 'and two kids', plop, plop. I spun the wheel as I listened to his story, trying to decide whether he would be the one selected for my giving game, or not. 'And now I've got one taxi, the one I drive myself', plop, 'no wife', no plop, 'and two kids on a Saturday only, which is a swine when the match is on: loses me no end of business.' Plop, plop!

The casino won, the electronics lit up number eight, black eight, and The Stiff did a massive sigh, just about collapsing his own lungs. He'd put about forty chips on in the time it had taken him to tell his fellow loser his life story, at £1 a chip, and I'd swept the lot away in four seconds. Red and gold, I thought, looking at my table, red and gold. Stories told. There were his windscreen wipers, gone down the chipper with the rest. Plop. The next spin took out his passenger seats. Plop, plop. And then another £40 was slammed into Mr Andreas' cash box and I replaced all of The Stiff's chips. One more spin and his car radio went. Plop, plop, plop. Thick as a brick.

I decided he was a lost cause. He was seriously dedicated to total self-destruction. It sounds hard, but the sooner The Stiff lived up to his name and hit rock bottom altogether, the better. There has to

*be a death before there can be a proper rebirth, don't you think?
A relighting of the tinder. Maybe then he could get a grip, give up
the gambling and get his life back together again. The fact that
he'd counted his wife and kids alongside or* after *his cars made
my mind up for definite!*

*Decision time. The next person, Foreskin apart, who came to
my table to place a Tier bet would be the lucky man or woman:
that was the best way. And that was the only way Mr and Mrs
Glum got some glamour injected into their lives that night, or
any other.*

Normally, £10 a night punters, between *them, are every
dealer's nightmare. To be fair to them, you've got to have a
pretty vast amount of money to make an impression on a roulette
table, and the customers we thought of as wankers, who spent a
few pounds on a game that was deadly boring to deal, probably
spent more like £50 a night. But that night, the Glums became the
Glams. They always came into the casino as a couple, his and hers,
colour co-ordinated clothes and chips. Most of the blokes came in
on their own. I used to feel really sorry for them at first, until
I found out that they had wives sat at home, businesses going
down the pan, and that all that they cared about was money.
Then I felt sorry for the wives, mainly. But little Mr Glum loved
his funny little Mrs Glum, so I reckoned he deserved a treat as
much as anybody did.*

*Mr Glum was about four foot nothing (animal, possibly gerbil?)
with a well-polished, ping-pong ball head and a shiny suit to go
with it.* Mmmm. *Dead trendy. And a barrel of laughs on top of
all that, he was. He didn't normally even back the Tier, but that
was his very lucky night. His first words to me were, 'Tier bet by
fifty pence, Christine, please.' Fifty pence. Christine? Please! Still,
a promise was a promise.*

*'Tier bet by fifty pence,' I repeated. I stuck Mr Glum's money
on the wheel, gave him a colour and changed his money within
seconds, and then I put my hand inside the wheel and aimed for
the Tier. Praying. 'Five, red five!' What a shot! First time, just like
training school. Mr Glum's face was a Christmas wreath of smiles*

as I pushed the chips across to him, and he wildly splashed eight of them back out again on the same third of the wheel. 'Eight, black eight,' it was that time. Another crashing victory for Mr Glum. Nothing glum about his face now: he was gleaming. Sixteen chips went down this time, doubling up, then it was, 'Thirty, red thirty.' Things were really looking up. It was time for Mrs Glum (animal, dormouse) to make her mousy-haired appearance and entwine her tail with his, stroked into place by her swarm of free-buffet-night friends, also rodents, who'd spotted Mr Glum's magnificent star shining from afar. Mr Gold was glittering across the room at me also, from his usual blackjack table in the corner.

Mr Glum's complete lack of imagination was his winning card, or rather his winning chip, that night. Seven times in a row he backed the Tier, doubling up as he went, and six out of seven times I hit it. His little paws were shaking so much in the end that he could hardly put his chips on. The shame of being taken off my table early because I was 'doing my brains' to Mr Glum was worth it when I looked at his face as I left. Sheer joy! He'd grown at least *a foot in minutes (from a gerbil to a rat?), and he had a stack of chips over a foot high in front of him as well. Transformed. It was like being a magician, making something happen instead of just doing what you're told. Mrs Glum was looking at him as if he was Richard Gere and she was Julia Roberts, while Angelo was watching me, free sandwiches in his hand and his special half grin on his face.*

As I cleared my hands (just to show my honesty) and left the table, Mr Glum topped the whole night off perfectly. He flicked a fifty-pence chip across at me, with a lick of his dry little lips and a wild wink of his eye, and said, 'That's for you, Christine!' Very *sexy. The top of his head was glinting softly in the lights, and a sliver of red tinsel had fallen down from the decorations near the ceiling right on top of his bald patch. A bald patch that was fairly sweating, now, with the excitement. At least ninety years of free dinners and gambling in British casinos behind him, and it was the first time he'd ever tried to tip anyone, because, of course, you can't tip dealers in British casinos. It's illegal. I left the chip lying there. Mr Glum could always add it to his mountain of winnings, or he could really splash out and buy Mrs Glum a whole new outfit, or a house or two, with it.*

Mr Gold glittered more brightly still from his comfortable corner. Did he have gold teeth? I wondered. I'm sure he knew what I was up to. He only shouted over, 'Good night, Christina. See you before Christmas,' as I left the pit, but his eyes were sort of dancing at me. I hoped none of the staff had noticed what was going on.

No chance! Peter the Pit Bull was killing himself when I got into the staffroom for my break. 'Chrissie,' he said, 'ye've left your Santa suit at home the neet. Owd Glum's got enough chips in front of him t' set up a Harry Ramsden's! Did y' see his face?' Peter could hardly speak for laughing. 'Aah've never seen owt like it. What were y' dein', man? Away with th' fuckin' fairies!'

'Just my brains, Peter,' I said, and smiled back at him. Best not to test Peter's loyalty too far: he'd already risked his job (and Jonty's lip) for me. 'Just my fuckin' brains,' I said, in my imitation Peter voice. Swearing felt so wicked now. He sighed and laughed again.

'I've never seen owt like it.' He shook his head. 'Away with th' fuckin' fairies.'

That was my first experience of making one of Angelo's visions come true.

17. Surprise!

'Dream on?'

Two days later, Angelo found a really original way of making one of my *visions come true.*

The last words he'd said to me on the night of Mr Glum's glory had been, 'Make sure you're ready on time on Friday, Christina. And make sure you're looking smart . . . As smart as usual, I mean,' he added, because my face had, 'Don't I always look smart?' written all over it. So I was dressed up to the nines, more make-up than Marilyn, as I waited for eight o'clock to arrive: nails manicured, hair combed, legs bald, the lot. Dead excited. Then I was off down the stairs and out of the door on the dot. Angelo had told me to meet him outside the flats, prompt as anything.

Amazed as anything. Because there, outside my grotty flat, looking like Howard Hughes (before he disappeared into the Desert City Hotel in Vegas, and drew the curtains on the world for nine years), was Angelo – dark, dark Angelo Paulillo – standing outside of a black-windowed, sexy, chauffeur-driven stretch limo, waving and grinning like mad. Dream on? But this time it was for real. Christina Rae, the second best-looking daughter, from one of the worst estates in Gateshead, and one of the worst families in the area, was the Queen of Cars! By the time I walked across to it, there were kids all around it, shouting: shouting at each other and Angelo. Two of them were touching it, and laughing, either checking that it was real or planning on taking a bit of it home each for a souvenir, but Angelo just opened the door for me and grinned some more. I couldn't believe my eyes.

Christina Rae and the Stretch Limousine

Christina Rae stepped straight from her apartment into the luxurious vehicle that awaited her, and settled herself comfortably into the J-shaped back seat with her partner, Angelo Paulillo, smiling at the chauffeur through the glass as she did so. The limousine purred its way out of Miss Rae's drive and headed for the centre of the city, as Mr Paulillo curled his arm around her waist, put a single red rose into her hand and said, 'I've booked us a table at a restaurant for nine o'clock. What would you like to see between now and then?'

That was what really happened.

Christina was so worked up that she couldn't speak, for once, so I took charge and we headed for the city centre. 'This was the nearest I could get to Chicago,' I said to her. 'The car, I mean, not Newcastle.'

'It's near enough,' she said. She looked radiant. And amazed. 'It's brilliant, Angelo.'

I leaned over to the minibar and opened the little fridge up. 'Glass of wine?' I asked. It was perfectly chilled and ready for her, *Vin Santo*, along with some *cantucci* biscuits. As I touched the biscuits, they reminded me of how much my old aunts in Certaldo would love her. She looked like she needed a drink. Shocked silent.

That shut me up, for a few sips, at least. But by the time I was on my second glass and the limo was on its second round of the Tyne Bridge and the city circuit, my tongue was getting itself back together again.

'How did you get the money for this then, Angelo?' It was

something I'd often wondered about, but I'd never dared to ask before. This was outrageous, though.

'Don't worry about it, Christina,' he said, looking a bit annoyed.

'But I am worried about it,' I said. 'You didn't rob a bank, did you? Or Mr Andreas?' I was trying to make a joke of it, but I needed to know.

'All right, then,' Angelo told me. 'I inherited a couple of thousand pounds from my grandmother. OK?'

'OK.' I took the hint and buttoned up, but the way he spent money sometimes, the couple of thousand wouldn't last much longer than a couple of months. Still, that was Angelo's problem. And he was trying so hard to make my dream come true that it would have been awful *to spoil it by arguing with him. So I didn't. I curled up in a corner of the limo instead, my glass of wine in my hand and my dreams shining out of my eyes, and watched all the poor people through the window, the poor people who were dead jealous of me, nestling into these gorgeous leather seats with this gorgeous-looking man.* La Vita E Bella. *(Remember Roberto Benigni at the Oscars? Wild!)* La Vita E *really, really* Bella. *Roberto and I understood that. Dead simple. Everything that can be imagined can be made, but you only imagine a mixture, or an extension of, what you've seen, or read about, or known. So there's no difference between the real and the imagined, only the effort it takes to turn one into the other. And the more that you know, the more you can imagine, and the more you can do. Dead easy. But I felt so free, so excited by it all, that it was weird. If Angelo had only given me that one experience of turning the imaginary into the real, then he'd given me more than some people ever had.*

Then he opened up the fridge again and took out this silver box of handmade chocolates. He kissed me on the cheek as he leaned over. 'Just enjoy yourself, enjoy the present, Christina,' he said, as he put them into my hands. His voice was as deep and as rich as the chiming of an old clock. Gorgeous. Peter's comment 'Bit on th' moody side' came into my head, but other people had no idea of just how good *the good moods could be! In private.*

I smiled across at him and put the box into my handbag to keep forever, like I wanted to keep the memory of the night, forever. Nobody had ever done such a thoughtful, lovely thing for me before in the whole of my life. Dead special.

And as we drove around, a scrappy little poem came into my head for him. I'm really good at poems, and better again at scrappy.

Stretch

I'm white wine high
And I'm chilli pepper hot
I'm leopard skin wild
And I'm lottery ticket lost

Chocolate, cars and Angelo
What a lot I've got!

I got a paper and pen out of my bag to scribble it down, handed it over to him, grinning, and he laughed, but folded it into his pocket later, when he thought I wasn't looking.

Later, we stopped the limo for a full ten minutes just so that we could stare up towards the Angel of the North in the night. Angelo looked like he was in a spell, and I was dead happy. No worries.

For the time being.

It was worth every penny, it really was. Even the chauffeur was smiling through his mirror at Christina; she looked so blissful. It was as if the limo was a carriage. Transportation, I thought. Transformation. And when I looked at Christina's face again, she looked freed. I knew my grandmother would have been pleased with the way that I was spending her money (not that there was a lot of it left). The limo pulled up at last outside the American diner where I'd booked us a table to carry on with Christina's theme.

What I was doing for her wasn't half as important as

what she had done for me before, when she'd listened to me so seriously and tried so hard to understand me. And it was only the start of my showing her how much she meant to me, and, even more importantly, showing her how she should think of herself.

My plans for her, for us – for our future – were more dramatic still.

18. The Stone Lion

'How can you enjoy yourself, how can you, after what happened to your brother?'

Christmas Eve, and I had to work at the casino. At least I was on an early. I was quite looking forward to it actually, although all the dealers and inspectors who'd been there a while had warned me that Christmas in Casinoland was nothing to write home about. 'Just the same old punters and the same old games, Christina,' as Gerry put it. 'Nothing special about it.' But after a lifetime of Christmases that involved Christmas club presents and an after-the-club row every day between my parents, Christmas in a casino still seemed very James Bond – very Bond Street altogether – to me. And then there was the very *definite magic of Angelo Paulillo to look forward to after work.*

I'd bought a real Christmas tree, put lights up everywhere, wrapped *The Scream* up in ivy and bought Christina loads of presents. We'd agreed that she would come over to the church after work on Christmas Eve and stay with me that night and all of Christmas Day.

Only one thought kept spoiling it for me: Christmas, the birth of Jesus. It couldn't help but remind me of my mother. And that couldn't help but make me feel down, spending my first Christmas without her. The night before, I'd had a dream about a woman drowning in the sea, or rather, she should have been drowning – the water was washing over her head – and I was just swimming along beside her, doing nothing to help. Water washed over her glassy eyes, time and time again, and then she slowly turned her head to look at me and laughed, started talking, smiling even, as if everything was quite normal.

Think about Christina, I said to myself. Make this the best Christmas she's ever had.

Mr Glum was all smiles that night. And Mrs Glum was more colourful than the Casino Club's OTT Christmas tree: new dress, new smile, new hairdo, the lot, totally full of it. She was almost not a dormouse any more. Tidings of comfort and joy, comfort and joy, and Mr Andreas wasn't exactly suffering either: he had a smile like a snowy swag on him when I walked out into the pit to start my shift. Father Christmas's sack of life was brimming over for old lobster-chewing, Santa-stomached Mr Andreas every night of the week anyway. He must have had more stomachs than a cow! Sometimes he ate two lobsters, you know, in one sitting. Incredible.

Old Mr Glum couldn't resist a bit of a bet at my table straight off, but he soon got the message that Jesus only rises once, at the Casino Club at least: I hit zero twice, and he moved on, figuring out there was no repeat performance in sight. The Neighbours of Zero sounded like all the Casino Club's customers at once now, as well as like a band. Too much talking to Gerry was the problem, I reckoned, making me cynical before my time, so I homed in on the nearly zero possibilities of my miniature roulette game and the many possibilities of my beautiful Angelo to come, and forgot about the rest of it for a while. What sort of preparations would be going on in Stephen King land? What sort of film would I be playing my part in later? I couldn't wait.

The voice of Debbie, who'd come off Jonty's training school, brought me back to the casino. 'Place your bets, please. No hurry there, Mr Fawcett.' She was smiling away at him, at old Foreskin, all friendly and relaxed. As if he was a normal person! It was an amazing achievement and he was kind of slavering back as best he could through those sausagey pink lips of his, with a gruesome drop on the end of his snout shimmering away in the light of the chandeliers. Then he spat a yellow puddle of old whisky into the ashtray, a nice strand of old lamb or beef floating on the top of it. And still Debbie smiled. She was half-Italian, half-Geordie: all flashing eyes, like Angelo, and also all blonde and chatty like me. Debbie was how our children might look, I thought, half Angelo and half me. All gorgeous.

The best part of the night was the last part, when the pit boss put me on the blackjack table, dealing to Mr Gold. 'The jewel of the Casino Club, Christina here is, Mike,' he said to Mike Turner. 'I hope you appreciate her!' Fat chance! But then he shook his head at himself, knowing it was a corny line. I'd got to quite like old Mr Gold really, not in the way that I liked Angelo (hot), but he always smiled at me and had a chat (cool). And whenever I dealt to him, I sort of watched what my body was doing, how I was standing or speaking, that kind of thing, which was funny because he wasn't my type at all. I suppose I was aware of him watching me.

Peter came to take me off my game at nine. 'Aal reet for some, Chrissie,' he whispered, or thought he whispered. His voice was as hearty as the rest of him. 'Fuckin' part-timers, leavin' th' lads t' de th' heavy shifts! Y' must've been shaggin' old Andreas t' get this shift off!' Mink knickers. Yuck! He grinned at me and shoved me out of my place at the blackjack table with one massive elbow. 'Hev a few beers for me, like, Jack Russell heed.' (This was Peter's revenge for my naming him 'Peter the Pit Bull'.) He heaved a massive sigh. Mr Gold, earwigging away, laughed, and the inspector tutted at me and Peter, shaking his head, all serious. I grinned up at Peter, rubbing it in, cleared my hands of the game and left. I was quite glad it was going home time.

I'd arranged to meet Angelo at the church, so it was a real surprise when I got outside the casino (the Red Jersey safely captured in my bag) and found him waiting there for me.

*'Angelo!' I ran up and kissed him. 'What are you doing here?'
And he seemed really happy, slinging his long arm over my
shoulders, hugging me in and smiling down spectacularly into
my face. He looked like Tom Cruise, only full-sized and better
looking. Then he bit my ear and did a growl: I think he was
being a tiger, or a puma, or something.*

*'You've survived, then?' was all he said. 'Didn't get eaten alive
by old Foreskin, or any of the other vultures?' For one weird
second, I thought I saw Jonty's square shoulders disappearing
around a corner as Angelo automatically took my bag, but then
Angelo nipped the side of my neck, being a bee, now, and stung
Jonty right out of my mind for good. 'Surprise,' he said. 'Your
first Christmas surprise.'*

I wasn't going to let Christina walk to the church on her
own, and sometimes I had these tiny doubts about her,
about her and Peter in particular, and one or two of the
punters as well. Persistent doubts. Do you remember how
concerned Peter was about her, the day of the Jonty affair?
But she'd walked out of the casino alone, so I could relax.
I had turned over the Star in my tarot reading, just before
leaving the house, too, which meant a new start, optimism
and hope – the perfect card for the night.

We left the casino and dropped down towards the row of
busy pubs and clubs and restaurants that line the Tyne. The
Quayside. The streets were full of other couples and young
people, all dressed up in next to nothing and carrying on,
laughing. A woman's voice was whispering away in my ear:
*'How can you enjoy yourself, how can you, after what happened
to your brother?'* I ignored it. I always ignored it. I killed her
again every time I ignored her voice, but I had to ignore
her voice if I was ever going to hear my own.

When we got to the Stone Lion, I made sure that Christina
was comfortable, in a seat that looked over the river to
the front, then I went to the bar and came back laden
down with my bottle and a cocktail and all the usual

paper paraphernalia with swizzle sticks and silver stirrers attached, for her. She looked up, smiling and tilting her head again in that way that made her hair look like a waterfall. Sometimes it seemed like no one had ever done anything nice for her before me.

'It's a Flaming Lamborghini,' I said, stupid name, assembled in layers of colour and lit up, just like I remembered from a time when I'd been there with a crowd and all the girls had ordered the most ridiculous drinks. The flames made the happy glow on her face seem even more intense as she looked down at it, laughing and excited, and then she looked back up at me again.

We were sitting at this tiny little table, with our backs to the rest of the pub and it was as intimate and cosy as a booth in a 1950s American diner. But it was very *Y2K+. There was a huge fireplace to my left, and its surround was a roaring lion with the fire blazing away inside its mouth – the Stone Lion, I guessed. The Polystyrene Lion, more like, I thought, like Angelo's black moods and dreads. Manageable. I looked out of the window. The curve of the Guild Hall was to my right and the line of stone buildings to my left was as smooth and well-decorated as the icing on a wedding cake. Dead classy. The buildings were like a frame for the river and 'The Boat', a floating night-club, was smack in the middle. There was a roundabout in front of me, with two young blokes sitting on it, meditating or something, and cars and taxis were twirling around it, a Lotus and then a TVR (Blackpool man), and the occasional young lad in a broken down old Mini with his mates. Mad. A full bridal party walked past, veil (net curtain), flowers (plastic), jewels (tinsel), the lot, singing Abba songs, all out of tune. What with the lights flashing, the river flowing and the traffic circling, the view from the window was almost as hypnotic as the view of Angelo's face. Almost.*

I turned back to him, my head full of weddings, and he smiled over the lip of his Stella bottle. The giggling behind me reminded me that I was sure the big chattering group of girls sitting to our right were all watching him and wishing they were me, so I kissed him full on the lips, just to make the point that he was altogether mine. Then he yanked my dress down towards my knees, hard (it had quite a way to go), to make the same point, I guess.

I couldn't wait to get Christina home with me. We hadn't made love since that night just after the Jonty incident; it had been sexier on the night of the limo to leave without anything intimate happening. But memories of the fine lines of her body, the softness of her hair and her face and the strength of her reactions to me had been tormenting me for days. Gorgeous. I needed to get inside her body, I really did, and I had to will an embarrassing erection away more than once in the pub. But I could take nothing for granted with Christina. Despite my careful choice of seat, half the pub had its eyes on her legs. The male half. Very female legs. I had a good look at her shoulders, checking there were no strange hairs or anything from Peter lying there. Nothing.

Surely she wants to be alone with me as much as I do with her? I thought. Surely? I had to know.

Of course, all I really wanted to do was to rip Angelo's clothes off, right in front of that admiring crowd of girls, but going back to the church first was probably a better idea. It was just that I needed a bit more Dutch courage before I could face Stephen King land again – and the cocktail was going down a treat.

'God, Angelo,' I said to him. 'I'm going to end up plastered.' Not to mention, I really had the hots for him. 'We'd better go!' I said. Christina Rae, the Queen of Romance.

Angelo must have felt the same, because as soon as we were out of the public rooms he slipped his hand down from my waist to my bum, over my dress, and kept it there all the time we were walking down the stairs together to the door, feeling me move. Just before we got to the exit, he pulled me towards him and kissed me, hard, holding me close to him with both his big hands. Dead

passionate. I felt like I was in a swirly, swirly dress, in West Side
Story *or* Grease *at least. Dead glamorous. And Angelo Paulillo
was John Travolta, without the 70s flares, the finger or the slick
fringe. Dead erotic.*

*His fingers burned right through my clothes to my skin, not
that I was wearing much for December. In the street, he moved
his arm up to my waist, very gentlemanly, but all the way home
I thought of the feel of his hand on my backside. What a tart!
It even affected the way I walked, the memory, made me kind
of sway, all powerful and womanly and slinky, because I knew
how much he wanted me. It was brilliant.*

I couldn't wait to get inside the church.

And I remembered the day when Christina first tried her
dress on, how Jonty went to put his hand on her behind
and she started away from him, instinctively. She hadn't
wanted him to touch her. But she wanted me to touch her.
That was vital to me.

I couldn't wait to open the door to the church and show
Christina how it all looked; it was just so different from that
first day she saw it. Because I felt different now. All her
doing. She had chased the darkness, the underworld, away,
and I felt the oldest, strongest optimism rise up at last.

I *almost* forgot about my erection.

*I just laughed. It was hilarious: it looked so totally different from
the bleak, frightening hole I'd first seen. There were presents
under the tree, a good half dozen lamps on, twinkly lights
all over the place, and best of all, Angelo was grinning his
head off at me, obviously dead proud of himself. 'What do
you think?' he asked, with his head all tilted to one side and
his black semi-curls shining. You could tell he thought it was
just great.*

*I spun him around by both hands. 'Fantastic!' I said. 'Absol-
utely fantastic.'*

'Wait until you've seen the bedroom,' he says, even more full

of himself, tilting his head towards it, with his eyes all questioning but confident.

I ran upstairs ahead of him to see what he meant. Again, he'd put fairy lights on the walls, and he'd piled chocolates and those little sugar cane candies, and tiny shiny presents, all wrapped up, on the bed. Excellent. I turned around and laughed in his face, shaking my head. 'What makes you think I'll be spending any time in here, then? With you?' And I poked him in the stomach. 'No chance!'

Angelo did this deafening, tiger's sort of roar, shouting his head off. A real bellow. I told you he was brilliant at sound effects.

Still roaring my tiger roar, I picked Christina up off the floor, swung her on to the bed and dropped her down bang in the middle of all the bits and pieces like a prize. She squealed, her hands flew up to her mouth, her dress slid up around her hips, and my cock stiffened instantly. 'Wait a minute,' I told her, noticing that she didn't smooth her dress back down, and a minute was about as long as I felt I'd be able to wait before touching her.

I belted downstairs, grabbed a chilled bottle of Mumm's from the fridge, slammed two tall, slim glasses on to a tray with the bottle and was back up the stairs and on to the bed with Christina well before my sixty seconds was up.

My dress was right up around my hips, just like Marilyn Monroe over the air grille, but without the excessive highlights and the size 16 bum. Told you I was a tart! I didn't know what to expect that night, but champagne was the perfect start. But when Angelo put the tray on the bed, his face went all serious and my giggles died down. Shit.

Wait for it, I thought, and suddenly felt much less sure of myself.

I don't know what made me say it; I think that it was Christina's eyes. They were as round and as bright as new pennies. 'Take your dress off,' I said to her. She didn't say one word: she just began to unbutton the dress down the front and shrugged out of it.

Then she sat back on the bed in nothing but her underwear, with her narrow spine pressed against the bed head, staring at me.

With just the coloured lights on, my body looked like I was in a church, which I was, of course, with the light flooding through the windows, painting colours all over my skin. And Angelo was really spooking me. He filled the champagne glasses dead slowly, letting the bubbles subside one by one, it felt like, brought a glass to me and sat down. When I reached out my hand, he shook his head, the dark eyes as magnetic as ever, then the slow half grin came, so slow this time that I wondered if it was coming at all. But it did, warming his eyes and his face. He lifted the glass to my lips, letting me sip it from him, like that. He was still fully clothed. Putting the glass down, he touched both of my boobs with his freezing cold hands and I jumped. He shook his head again and touched my nipples quite firmly, his lips a centimetre apart, his eyes fixed on mine. I tried really hard not to wriggle, and just about managed it, making Angelo smile, pleased with me.

The champagne glass came up to my lips again and my head started to swim.

Christina had the skimpiest knickers on, dark blue, and a little bra to match. She was wearing stockings again, making a sharp black line around her legs, and a suspender belt this time. There were tiny diamonds around her thighs at the top and the coloured lights were catching at them, turning them into different-coloured jewels. I touched the private white skin at the tops of her stockings, feeling her legs. She was still wearing the new shoes that I'd bought her.

I slid the base of the cold glass down an imaginary line between Christina's breasts, to her stomach, and then all the way down to her pubic bone. Her eyes never left mine. I pressed the glass circle of the base, hard, against her knickers. Her eyes just widened and she breathed in sharply. A few drops of cold champagne spilled against the front of her pants and I shook my head again when she went to touch herself there. I bent down and bit at the front of the silky knickers, once, loving the feeling of the small fold of her skin between my teeth and the smell of her warmth.

Warm for me, needing me. Wanting me. Don't you love that?

And I turned her over, so that I could see if she was still hurt on her back. The pale bruises looked like wisps of leftover grey cloud. Healing. I touched her very lightly, with all ten fingers, and then I explored her behind, which was pouting up at me: perfectly small and round and very, very female. The little knickers were all rucked up at one side, but I was glad that Christina was confident enough not to bother about that, and I could see, then touch, the sweet, tight curve of one cheek, white against the blue. White, cold skin. I bit her there too, not hard, rubbing her and making a tiger noise into her skin, and she laughed and turned around. There was squashed chocolate everywhere.

He was so bony and male. I put my hands to the sides of his head and stroked his cheekbones with my fingers. His eyes grew darker again and he pulled his shirt off and unbuttoned his trousers. I helped him take them off: he always needed to know that I wanted him. Always. Then he got back on the bed with me, wearing just some black boxers, a superb set of muscles and a massive hard-on. Good news. But I needed some reassurance before things moved further and, being Angelo, he read my face at once.

'Hey,' he said, sounding half-American, half-Italian, and totally sex-on-a-stick, all in one. He picked a round, melting chocolate off the bed and slid it into my mouth, smiling. 'I love you, Christina.' He was doing his dark chocolate voice and his hand was still in my hair. He pressed his dick against me, but gently.

'Are you ready?' He nodded into my eyes. I nodded back.
'Sure?' he said. I nodded. The boxers hit the dust.

The look on Christina's face told me – both that she loved
me and that she loved my body, even though she was still
building up to saying it. Maybe she needed to build up to
admitting it to herself, even. I could understand that.

I slid her knickers down her legs as she unhooked her
bra, and this time I let her take the stockings and shoes off
as well, so that she was naked on the bed before me, apart
from that clasp. Even her toes had a vapour of varnish and
polish and newness around them; she was always so smart
and clean. I pulled her down on top of me, in the middle of
all the crinkling wrapping paper and everything, grabbing a
condom, then guided her body down to mine. The skin on
the tops of her arms when she lifted them smelled of sugar
warming its way into caramel and I breathed in her smell.

'You feel massive,' she said, touching me with her little
fingers at the same time as she spoke. 'Huge.' She smiled and
raised her eyebrows. She really was great: she looked all sort
of interested and curious. Open. The swelling, the urge, in my
balls was overpowering, it was hard to think of anything else,
but I made sure that I touched her carefully, made sure that I
didn't jar her skin where she was so sensitive. So pink.

I wanted to soothe and excite her both, soothe with my
fingers and excite with my cock.

It was hard to push him all inside me, but it felt so good there,
brilliant, and Angelo kept touching my clitoris so gently that it
was tickly, almost. His fingers were like feathers. And eventually,
in about three goes, he was right inside me. I leaned down then
and laid myself against his lovely chest, just enjoying the feeling
of fullness for ages. Then I lifted back a bit, so that I could see
his face. His eyes were closed.

I touched his face and began to move.

*   *   *

It was nice when Christina leaned against me. More than nice. Slipping my hands around to her bum, I massaged her there slowly, and I played with her breasts. When she started to move against me, the tension built at once. I pretended, I always pretended, that there was no condom there. Pretended I was about to fill her with myself.

I held myself back, because I wanted her to have the most shattering orgasm with me.

Angelo's feathery fingers were making me feel really *hot at the front, and his big dick felt so right inside me. Beautiful. I felt warm and wet and safe, and full of love and strength. He kept one hand on my clitoris and put the other hand on my backside, just like at the start of the evening, holding me to him.*

And that was what finally made me come, with my arms wrapped around his neck.

At last I could let it all go. It was like being in another world for me, a real world, full of the passion and dark intensity that I could only express at those rare, raw, tenderest times. The truest times, for me. Red, red tenderness.

And for Christina too. She literally fell against me at the end, with her eyes closed. I pulled out of her, dropped the condom and wrapped my arms around her, easing her down on to her side beside me, my arms never leaving her. I knew the intimacy, the extent of her passion, embarrassed her still. Her head was in my hand, cradled to my chest, and my other hand was rubbing her back. 'Hey,' I said again. 'Calm down. Just relax.

'Trust me,' I said. 'Just trust me.' I took the clasp out and kissed the place in her hair where it had been. Trust. Mic's arms around my waist. Corners. I needed so much to be a man that a person could trust again, if I ever could be that sort of man again. Only Christina could give me that chance, I knew that. 'I'll look after you,' I said.

*   *   *

And the funny thing was that although Angelo had put all *of himself into having sex with me, I'm sure there were tears in his voice afterwards. 'Trust me,' he said, sounding like Jack with Rose, just before he slipped underneath the water. Icy water. Angelo seemed so alone, sometimes. Often. And his voice cracked, ice dry, when he spoke again, in a whisper almost. 'Just trust me.' It meant so much to him. He would never hurt anyone, except maybe himself: I had always known that. 'I'll look after you,' he said. It was* exactly *what I needed from him.*

'I love you,' I said. I hadn't meant to say it, but it was honestly what I felt most at that second. It just came out.

Angelo really laughed, right in my face, and sat up in the bed, pulling me up with him and kissing me, everywhere, face, eyelids, hands. I'd never seen Angelo so happy, never imagined that anybody anywhere could look so happy, so purely *happy. It just lit him up.*

'I love you,' she said. The rarest words of all. I started to believe that she meant them. If she'd said it when I'd first told her, it would have been harder to believe, in the middle of all the drama, the distress. Now, I could let myself believe in it, believe in Christina. I knew she must have been thinking about it for ages, thinking about me.

She'd thought about it, but she'd said it right after we'd made love.

She loved me. Christina really loved me.

19. Christmas

'But they were perfect children . . . I was so proud of them then.'

Christmas morning. Christina was fast asleep when I awoke at around seven, not surprising really, but once I'd awoken, I knew there was no chance of getting back to sleep. Christmas Day.

Creeping down the stairs, the first thing I saw was my print of Michelangelo's *The Creation of Adam* fresco. Adam always looks like he's got just about enough energy available to face Creation, a feeling I can identify with at times. But these were new times, and my relationship with Christina was a creation I could pour so much new energy into. I had a quick look in her jacket pockets, just to check there were no letters or notes in there from any of the dealers or punters. There was nothing. I knew that I could trust her.

And there was one thing I definitely wanted to read, by myself, before Christina awoke: I know you'll have guessed. The red notebook. Even having no presents from them both might take a bit of getting used to, I knew that. The red notebook usually helped. I put just one lamp on in the darkness when I got downstairs, and then I drew the notebook out of its hiding place in the candle box.

This time I cheated, and I turned the pages until I found the section that I wanted.

Christmas was the best time when the boys were young. They were both so dark, so dark and yet so filled with energy and light. Every year, they would insist on an old-fashioned treasure hunt, and every year the clues had to get a bit harder and the presents a bit bigger. But they always loved it, even if they did fight like mad all over again as soon as one of them found something.

But they were perfect children, absolutely perfect. I used to love buying them a new outfit, not that either of them cared at all, or noticed what they wore until they were in their teens, and I loved making them put their new things on and taking them for a walk. We'd see Anthony's mother, and maybe Irene, and my sister. But even strangers in the street would say how lucky I was, how gorgeous both the boys were, with their dark hair, their bright faces and their Italian eyes. Their cheek, even. Angelo's hair was all curls (until he insisted on cutting it off, himself, in the bathroom, when he was about six) and Michael's would be flying around, or flopping straight down into his huge eyes. Perfect children. Old ladies used to give them both sweets, or presents, just because they'd seen the two of them running past their front doors. I was so proud of them then.

So proud of us. Then. When we were *'perfect'* children, then reasonable teenagers, even. I knew that was how she saw it. But what an imperfect adult I'd turned out to be. *'Moody.'* Flawed. *'Maybe a genetic thing.'*

That was partly why I kept in touch with old Irene. My contact with Mic helped to stop the past from hardening into a solid, bitter memory. His humour was the only way to jolt me out of the feelings, sometimes. And this red note-book helped as well, because it reminded me of the better times, the *'perfect'* times, the 'normal' times, as my mum might have said. Mic connected my past and my present, and he also made me aware that the future was still there for me. Michelangelo's *Pietà* caught my eye from its corner of the wall, and however hard I tried to think of creation, of birth, at different times of the day, it was Mary's sad, bowed, helpless face, with Jesus lying over her lap, that I saw off and on throughout that Christmas. Pity. It haunted me.

Thank God I had Christina to think of. I put the notebook away and headed for the kitchen.

And then all at once it was Christmas. What sort of a Christmas exactly, I wondered, did Angelo have in mind for us? Christmas Eve would be pretty hard to follow.

The smell of cooking, and a lot of noise, woke me up. Angelo obviously didn't go in much for silent, solo suffering in the kitchen, and who could blame him?

'Angelo!' I bellowed down the stairs to him, over the racket. 'Happy Christmas!'

'Not awake, are you?' he called back up.

'Well, of course I am,' I said to him. 'Isn't that the idea? What have you got in that kitchen, a drum kit?' I leaned over the top of the iron staircase to find out what he was up to. Immediately, Angelo appeared at the bottom, grinning, with a very loaded tray in his hand.

'Just some croissants and some juice. Are you starving?' he asked, heading up the stairs with the tray for me.

Breakfast in bed! I scuttled back under the covers before Angelo could change his mind and force me to dress. Food. Then he let me open up all the tiny presents that had fallen, or been thrown, out of the bed before. There were earrings, and hair slides, and a bracelet, and hand-made glass bottles – so many gifts, so carefully chosen by Angelo. All for me. Imagine me, eating croissants and chocolate and pink sugar mice, one after the other, like a six-year-old, with my new earrings and hair band in and nothing on but a nightie and some knickers. Superb. I soon felt sick, naturally, but it was well worth it. Except that when I really was six, Christmases for my sister and brother and me had been nothing like that at all.

And just as I was deliberately not thinking about all that, what should happen? We heard the very insistent ringing of the phone, by someone who did not *want to be ignored.*

I was off down the stairs to the phone before Christina could look at me, and I turned the volume down and clicked the answer phone on before a word could be said by anyone. I could relax now, sort of.

One look from me told her that this was one subject that was not to be discussed.

What a reaction from Angelo, I mean, thunder *face, honestly. Then I thought, Let him cool down, open up his presents, and maybe you'll both survive the day intact. 'Look,' I called to him as he walked back up the stairs with that look on his face. 'Have some more breakfast and then open your prezzies with me. I've got them all wrapped up for you!' I scrabbled beneath the bed to where I had them hidden away in my overnight bag.*

Except that Angelo's presents were starting to worry me in themselves. Hard to play Santa when you're funded by the Ebeneezer Scrooge of the entertainment world. The fact that Angelo managed to be so generous with me only made my poverty even worse. Or rather, the poverty of Angelo's Chrissie presents. And I'd had to buy some new underwear and make-up for myself, to wear over the holiday, which hadn't helped matters financially.

Watching Angelo's face as he sat opposite me on the bed, chewing away at his croissant, I thought, He looks miles away, he often does. Christmas must remind him of his mother. Pity I hadn't thought of that when it came to constructing my Christmas list. Still, men aren't always bothered about a load of presents to open up, are they?

Stop worrying, Christina, and just let him open his parcels.

I ripped open the presents straightaway. Christina had bought me some chocolates and a bottle of after-shave.

I knew she never had any money so I didn't mind about that, really. And I was looking forward to seeing her open her main presents from me. (I'd spent a big chunk of the money I had left from my grandmother on those presents, but I knew she would have understood.) More often than not, Christina wore dresses, so I'd bought her this classy, yet quite short, black dress, fine velvet, with some tiny, sharp-toed shoes to go with it. There was some *Dolce Vita* perfume, a handbag and some sparkly little earrings as well, not too Casino Club because Christina and half the other dealers were constantly taking the piss out of all the 1980s 'Save the Sequinned Whale' look, as they called it, that the punters loved. But I knew she liked to look smart.

She put the dress on straightaway. 'I'm wearing this *all* day,' she insisted, and it fitted her really well. 'And the best Christmas present I've bought for you,' she said, 'is all the new underwear I've got with me in this bag.' She got this scrap of a bra out, and waved it around in front of me, loving the attention, and then she pulled this cherry-coloured teddy affair out with the other hand. 'Which of these do you think I should wear tonight, underneath my new dress?'

I was so pleased with Angelo, and with the clothes he had chosen for me. He was so thoughtful: the handbag was lovely, a boxy Italian one. It turned into a carpet, swirling around above my head, flying on Angelo's palm.

'It's a magic handbag,' he said, dive bombing me with it. 'It's a bird with feathers on it, or a safe with treasures in it. It's the Skeleton Woman's treasure chest, with all the chocolate shells and a map inside. Magical!' He dropped it suddenly and went all serious, kissing me on the cheek. 'You will get to America, Christina. Don't forget.'

'I won't, Angelo!' I said, and kissed him back. I was so lucky! I mean, I'd already seen the red nylon nasties that Ben had in mind for his latest snog – not jealous. Geordie men are notorious

for the bad taste factor when it comes to their girlfriends' clothes, underclothes especially. They're much sharper with their own wardrobes. Thank God I'd found the only genuine exception in the present-buying category. Must be that Italian blood, I decided. Half of the world's top designers are Italian, aren't they? Gucci, Prada.

That reminded me of my mother's 'Eyetie' comment. Boxing Day night, I was seeing my mother and my sister. It was better not to ask them over to the flat: my mother would only moan on about what a nice bedroom there was waiting for me at home any time I wanted it, and my sister would make some really funny jokes about what a dump my flat was. A scream! Speaking of which, the man with the mouth had that much ivy all over him that his bridge was better dressed than the one in Jesmond Dene. There was nothing spooky about the church now, really. Except for those phone calls.

Later it was Christmas dinner, or Christmas tea, or whatever the right word is for salmon, in the afternoon. I'd never had real salmon before, Gateshead girl and Gosforth boy, although I'd seen people eating it in the casino restaurant. Then a walk through a park near the church, wandering hand in hand together.

It was probably the darkness that deepened our mood, I don't know, but by the time we were heading back to the church there was a real atmosphere building up. It was time to talk. I knew little more about Angelo than I'd squeezed out of him that night at the Italian restaurant.

Now was the time, whether he liked it or not.

When we went for a walk together that afternoon, it reminded me so much of the extract from the red note-book I'd read that morning that conversation ran dry. I ran dry. Even the way Christina looked at me occasionally, which was great, as if she was proud just to be with me, reminded me of what my mother had written about our walks when Mic and I were little. Christina and I only stayed out for about half an hour, just long enough to watch the worn bone of a moon rise up in the sky.

I couldn't help but think about Mic. Mic is always hyper on Christmas Day, waking up at five, full of stupid carols and jokes, spreading food and presents and paper all over the house, tormenting the life out of my mum. Only two years ago, he'd borrowed a karaoke machine from a mate with a pub and we'd sung all the worst Elvis songs all Christmas afternoon, *Wooden Heart*, *Jailhouse Rock* and *Hound Dog*, for hours, days, on end, it felt like. I missed him. My bones ached and I rubbed at my arms. I couldn't get used to it. I had to get used to it. But I also had to talk. Christmas night, with Christina. The least silent night that I'd spent for nine months or more.

Not that it started out that way, me being me. And not that the conversation began, or ended, in quite the way I would have liked it to.

Still, maybe the whole of Angelo's past would never have come to a head if those spooky phone calls hadn't suddenly become such an issue. Because when we walked through the door after our walk, guess which little red light was flashing out in the darkness? Angelo jumped across to delete the message, as per, and this time I had to tackle him about it.

I started off gently, or so I thought. 'No other women in your life, are there, Angelo? Nobody I need worry about?' I kept my voice really light and playful.

'Nothing you need worry about at all, Christina.' Angelo's voice was anything but light. Very heavy indeed. Angry, almost. Still, I needed to know.

'Who's the caller, then? A jealous ex-girlfriend who might have seen us on our walk? A friend you've fallen out with?' Again, my voice was light, but these were possibilities I'd thought about. And I wasn't giving up.

'Leave it, Christina. Just leave it.' He was giving me the real

eye treatment, daggers, towering over me, but I wouldn't be warned off.

'Just tell me one thing then, Angelo. Please.' I had to know. 'Is it another girl, another woman? Have you been seeing someone? Or is it an ex?' I waited.

'It's not another girl. What do you think I am, Christina? Stop it! Relax!' He was more or less ordering me. 'And can you please stop the cross-questioning now?'

What made me bring an even thornier subject up, I don't know, but out it came. 'What about Mic then, Angelo?' Angelo's head turned away from me the second I mentioned the name, and I continued as gently as I could. 'If you can't tell me about the phone calls, can you tell me exactly what happened to your brother?' The whole upper half of Angelo's body was twisted away from me now. I tugged on his hand. 'Don't you want to talk to me about that?' He nodded, eventually, but made no move to come closer to me, and his body seemed even stiffer than usual if anything. I tried to draw Angelo down on to the settee to sit with me, but he shrugged me off and stayed standing. Suddenly, something I'd been told as a child came into my mind, something about angels being the messengers of death, and I shivered. He wouldn't have hurt his brother, would he? I thought. Angelo withdrew altogether then, as if he'd read my mind, and went banging off up the iron steps to the loo. Leaving me alone.

Turning the convector heater on for some extra warmth in the chilly little church, I decided I would make this as easy for him as I could. I plumped up the single cushion on the old settee for his back, I sat down on the other half with my arm around the cushion and I waited. Christina Rae, the Queen of Hearts. Not really, but I was doing my best. But there was no sign of his return from upstairs.

Splashing my face with cold water, I made sure my eyes came nowhere near my reflection in the mirror, kept my head well down. The night was going badly enough with Christina to start with. Why had she thought the phone calls were from another girl? Guilty conscience on her part? How much exactly should I, *could* I, tell her?

Orpheus. The dark, lonely water. If I told Christina the *whole* truth, would she still be there behind me when I turned?

At last Angelo emerged from the bathroom, but I deliberately didn't turn to watch him walk downstairs. It was important not to make too big a deal of the discussion or he wouldn't even begin to be able to speak, I knew that. So I waited.

And eventually, after several deep breaths and two sideways glances, the story of Mic and Angelo really began.

Blood Brothers

20. The Duke

'Who do you think makes all those phone calls?'

'She always hated motorbikes – my mother, I mean. I suppose they all do. But we had to have one anyway, Mic and me. We'd bought one as soon as I was old enough, and this one was the second one, a more powerful one. A Ducati.' I laughed, once, remembering Mic touring the second-hand bike shops on Westgate Road, scouring the bike magazines endlessly, playing Bruce Springsteen, *being* Bruce Springsteen, looking at photos of the factory in Bologna and going on about 'The Duke' the whole time. 'The Ferrari of the motorbike world.' I could see him clearly, wiping bird shit off his shoulders and complaining about his sore arse as he stepped off the Duke. 'It took us ages to get hold of one. We couldn't buy it out of our university money, because our mum gave us some of that, so we saved up money from our part-time jobs instead, traded the old Honda in without even telling her, paid an insurance bill like a mortgage and we were on our way, on the road.

'We used to argue about it all the time.' I smiled across at Christina. 'I told you about all that before. Mic had got a job working for a printer's in Sheffield, straight after he graduated, and he'd started designing CD and book covers and other stuff freelance as well. But because I was still

at Newcastle Uni then, and Mic was in Sheffield, sharing
the bike was sometimes a bit of a nightmare.' I stopped
talking for a second. 'Anyway, the best times of all were
in the Easter and summer holidays. Even Newcastle gets
the odd bike-friendly sunny day when the only thing we
could argue about was who'd be on the front and who'd
be on the back . . .'

Angelo carried on. 'Mic's the eldest, of course.' That 'of course'
showed this was a sore point. Was that why Angelo always had
to be in charge of me? I wondered. Anyway, he continued. 'Still,
it had to be rowed about and discussed every single time. And that
day Mic won: he'd just paid for some repairs on it so I was riding
pillion. He was hooting his head off as we pulled away from his
flat in Sheffield; I'd been staying there with him for a few days
and we were on our way home together. We'd been to Leeds as
well, and he'd just bought some awful, pointy shoes. He insisted
on wearing the things, kept looking down at them all the time
and practically totalling the bike.' Angelo stopped in his story,
turned towards me and right out of the blue, he grinned. 'He
loves awful old things altogether. You know, he even took Irene
out on the back of the Ducati a couple of times. Clinging on to
him, shrieking her head off round all the corners, she was.'

'I bet she loved it.' I couldn't help laughing myself. 'Pensioner
Power.' I could just imagine Irene, false teeth and lower jaw set
against the wind, perm flying in the breeze, and her deafening
cackles streaming out to all the traffic behind her.

Angelo smiled. 'She did, except for the helmet; she would never
wear a helmet.' I swallowed the obvious 'Beware of danger!'
comment, then Angelo thought of something else and smiled
again. 'Mic's like you in lots of ways. Obsessed with America
for a start. He wanted to visit all the bike dealerships.'

Angelo was right. I was saving up to go to America. Not to see
bikes, of course – to see everything. Miramax. I pictured myself on
the back of some mega-bike with Mic, riding through Memphis or
Texas with my arms wrapped around his waist, then scotched the

idea, quick, before Angelo could do his mind-reading act. Anybody could see there was a fair bit of jealousy there, alongside the real closeness they'd obviously had as well.

Angelo's grin faded and he continued. 'We got all the way back from Sheffield with no trouble, no trouble at all. And then Mic decided that he hadn't seen the sea for ages. It was Easter, and he said that everything was "alive, kicking and laying eggs, including every single single woman in the area", and he had to cruise around some to see it all.' Angelo shook his head and took hold of my hand. 'Mic can be a complete pain in the arse, never takes "no" for an answer; I don't think he ever even hears "no". So we were there, "cruising" around Whitley Bay, cruising Cullercoats, cruising Tynemouth, cruising North Shields, The Bottlenose, even.'

Well! 'Cruising by The Bottlenose?' I said. 'You'd be lucky to pick up an old kipper there, yuppie flats or no yuppie flats.'

'I know,' said Angelo, shaking his head and sort of smiling. 'Mic knew, too, but he still insisted we rode past all the old haunts; he was waving at every woman under ninety too slow to look away, flashing those stupid shoes. Not that he was interested in meeting a girl; he was just messing around – enjoying the day, the sun.

'Anyway, eventually even he had had enough. We'd done the whole of the coastline – and at long last we turned around and headed towards Gosforth, headed back towards my mother's house.

'We were in Tynemouth, waiting at a junction, stuck behind this gigantic lorry. Mic kept singing Born to Run, doing a Bruce Springsteen, with loads of bike noises.' Angelo looked down and swallowed. 'It was getting late. I was looking in a shop window to my left, thinking about nothing I can remember. Nothing.' He swallowed again and looked away from me. 'I played a big part in what happened: that's the truth of it. Next thing I know, Mic shouts, loud, a funny shout, turns around all at once, pushes backwards and shoves me off the back of the bike, all in one go. Instinct. Good instinct. I was too surprised to take in what was happening, but when I sat up, I saw that the lorry had

reversed into the bike. It wasn't really even the lorry driver's fault. He says he took a quick look behind, a shaft of light hit his eyes, he just couldn't see us, maybe because of the way Mic had been leaning on the bike.'

Chaos and destiny. Terrible, terrible chaos. 'And Mic was on the ground, half on the road and half on the pavement.' Angelo stopped. I knew from the unevenness in his voice and the tension in his face that he was trying really hard not to cry in front of me, so I squeezed his hand, and deliberately didn't look at him as I spoke.

'Curled up on the pavement,' I continued for him, squeezing harder, watching my fingers wrap around his bigger ones, remembering what he'd said after his nightmare and seeing my original meeting with Angelo in a totally different light. How awful, for him, for Mic, and for their mother, waiting at home for her two boys to get back for Easter. 'Like a baby.' A tiny, vulnerable baby. Guilt.

Angelo nodded and it was ages before he could carry on speaking. 'He didn't look bad to me; his face was fine. And I was perfectly fine.' Angelo's voice was bitter and he was still looking away from me, his face warped with self-disgust. 'So I grabbed his hand, shook it. "Mic, Mic!" I was shouting at him. I dragged him off the road so that he was fully on the path. I shouldn't have moved him they said later, at the hospital. Bad instinct.' Angelo's eyes were hard, and he was being hard on himself, I thought and nearly said, but I didn't want to interrupt him.

'There was one line of blood coming out of Mic's mouth, just one line, and his hair was sticking up. Then the lorry driver was there, took one look at Mic and went back around the side of his lorry to throw up. Nobody came, not for what seemed like forever, though it was probably only seconds, a minute. And I didn't know what to do, just kept shaking Mic's arm, Mic's body, trying to wake him up. His shoe had come off. It was lying in the road.' Angelo tried, and failed totally, to smile. 'Those stupid shoes. The bike was mangled, I kept thinking about that, the whole of the front was gone. Kept thinking of how Mic would feel about that

later, when he'd only just had it fixed.' He sighed and rubbed his eyes with the back of his hand before looking up with something defensive in his expression. He broke away from his thoughts and spoke in a cold, cold voice, yet I knew the hot pain behind it. 'He'd had a haemorrhage. That was it, really.'

Angelo's words had finally dried up. I kept thinking of James Dean and River Phoenix, the awful waste and the wrongness of the dead body of a young man. It was so romantic, but so horrible. One of Angelo's prints was staring right at me again, a religious one this time, of a sculpture of Mary, cradling the dead Jesus in her lap. Just so horrible. Easter and Christmas, death and birth, mother and son, I thought. Dead babies. Poor mother. Poor *Angelo. No wonder he'd been feeling so disturbed lately. And alone.*

'It's gone, Angelo,' I said to him. 'It was one of those split-second things and it's gone. It's in the past. Let it lie there.'

'It won't *lie there,' he flashed back at me. 'And I don't want it to. I'll be with him, with Mic, again. He's not gone. And you don't* choose *whether a memory, a feeling, will stay in the past or whether it lives over and over again. You don't choose that.'*

I knew all about this, but there was no way I could tell Angelo how. I thought for a minute. 'If Mic was able to, he would pull that memory right out of your mind,' I said. 'He would put all of the other memories of himself in there, the ones where you were enjoying yourselves together, having a laugh. You have to turn all of that looking back, that wasted energy, into moving towards the future. Your future. Because you aren't just yourself now. You're you and Mic. You're all that's left here of Mic's energy, Mic's life.' I had *to make him see it all in a different way. 'You have to* do *something with all of those feelings instead of just letting them destroy you. Like when I turned the whole casino thing around, and made Mr Glum win, remember?'*

I curled myself up on to Angelo's lap and tried to hug him close to me, but he was so distant, his body all strung up, tense, and one of his hands tugging at his hair, hurting himself even more than he had to, like he always did. His eyes were staring out

over my head, as if he was looking for something, you know?
Someone.
He was way beyond me.

'Come with me,' Mic had said. 'America! Philadelphia, the
city of brotherly love.' He'd punched my arm twice as he
said it. 'We should go together: the Paulillo brothers on
tour! Take the world by storm! I've got the route planned
out and everything. I'll show you it later.' He laughed,
patting his pocket. 'Come with me, Ango! You wouldn't
make me go on my own, would you?' I'd been thinking
about it, dreaming about it, on the bike even, the day that
he died. I would give anything to go with him now. How
could I carry on with my family as deformed and shrunken
as it was now? I sometimes thought that I'd rather die at
once than struggle on in a crippled, weakened body. How
do other people get over it?

Thank God I had Christina to give me a future. *'Come
with me, Ango.'* I wouldn't make the same mistakes with
her, ever.

But what I hadn't told her were the worst bits. Why is it
that it's always the dirtiest secrets that we hug to ourselves,
rather than the treasured memories? Do you want to hear
some of the dirt, the truth, the words I can't say to anyone
except myself?

I didn't say to Christina that I didn't even try any first aid
on Mic, that I didn't know how, then. I didn't tell her that I
cried in the street like a child when I gradually realised that
he was dead. Except I was sweating shock, fear and guilt
at the same time as the tears. Is that crying like a man? I
looked up at the print of Christ on the wall opposite me: *Ecce
Homo*, 'Behold the man', Christ with the wreath of thorns
around his head, the Virgin Mary weakened by grief. No
sign of tears there.

And I definitely didn't tell Christina that when I got
to the hospital with Mic's body, and I was taken away

and checked over, my mother came into the side room, screaming at me that I hadn't looked after my brother, screaming at me that she couldn't cope with Mic gone, couldn't accept what had happened. And why hadn't I done more?

The questions shouted themselves out again in my head, as violent and as furious and as full of pain as the first time that I'd heard them, the first time she'd said them. Spat them. *'Michael dead?' 'You could do nothing to help?' 'You didn't see it coming?'* Her head was shaking in rage and disbelief. *'My special son,'* she kept saying, over and over again. *'My special son.'* What did that make me? Was she shocked out of her right mind that day, or shocked into it? *'And is there really nothing wrong with you at all?' 'You haven't been hurt at all?' 'You didn't even try to look after him?' 'And Michael's dead?'* Over and over again. The memories and the whispers merged in my mind. I could never let my mother touch me again after that. Never. Do you understand that? Or do you think that makes me even worse than her?

And the worse scene, the scene of the funeral. The coldness between myself and my mother. Her back turned towards me when I went across in the end to try to talk to her. *'And is there really nothing wrong with you at all?'* And Mic gone. *'My special son.'* Forever. And then the shocking, the unimaginable appearance, the appearance that I just could not cope with that day.

Mine was the back that was turned now – turned away from the truth. I could not tell Christina the part I had really played in Mic's accident. I'd had enough.

I cuddled into Christina's arms and looked down at her face; she was all curled up in my lap. Her head was tilted over to one side. Even after all that, there was obviously something else she wanted to know.

One point had been puzzling away at me since about halfway through Angelo's terrible story but I hardly dared to ask him about it, he looked that preoccupied. Then he smiled at me, so I lifted my head and took my chance.

'Angelo, it can't be that long since your mother died then, if she was still alive when Mic had his bike crash. It must have been terrible for her. She didn't have some sort of an accident as well, did she?'

Angelo looked at me as if I was stupid. He moved both of his hands away from my body before he spoke, then he spelled out his words slowly, as if I was a moron.

'My mother's not literally *dead, Christina.' That 'literally' was so scornful. 'Who do you think makes all those phone calls?'*

21. One Venetian Bridge

'What is the matter with you, Angelo?'

Well, I think the next chapter should be just silence, the whole chapter. Stunned silence.

Followed by quite a lot of words, quite quickly, mainly from me. Funny, but all the sympathy I had been feeling for Angelo went right out of the window, or rather, it got turned into a load of different feelings altogether. Anger was the first one. Anger then disbelief.

'You lied to me, Angelo!' I know, I know: Christina Rae, the Queen of Truth. But this was such a huge one. 'Why did you do that? Lie to me?'

'I didn't.' Angelo looked that surly, all eyebrows and frown, it was practically killing him to say that much.

'Of course you did.' My voice went up: very unattractive, it was. 'Nearly all the time I've been seeing you, I've thought your mother was dead. Why did you say that to me?'

'I said it because it's true, Christina. She is dead to me. I haven't seen her in months, and I'm not going to see her again. It's not exactly a living relationship, is it?' His face and feelings were set against her, and against me now. Closed. He snapped his head away from me and stood up, walked over to the kitchen area and called over his shoulder in his clipped, 'fuck right off' voice, 'Do you want a coffee or anything?'

'Coffee?' He wasn't getting away with that one! I jumped up, grabbed his arm and made to pull him back over towards the settee. 'Forget it! What happened between you? I could understand a row,' I'd had plenty of those with my own mother, 'but never to speak to her again? I don't understand that.'

'No, I can see that.' Angelo held my wrist as I'd been holding his, making me remember him that first day, with the boy. Hard. He shook my arm with every freezing cold word he said to me. 'You don't understand it and I can't explain it to you because I still don't think you would understand. And you can't judge me because you can't know what happened between us. That's why I didn't tell you. So can we drop it now?'

Angelo's fingers were as hard as the lines on his face. But still I questioned him, not wanting him to close down on me like that. 'Try me, Angelo. What happened between you? Why shouldn't I understand? Just try to explain.' The fingers dug in more and he stared at me. His expression was awful. Sometimes having the contacts in was more like having a layer pulled off than a lens put in. Then I remembered his voice in the night, 'Michael. Michael', remembered the despairing expression on his face at some times and the distance in his eyes at others, and I understood the distress behind his mask of icy anger. I thought of the four hundred bridges in Venice, with only one connecting to the mainland, connecting woman to man, me to Angelo. Or was that me connecting Angelo to reality? To the present? To safety, even? I thought of his arms around me after he had explained his visions to me, his relief at having finally been understood. Salty, islanded Angelo Paulillo and solid, connected Christina Rae. Needed.

I had another go. 'Explain it to me then, Angelo. Try at least. Was it after Mic died? Is that when it blew up between you and your mam?' I tried to be as gentle as I could, dropping my tone of voice, but his stare grew harder still. Frightening. 'Angelo,' I said, shaking at the bulldog clamp of his fingers, 'you're hurting me.'

Shit, I thought, I'm as bad as Jonty, but Christina was

pushing me, questioning me, the whole time. That didn't mean I had to be such a bastard. I released her arm and backed off, but that only made it worse, only lengthened the distance between us. Because what could I say to her? If I told her about my mother's reaction when Mic had died, how would she see me after that? She'd see me through my mother's eyes, and I couldn't stand some of the images of myself that I'd seen through my mother's eyes already. If Christina were to view me in that way, it would cut me in half. It would also be the end of us. And if she knew what my mother had said about the other things, about what I'd seen and heard after Mic died, if she, Christina, were to know how my mother had seen all that, I would never be a whole person again to her.

I looked down into her open, question mark of a face. Questions I couldn't answer. Questions and criticisms – that had been the cause of the problem in the first place. Any half-light, half-trust, is dangerous to me, and Christina had to remember that.

I couldn't stand it. And I definitely couldn't explain any more of it to her. Christmas night. And now, because of me, it was a night full of death, destruction. It was happening all over again. What could I do or say that would make Christina understand?

I spun around, away from her, useless again.

And he left. Angelo left, just slammed away, leaving me staring like an idiot at the door banging behind him.

22. Tears

'Don't forget your oldest friends.'

What do you think I did in that hour after Angelo left? I'll never tell anyone else about this for as long as I live, because I don't think I'd live long if Angelo knew about it. I ran to the door, watched him stamp off around the corner, then I fought with myself for a minute before going over to the answering machine to hear what it had to say. Dead sly, I know. Well, Angelo had kept me pretty much in the dark *forever* about the situation within his family. I mean, it was *totally confusing, and I reckoned if I knew exactly what was going on, then I could help him more. I could understand.*

Anyway, I'm not proud of it, but that's what I did.

I began to feel ashamed almost immediately after I'd left. What was the point of spoiling Christina all day, spending the last of my grandmother's money on presents for her, taking the big risk of telling her part of what happened to Mic, and then arguing with her about my mother, a situation I was sure she wouldn't understand anyway? No point. I'd never had a serious girlfriend before Christina. I sometimes think that twins don't see, don't *need*, other people as much as most, and I often think that Mic and I are as near to twins as you can get. But I needed someone now, needed someone to need me now.

I walked around in the freezing cold for about an hour, thinking about Christina and the night before, thinking about other nights before, and it seemed to do the trick: I worked some of my temper off and a bit of the distance back in. I started to think about it from Christina's viewpoint a bit more. How could I expect her to understand why I had reacted to my mother that way if I couldn't begin to explain it to her? I couldn't completely explain it to myself. But I'll try to explain it to you.

You see, the past had hardened into the present. If I'd kept on seeing my mother regularly, the past and the present would have stayed flexible, and the whole relationship would have been moving, changing, living, in colour. Now it had fixed into black and white, a dark old photograph of the past. Finished and filed. There was nothing I could do about it. Really. I just couldn't forgive her.

Christina would have to learn to accept me, and accept the way I felt about people, without criticising me and questioning me all the time, I decided. Otherwise we could have no future together. Because if she saw me in the way some people did, she'd have no respect for me at all. I needed her faith and her trust, and I would fight for those things, but I wouldn't fight like Jonty, wouldn't fight with my fists.

By the time I was heading back to the church, I knew exactly how I could make Christina understand.

By the time Angelo got back to the church, I understood a few things about him and his family much better. I understood that Angelo was stubborn, unforgiving, that he should have been finishing his course at university, that he was wasting himself in the casino, that he had loved his brother very much, that he needed to see a doctor, and that he hadn't even sent his mother a Christmas card. All of that, I'd just about worked out in advance, but it was really strange hearing so much relating to Angelo in one go, or rather about four goes, four messages. Want a replay? It went something like this.

Message number one. 'Angelo, darling *(she was quite posh)*, it's just me. Surely, we aren't going to fall out at Christmas, Angelo, are we? Because, you know, that's not what Michael would have wanted: he'd have wanted you to ring me. *(That sounded like a definite lead balloon job, to me.)* And don't worry about what happened in Mic's room. *(What?)* Maybe it was for the best. I've sent you a card, but I'll keep your present until I see you. Call round any time, Angelo. Enjoy yourself at the casino.' *Click. She had the maximum length of time available for her message worked out to a T. Dead practised. I could tell from the pitch of her voice on the last word that working at a casino was* not *the career path she had in mind for her son. And that first message was about the best.*

The subjects of the other calls swung from suggestions of careers' guidance and House of Fraser management training schemes to the very polite suggestion that perhaps, if he saw a doctor, she might feel happier about him living on his own. Multi-*lead balloon. I mean, I could understand her concern, but Angelo seemed to be managing OK, as far as I could tell, and I would never have* dared *suggest that he visit a doctor. You could tell that much by instinct. Either her instincts about her own son weren't that well developed, or she was deliberately trying to wind him up. Surely not? And I'd thought he was quite happy in the casino; loads of dealers and catering staff travel all over the world once they've trained in English casinos. I couldn't see him in a polyester suit, his 'Angelo Paulillo, Assistant Manager' badge stuck to the front of it, stacking shelves, sorting shoplifters and setting targets for sales. Worse, I couldn't see his mother being impressed by his just-about-unqualified Gateshead girlfriend from the dreaded casino. Remember* Titanic? *There were no lifeboats for the third class people and the people in first class sure as hell wouldn't let you share theirs. A sneaky voice was saying to me that maybe, just maybe, it was better for me and Angelo if the distance between him and his mother stayed exactly as it was.*

The message that had come through earlier that day, Christmas Day, was really sad. 'I hear you've been to see old Irene,' *his mother said, her voice less confident altogether,* 'and she tells me you've got yourself a new girlfriend.' *She was* dead *put out to have to hear it from old Irene, was my guess.* 'Just enjoy yourself, Angelo. The door is always open. Oh, and don't forget your oldest friends. Pop in and see Katy over the holiday. She's having a difficult time. She's at 124 Osborne Road still.' *Then there was this little pause.* 'Happy Christmas, Angelo.' *She ran out of time. Poor thing had obviously given up on a festive family reconciliation, for the time being, at least. But I couldn't help feeling sorry for Angelo as well. The distance between them must have been tearing him apart as much as her.*

But who on earth was Katy? Katy! *I hoped she was fatter than Kate Moss and Kate Winslet put together!* 'Don't forget your oldest friends.' *She was such an old friend that he'd never mentioned her to me* before. *I rewound the tape to where it had been at the start of my snooping: there was no chance he was getting that message, he'd already rewound it himself anyway, and I headed up the cast-iron stairs to try on my brand new undies with my dress. I had to try to work out how to unbend, unwind, entrance a fairly cast-iron Angelo Paulillo: take all thoughts of* 'Katy' *right out of his mind. I jotted her address down, Jesmond, but it wasn't the time to mention her to Angelo. I knew now what he was like when he fell out with you properly. Not pleasant.*

I'd decided on one of the oldest but most reliable methods known to croup-kind to soften him up. I'd spent quite a big chunk of my salary on undies since I'd started at the casino and I couldn't face an all-nighter of a row. Well, I had to get the old Christmas spirit back into the church somehow, didn't I? And maybe I was being selfish, but it didn't look like there was much I could say to make Angelo change his mind about his mother, if and when he got back, anyway. Didn't look like there was much anybody could do about that.

I was starting to think that he never would – come back, I mean – which was probably exactly how he wanted me to feel. And it was starting to rain. Shit.

Shit. What worried me, as I turned the corner and saw the church come into view, was that Christina would have got sick of waiting for me, and that when I walked back in it would be empty. An empty house would have been too hard that night. So why had I left her like that, then? Why did I always walk away?

Even as I started to open the door, Christina's face appeared at the window, worry creasing her brow. Then she jumped out into the porch and straight into my arms like a cartoon woman, spinning me around and kissing me, which was the very best present that she could have given me, ever. Wrapping her arms around me, she dragged me inside the church after her. She was really warm and fresh, with her *Dolce Vita* perfume on, and her *Dolce Vita* mood, and she was wearing her new dress and shoes, and her hair had just been combed. There was this light but layered depth to her fragrance, to her, and I sometimes sensed that there were layers I hadn't touched on, hadn't even suspected within her. Best of all, she bore no resentment whatsoever towards me when she spoke: her voice was as warm as her body. She didn't seem to suffer from my problems about forgiving and forgetting.

'Angelo! Angelo!' she said, practically singing it. 'You've been *ages*. You've practically turned into a snowman.' She laughed, and rubbed my arms, and hummed a few bars of the theme tune to *The Snowman*, reminding me of Mic again: it was just the type of rubbish he used to do. 'No jacket or anything!' She pulled my wet jumper off and dragged me across the room to the fire and the settee. Then she jumped straight on to my knee, kicked her shoes off and started to rub at my hair with her fingers. 'It's gone all curly in the wet.' She was smiling at me, nuzzling at my cold face, pulling strands of hair and kissing my nose. She sang a few words from *Frosty the Snowman* as she teased my hair and then looked me straight in the eye. 'I'm not arguing with you any more, Angelo, I'm not. It's Christmas, and I've got a new dress, and you've got me, and everything will be fine. More than fine! Honestly.' I felt her fingers, tugging on my hair again. It was hard to agree with her logic, but harder still to stop from smiling along with her. 'Say we're not going to argue any more, Angelo? Go on.' She started yanking on the buttons of my shirt with every couple of words. '*Say* we won't row tonight. Say it!'

I laughed. 'Okay, then, no rows. But we might need to talk later, Christina,' I told her.

She rolled her eyes. 'Talk, talk, talk. Haven't you blown off enough steam already, tonight?' Every word was a heavy bounce. I had to steady her, smiling, holding her ribs. 'We can't seem to talk at all without arguing today, so what's the point?' True enough. 'Forget talking, Angelo,' she said, lifting her thighs and then pressing herself down into my lap, softly now. 'Forget thinking, especially.' Her mouth was on my neck, breathing into my hair, her fingers undoing the last three buttons on my shirt. 'Forget everything now except for me and you.' Her lips were on my ear. 'Don't move, just feel. Feel me.' I let my head fall back on to the settee, it always seemed so heavy, and I felt Christina's velvet-wrapped behind moving against me, warming the tops of my damp thighs as her little hands warmed, teased at, my chest.

My eyes closed. I pictured Christina's white velvet petals of breasts rising up slightly out of the sepal of her close-fitting, black velvet dress that I had chosen for her, as she leaned over me, letting the skin of her breasts and her dress fabric graze my chest. I wanted to touch her, strip her, but as soon as I moved my hands, she pressed them back to my sides, whispering, 'Just feel. Don't remember, don't think. Just feel, Angelo. Feel.' What I was feeling was gorgeous – black velvet – and Christina's warm smell was everywhere.

She twisted herself around on my lap until she was sitting on my knee, her luscious arse rubbing my legs. Clumsily, she unbuttoned my jeans and pulled my boxer shorts and socks off. I opened my eyes and saw the tops of her breasts pressed against my chest, the tiniest line of cherry silk fringing them within the v-shaped velvet neckline.

'Shut your eyes,' I said, making the most of the feeling of control over Angelo. 'I want to spoil you tonight.' My boobs looked brilliant *against his cushiony, muscley chest and my new teddy was as tight as anything. I pressed him back against the settee. Most men, in my medium, but not vast, experience, love being pampered and babied by a woman. But Angelo is not most men, and his reactions were not what I expected. I noticed that the brown irises of his eyes were almost covered by his pupils, the blackness of his eyes filling me with their force. 'Shut your eyes,' I said again, but my voice was smaller now. I was testing him, looking forward to finding out how he would react.*

Because I could tell that a pretty powerful reaction was on its way.

I blinked once, slowly, and then I focussed. Christina tried it one last time. 'Shut your eyes!' There was a break in her voice. 'Go on.' I shook my head, still holding her gaze. She looked scared – wide-eyed, silent. But the top half of her body moved towards me fractionally. That slight edging forward made it easier for me to put my arms around her, pick up her supple, velvet-and-silk-wrapped body, and carry her over towards the black iron staircase. Her dress slipped up over her thighs.

I'd always thought that that old 'weak at the knees' saying was a joke, but when we reached the staircase and

I lowered an arm to ease her into a standing position, I was shocked to find she had trouble standing up.

'Sit down,' Angelo said, in his richest, gentlest voice. I was glad to. My dress was up over my thighs and the iron step felt ice cold and hard beneath the softness of my hips. I was wearing hold ups again, to go with the teddy, and Angelo must have seen them, together with just about everything else. It was a less than elegant position, sitting down as I was, with my knees in the air, and I felt more naked than Angelo then, which was the whole idea, I think. I met his eyes and pulled my dress down over the tops of my thighs, deliberately winding him up. He tilted his head and frowned, but I shook my head at him.

I wanted to see what he would do next.

I'd always had the feeling that Christina was amenable to a deeper kind of intimacy. And I needed her to understand that she was not the one in charge, she was not the one to question or control me. The sparkle in her eyes as she pulled her dress down showed she felt the same.

I pushed her down on to the staircase, turned her around, and tore the long cold zip of her short velvet dress down in one yank as she twisted beneath my hands, trying to pull herself away from me. The dress opened up and exposed a triangle of Christina's body, wide at the shoulders and narrow at the base of the spine, where the zip ended (just inches above the hem of the dress). She was wearing the silky teddy. It looked tight around the bottom part of her body as well as the top and I could see just to the top of her hips.

I slipped both hands inside the smooth lining of the dress and felt her back, her shoulders and then her waist. I felt the new silk of her underwear, which I knew no one but me had ever touched before, or even seen. That stirred me, and so did the catch in Christina's breath as she lay beneath me on the stairs, not moving a millimetre now. Inside the velvet, gripping her waist with both hands, I lifted her up from the middle, so that her backside rose slightly from the stairs, then I held her up with one arm, while with the other hand I pulled the dress down over her arms, her waist, her thighs and her feet. Still, she didn't move.

She was wearing nothing but the teddy then and a pair of fine black stockings with small square patterns running around her thighs. My face was just inches from the tender tops of her thighs, her behind. She tried to turn around, struggled to turn around, and just managed to twist her head towards mine and meet my eyes.

'Angelo,' she said. She looked pink, uncomfortable and tense. Intense. The silk teddy had got itself caught up in the cheeks of her arse in the struggle, and her hand went behind her back, trying to hide herself from me. What I always wanted to see most was her secret side, not her best, her most public side. She knew that.

'Shut your eyes, Christina,' I said, squeezing her waist as I was pulling her hand away.

'Angelo,' she said again, louder, and her voice sounded strained. Worked up. Which was exactly how I wanted her.

'Shut your eyes.' Angelo was getting his own back, or was he? Because with my eyes shut, the shame of being bare in front of him eased a bit, and then I felt one palm on my bum covering up where my teddy was caught and feeling me, knowing me, at the same time. The other arm was still around my waist, more or less holding me up. I imagined a blind-folded Christina Ricci kissing Johnny Depp's cool cheekbone. Sleepy Hollow. *The teddy was laced closely at the front, making more of my cleavage than the Red Jersey had ever managed to do, and as I breathed more and more heavily, it got tighter and tighter there. The rain was thudding away, hypnotising me into forgetting about Katy. Angelo's hand moved down from my backside to the tight line of silk between my legs, making me jolt. His grip on my waist tightened.*

If he doesn't move his hand from there, I thought, I'm going to come, right now, bent over in front of him like this.

The way she was practically collapsed over my arm was enough to make me just about come myself. All she was aware of, I guessed, was the burning in her breasts, her behind and between her legs, a burning she needed me to release her from. She'd forgotten what the situation between us was, everything. But I hadn't forgotten.

Can you see who was the stronger now?

I moved my hand from the warm, appealing folds between Christina's legs around to the front of her body, to her breasts, which were laced up and rounded. I handled these more firmly than I had done in the past, knowing how excited she was, but still she cried out, squeezing her eyes together more tightly. I bent my head down so that my lips touched her ear. 'Quiet,' I said, and she opened her eyes, staring straight ahead, frowning, looking genuinely uncertain. I put both arms around her and held her to me, kissing the side of her face. 'You look gorgeous,' I said to her. 'If you want me to stop, just tell me.' One hand went around to her clitoris, teasing it, until she closed her eyes again. I thought of the eyeless, yearning face of the Angel of the North. If we couldn't talk our way to the truth, to trust, perhaps I could move her to trust, physically.

The last thing I wanted to do was to really hurt Christina, or to frighten her, you know that. But still, I had a point to make.

And in fact, the way that Angelo was touching my breasts was making them swell even more, despite the fact that he was being rougher than usual while they were as tender as ever. I kind of moaned. He put both hands on my breasts this time, and I relaxed. He squeezed and squeezed each breast, ignoring the throaty sounds I made as it grew more and more intense. He was still standing over me from the back, with a good view of my behind and between my legs, so I knew he would be able to see from the slackening of my body and the pinking of my skin, the effect he was having on me, whatever little noises I was making.

Then I felt Angelo's fingers at the straps of my teddy, unfastening them and uncovering my boobs, before drawing the shoulder straps down and pulling the teddy off me completely. The stockings went next. I tried to turn around, but he pushed me back on to my front, with his hand in the small of my back, saying, 'I want you like that,' in a voice that was deep and starving. Starving for me. Excellent! I wanted to face him, and yet the nervous edge that his forcefulness was creating was a real turn on.

But one thought worried me. I remembered how he'd kissed me as I'd stood in front of him on the staircase once before, how embarrassed but excited I'd felt. How surprised.

Just how far did Angelo intend to go now?

I never could forget that night I'd kissed Christina on the staircase – kissed her most intimate and virginal, I guessed, opening. I'd felt like I was parting her and entering one of her most secret places. Although she'd wriggled slightly, as if she was enjoying being touched there, she'd also moved away so quickly that I was pretty sure that full anal sex would worry her. Well, I needed to worry her now. I had to show Christina that she could be disturbed by what I was thinking and doing, and yet, however uncertain she was, it would turn out that I was the one who was right. Not her.

'Don't move,' I told her, and went over to the settee and came back with a condom and four cushions. To protect her breasts, I put two cushions between her skin and the stairs, and then I kneeled behind her and stroked her buttocks. 'Lift your hips up, Christina,' I said, and pushed the biggest cushions down between her hipbones and the stairs beneath, forcing her to arch her back. Like before, the soft whiteness of her skin contrasted with the hard blackness of the iron stairs where she lay, but this time her hair, her cheek and a part of her face were all actually touching the blackness. I stroked the blonde strands away from her mouth and kissed her lips, explaining to her, 'You don't need to move your arms. I know exactly what you need: I know it better than you do.' When I put my hand between her legs, there was dampness in the tangle of fair hair.

My point was made.

Did I want to be with someone who knew better than I did what I needed? Would you? I really wasn't sure. What I was sure about was that the combination of all the macho stuff, the attention and the preparation, was really getting to me. I was getting so frustrated. God knows how Angelo was managing! When he pushed his hand between my legs, I tightened my grip on the stair rail with both hands instinctively and clenched my thighs together. Despite myself, I began to move my body around Angelo's hand.

The more I rubbed at her, the more she rocked against my hand, her luxurious arse and thighs tightly circling my wrist. Her expression was one of the purest concentration. I was desperate to penetrate her, my cock was practically screaming, but I wanted her to be almost tormented, maddened, before she came. I wanted her to know exactly how much she needed me. I took my hand away from her, all at once.

She raised her buttocks higher in the air, her elbows crooked as she clung to the rail and her mouth slightly open. A tiny, impatient noise came out. Her bottom parted for me and I could see both of her rawest, her tenderest places. Asking me. My cock twitched. Asking me to take her in the backside, but I knew she wasn't. I pictured it, though, pictured myself roughly splitting her plump little cheeks and riding her arse hard, pushing her towards real excitement through the pain. Maybe too much pain. Christina.

I had to feel her there, to know her there, though.

*   *   *

The rain was streaming its way down the windows as I waited for him. I thought he was going to put his dick inside me, I really wanted him to put his dick inside me, some fluid was running down inside my legs a bit, which had never happened to me before. As I waited, I actually felt his breath on my buttocks. Then it was on my cheek again. 'Has anyone ever made love to you from behind, Christina, here?' he asked, fingering the tiny opening in my bum with his fingers.

Don't you get torn? 'No, Angelo, they haven't. I don't want to.' I went cold.

'I know that.' His fingers were teasing and tickling at the nervy circle. 'But I also know what you do want.' I heard him rip open a condom and put it on.

As soon as he touched me, I knew that no matter what I had just said, I would let him do whatever he thought was right. It was mad, really mad. I was arching my back as much as I could. It was awful, animal, in a way. It was wonderful in another way. It was what I wanted.

I opened my legs for him and I felt him move to kneel between them at once.

Christina's body was weeping as I reached between her legs and lightly pressed her clitoris. I held her hipbones in my hands, positioning her precisely, and then I touched her clitoris again. Suddenly, I jammed my middle finger, hard, into her backside, just an inch, and she pushed her hipbones into the cushions, her eyes closed tight. The rest of my hand was flat against her backside, and I felt her arse clench, tight and hot, around my finger, welcoming me into her body. Good. I adjusted my hand so that I'd be able to enter her from behind, and her body tensed more against the cushions. I pushed the thumb of my other hand into her sex. I was holding her in the most intimate way possible. She was twisting with every movement of my hand.

I was all body now, following Angelo completely, wrapping myself around his hand. I half braced myself on my knees for him as he felt my womb and my behind with his fingers. Wherever his fingers moved, I moved. He was right, I did want his fingers inside me, everywhere, but I hadn't known it myself. I wanted him so much I couldn't stand it. His fingers eased out of me, and his hands came up to my hipbones.

What next? I thought.

I touched Christina's clitoris just once, and she moaned, but she braced herself even more firmly. She was more than ready. I gripped her hips, rubbed myself along the heated split of her uptilted arse, and then I pushed myself into the hot, red tightness between her legs, hard. She was worked up enough already, but as I pushed into her in long movements, almost pulling out of her and then pushing myself back into her harder every time, her hands fell away from the rail, she made a noise, and then she tensed and tensed and tensed. And then relaxed. I was so close to her like that, right inside her belly.

It was all friction and heat, fierce. Too fierce, as it turned out. Too heated.

It was as if I was a completely different person: it was as if I was Angelo's person. My mind had shut down. Even my face felt flushed and alive as his body pushed me to orgasm. I wasn't even aware of whether he had come or not. For a while, I wasn't even aware of who, or where, I was.

It was really, really frightening.

It was one of those experiences that changes things forever. 'The terrible night that Angelo was born,' I thought. The terrible night that Christina and I were born. The power of my orgasm turned automatically into equally powerful feelings of protectiveness and love for Christina, as I pulled carefully out of her and lifted my eyes from the back of her body to her face.

She was lying against the cushions now, looking ahead. But when I turned her around and pulled her into my arms, she started to cry – not just crying, but sobbing her heart out, just like after all that crap with Jonty, when she fell down the casino stairs.

For one black-dark minute, I thought that I'd got it completely wrong; I thought I'd really hurt her. *'You didn't even try to look after him?' 'You didn't see it coming?'* She'd trusted me and I had hurt her. *'And is there nothing wrong with you?'* Again. I put my arm around her shoulders. 'Christina?' She cried more, her shoulders hunched with a terrible tension. She wouldn't look at me. I was terrified of losing her. There was pain in my face as I waited for her to tell me what was wrong. I put my other hand down between her legs. God, what if I'd torn her skin? But there was no blood. She was just a young girl; I should have been much gentler. *'What is the matter with you, Angelo?'* I tried to get through to her again, putting my face close to her temple. 'Christina?' It wasn't until she put her arms up around my neck and cried wet gulps of grief into my shoulder that I let a deep breath go and realised I hadn't breathed out for ages. Thank you, God, I said to myself. Whatever was wrong, she wasn't blaming me for it. It wasn't my fault. Or was it? I held her as closely as I could, my mouth lying against her hair and guilt pressing hard against my chest.

'Angelo!' She sounded tragic. Her back was shaking with sobs and I stroked her spine, trying to work the distress out of her bones. She would not, or could not, be soothed.

'Wait a minute,' I said, and ran upstairs, pulled a few clothes on myself, and got some knickers and a nightie out for her. When she took her hands away from her face to put her arms in her sleeves, I saw that her skin was pink in patches and her eye make-up, what was left of it, was a mess. She was so upset and she hated looking ugly, not that I cared how she looked right then. But I did care that she was so distressed.

'Come and sit down,' I coaxed her, guiding her across the room. 'Tell me what's wrong.' When we reached the settee, Christina curled her legs in towards her and wrapped her arms around her knees. She'd finally stopped crying; it had finished as suddenly and as strangely as it had started, although there was the odd leftover catch in her breathing. Her fingers combed her hair, like a cat, grooming herself, making me smile at her at last. But her eyes were earnest.

Typically, the first thing she said was, 'Do I look all right?'

'Don't worry about that,' I said, but I traced my fingers below my eyes to show her where her make-up was smudged.

'Shit,' she said, and rubbed at the thin skin below her eyes with her sleeve, as if her face was a window she was cleaning. I'd never heard her swear before, not even in the casino where everybody swore, and I smiled. 'Is that better?' She lifted the backs of her knuckles to her bloodshot eyes, her open fingers echoing her question.

'Better than it was,' was about the best I could manage. 'I'm more interested in whether you're feeling any better,' I said, and it was true. 'What was the matter, then?'

Talk about fucking your brains out! Christina Rae, the Queen of Cool, blaring her eyes out in front of her loved one, again. *Bet Jesmond Katy never did that! But I never knew I could feel so much for someone. Brains were something else completely.*

Angelo knew my body well enough, but what about my head? My body liked having sex like that. Deep. Intimate. Too intimate? (He couldn't tell things about my body, could he, from being so deep inside it like that?) My head was much less sure. Physical. Primitive. My body liked just about anything where Angelo was involved, that was the trouble. That didn't mean I wanted him taking charge of what went on in my mind! Was that how he seemed so psychic? Because he was so tuned in to what people needed?

I couldn't explain any of that to Angelo, or mention my new, Katy-related, dread. 'I hate you seeing me when I look such a mess,' I said instead, which was true enough. My main selling points, I reckoned, were my reasonable-but-not-spectacular, B but rarely A, looks and now I'd blown even that. I mean, my brains were never exactly going to impress anyone, were they? I nearly blubbed again; got away with a Gwyneth gulp.

'And?' he said. 'Tell me, Christina. I need to know.' Angelo's burning needs!

'All right,' I said, trying to put it into words. 'It was all feelings to do with my body, not my mind, not even me.' There was one more point to make as well, but I didn't know how he'd like it, so my voice went all hard, high and edgy. 'And it's dirty, isn't it? Touching me inside, like that.' I looked down. 'Inside there.' Angelo looked blank. I tried again, impatient with him now. 'I mean, how can I be clean, there?'

And he hadn't even looked at my face.

Christina was so disgusted, so funny. She'd loved me touching her. Hadn't she? I needed to know her feelings exactly. 'How did you feel when I actually touched you? Did you feel dirty then?' I asked her, rubbing her arm. She insisted on mutely destroying a button on the quilt cover. A minute passed and I spoke again, gently. 'Christina?'

Her body juddered, trying to refuse me my answer, but when she finally lifted her head, she said, 'It felt nice.' I pushed her to elaborate with a shake of my head, waiting. 'Exciting. Private,' she said, then her mouth drooped and her eyebrows rose, appalled. 'Angelo, you wouldn't tell *anybody*, would you? At the casino or anywhere else? You wouldn't!'

I could have hit her. 'Do I look like Jonty? For God's sake, Christina, private is the point! I wouldn't dream of telling *anyone* about that sort of thing. What kind of idiot do you think I am?' I looked down at my hands before just about spitting my last words at her. 'I'll get a wash then, shall I? Before I buy my amplifier and club and start broadcasting.' And I left her sitting alone on the settee while I went upstairs to clean myself up and cool down.

I generally avoid looking in mirrors because of Mic's face, Mic's eyes, so similar to mine. But this time, I looked in the mirror and I thought of my mother. At first, I thought of how Mic's death had just exaggerated her normal personality – the energy, the criticism, the advice – and my anger at Christina stayed. Grew even. But then I thought of her face, the twisting pain as she shouted at me in that side room, hurting herself as much as me. And I thought of one night, shortly after Mic's accident, when I'd heard this animal, breathless crying coming from her room. One night, when I'd stayed in my room, waiting for the noise to stop, because I couldn't cope with the grief that my mother was going through. A grief so powerful that her body, her lungs, couldn't keep up with it.

I started to think of Christina again, hating myself and softening towards her now. I could hear her turning switches off downstairs, then climbing up the stairs. What she'd said about me loving her body rather than her was really starting to hit home. I'd mixed up feelings of real love with feelings that were just erotic, just 'body', as she'd put it. I had to make it clear to Christina that my feelings for her were deeper than that, because they were. I walked back into the bedroom, ready to explain it all to her.

She was lying with her back to me. I sat down beside her and she turned towards me at once. She never bore a grudge. I tried to express it as truthfully as I could. 'All I wanted, Christina, was to touch you – really touch you.' She still hadn't taken her make-up off, and the black smudges underneath her eyes made me feel so guilty. 'I wanted to move you, to connect with you. To show you that in some ways, I know about what's best for us. You and me.'

'It worked,' she said. But she sounded sad. Distant. She was fading right away from me.

'Tell me what's upsetting you the most.'

She took a deep breath and then out it came. 'My face,' she said. She looked down towards her hands. 'You weren't looking at my face. You ignored me.'

I understood at once how she felt, how I'd made her feel. Terrible. 'No, Christina, no. Don't think that.' I held her tired, smudged face between my hands. 'I didn't look at your face because I knew how you were feeling. Your body told me. I nearly always know how you're feeling. Didn't I touch you the whole time, talk to you the whole time? I would never ignore you when I was making love to you. Never. And if part of you is, as you say, dirty, different, from other parts of your body, it's still you. It was the intimacy I wanted with you. Didn't you feel that?' She nodded, looking more tired than ever. 'You're worn out,' I said, 'and I never meant to hurt your feelings. You need to trust your instincts about me more, rather than thinking too much about things. Do you feel better now?'

'Some,' she said, but she didn't look any happier. 'But you have to look at my face.'

If she'd known how it looked at that second, that was the last thing she'd have wanted. 'I know,' I told her. 'I will. I'll go and get all your stuff, so that you can clean yourself up without getting out of bed, and then you can sleep. Okay?' She nodded. I went into the bathroom for her make-up bag, mammoth, of course, toothbrush and a mug of water.

When she'd finished with all that, and was feeling and looking more human, I pulled her down beside me. 'How can I make you feel better before you go to sleep?'

'A story,' she said at once, brightening. 'Like the Skeleton Woman story.'

I had to think about that, running my fingers through the gold-red strands of Christina's hair as my story warmed and grew. By the time I was ready to begin, she was really sleepy.

'Once upon a time . . .' Christina went into auto-snuggle again, '. . . there was a young princess, with blonde hair.' I teased at a lock of Christina's hair as I spoke. 'Blonde hair with just a touch of reddish-gold in it.' I pulled at it a bit.

23. Gold-red Hair

'He was so much stronger than the princess that there was nothing she could do.'

'Ow!' *He'd woken me up now.*

'And because the princess was very beautiful, and because she had hair like pure spun gold, many young princes from other kingdoms were attracted to her.' Mr Gold, I thought, and hoped that Angelo's psychic tendencies weren't *that* well developed. *'These men would visit the kingdom of Northumbria,'* he went on, circling my temple now, *'and they would try to persuade the princess's father, the king, that she should marry them. But to the king, the princess was a very special daughter, because of her lovely, cheerful nature. Because she was so special to him, the king had told his daughter that she must never wander in the woods around the castle alone.'* He doesn't know my dad or me at all, I thought, wishing that I'd wandered less and been loved more a few years ago, in particular. I quite liked Angelo's version anyway, although it could get boring if taken to extremes, and I waited for what was to come next.

'Meanwhile, living in the forest beside the palace was a handsome young woodcutter, who loved the princess for herself, as well as for her amazing hair and face, a man who wanted to protect her and give her just everything she needed.' Enter Angelo, obviously. How nice! *'But because he wasn't a prince,*

he wasn't allowed to approach the palace to court the princess.'
Typical!

'One night, the greediest prince of them all, an ambitious prince
who wanted to extend his kingdom, which was already rich in
fertile land and gems . . .' obviously a punter *'. . . visited the*
palace when the king was out. He watched the princess reading
and dreaming in her room . . .' (Hello! I thought) *'. . . and*
eventually, as night drew near, he watched her leave the castle
and begin to walk in the woods.' Big mistake, I thought. Anybody
who'd ever read a fairy story could have seen that one coming.
'And he followed her into the woods, picked her up, and carried
her further and further into the forest and closer to the dangerous
heart of it.' Could be fun, I thought. Angelo continued. *'However*
hard the princess struggled, she couldn't stop the prince from
taking her away from her home. He was so much stronger than
the princess that there was nothing she could do.' Also Angelo?
'How could she protect herself?' Swift knee to the bollocks? I kept
that little pearl to myself. *'But she could refuse to marry him and*
she did.'

'What did the greedy prince make of that, then?' I interrupted,
quite pleased at her, my, refusal. Just because I'd liked Angelo
taking charge in bed didn't mean that I wanted that to extend
to any other parts of my life, real or imagined! *'Not much,*
I guess?'

Angelo lifted himself up on to his elbow and shook his head:
he was really getting into it. *'Not much at all. He took the*
beautiful princess deeper into the forest,' his voice dropped deeper,
'and when they were totally *lost . . .'* Slash! Angelo slashed
at his throat with a pen that lay beside his bed, his eyes
bulging as he, I, gurgled away his/my last, like Keanu Reeves'
wife in The Devil's Advocate. Dead theatrical. I spliced a
few shots of Katy, as I imagined her, on to the image and
started to enjoy myself. I wasn't quite so sure about having
my throat cut, though, just for turning down one grotty proposal.

'What happened after that, then?' I asked. *'That's not exactly*

a restful bedtime story, is it?' Having my throat cut was getting on my nerves a bit.

I laughed, she sounded so pissed off, and decided I'd better build up her part. 'After that,' I said, 'came the very best bit of all. After a death . . .'

'. . . a life,' Christina chimed in. 'After a death, a life.'

'A life,' I agreed. 'But first of all, the greedy prince cut off all the princess's hair.' I scissored away at Christina's pride and joy with my pen, making her shriek and push my hands away. 'And he put it in his purse, as if it was money, because he was also a very stupid prince. And then he buried her.'

'Great.' Still sounding pissed off.

'But every night,' I continued, 'the woodcutter dreamed of the princess, and every day he searched for her. He dreamed of her in the black, black night.' Click.

I switched off the light. Black dark.

Black dark. Dead effective.

'What did he dream?' I whispered. I was getting pretty involved myself by then, and I was definitely looking forward to my rebirth. The best bit.

Angelo crawled across the bed to me in the dark. 'Every night, as the moon rose high in the sky, and the woodcutter's sleep grew deeper and thicker, a panther stalked the land of the woodcutter's dreams. Rrrrrrr!' A panther stalked me across the bed, pouncing with low, soft growls, attacking my neck and my ribs and my stomach.

'Panthers don't tickle,' I said, smacking the panther's paws away. 'They don't.' Angelo made quite a good panther actually. 'And their claws are sharp.'

'Well, this panther had nice claws; I think he'd been using the princess's emery boards.' Angelo dug his, totally unmanicured, fingers into my ribs again, waited until I stopped giggling, then carried on. 'The panther stalked the forest in the woodcutter's

dreams and he showed the woodcutter the place where the princess was buried.

'So the next day, the woodcutter searched the woods, but it was impossible to find the spot he had seen in the dream because there were so many trees and so much undergrowth. He sat on a tree stump with his head in his hands and he sighed. Would he ever find the princess? And at the very second that he gave up, he heard a whispering song join the sound of his own breath. He followed the sound of the singing until he saw long, gold-red hair growing out of the floor of the forest, curling up towards the light. Walking across to the hair, he heard the voice of the princess singing. "The greedy prince killed me and cut off my hair," it sang. "Find me. Find me."

'But all of the hair, and quite a lot more of it, had grown back.'

Well, that was a relief. I lay back on the pillow, arranging my own hair, and smiled.

I knew she'd like that part. 'The song had to come out,' I said, 'because carrying secrets is exhausting.' My own half-buried secret weighed down on me, stopping the story for a second, then I carried on. 'So the woman grew stronger as she slept beneath the soil, singing out her truth to the woods, freed from the burden of the secret.' There was a slight tension in Christina's body when I said that, a slight drawing away. Maybe she had secrets of her own? I hugged her and carried on.

'The woodcutter dug away at the soil with his axe and his nails until he found the princess's body, and he moved all the earth and the bracken before he carried her home. In the woodcutter's cottage, he cleaned the princess up, wiping the mildew from her face and her mouth, and then the princess began to breathe.' I couldn't resist adding a bit of mouldy Keats to the story, imagining Christina's face. Horrified! She would much rather have her throat cut than her face mildewed. I took pity on her and decided to give her a happy ending.

'For seven days and seven nights, the woodcutter looked after the princess in his warm, wooden house, feeding her chocolate, telling her stories and singing to her. Feasts all day and stories all night – just like us.' Christina's body relaxed back into mine again, imagining all of that attention and warmth. 'At the end of the week, she and the woodcutter returned to the palace to tell the king the whole story and to ask for his permission to marry.

'The king was so delighted to see his princess alive, and so impressed by the woodcutter's bravery that he gave the couple his permission to marry at once. There was a big party in the forest that night, and the next night the greedy prince was hunted down and hung.'

'A bit savage, don't you think?' I said, all curled up in the arms of my own sexy, storytelling woodcutter.

'Well, in the greedy prince's pocket, the king found the long rope of the princess's gorgeous, golden-red hair. After that, he just couldn't forgive the prince and insisted on the hanging.' Angelo brushed my hair out of my face.

'Fair enough,' I decided. It was *a pretty bad crime and I was just about asleep.*

But one last nasty flash of reality pushed its way into my mind, just before I closed my eyes to rest. 124 Osborne Road. Katy. Katy, Katy, Katy. Katy and Angelo.

24. Mount Pisgah

*'A woman, clothed with the sun, and the moon under
her feet, and upon her head a crown of twelve stars.'*

I lay there in the dark beside Christina for ages as she slept and
I was just charged up with everything that had happened that
day. Christmas has one of the longest, darkest nights of the
year, perhaps that's why we need all the glitter and the snowy
cards, but that Christmas *Day* had been one of the longest,
brightest and darkest days I had ever known. I was glad
Christina was asleep. I thought of her white skin against the
black steps, the light of her skin against the dark of my night.
My buried secret. Mess. I stroked her arm. My ideas turned
into circles, spirals, connecting and disconnecting, shaping
and distorting. Becoming more and more intense, important.

I looked up towards the skylight above my head, memories and ideas buzzing around my head in coils. Rain was
dropping down on to the velux, there were tears in my eyes,
and then the drops became lights. And the lights became
words, pattering down above my head, around my ears.
'Mary. Mary, Martha, Medea, Mene, Mount Pisgah, Mary.
Mary.' The words circled and circled into a ring of spinning
metallic voices, 'Mary, Mary,' and the golden droplets grew
and grew, and then they swirled together. The voices were
loud, I was loud, repeating them. The droplets joined. I

was shouting. A bright light flashed on, buzzing, blinding. Christina was shouting beside me, annoyed, alarmed, pulling my arm. The room was full of blinding white light, then it was black again, but still the drops spun and the names carried on, with me repeating them. It all carried on and I carried on repeating the words, joining the metallic chant. And then it went, and there was just me and the words, repeating them, adding to them, trying to work out exactly what they were telling me.

'Mene. The writing on the wall. A string of women. Mary and Joseph, Medea and Jason, James and John. Minerva. The Promised Land. Mount Pisgah. Moses. Moses climbed to the top of the mountain to see the Promised Land. Mary. Many mothers and future mothers. Mary. The mountain of hope. Mount, mounds, curves, women's curves. Women's bodies. Women's breasts. The hope of a woman's breast. Mary. Sex life, child life, the life of a child through sex. A woman's body. Hope. Christina.' The image of the *Pietà* had filled my mind all day and now light and energy and life were filling my night. Christina.

Christina. At last I turned back to her, turned back into a different world, a lesser world, a darker world. Except for Mary. Except for Christina. Christina. I calmed down. She would think that I was mad. Mene. The writing on the wall. Babel.

Babylon.

He gave me such a shock. The light and his voice woke me up; they were switched on together, somehow, but the light flashed on for just seconds and then everything fused. The darkness was back and Angelo's voice spoke, 'Mary,' followed by talk about mountains and women and then my name. I hadn't a clue what he was on about, but the flashing of the light had been real enough.

At last he was silent. I felt totally inadequate, scared. I didn't know what to say to him.

I didn't know what to say to her. She lay beside me on her back, silent but definitely awake. I got up and walked into the bathroom to wash my face, to wait for my heartbeat to slow, my breathing to calm. To wait until I wouldn't frighten Christina any more. The words were still running through my head. When I pulled the cord to put the bathroom light on, nothing happened, so I had to make my way in the dark back to the bedroom again. The whole building must have blown, the whole street, for all I knew. Shit. It compounded the whole weirdness of the last twenty-four hours.

There was an old oil lamp beside my bed so I fumbled around for matches, removing the tulip-shaped glass shade before finally lighting the wick. Had she gone back to sleep?

No chance. Her question mark of a face was the first thing I saw as my match touched the broad, oily wick of the lamp.

At least I understood Angelo's mother some by then. One minute he was shouting his head off at the ceiling and the next he was lighting up a lethal-looking paraffin lamp. Definitely a danger to himself, and maybe to other people as well. But was he mad? I thought. What about the light? Could it have been his energy that had blown it somehow? Or was it something else? Fire was Angelo's element and it looked like he'd torched the whole house, the electricals at least.

Or was I *the one starting to go mad? I* hadn't *imagined it. Did that make it madder?*

I shook myself. 'Let me put that at my side of the bed,' I suggested, sitting up and taking the Olympic flame of a lamp out of his hands, then clicking the shade firmly into place. 'Get into bed and calm down.' It was a wicked-looking thing, exactly like the one Chris Eccleston had in Jude. *Calming him down had the effect of calming myself down at the same time. I was less frightened than I had been the first time, but I was definitely more concerned about him and the state of his poor mind. He just seemed to be torturing himself, to me.*

I pulled Angelo's side of the quilt back and waited for him to climb in.

'There's just one more thing I have to do,' I told Christina. The words were spinning around in my head. The Bible. The Bible always helped me. She put her head to one side, as if she was going to say something, but then she thought better of it and lay back, pushing a tiny sigh out of her lungs as she hit the pillow.

It took me a while to feel my way around the dark corners of the room in the dark to find a torch (leaving the lamp by the bed for Christina), and then I had to get the box.

At last I had the Bible in the one hand and a torch in the other. I looked up towards the skylight and blindly picked a page, or rather, I let a page pick me.

'A woman, clothed with the sun, and the moon under her feet, and upon her head a crown of twelve stars.'

A woman's body. Hadn't I always known it was the key to everything? Christina.

I took the last two hair clasps and all the rings and the Burano lace out of the box and then went back up the stairs to Christina. I laid the rings and things on the table on my side of the bed. I put my hand on her lips when she opened her mouth to question me. Then I took her lipstick and comb from her make-up bag.

'"A woman, clothed with the sun, and the moon, under her feet, and on her head, a crown of stars."' I recited it to her, almost. 'Trust me.' A ceremony. She shook her head just once, moving her hair on the pillow, but she didn't move away or speak.

First, I combed the hair on her head and then I combed the fine tendrils of hair between her legs with my fingers. Strawberry blonde, I thought, but those were the wrong words. I looked at the curly strands between my fingers.

They were the colour of the newest, palest bronze, a freshly minted coin, shot through with gold. Valuable. Rare. Just as Christina and I were ourselves: clean, new, shining in valuable love. Maybe the prince had been right to put the gold-red hair in his purse and keep it.

I drew a red line from the bone between her breasts to the skin just above the strands of hair, a long red line. I put the jewelled, starred clasps in her hair and slid the rings on to her fingers and toes, and then I tied the black and white lace to her wrists and her throat. *'Mene. Mary. Minerva. The writing on the wall. Mary, Minerva. Mene. Mene.'* In the flickering, fluid light of the oil lamp, I drew red and black waves, red and black circles, around her body and her white, white breasts.

When I touched her bright blue eyes and kissed her eyelids, they smelled of flowers and sweet, wild herbs. She was magical. She was so close to experiencing what I did.

Hadn't I always known that a woman's body held the secret? The magic?

You would think that the whole episode would have been totally embarrassing, or weird, wouldn't you? Well, telling you about it is definitely pretty embarrassing, seeing it through your eyes. But it wasn't you who was looking at me. It was Angelo. And that changed everything, always. Angelo's eyes. Angel eyes. And coming as Angelo did after Jonty, that made the whole affair with him much more intense. For Jonty, I was just a little something he slipped into when he was feeling horny. A little nothing. What exactly was I to Angelo? To him, I was all the myths of womanhood rolled into one: soft, fertile, beautiful, vulnerable, mystical. Fantastic.

But was I Christina? Was I scarred, secretive Christina, with a head full of things that I knew I would never tell him – could never tell him? Christina, with a stomach that was a real woman's stomach, with aches and pains and a history all of its own? No.

Is he mad? I thought, as I lay there with my eyes closed, feeling

Angelo paint me, touch me, revere me. Mad or magical? He was whispering over me the whole time, like a spell, 'Mary' again, and so much more besides, and kissing me or touching me with his tongue. But the touches of his fingers and his tongue were so gentle, so loving, that I was warmed, loved right out of my questioning. Hypnotised. Adored. I put myself completely into his hands: it was the only way with Angelo. Actually, it felt gorgeous. It felt like home. If I'm really honest, more honest than usual, it felt like heaven. Maybe I was as mad as Angelo was, or on my way to it? Or maybe I was just nearer to the truth, nearer to the centre of things, than I ever had been before? What do you think? Folie à deux.

At last, whispering to me that my eyes smelled of flowers, Angelo kissed my eyelids closed, kissed Christmas closed, and I slept, with just the tips of his fingers touching my belly. Magical.

Why should I listen to the voices of people but ignore the voices of angels? Could a doctor have something better to say? Is it sick, or weak, to turn your face to angels, however weird people might think you are, or is it weak to pretend that angels don't exist, even when they've spoken to you? It felt like since Mic's death, the flashes of light, of understanding, were almost joining, like animation, showing me completely different pictures of the world to those I'd seen before. All this was running around my head as my fingers ran still around her half-asleep body. I wanted to be sure that she was dreaming of me.

I lay there, and a line of a poem came into my head. I arranged and rearranged the words in my head, thinking of the words that I'd written around the windows before, and then I wrote it all down on a piece of paper beside the bed, planning to put it in the handbag that I'd given her, to surprise her whenever she opened it.

Christina slept before I did, but when I did eventually fall asleep, my hand still on her belly, I slept like somebody numbed.

25. Katy's (and the Melting Wings) . . .

'Maybe Angelo had trouble with a lot of things after a start like that.'

The bits of lace digging into my skin woke me up the next day; otherwise I think we'd have missed Boxing Day altogether. When I did wake up, Angelo was still in a deep sleep. I kissed both his eyelids, but there wasn't a flicker. No wonder, I thought, looking down at my watch. It was half-eleven, but we hadn't exactly had a restful night, had we? And it must have been more exhausting for Angelo than for me. I stroked his lovely, crispy hair. La Vita E Bella, I thought; then Angelo E Bella, very bella. And very, very tired. He was the most intense person in the world, or in my world, at least.

And I was the most uncomfortable person in my world. Three or four of the rings were lying around me on the sheet, one of the hair clasps was on the floor and the other one was clumped up in some hair at this wild angle to my head. Not to mention the marks, which felt totally mad in the cold light of day. A lot of the rest of it was less worrying in daylight, like all that stuff about what I represented to Angelo. It took him all his time to sort out his own globe of a head; there was no need for him to worry much about the one-page street map of mine, was there? Better have a shower, I thought, taking off the rings and bracelets of lace one at a time as I sat up.

But of course the shower was electric, the water was cold, and Angelo was asleep, so I had a nice chilling rub down in the gloom with a sponge. As I sponged my face, I remembered the elderflower eye cream that I'd put on the night before, trying to make my eyes look less of a sight. Flowers. That was what Angelo had smelled on my eyes. He must have been really spooked. Poor Angelo. I stuck my contacts in, and it felt like being a different sort of God, opening your own eyes wide, looking straight at yourself and putting in an improvement. If only Angelo were as easy to heal!

I blinked twice, walked back into the bedroom and quietly got dressed, watching Angelo's face as often as I could while I found my clothes and put them on. He was curled around the warm gap that had been my body. He wouldn't wake up for ages. Angelo was one thing that I didn't want to separate myself from, I knew that now. Because I couldn't have separated myself from him then if I had tried. I had no intention of trying.

What I did want to try to do was to look after him better. Everything that had happened the night before had proved to me pretty conclusively that he needed to be looked after a bit. More than a bit. He was dead vulnerable, living there on his own, at the mercy of his weird imagination, his messages, his brooding about his mother, the past and Mic, and blaming himself for everything. Jude's smelly old oil lamp had to go, for a start; I've never seen a more depressing film in my life! I picked it up from my table and walked downstairs in my stockinged feet to put it beside the bin (didn't want to tempt providence by putting it inside and risking total incineration), deciding that I would potter around the church for a while as I waited for Angelo to wake up.

Then I reached the living room, and my plans for the morning shifted. An open wooden box was staring at me, half stuffed underneath an old chair in a corner, spilling out letters and postcards and an old red notebook. So that was where all those rings and bits and pieces had come from! I knelt down and fingered the smooth sides of the box. How strange that I had found it just as I was realising exactly how many secrets the Paulillo family *harboured. I sensed that this might provide some answers. It had to. Well, who could resist a quick look? I pulled out the book. I knew by instinct that it was the most revealing piece in the whole exciting little collection. Listening out for Angelo, I opened up its pages, hearing the words whispering their story to me.*

Angelo's birth was like something out of the Middle Ages. I carried him for a lifetime — an adult's lifetime rather than a baby's, it seemed: he was a week overdue and I felt like a warship. My body had barely recovered from Michael's birth when I became pregnant with Angelo: Michael's milk was Angelo's milk, but that was exactly how I wanted it. I thought, wrongly, that there would be less jealousy between the boys if they had each been in the other's memory from babyhood, and certainly they were always very close. But it meant that the pregnancy was exhausting, carrying Angelo in my belly like a heavy secret and holding a wriggling baby Michael in my arms at the same time.

I knew when Angelo was on his way. It was different from the pain I had known with Michael, but I knew that it was the pain of this new baby, of Angelo. The hospital didn't agree and they sent Tony and me back home to wait. I was full of irritation, impatience and then agony. The waters broke, some blood appeared, and we were flying back to the hospital in a panic this time, in the pitch dark.

By the time we got back to the RVI, I knew there was something wrong. It just felt wrong. Angelo was in an awkward, twisted position and the labour was endless and gruelling. I couldn't push him out, the midwives couldn't coax him out and the consultant couldn't even pull him out. And all the time, I could feel his little body, struggling for life and independence inside me.

The forceps dragged him out in the end, tearing me and bruising him. By the time Angelo was finally born, he looked like he'd been beaten. His first experience of life was of pain. Does that explain what came later, in part at least?

Maybe Angelo had trouble believing that he was loved, after a start like that.

Maybe Angelo had trouble with a lot of things after a start like that.

Carrying heavy secrets. I rubbed my stomach as I thought. I knew all about those.

I started to tidy the church up. Maybe I would cheer the place up more permanently, help him to decorate it or something. Whatever Angelo thought, and it was pretty clear and sometimes quite unflattering, what he thought, I knew that in my own way, I was actually stronger than he was. Much.

Something about that worried me.

The noises from downstairs woke me at last, and I smiled because I knew Christina was there. When I looked at my watch, it was after noon and I hadn't woken once in the night. The easiest time for me to sleep was always after it was light, when I'd broken the back of the night for good: that's why casinos suited me. I grabbed a few clothes, put them on and made for the stairs, slowing down as I went, rubbing the bristles on my jaw. How would Christina be feeling after the weirdest Christmas Day in history?

But she was doing some kind of 1920s American soap-opera impersonation in the kitchen. (Mic flashed into my memory: how he'd imitated the American girls' whiny voices and taken all the parts when Mum was trying, unsuccessfully, to watch one once.) Christina turned her head to smile at me as I walked up behind her, and shook some flour off her fingers. She was all made up and everything, as usual, all fresh. 'I thought you'd never wake up,' she said, raising her voice on the 'never'. 'I'm just making you something to eat. Do you feel better?'

'Much better.' Now. Her face was as soft and beautiful as Botticelli's *Madonna del Mare*. I put my arms around her from behind and cuddled into her, pushing my face into her white perfumed neck and kissing her. I put my hands on her belly. Imagine Christina with my baby inside her! I squeezed her waist. Some flour was winding itself around the crown of her head, and I touched the dusty blonde swirl. 'What are you doing?'

'A sort of salmon pie,' she said, looking down at her hands. 'Making the best of a bad deal is my speciality. Except with you, of course.' She turned around to give me a powdery kiss and flicked a hand towards the fridge and the cupboards, sprinkling more flour everywhere. 'Not exactly a Delia Smith experience in there, is it, Angelo?' It was a good job she hadn't seen it before Christmas. 'I'm doing a kind of shepherd's pie, only with white sauce and salmon instead of meat and onions. I've gone just about as far as I can manage without some electricity!'

So I fixed the fuses, Christina fixed the food, the church was full of the smell of perfume, cooking and Christina herself.

I had a lovely day with Angelo, a really lovely day. It was like being in The Waltons *or something. I think I was Mary Ellen, up to my elbows in flour in the kitchen, cooking for my beloved Kurt, who was way up a mountain, saving somebody's life, or delivering somebody's baby or both.*

And then amazingly, I was quite looking forward to seeing my family and having a bit of a laugh with them. I mean, I loved going to the church and I loved seeing Angelo, but sometimes all that intensity wore me out. Too much night. While I didn't much like the idea of leaving Angelo in the church on his own on Boxing Day, taking him to my mam's house in Gateshead with me would have worried me even more, not to mention, Angelo thought I came from Jesmond, à la Katy. And then, the house was not quite as I had described it to him, and neither was my family.

Best if he stayed with the fictionalised version, for a while at least. And so far, he didn't suspect a thing.

'You can always come to my mother's house with me,' Christina said to me, just before she left to go there herself. Every feature on her face showed me that she was praying I would say no. And I knew why, of course. I'd seen the house.

Ever since I'd seen Christina's flat, I'd known that she'd been giving me a very rosy, a very soft-focus, picture of her life. She even smelled soft, of flowers, but there was much more to her than that. I needed to know the whole truth about her. So I'd followed her in my car. Three times now.

There was no big secret, not that I was aware of. I'd already known she had a brother who was always in trouble with the police, one of the other dealers who knew of the family had told me, and I knew she never talked about that. Fair enough. But I think what was bothering her most was the house itself. She was always trying to dress as nicely as she could, talk as nicely as she could, present herself as nicely as she could. And the house wasn't nice. It certainly wasn't in Jesmond. I didn't mind that (fantastic to be so close to the sky-stretching Angel of the North, was my opinion) but I guessed that that was what was bothering her, what she was shy about.

It was a cluttered, tired house, with bare lightbulbs blazing away any warmth or comfort the house might otherwise have had to offer. And the mother had a dry, bleached little head, a dry, cracking voice and a dry, cracking little soul. Narrow vision. Nobody there would have taught Christina to dream, or even to think much. It was the equivalent of *Hansel and Gretel*, being brought up in a house like that. All of the roads, the dreams, are open to you, but you have no idea that you've got the power to make them come true. The danger is not of losing yourself in the woods (a bit of imagination and some bread sorts that out). The danger is of staying at home and not realising you're lost. Dead inside. Christina had braved the woods, lived, without so much as Gormley's Angel to guide her when she was young. So it didn't bother me that she hadn't told me the truth about the house. Lies like that didn't bother me: in a way, it was proof that she loved me, the way she was always trying to impress me.

But if she ever lied to me about anything else, anything personal, I mean, that would be different altogether.

Boxing Day night was the time to pay a visit to Katy, I reckoned, whether Angelo liked it or not. Well, if he was having a fling with this Katy then I needed to know, and if it turned out that she was just a friend, I could always say I'd overheard the phone message when he was out and I'd known he wouldn't listen to it, so I'd had to do something. I just had to see for myself what was going down.

But first, I had the day to get through. Life at my mam's was certainly different from life chez Stephen King.

My sister still lived at home so she and my mam had prepared the dinner together. What with my mam and sister in and out of the kitchen, my sister's boyfriend in and out of the house and my mam's friends in for a Christmas drink every five seconds or so, there wasn't any time to think. It was quite nice, really. And the presents were very welcome, of course, gloves and slippers and a top and chocolates and so on. I won't give you the whole list. My dad was between families – between a divorced woman in Leam Lane and my mother, to be exact – so he'd had his Christmas meal at home the day before and then left, which meant that the atmosphere in the house was quite civilised. (My mam had given up on trying to change him, lifetimes ago.)

But in the middle of all this action, I kept, of course, thinking of Angelo. Angel eyes. Was it because the church was so quiet that he was sensitive to sounds only he could hear? Dead special. My Angelo. Black eyes and the blonde. My Angelo? My visit to Jesmond Katy was never out of my mind all day long. He wouldn't deceive me, would he? I trusted him. Still, 124 Osborne Road was printed on my brain, Katy's name was on my lips, and whatever I found, I was going to get the situation sorted.

So I left my mam's house early and off I went on the bus over the Tyne.

Osborne Road is easy enough to find, it runs through Jesmond like a bone, but as my fingers rapped on the tatty panelled door, I really couldn't say who, or what, I was expecting to find on the other side. Some kind of a sad, mad, magical, tragical drama queen, I suppose, after Angelo's mother's message. But all I got at first was this bellowing voice, half drowned out by a radio playing. 'I'm in the kitchen!' Didn't sound much like she was having a hard time, all those decibels.

I waited a few seconds and then I opened the door to face a long, thin corridor, with one door off the end of it and another to the side. 'Katy?' No clues in sight. Apart, that is, from what was staring at me from the end of the corridor! It was a man's head and shoulders — is it a bust, they call it? — sticking right out from the wall like those grotty, mothy old deer's heads in pubs. It must have had its ears pierced about seven times at least because there were all these dangly metal earrings dripping off its earlobes, not to mention the row of nose stones it was sprouting and the necklace of silver tinsel wrapped around its neck. Despite all this, the moosey man had a funny kind of dignity. I suppose it was the Elvis lip, curling its way nastily away from the tinsel noose. I squinted up for a better look at him. Good job he was made of plaster: with all those piercings, he'd have been more than a bit prone to the old hepatitis and germs.

'I'm in here!' The bawling voice was a bit of a shock and there was a kind of roaring noise as well. There was some music going, 'Road to Nowhere . . .' *'Who is it?' she shouted through. What could I say? I just followed the din to the room at the end.*

The kitchen was totally unlike anybody else's kitchen I'd ever seen, and Katy was totally unlike anybody's idea of a kitchen maid. 'Pineapple heed!' jumped into my head, in Peter's loud, hooting voice — he'd called Shelley that when she'd done her hair a bit the same. This girl's yellow-blonde, tufty sort of hair was bunched up into diamond-shaped segments all around her skull, I don't know how she got it like that, and she was holding a flaming blowtorch in her fingers, cheerfully blasting a few blameless-looking bits of metal on the top of her cooker practically into oblivion. She was about my age, I guessed. The radio blasted on. She turned around, torch in hand, and focussed on me.

What on earth was I going to say to her?

'*Just a bit of an experiment,*' she explained, then she switched the blowtorch off as she focussed on me. '*I thought I heard my name. Aren't you after Emma?*' Turning the radio down, she lolled back against a kitchen cupboard, waiting for me to speak. '*She's working at the Lonsdale tonight, double time or something.*'

'*No,*' I said. '*It's you I need to talk to. My name is Christina Rae. I'm here on behalf of Angelo Paulillo,*' I told her, all posh, because her own accent was quite posh, not Cockney, but not Geordie either. Maybe Yorkshire.

'*You sound like a bad solicitor, Christina Rae.*' She was laughing at me, bit of an Elvis lip of her own there. '*What the fuck does "Angelo" want?*' But she looked sad when she said his name and she hesitated before saying it, as if she didn't want to have to think about him. Until she sneered a bit more, that is. Special ex-girlfriend? I thought, and swallowed. Special girlfriend, even? I had to make sure she wasn't as special as me.

'*It's just that I took a message,*' like I lived there, '*from his mother about you,*' like I knew her, '*and Angelo is really busy at work at the moment,*' like I knew his busy schedule inside out, '*so I thought that I'd better come around to . . .*'

'*Snoop?*' she interrupted me, pineapple head all tilted to one side. '*His mother passed on the message then, did she?*' I looked away. '*What are you here for, exactly?*'

'*Nothing. I just wanted to check that you were all right.*' It was half-true. '*Angelo's mam sounded really worried about you.*' The head tilted even more, her Elvis lip heading for the ceiling. I looked away from her, feeling all lost, and noticed a photo on the wall of her with another bloke, nice-looking as well. Courage. '*Angelo and I are pretty close.*' Out with it. '*I suppose I was curious.*'

'*Nosy, more like!*' she snapped. '*I bet Ango doesn't even know you're here.*' I said nothing. It was the best way, as it turned out, because then she stopped being quite so poisonous. '*Relax,*' she said. She even smiled. '*So what did the old witch have to say about me?*'

Old witch? '*She was worried about you actually.*' Katy stared. '*Quite concerned.*'

'Now you're starting to sound like a solicitor again,' she said, levering her back away from the cupboard and putting the blowtorch away, thank God. 'She doesn't need to "worry" about me, you don't need to "worry" about me, nobody needs to "worry" about me!' Her voice went up a bit with every 'worry' and her eyebrows went down. 'And certainly not people I don't even know. You can go now, and take your little "worries" home with you.' Then she was out of the kitchen and back to the front door, opening it for me, very thoughtful. A sharp draught came through. While I just stood in the corridor, looking at the door like somebody not right in the head, she stalked back to the door by the kitchen, slamming that behind her. I trailed over to the open front door like a snail with no steroids, slithered one hand across to the handle and opened it further. But I still didn't know who she was. Angelo's haunted black eyes stared into my mind. I couldn't stand it. I had to know what was going on.

I turned back, closed the front door loudly behind me, faced the moose man head on, and walked back down the corridor to the room she'd disappeared into.

I had plans of my own for that night, anyway. Plans that didn't involve Christina at all.

Plans that involved Shelley.

Not in a sexual sense, of course, you know that. I know that Christina had always sensed a bit of chemistry between Shelley and myself, and maybe if I hadn't been going out with Christina, I might have been interested in Shelley, to be honest. But I was going out with Christina. And whatever I said to her about my reasons for going to Shelley's house, all that she would have been able to hear would have been the name: Shelley. I didn't want a load of earache about her and I certainly didn't want to hurt Christina – I was really starting to rely on her – but my business at Shelley's house was important.

That was why I had had to keep it so quiet.

*   *   *

I was hovering at the door. The shut door. I mean, it's not that I didn't trust Angelo or anything. And I'm not being spiteful but Katy didn't exactly seem his type, pineapple heed and all that, not to mention the attitude. I thought of my lovely old hair clasp, and of Angelo's lovely young hands winding it gently into my hair. Wouldn't get very far trying to push it into Katy's straw nest of a head. But who was she, then? The shut door stared at me. Bothered me. Sometimes, it seemed like life was full of doors that were closed to me. Snotty university types like her often held the keys. I wasn't going to turn myself into a Paltrow puddle for the likes of Katy – she'd only step in me – so I grabbed the handle and pushed. And got the shock of my life.

The sound of the radio from the kitchen must have drowned out my entrance because Katy didn't turn around, so I had time to take in some details of both the room and the situation. There were photos of Katy on the walls, some of her with her friends and some of her with the bloke that I'd seen before in the first photo. There was a life-sized model of a naked man standing beside her, with a string of pearls draped around his neck, a white-grey bride's veil over his head and all these handmade necklaces hanging off his Day-Glo pink, condom-covered prick. There were a thousand coffee cups spread all over the room. The settee was made up of a pair of tarty, blown-up balloon lips in dazzling 1950s red: bad, bold and very, very puncturable.

A bit like Katy herself, I realised now. She was all curled up on this blow-up settee with a photograph in her hand and her clumpy head bent over it. When she heard the door open a bit further, she turned towards me and her brow was all wavy lines. The Elvis lip had definitely lost its tone. She looked like she was too fed up even to bother with her usual 'I'm a total bitch' routine.

'Katy?' I walked across to her. She stared up at me, dead upset, and the brow lines got wavier again. Then, without saying a word, she twisted round altogether and passed the photograph over, looking up at my face as I stared down and took the whole picture in. Slowly.

It was a photograph of two men and the pair of them had

their arms wrapped around each other's shoulders. One man was young, one was old; one man was smiling his head off, the other was all serious. Both of them were attractive, both dark. They were staring straight out at me together. Weird.

Because they both had Angelo's eyes.

26. ... and Shelley's

'There are two very big opportunities that I am going to put to you today.'

This night was just getting stranger and stranger. They were so, so similar, Angelo and the young bloke, the smiling bloke, especially. He could only be one person.

I sat down, carefully, on the blown-up lips and put the photo back into Katy's hands. 'Mic?' Making her Mic's girlfriend, or ex-girlfriend, or whatever, of course. Of course?

The clumpy head came straight up. 'Obviously Mic! You didn't think I'd be going out with Ango, did you? No chance!' The Elvis lip was back and the sofa lips practically split as she bounced in disgust. 'You did think!' She laughed. 'Not my type, Christina Rae. Too much like hard work! Although you don't seem to think so, I reckon.'

Secretly, I agreed, you know. Secretly. ('Bit on th' moody side,' as Peter had said months ago.) Hard work, but worth it. 'Not at all,' I said. 'Not for a minute.' I cut myself off there before I started to sound like a solicitor again, that or a total hypocrite. 'And this?' I pointed at the older man.

She settled back into the settee again, peering at the photograph. 'His dad.' I frowned. 'Mic's dad!' I frowned again. 'Ango's dad!' Katy's voice went up. She pulled the photo right across to her, as though she was checking it, as if I was too thick to be allowed to *look at it again if I couldn't even work out something as obvious as that.*

What? 'But I thought he lost touch with them both? Years ago!'

*'That was years ago. Didn't Ango tell you that Mic had got back in touch with his dad before the accident?' I shook my head, trying to take it all in. 'Look,' said Katy, and she sighed this massive genius-forced-to-consort-with-a-*complete-*imbecile type of a sigh. 'We'd better have a coffee.' Grabbing two of the less mossy-looking numbers from the floor, she clinked back towards the kitchen again, dropping the photo into my hands on her way out. 'Seems like this could take a while to get through.'*

I had decided to try a different way of getting through to Mic.

It was one of the few channels of communication I had avoided up until that point. I was more wary than most of opening myself up in that way, and especially of the risk of opening myself up to evil, to hell. But what is hell? What kind of God would invent it or allow it to exist? Every hour, I thought about Mic, every hour of every day. Nights too. And so often, the image I had of him was that last one, the one of him lying on his own on that pavement. That was hell.

So I'd decided to take the risk.

Katy's definitely got her eyes fixed to the future, I thought, looking around her living room at the photos of her in clubs, at barbies, parties, and at the jewellery she'd made that was spread all over. In a way, I wished that Angelo was the same. Coffee mugs clashed in the kitchen. But wasn't it his intensity that I loved most? His passion?

Just as I thought that, I saw a poster on Katy's chimney breast.

It was called The Lament For Icarus *and was by somebody called Draper. I couldn't believe it. It was of a young bloke,* well *muscley body, and he had these* huge *angel's wings attached to it. Looked like he'd come down into the sea (even I could remember that part of the Icarus story from school), then there were these three very white water nymphs trying to look after him. No wonder they were lamenting him, Icarus, that is: he was gorgeous. Well worth pulling out of the sea. But it looked like they'd got there too late. I thought of Angelo's description of Mic's death, of his singing and his shoes, and then of the shaft of sunlight that had caught the lorry driver's eye. Flew too near to the sun. I looked from the poster to the photo and from the photo to the poster: Icarus and the smiling man were identical, give or take a curl. Mic. I looked again; I couldn't get over it. Mic, but with wavier hair.*

Seemed like Mic was pretty hard to forget, even for someone like Katy who was trying really hard. I thought of the way that Angelo always talked about Mic as if he was still alive. What chance did Angelo have of ever forgetting him?

I had my questions worked out as I walked through the centre of the Town to Shelley's. They were the same questions I had tortured myself with for the last months, over and over again. Can you forgive me? Can you ever forgive me? Will I see you again?

That last one was pretty hard for anybody to answer and Mic had never been exactly the religious or spiritual type. Mind, neither had I until all of this had happened to me.

I knocked on the door.

Katy walked straight in, two mugs of coffee slopping about in her hands. She was wearing dazzling green party contacts, I noticed, as she shoved a mug into my hand, and she looked about my height too. We've got a few things in common then, whether she likes it or not, I thought: blonde hair, bad eyesight and small bones. Except my *hair was natural. Even smart-arsed Yorkshire student types have their problems! Now who was being a bitch? Maybe she could read my mind. There was a hint of a sly smile on her face as she passed the coffee across, which was the closest she seemed to be able to get to doing friendly, as far as I was concerned, at least, so I seized my moment and opened up with the questions. 'How long did you go out with Mic, then?'*

'Oh, it was about a year, on and off,' she said. 'We met at a friend's house here in the holidays. We were both in our last year, me at Birmingham Uni, Mic at Sheffield.' She tugged at one of the naked man's chains, hard. Good job his prick was made of good, strong, very pink stuff. (He was well suited to make love to that settee any time he felt like it. Pink passion!) The chain was covered in big, coppery crosses, like kisses. 'Jewellery and graphics. Me and Mic. Then I came up here to try this,' she twisted a link, 'and he got a job down there. Not that I always saw a lot of him, what with his course and then his job.' She grinned. 'Not to mention, him and Ango were practically joined at the hip. They burned more rubber on that precious bike than Mic and me burned together in a whole year in bed.' She tugged harder still on the chain; I'm sure his gemstone eyes were watering. 'But he was great for a laugh – Mic, I mean.' She stopped fiddling with the chain and looked away from me. 'More than a laugh.' She looked up at the poster and then back at me. 'How's Ango doing these days? Still going to the gym every spare minute?' Her gaze flickered up to the muscley angel. 'Still at the dreaded casino? Is that where the two of you met?'

Must have had 'croup' tattooed on my brow. And Angelo never went to the gym now, ever. 'He's getting by,' I said. ' "Dreaded" casino? Why do you call it that?' It's a really smart casino, I thought.

'Mic's mother, of course. She rings me occasionally.' Katy pulled off his strings and swivelled a pearl. 'Not what she had in mind for one of her boys.' Then bit it. 'Uugh, pure plastic. Ango's pretty bright, you know.' As if I didn't! 'I think she's a bit lonely, to be honest. Have you met her yet? Can't she be a pain?'

'Then why did you ring her the other night?'

'Usual reason: a bout of maudlin depression I was too pissed and too pathetic to fight off. And maybe I "worry" a bit about her

myself!' She grabbed the kiss-crossed coppery chain off the hard man's prick, edged it gently over his veil and hung it around his neck, where the biggest kiss of all lay flat against a pinky-purplish love bite that somebody had drawn on his neck with lipstick. 'And one other reason, a really unusual reason.' The photo was plucked out of my fingers. 'Mic's dad. Christmas and all that. He's even more cut up about Mic and Ango than usual. We exchanged phone numbers at the funeral. Didn't seem to go together, Mic and funeral.' I looked up at the gorgeous drowned man on the poster and knew exactly what she meant. 'He's desperate to see Ango. He's spending a lot of time in the States. He's got a couple of kids from his second marriage, a girl and a boy.'

'But that's brilliant.' I was really pleased for Angelo. 'Surely this will help Angelo to come to terms with losing Mic? A whole new family! And if his dad is keen to make a go of it, then ...'

'Shut up, Christina!' Katy did not suffer fools gladly. 'Just for a minute.' My teeth clicked closed. 'A word of warning. Ango finished with his last girlfriend for that little suggestion.' My bottom lip dropped a good inch. 'And the next day, he left university.'

They were all in there already: Shelley, her friends – mainly girls – and a couple of blokes I could tell from the off were pissed. I was the only person there from the casino, apart from Shelley herself. She had lit some candles and put some black sheets all around the place, and there was music going in the background. The ouija board was there, a proper one, right in the middle of the table, and they were all sitting around it.

I walked across to the table. 'Only one seat left to fill now, Angelo,' Shelley said. 'Make yourself at home.' She stuck a pint glass of beer into my hands, which was the last thing I wanted. 'Then we can make a start.'

'With Ango, I think that it's when there's a combination of different things going on that he blows. You know, goes right

over the top.' I nodded. Katy carried on. 'I mean, losing Mic was devastating for him. Then there was the falling out with his mother.' So she knew about that. *'And on top of all that, his dad makes an appearance at the funeral, wanting to take part in some kind of an Italian Cilla Black-type reunion! Bad timing. Ango just told him to go and fuck himself!'* That didn't sound like Angelo at all. I caught Katy's gaze. *'Well, not in so many words.'* She shrugged. *'But he didn't want to meet up with him, or even speak to him. Definitely not.*

'Mic had wanted him to, though. He was always on at Ango about it, telling him to let the past stay in the past, all that stuff. And you can see it from their dad's side; I mean, the guilt is just about killing him, especially after what happened to Mic. And he can remember them both from when they were cute little kids, you know?'

'But Angelo doesn't remember his dad from that time at all,' I interrupted her.

'I know,' said Katy. *'I had to tell him who his own father was at the funeral. That was shitty. His mother was away with it, really upset, so she didn't notice her ex, and Ango wasn't much better himself.'* I could imagine. What had the atmosphere been like between Angelo and his mother that day? I wondered. *'Mic's mother had no idea that he had been seeing his dad anyway, I think he was building up to that one* very *gradually, and so his dad sat right at the back of the church all the way through the service, lowest profile possible, naturally enough. But even when I took him across to meet Ango after the service, Ango just didn't want to know. Blanked him completely. And he hasn't wanted to know since. The combination was too much for him to cope with. He never could stand Mic bossing him around to start with. Mic could be a bit of a wind-up merchant, really.'* Katy grinned, and then started to fiddle with the pearls again, her grin fading. *'Maybe Ango even connects his dad with Mic's death, what with meeting him for the first time, in a sense, on the day of the funeral.*

'Anyway, Mic's dad . . . Ango's *dad . . . wrote to him at*

the church, three or four times, but apparently Ango just never replied. His dad doesn't even know if he opened the letters. He can hardly go through Ango's mother, can he? And this isn't the first time he's tried to pass a message on to Ango through me.

'There's only one person Ango wants to get through to now – more than ever if anything since he died – Ango's completely obsessed with it, and that's Mic himself.'

It was so hard just to sit there and wait for the last person to arrive with all those strangers around me, and know that I could hear from Mic in a short time. I ended up drinking that beer anyway. I wanted to get out of my chair and walk around the room, around and around the room, again and again, until I'd stirred up some energy, made some changes happen. But I couldn't do that in a room full of strangers. Anyway, it was all of our energies that would be needed to stir up something real between us on the ouija board. Together. They all seemed pretty chatty and friendly with one another, handing around the wine bottles and messing about with the ouija cards, doing the usual stupid, 'Is there anybody there?' sort of crap.

I sat there on my own. First the beer went down and then a glass of wine. Shelley came across with the bottle. 'Chill out, Angelo,' she said. 'We'll have a great laugh when Tim gets here.'

'I haven't come for a "laugh", Shelley,' I said to her. 'I told you that.' I had told her a little bit about Mic when she had first mentioned the ouija session to me, one night in the casino, but I certainly wasn't going to talk about him in front of these strangers.

'I know, Angelo,' she said, and filled up my glass with more wine, pulling her chair in beside mine at the same time. Her arm touched my arm, and her sleeve smelled vaguely of onions and old, vanilla-scented cigarette smoke. I thought of Christina and caramel, of Eurydice and the Maenad women. 'Have a drink.' The Maenads tore Orpheus to pieces. Orpheus, *orphne* – darkness. At last the final person arrived and we could start.

Obsessed. Angelo's imagination moved backwards, trying to turn a spirit back into a body, and Katy understood that. She knew she could turn a man into a moose, a prick into a jewellery stand and, I looked down at her 'coffee table', a foul 1960s wardrobe mirror into a table. But she knew she couldn't turn a corpse back into a lover; knew she had to get herself a new man, however hard that was.

Yet surely a relationship with relatives, without any old grievances attached, could only help Angelo to move away from his old obsessions? There was even a new little half-brother and half-sister to get to know. And surely our relationship was too close now to be threatened just by my making a suggestion about his father that Angelo might not like? I was determined that he should make the most of this new chance.

'What's he like then, Angelo's dad?' I asked Katy.

'Well, you can see from the photo what he looks like,' she said. 'I don't know exactly what went down between him and Ango's mum, he didn't go into that at all, which in itself is a good sign. At least he didn't try to blame anybody else for the fact that he lost touch for all that time. He designs cars, works for Alfa Romeo, amongst others, spends part of his time in England and part in America – pretty well off, if you're interested in that kind of thing.' She grinned when I scowled at her. 'Like I said before, he's very interested in Ango – doesn't want to risk cocking it up with him now. What happened to Mic has made him doubly sure about that.

'Anyway,' she said. 'There's a bit more information for you here.' She got up from the lips and walked towards a chest of drawers, pulling out a fat letter. 'That's why I was working on Ango's mum to get him to contact me. I haven't got his phone number and I hoped she'd be able to get through to him somehow.' She waved the letter at me.

'Mr Paulillo's written to Ango again,' she told me. The

letter – package – was all lumps, bumps, American stamps and excitement: I couldn't wait to give it to Angelo. 'It arrived last week. And he said in his letter to me that this time it was really important that Ango should read it.' She squashed up the party contacts, trying to remember properly what he'd said. 'Mentioned something about there being a "big chance" waiting for him.'

I was that excited, I even smiled at Katy. 'I'm sure Angelo is ready for this. This will really cheer him up.' I grabbed the fat package from out of her fingers.

Ever made a *complete* arse of yourself? In public? Well, you might as well hear about how I did it.

The second their fingers were on the glass, the messing about got worse. What with the stupid music, the blackout material and all of the shouting, it was impossible to get any sort of atmosphere going at all, apart from that of a kids' playground, that is. To them, it was just a joke, the whole crowd of them. But to me it was deadly serious, partly because I really needed to talk to Mic, and partly because I knew that you don't even mess with mirrors and dreams, let alone ouija boards, with seven people concentrating on them. Still, that's no excuse, is it?

The first few times that somebody took the piss, I just gave them the glare and hoped they'd take the hint. I waited for them to get into it properly. There was a lot of shaking of the blackout material and 'shivering' of the candles and every time there was so much as a word spelled out on the board, they all went into spasms. I took another swallow of my wine and waited for the novelty to wear off. One of the girls, Joanne, was 'talking' to her grandfather and she was shouting her head off at every stupid word he 'said' to her.

'What do you mean, what colour knickers am I wearing? Oh, yeah, that's *exactly* the kind of thing he used to ask me when he was alive,' she was saying. 'Fuck off, Granda!' More giggles. 'And that's exactly the sort of thing I used to say to him. Not!' More and more ridiculous messages. The glass was getting so much pressure that I'm surprised it didn't crack there and then, and I was beginning to feel the same way myself. 'Becky, stop shoving that glass! I can see it's you!' Joanne said.

I had to say something then. 'Look, this isn't a kids' game. You tap into some powerful forces with these things. Show some respect.'

'Yes,' said Becky. 'Angelo is right . . .' Silence, for a second. 'Don't you know that if you break the glass, the evil spirit comes out of it to get you?' She turned into her idea of a spirit and waved her arms at them all. This made her practically piss herself with laughter and the rest of them joined in.

'Maybe the spirit wants a drink,' another one of them said and she spilled some red wine over the top of the glass and on to all our hands. I pulled my fingers away from the glass and reached back for my jacket, ready to leave.

'Wait a minute,' said Becky. 'Something really is happening now.'

The movement of the glass was different, jerking and angry, jarring Becky's wrist, so I dropped my jacket at once and watched. It moved around all of the letters one by one, randomly, crazily, then for the first time that night, it looked as if it was floating, almost.

It was a slow, a painfully slow, process.

'A-n-g-e-l-o . . . m-y b-r-o-t-h-e-r . . . i-t i-s M-i-c . . .'

Angelo's family! I twisted the letter in my hands. 'I'll give it straight to him when I see him. We'll have a talk about it: I'm sure it'll be great.'

'I'm not,' said Katy. 'Not unless he's made a hell of a lot of progress since I last saw him. Go easy on him, Christina. You know he can't stand being told what to do.'

Neither could I, not where Angelo was concerned, anyway. 'He has made a lot of progress!' I said. I knew he had. 'I'll go round to the church now.' Angelo's place was just a walk away from Jesmond. 'This is a brilliant time to talk to him.'

'. . . M-i-c-k.' I really lost it then.

I spun straight around to Shelley: only she knew I had a brother whose name sounded like that. She evidently didn't know that Mic had never in his life spelled it with a 'k', or that he hadn't called me 'Angelo' for years, and she probably had no idea how much she had upset me with her stupid joke, but that wasn't how I thought of it right then.

'Think this is funny, do you, Shelley?' I twisted towards her in my chair. 'Is that why you asked me here? To take the piss?'

'She was only joking, Angelo,' Joanne butted in. 'Sense of humour failure, or what?'

'Angelo, I shouldn't have . . .' Shelley at least looked embarrassed. She put her hand on my arm. 'Look, you're right. It was stupid. I . . .' Seeing my face, her hand fell from my arm and she lost it. And so did I. The frustration of losing Mic was building and building more every day, the futility of trying to get him back, of willing him to come back to me, any part of him, any word. And now this. I felt like punching Shelley in the face.

I swept the board to the floor with one arm and upended the table with the other. The glass, spirit or no spirit, bounced to the floor and one of the candles fell too. Joanne shouted out, hot wax splashed against her skin, but I was past caring about any of them then. I left them to their squawking, pushed open the door and headed home for some peace.

I was glad when I got to the church. The mood I was in, I didn't want to see anyone. But the minute I walked through the door, there was a loud knock on the other side of it.

*   *   *

I burst through his door with the letter in my hand, a speech on my lips and not a brain in my head. What's new?

'Angelo, look at this! There was a message on your answer phone . . . I thought it might be from Brett or somebody, so I listened to it for you and it was from a girl called Katy.' His face blackened instantly, but I had expected that, so I rushed on and tried to chivvy him out of it. 'You'll never believe what she had at her flat for you!' I pushed the fantastic American package into his hands, distracting him, before he had time to analyse why I'd snuck off to Katy's without telling him. It worked.

He held the parcel against his chest, put his hardest, coolest expression on and headed for the iron stairs. And he didn't come down for at least thirty minutes. In all that time there was not a sound, except for the slightest rustling of paper occasionally. I knew better than to disturb him. When he did come down, his face was tight with tension. Tension and what else? Hatred. I couldn't stand to have him tap that hatred, have it spill out all over me: God knows, I'd done little enough to deserve it. But Angelo couldn't stand to hold it in: one look at his face would tell anybody that.

I had to begin some place, and so I started at the most obvious place. The most obviously wrong place.

'What did your letter say, then?'

She had never told me, my mother had never told me, that my father had had an affair. And Mic and I had been so tiny. There must have been no one for her to talk to at all.

What she had written in the red notebook, about me blaming her when I was a kid for losing my father, was right; I realised that as soon as I read his letter. All the time I was growing up, I had thought about my dad. My mother was under a lot of strain, with two boys, a job and a house to look after as well, so when she'd snapped, shouted or been impatient with Mic or me, at the back of my mind, I'd thought that that was what had turned my father away. Now it sounded more like *he* just couldn't cope with having kids. I understood some of my Italian grandmother's pithier comments about him now. But neither she, nor my mother, had ever badmouthed my father to me and I realised all at once what an effort that must have been, for my mother in particular. I saw the situation from a completely different angle.

I grew up. And I knew for the second time in one night what a complete arse I had been.

Still, I did not want to speak about it to Christina: her meddling, her picking my phone up, her meeting with Katy, these were all betrayals. Besides, I had so much to absorb, I didn't want to trivialise it with instant conversation. I sat down in a chair on my own.

Christina got brighter still then, like she always did when she was nervous, and the smell of her fear rose sharp above her perfume. 'Anything interesting?' she asked. 'Must be great to hear from him.' Great? She was making it worse and worse, but she didn't seem able to stop herself. 'I know it must have been a shock and everything, meeting him for the first time at the funeral . . .' Even Christina shut up then. She had been talking to Katy? About Mic's funeral? Then she blundered on. 'But Katy said that Mic was desperate for you and your dad to meet. She said that . . .'

'Forget whatever Katy said,' I interrupted her. 'Forget about what Mic said, all that time ago. When will you all realise, I am not Mic? I am *not* Mic!' Silence.

When Christina spoke again, she was quieter by far. 'What did your dad say, then?'

'Nothing to do with you. Stop asking me these questions!' I gestured at the phone. 'Does that phone belong to you? If you're so keen to know about it, why don't you have done with it and just read the letter for yourself?'

What I did next amazed me as much as him, but I was learning at last that if you lie down in front of men, flatten your bristles and smile, they just wipe their stinky feet all over you – without smiling.

I clattered up to Angelo's room and picked up the letter from the bed.

Dear Angelo

There are two very big opportunities that I am going to put to you today, and you can take up either one of them, or both, as you prefer. But what is worrying me most is that you may not have read my other letters. You have not replied to me and I can imagine several, understandable, reasons why that should be. So just in case my earlier letters are still unopened, or in case you have destroyed them, let me at least try to explain why I did not try to contact you in the years when you were a child and then a teenager.

Your mother was an excellent parent and from the second you and Michael were conceived, or even before, she adored her two sons. Our early marriage had been intense and passionate, and, as a mother, Jeanine was intense and passionate also. I was a young man, a spoiled man perhaps and certainly an impatient one, not mature enough to cope with losing the attention of my lover, as it seemed to me, and shortly after your birth, I began an affair.

Your mother sensed the change in me immediately. She was bitter, hurt and defensive, while my young girlfriend was sweet, patient and supportive. And I was an idiot. I gave your mother little time to recover from her hurt, we quarrelled constantly, painfully, and then I went to stay with my girlfriend. That affair fizzled out within weeks, but the damage to my marriage was fatal. I had not been able to convince your mother to convert to the Catholic church and I was not able to stop her from divorcing me. My own mother tried to reconcile me with Jeanine several times, but this only made me more determined to stay away. Perhaps we are alike in that trait, Angelo. After our divorce, I was unforgiving and hard, but I married my present wife soon afterwards and we have been happy together.

On the unspeakable day of Michael's funeral, anyone could see that your mother was a broken-hearted woman and I would never suggest that it was her fault that I lost touch with you. What actually happened was that at the time when I had to accept that my marriage to your mother was over, I did not realise that I had two sons who very much needed a father.

Twenty years ago, it was more common to consider a mother's role in child rearing than a father's and, as you know, your mother is an extremely capable woman. For the first weeks and months, I kept in touch with you both regularly, but then the gaps between seeing you grew longer and my reluctance to disturb you grew also. I convinced myself that Jeanine would cope so well with her two boys that it was better for us all if I kept my distance. I am ashamed to say that, if I am painfully honest, the fact that I fathered two more children within three years of leaving you also made it easier for me to think that a clean break was best. But, Angelo, I never did quite manage to convince myself that I had made the right choice. The growth of the children of my second marriage reminded me so much of your infancy and your brother's, and as my third and fourth children grew, I was aware that I was missing important stages of your development and Michael's. I never forgot you, Angelo, and I never will. And I always knew, through my mother, that you were both well. But I am a man who has made mistakes.

As time passed, it became increasingly difficult to imagine a relationship with you, to imagine what you would both think of me, and to work out how to bridge the gap between us. When your mother took you back to Certaldo to meet my old aunts, I was so sad that I had not taken you myself. I knew that I had lost my two first boys.

Only one year ago, I owned up to myself what a huge

mistake I had made. That, as you know, is the time when I got in touch with Michael at university and tried to get in touch with you also. Of course, I am filled with relief that I got to know my eldest son for those months. The more I grew to know Michael, the more I realised that my two eldest sons needed a father every bit as much as my two youngest children did. This is the biggest thing I have to offer you, Angelo. Because whatever mistakes I have made and however much you despise my judgement, I am your father and I am your own blood. I would love it if you could let me try to make up for what I have done wrong and the ways I have hurt you or shocked you in the past.

I would not criticise you, Angelo, I would not criticise you at all, but I could see that on the day of the funeral, there was some difficulty between your mother and yourself. Perhaps you need a father now more than you ever will again.

Please write to me, Angelo. That is the most important point.

The second opportunity is much easier to write about and it may be that this is the perfect time for you to take up this chance. As you know, I am a car designer and for many years, off and on, I have been working here in America. The children of my second marriage are growing up now, and my daughter has left school. The youngest child would like to finish his education in America and so I have just bought a house over here in the States. (My address is enclosed.) At last I have been making some good decisions. There is a room in this house for you, Angelo, and I swear to you that even if you never contact me and never come to America, the room will remain yours and no one else will ever be allowed to sleep there.

Michael told me that you were happy when you were studying at your British university but there are many excellent universities here. I have enclosed some of the prospectuses in this parcel so that you can see the choices open to you. I would be happy to assist you financially, if this would help. And now Katy tells me that you are working in a casino in Newcastle. Once again, I would be happy to help you in this, and I enclose addresses and advertising material for the big American casinos within travelling distance of this house. I also enclose two, open, return tickets to the airport nearest my home.

You may decide to enrol at an American university, but to live in a flat or a shared home of your own. You may decide to work in a casino here, but to travel with your English colleagues and perhaps set up home with them, or with a girlfriend. You may decide to remain in England so that you can be near your mother and your friends. Perhaps you will even decide to return to Tuscany; I have often thought of doing this myself. Angelo, you must, of course, make these decisions yourself. The most important thing to me is that you make me a part of your life, even the smallest part. I would be so happy to see you, even if you simply decided to visit me for a holiday.

Please write to me, Angelo. Those people who have betrayed themselves and the ones they love must be more careful than the innocent to avoid betraying again. To avoid hurting again. I understand what I have done, believe me. If I do not hear from you, then I will call in at the church to see you when I come back to Britain, on the fifth of January. Write to me.

Anthony

The poor bloke! So this was how Angelo reacted to people who made mistakes and told him about them? I thought back to his sexy woodcutter's story, that night, singing secrets through the soil! I had been right all along to bury my worst secrets.

I felt like he had really let me down.

And I thought back to our Seven Wonders of the World conversation, when Angelo had mentioned, casual as anything, that he'd been to 'The Carolinas', that he'd worked in America for a while. It was easy enough for him to ignore two free tickets to America, but nobody had ever given me more than a new top, or a nightie, in the whole of my life! He took so much for granted because he'd always known that fresh opportunities would be coming his way: university, travel, books, inheriting churches, furniture, money. He expected that sort of thing, could make it happen himself, too, because he'd come to expect it. My life wasn't like that. You can't very well inherit a council house, can you? And you can hardly expect two people without a GCSE between them to help you when you're stuck with your homework, then stay up all night writing The Which Guide to University, *either. Angelo had been given so much more than he knew. Best of all, his dad wanted to make up with him more than anything else in the world. And he sounded lovely.*

I stalked my way back down the stairs. 'And this has nothing to do with me? Two tickets to America and the chance of making contact with casinos in the States, not to mention a family over there waiting for you?'

The look on his face, you'd have thought there'd've been a hurricane, not the offer of free tickets to America. 'That's not the way I want to take you to America, Christina,' he said, quite quietly.

'I don't need to be "taken" anywhere. But I just don't see the point of giving a massive opportunity like this away, either. Giving two massive opportunities away!' He was trying to keep his face all still, and his eyes were cold. 'Aren't you even curious about meeting him? Meeting them?'

'No.' His response was so quick – so quick and such a lie.

I tried my first tactic again. 'What about me, then? You know I've been planning a visit to America for months, then all of this falls into your lap and you weren't even going to tell me about it, were you? This is a present – not a punishment. Grab it!'

'No.' Again. 'This is nothing to do with you.' He shook his head. 'It's between me and my dad. There's no need for us to be having this discussion at all.'

*　　*　　*

But have it we did. Hour after hour, it seemed. And the more that Christina interfered, the more layers of resistance I built up. I'd always thought I'd got that hardness, that distance, from my mother's side, my English side. Now I knew differently.

Round and round the old arguments Christina and I went. How about a visit, for just a few weeks? Then, Would I consider just going there for a holiday? What about reading the material and considering the casinos and universities there, just *thinking* about them? Was even writing a letter a possibility? A phone call?

But how could I fit in with a family I had never met? And a family that had shown little interest in meeting me until after Mic's death? Even his signature, Anthony, made him sound like a stranger. Twelfth Night. The end of the celebrations and the eve of Epiphany. What would I do if he just turned up at the church? How could I even start to explain to Christina exactly how awkward I felt about meeting these people? *'Difficult.'* Not like my brother, of course – *'confident'* Mic, *'sunny'* Mic, the *'special son'*. And how could I tell her that I was especially wary of reliving the clumsy, nightmarish horror of Mic's funeral? I knew more than anyone about betrayal, so why couldn't I forgive my father easily? Because it wasn't easy – it was very, very complicated. And the more Christina questioned me, the more she tried to simplify it, the more I clammed up, until I ripped the tickets to bits and she admitted defeat, called a taxi and went home.

Why couldn't Christina understand? I thought, as her taxi juddered away. And most importantly, most horribly, of all – why were we always arguing now?

I was pretty depressed, sitting there in that taxi on my own. And I'm dead ashamed of this, but when I lay down in bed at home, I had a mega-Paltrow moment at last and practically drowned my poor pillow. Because there was Angelo, wasting every chance that he got, talk about elephant memory, and there was me, dying for any chance to make a difference to my future. Christina Rae, the Queen of Opportunities!

Anyway, by the time I got to sleep I felt a whole load better. The only person who could make any difference to my life was me, I'd always known that. Seeing Angelo close his eyes to chances like that made me more determined than ever to make the most of mine, if and when they came.

The Hot Spot

27. Flaming Lamborghini

'Watch yourself. And watch her.'

Why couldn't I sometimes, just sometimes, be a bit more like other people? Looking back now, I see that this is when I should have cooled the situation right down, not stepped it up. But after one of those big days, and bigger let downs, the first thing I wanted to do when I got up was to see Irene. She was one of the few people I knew I could still rely on. It was noon before I woke up, I was off work, and by the time I was heading for Irene's, Christina must have been just about at the casino.

Work. Again! Christina Rae, the Queen of the Workhouse. But it wasn't really like work in the casino, not like hard work in a factory anyway. It would be a good laugh.

For a start, there were a few others from my training school on the shift: Peter, Shelley and Alex. (Susie Stuffer had left by then: couldn't take the hours and the clean air!) It had been ages since that many of us had been on a shift together, so I was really looking forward to the gossip in the breaks. They were together in the staffroom when I walked in that night, with the Red Jersey bearing a few new scars from an over-enthusiastic battle with the iron on a soft-focus day. I knew I looked a mess, but I didn't want to lose brownie points with the management by admitting my cruelty to the prized, mutilated Red Jersey. Please don't let anybody notice my dress, I thought to myself, as I walked through the staffroom door.

Fatal. Peter started to laugh the minute I appeared and didn't stop until choking was a definite possibility. Please. He pointed his finger at the mark, shaking his head as if he couldn't believe it, until he recovered his breath enough to speak.

'Chrissie, what the fuck's happened to your dress there? Fuckin' Jack Russell heed. Cannet even iron her own dress.' He walked across to me and took a closer look, hooting at me deafeningly – Al Pacino, only a foot taller and with much bigger lungs – then he went to slap me a high five but I slipped in a quick stomach punch. 'Ha! Fuckin' melted her own dress down, got the cookin' mixed up with the ironing. Fuckin' hopeless, man. Lasses!'

I rolled my eyes at him. 'Talking a load of crap, as always. Just because you think you're some sort of male model!' Peter was a pretty snappy dresser himself, no burn marks there. I poked his arm as hard as I could, but he just soaked up the attention, laughing and jabbing me back. You couldn't get annoyed with him, however hard he tried to make you. 'Happy Christmas, Peter,' I said, and stretched up to give his chunky cheekbone a kiss. He wiped his cheek, dead dramatic and male, but still looked pleased.

'Aal the old trainin' school is here, Chrissie,' he said, waving his arm over to the corner where they were sitting. 'Beamish Heed, Museum Mooth is here.' Alex was twenty-five, the oldest from our training school, and brainy. 'Even fuckin' Sasquatch is here.' Shelley was a bit self-conscious about the size of her feet. 'We'll hev a great neet.' It felt like we were a family, the old training school. It always felt like that.

For most of the night we did have a 'great neet'. It was when I left that the real trouble began.

'Season of goodwill?' said Irene, as I walked through her door. 'Ne chance. That Mic hes been givin' me ne peace at all.' Her grey sleeve waved me to my seat and she didn't even pause to make a cup of tea before she started talking. 'Am I pleased t' see you!'

She sat down beside me and started to talk. 'Well, th' first thing that's been happenin' is that he's been singin' to us, th' same song as before. Eeh, but he sounds that sad, Ango. There he goes again. Aye, we know, son, we know. "Female of the Species" . . . I'm tellin' him, man! Let us get a word in edgeways!'

Mic must have meant Christina. Remember how he'd sung that song when I first met her? *'He was so protective of his brother.'* Too protective? More information would help. 'What's he trying to warn me about, then?'

Irene, or Mic, was pretty direct. 'He sez y've got t' watch her with the men, Ango. I think that's the gist of it. "Watch yourself. And watch her." That's what he's sayin' t' me, word for word, Ango. "Watch yourself. And watch her."'

I must admit, I enjoyed the attention when Peter, Alex and I did a shift together. Not that Peter's attention was exactly flattering; he spent most of his breaks insulting us as per.

He started on Shelley the second she walked into the staffroom for her first break. 'Hoy, Sasquatch! How're ye managin' a real job, like? Withoot the workin' lads t' help' y' oot and pay y' grant f' y'?'

Shelley was too used to this attack to bite properly, but she had her defence pretty well sorted by then. She smiled at me – she was dead friendly to me that night. 'I didn't get a grant: it's all loans now. And do I look like a hippie?'

'Aye, well, y' hair's a bit on the slippy side, like!' Shelley had her hair gelled back. Peter leaned across and scrumpled a bit of it up before she smacked him away with her hands. 'Tryin' t' cover it up. That's aalways a sign. And then there's y' fuckin' Linda McCartney eating habits. Cannet gan oot o' th' hoose unless y've got a veggie burger in y' hand. Aalways a sign!'

'Just because you eat an ox every day doesn't mean the rest of

the civilised world has to, Peter! Get off my head!' She swatted him like a fly flapping its wings at a bull.

'Ye lasses want to eat more meat,' he said, patting Shelley's head with his dinner-plate hands then pointed a finger at me. 'Fuckin' Jack Russell heed there might've been more've a proper size if she'd have got some proper food into her, like!' Then straight back to Shelley. 'Fuckin' leisure centre life! We cannet aal hev rich mams and dads and massive hooses like ye, y' knaa. Fuckin' royalty!' Shelley's parents lived in a three-bedroomed semi in Hull, which Peter knew. 'If I'd've hed your chances, I'd've been Prime Minister noo, Shelley! And what are ye?'

This was one of Peter's favourite lines, and Shelley and I joined in with him, in our (quite good by now) versions of his booming voice and accent. 'A croupier, Peter. A fuckin' croupier! Exactly the same as ye!'

Peter grinned. 'Aye. Exactly. Well, that's aal I'm fuckin' sayin', Shelley. Reet?'

'Reet!' We shouted it at him, praying for it to be true. Then he started up again.

'Aal I'm sayin' is, reet . . .'

'*Watch her.*' Those words were in my head during the rest of my conversation with Irene. '*Watch her.*' They followed me down her path and into my car. '*Watch her.*' Irene's voice in my head, Mic's voice in my head, repeating it over and over again.

'*Watch her.*' '*Watch her.*' '*Watch her.*'

Watch her.

They were a pretty miserable lot, the punters, considering it was the festive season and all that. Mind you, they were dressed up like they were off to a wedding at the least, not a casino. That set me off thinking about my *wedding,* my *beautiful white wedding, to my beautiful dark Angelo, naturally. Our wedding, the meeting of the Old World and the New, Naples and New York, fashion and fast cars. Naples has got a* massive *shopping centre, you*

*know. Maybe Angelo would take me there to buy my dress? Our
wedding.*

Dream on.

Wedding of Christina Rae and Angelo Paulillo

A wedding took place today between Miss Christina Rae, the
Stateside celebrity, and Angelo Paulillo, her delectable long-term
partner.

The ceremony was held early this morning on an isolated Caribbean
beach. The air was heavily scented by the dark red roses and white
roses which were scattered around the pale sand, arranged in Miss
Rae's waist-length hair and in her extravagant bouquet. Miss Rae wore
a short, voile, Italian wedding dress and a floor-length veil. Angelo
Paulillo looked magnificent as usual, all dressed in black, except for his
very white grin. The beach was crowded with glamorous guests.

OK? *Dead excited, Angelo would be, underneath his* Godfather
*hard act. Would his dad be there to see it? I wondered. And
his half-brother and sister? There'd be tiny bridesmaids, big
bridesmaids, pageboys, guests from the casino, family, friends,
ushers, the lot. Dead carried away, I was. Maybe I'd ask Peter,
though he looked more like a bouncer than an usher. That made
me smile and remember where I was, and the second that I smiled,
I caught Mr Gold's eye. He smiled back, not realising he'd just
been to the wedding of the century.*

*I'd thought a few times that night that Mr Gold had been
watching me. He'd come in at about six, after his January sale
and before his journey home, I guess. Did he get lonely then? I
thought to myself. Anyway, for the last three hours of my shift,
wherever I was in the pit, Mr Gold's eyes were on me. I mean, he
was quite reasonable-looking really, for a thirty-year-old – blond
and tall – but not a touch of Jude Law in sight. Still, he was quite
nice in a business-manny, rather than a Hollywoody, way, if that
makes any sense. But it was Angelo I loved, and Angelo who loved
me. I hoped he was managing OK after our row.*

At half-eight, as I walked out for my last stint in the pit, Gerry told me to go and open up a new blackjack table, right beside the one where Mr Gold was sitting.

I thought about it all afternoon in the church. I thought about it all evening. Seven hours. I couldn't talk to Mic about it, I couldn't talk to Brett about it and I definitely couldn't talk to Christina about it. The very thought of my dad and his new brood of kids only made the whole thing seem even worse. What could I do, then?

'Watch her.' 'Watch her.' 'Watch her.'

Watch her.

He must have been watching me – he came straight across to my table. I spread the cards out on the red felt for the crowd and I spread the smile on my Ferrari Reds for Mr Gold. He was always so friendly and chatty, all the other dealers liked him. 'Dead canny' was what they all said.

'All right tonight then, Mr Gold?' I asked, as I carried on spreading the cards to show the world that there were no aces slipped in or out of the pack. Cross my heart. 'Had a nice Christmas?'

'Fine, Christina!' He never said much about himself really, not like some of the others. I think casinos were the only places some of them could go where anybody would listen to them droning on about themselves: their flashy houses, flashy women and flashy businesses. But Mr Gold wasn't like that. The bloke who'd just moved across to sit beside him was: Ricky Wednesday, a singer, I knew him from the Dunston dawn chorus days, but he was concentrating on the card checking so I could chat to Mr Gold.

'January sales do their stuff, then?' I asked

'Yes, they did. Thanks for asking.' He tilted his coffee cup at me like a glass of champagne. 'Nothing in the shop as valuable as you, though. Pure platinum.'

'Of course.' That was pretty generous of him, considering the clip of me in my red burn victim. I carried on spreading the cards,

thinking for the first time that maybe Mr Gold was a bit shy. Maybe that's why he came out with those terrible lines?

The noise of the shuffling had broken old Ricky's concentration and I turned to him with my next line in small talk, croup-style. 'How's it going with you then, Mr Wednesday?' We always had to talk to the punters like that, all formal; it was a rule. I hadn't been half as polite to him when he'd been a customer and performer (what a performer!) at the Dunston club. Farty Friday was the name he'd got there, and that was his name in the staffroom at the Casino Club by now as well, if he had but known it. Well, we had to get our revenge somehow!

'Fine until I came in here, Chris.' A massive sigh came out of his pursed lips as he spoke. 'You'll be having a hell of a New Year on my account, the lot of you.' I slammed the cards into the shoe. Slight touch of aubergine to the nose, I thought. Mmmmm. *Lovely! Old Ricky was obviously doing his brains. Why didn't he go home then, and eat Christmas cake, or cyanide, or something? I mean, you don't go into a really expensive restaurant and then start crying your head off when the bill arrives, do you? Then he twisted the knife. 'Bit classier than the club at Dunston, eh Chris?' I never told* any *of the casino staff or the punters where I'd worked before the casino, although Jonty knew, obviously. Ricky was deliberately winding me up – worm!*

Mr Gold rescued me. 'Will you be working here at New Year, Christina, or will you be off to one of these jet setting, casino parties I'm sure you all have?'

'With my *money!' Ricky was getting tricky. 'Nearly a thousand quid tonight.' He slapped fifty pounds' worth of chips on to his box like an idiot, and waited for his cards.*

'I'll be here, Mr Gold,' I said, smoothing it over as nicely as I could while I dealt the cards out from my pack. 'I'll be here for you. As faithful as the North East snow.'

Even old Farty Friday grinned at that. The game played on.

I would go to the casino to meet her, I decided. Just to check if she came out on her own and got into the taxi on her own. Or would she share a taxi with Peter? They both lived west of Newcastle, so it was possible.

Maybe Mic hadn't been talking about other blokes. Maybe he meant something completely different, like the little lies that I already knew about, and I was worrying about nothing but old Irene's actual interpretation of what he'd said.

'Watch her.' That was all that Mic had said. *'Watch her.'* *'Watch her.'* *'Watch her.'*

Watch her.

'Soft sixteen.' Always a tricky one. Sixteen soft millimetres, that was about the size of Farty Friday's manhood, by my guess.

'Pull!' he said. In his dreams. I slapped his card down, dead professional.

'Too many,' I said, in the mildest of mild voices, all calm, as I stacked his cards into the shoe. I dealt my own cards and clicked Mr Gold's winning chips up against his pile.

'Ball breaker.' This was muttered under Farty Friday's breath, having checked that the inspector was watching the other, busier, game at that second. It was a standard, slimy punter's technique when they were losing. 'Slut.' He'd have got a mouthful for that if we'd've been in the club in Dunston, but I didn't want to risk my job over an old wanker like that, so I kept my lips stapled, for once.

I pretended I hadn't heard and shuffled my pack, a bit harder on the cards than usual. I was hoping now that Ricky Wednesday would lose the next hand, of course. I was starting to hope that he would lose his hair, his teeth and his testicles as well: they were on their way out anyway, I reckoned, but I kept my mouth shut. There were flashy security cameras and flashier dreams to be considered. Play on.

I diverted myself. Animal, Mineral or Vegetable? Vegetable, definitely. There again, maybe Ricky was more animal than vegetable. One of my sister's Christmas presents to me had been a celebrity cookery book and we'd curled up on the settee together on Boxing Day, hooting over a recipe we'd found for bulls' penis stew. You can imagine what I was cooking up in my mind. Battered Bollocks and Chips. Ricky's Dicky, Deep Fried. He was really getting on my nerves. Bollock Burgers with Relish! Served him right for calling me a ball breaker.

I dealt the cards: a six for Farty, a nine for Mr Gold and a queen for the house. I kept my head down, out of the firing line of Farty's filthy mouth.

'Pull.' A king for Mr Gold. Good card.

'Pull.' It was almost torn out of Farty's mouth. An eight for Farty. 'Bitch!' he said.

'Do you want another card or not, Ricky?' He was even getting up Mr Gold's nose.

Farty ignored him completely, but he carried on with his game. 'Pull.'

'Too many,' I said, all quiet still, tucking Farty's cards away, and he made this really loud snort. Although I was trying not to let him get to me, I was starting to feel upset.

I dealt myself a king and Mr Gold really smiled at me, even though it meant he had lost.

It was nearly ten to nine so I set off for the casino in the car. If she came out on her own, I would jump out and offer her a lift. If she came out with Peter, or one of the other dealers, I would follow her. And if she came out with a punter, what would I do then?

Watch her.

The next hand was worse, or better, still. Because my first card was an ace, and then my second king arrived. Blackjack. I really am in mink knickers tonight, I thought. Or rather, Mr Andreas was. Gruesome image! I tried not to smile. I was also desperately trying not to look at Farty Friday's face as his cards went back into the shoe, the bin.

'That is enough!' Ricky exploded, nose more aubergine than ever, as I swept his chips away again. 'I haven't had a decent

hand since Chris opened this table. Gerry! Get this girl off my table. Gerry!' He was waving his arms, looking as though he was about to have a heart attack at any second. I wish.

'I'm sure the feeling's mutual, Ricky!' Mr Gold, telling old Farty Friday off! 'Pity Christina can't have you taken off the table.' I nearly had a coronary myself. 'It's not the girl's fault.' Mr Gold, sounding like a real, mature adult – not the kind of behaviour I'd come to expect from a punter at all. Dead canny, Mr Gold. And maybe more.

Meanwhile, I was pretending to be somewhere else, the inspector was working out whether he dared say anything or not and Gerry was running across the pit towards us in a right panic. Ricky Wednesday sighed, thumped the table and threw the last of his chips down on the floor as he stropped his way out of the casino.

Once the wobbler was well and truly over, everybody turned back to their games and their dealing, and my shift was soon over. I smiled up at Mr Gold as I was taken off my game at nine o'clock. He gave me a big smile back and a dead cool nod. Apart from Ricky Wednesday's performance, it had been a good shift, but the rest of the night ahead was starting to look a bit bleak, to be honest.

The last thing I was expecting as I stepped out for my taxi home was to find myself back in the Colosseum again.

I waited outside in a corner of the car park with a good view of the doors. I stared through the smudged glass of my car window at the casino's red and gold interior.

What exactly would I say to Christina when she came through those double doors?

Watch yourself. And watch her.

As I came out of the casino, still in the flaming Red Jersey, Mr Gold came running out behind me.

'Sorry about that, Christina. Bit unpleasant, wasn't it?'

Wasn't he *unpleasant? I thought, old Farty Friday, I mean.*

'You *don't have to apologise for anything, Mr Gold,*' I said. 'You *were the perfect gentleman in there.*'

Christina came out on her own. She walked outside to wait for her taxi with all the lights from the outside of the casino lighting up her hair like a nimbus. She looked glad to be out of the building, looked a bit tired. *'And upon her head, a crown of twelve stars.'* I was just about to run across to her and take her in my arms, forgetting everything Irene had said. I opened the car door.

Then that smooth blond jeweller guy walked out behind her and she looked up at his face and smiled. She actually *smiled*. At him. Twelfth Night, the bitter end of the celebrations, was on its way for me. Watch her. And watch yourself.

That was the moment when I started to lose everything.

'People who can't afford to lose shouldn't play,' Mr Gold said, *shaking his head a bit. 'He should be barred from the place.'* I *wasn't going to get into that one, very unprofessional, so I just smiled until a staple hurt. Mr Gold, the King of Diamonds, I thought. The Red Jersey's burn scar glittered fetchingly as it caught the exterior lights of the casino like a jewel.*

'Listen,' he said, and the eye contact gave me the warning that he was going to move in on me, 'do you fancy coming for a drink with me tonight? A meal even, Christina? Say no if you'd rather not, but I just don't feel like going home yet and the company at the casino's not fantastic this evening.'

I started up my 'no sex with the punters' speech. 'I'm very sorry, Mr Gold. It isn't that I wouldn't like to go for a drink with you, but the dealers just aren't allowed to see customers outside the casino.' He shuffled his feet a bit, and I knew that he knew he was getting the brush off. 'I'd be risking my job if I were to . . .'

My speech would have saved both his face and mine, but as I was halfway through it, I noticed a pretty long-looking face, more

*long than pretty, it has to be said, at that exact point, heading its
way across the car park towards us.*

Watch yourself, I thought as I walked across to them.
Christina wasn't the only one capable of making mistakes,
I knew that well enough.

But listen, I felt that there was so much energy, heat,
red pain and anger, coming off me, coming off me in
waves, that they'd be able to see it from where they were
standing.

*Angelo? What was he doing there? He stalked across the asphalt
towards us, dead slow, dead moody, looked* daggers *at poor Mr
Gold, and then he came right over to my side. He looked at me
as if he couldn't stand to speak to me, then glanced away from
me and spoke to Mr Gold instead.*

'Christina's coming home with me.'

*Poor old Mr Gold looked as if he wished Christmas, the Casino
Club, croupiers and Christina Rae had never been thought of. But
he didn't move away from Angelo.*

*'Get in the car, Christina,' Angelo said, turning his back on
Mr Gold completely. 'I'll tell Paula you don't need a taxi.' He
waved at her through the doors, gesturing at his car.*

*I looked across at Mr Gold, I felt so ashamed, and he lifted
his eyebrows, meaning, 'Are you OK?' They were nice, Robert
Redfordy, eyebrows.*

*'I'm fine, Mr Gold,' I said, shaking my head and feeling a
complete fool. 'Fine.' I wondered what his first name was. He
nodded once, walked* slowly *past Angelo, and got into his big navy
Jag, all leather inside. All warm inside. A Brown's Lane man.*

*'Get in the car, Christina,' Angelo said again. 'Now!' It's a
wonder he hadn't suggested I sit in the boot! And I was such
a doormat it's a wonder I didn't just open it up myself, climb
in and have done with it, because I was sick of the rows and
the hassle with him. So I walked across to that old Fiat without
saying a word.*

I just nodded. That worried me too.

You won't believe *what Angelo did next, for all his posh Gosforth upbringing. It was the most humiliating moment of my life and I could never once discuss it with him later.*

Christina actually spoke to him first, 'I'm fine, Mr Gold.' As if *I* was bothering her.

That really got to me. I walked across to his car – he didn't move off, just sat there looking at me – and I tugged down my zip in two goes and pissed, washing his car door in hot piss, bathing him in contempt. I did my jeans up slowly, looking through the window at him, willing him to come out to me. He stared at me, just stared, then he twisted his head away and clicked the ignition key.

'Don't look at him,' I said to Christina as I climbed into the car beside her. 'Keep your eyes on the road.' I couldn't stand it that she had looked up to him and smiled.

Neither of us spoke for a while after that. I couldn't bear to speak to her, my mouth was full of acid and so was my mind, but as I headed towards the church, she turned around to me and said baldly, 'I'm going back to the flat.' It was as if she couldn't stomach saying my name out loud. I hated her then. She looked cold and small and pinched and hard. Ugly. I hated her.

I loved her. You know that.

The car wrenched its way along the road and hurled itself into the kerb, scraping at the paintwork and the bodywork sickeningly before I yanked the wheel away and got us out of it. Shit! Fucking jeweller. And I'd spent the very last of my money.

I jerked the car into a parking space beside her flats and turned the engine off. 'Was it the blond hair that did it, or was it the thought of a more mature man?' I asked her. Her silence needled me. 'Or is it his six jewellery shops? That the attraction, is it, Christina?'

*   *   *

Those were Angelo's last words, after he'd put the pedal to the metal, flat out, practically totalling his old car. Hung like a horse, is he, Teen? I thought, as he pulled away. That the attraction, is it? Jonty's voice and Angelo's joined. Fused. My voice was silenced. A bit of Angelo's spit lay in my lap. And I realised for the first time that I was actually frightened to look into his eyes. I couldn't let myself be frightened of his eyes.

I got out of his maimed car, talk about flaming Lamborghini, slammed the door just about off its hinges and headed for the lift.

Days of Thunder. *But I was Kidman without Cruise. Did I want him to follow me?*

Did Christina want me to follow her? I didn't know. I didn't care.

I sat outside her flat for over half an hour. For most of that time I was looking at the floor of the Fiat, fuming. Looking down, always looking down. And looking back. I felt like I was leaking poison and hate. I knew the number of her flat from when I'd sent the roses. Red-black, bleeding roses. It took me forever to calm down.

And then the doubts started. What if Christina slipped out through another door and I lost her? What if she was gone by the time I tried to find her? I should at least have walked her to her door. In the time I sat out there, I saw a dozen people go into the flats and quite a few go out. They were a rough crowd, the lot of them. I didn't want one of them anywhere near Christina, let alone in the same building as her.

I couldn't stand it. I had to talk to her.

I thought that Angelo had gone. There was no way of seeing the parking spaces from where my flat was. I changed into my ordinary clothes, thinking about him all the time. Black eyes and the blonde. What had happened to them? So much for trust, a one-way road for Angelo's battered car only. I waited for his knock at the door. No knock came. The shame and the anger were burning me up. Maybe some bubbles and some warmth would make me feel better, 'Wash that man right out of my hair' and all that. Wash Angelo – and his self-destructive streak the size of an open-cast coal mine – out of my hair. It works sometimes.

Not that time. Too many feelings to be cleansed. Angelo. I was trying to rub him out of my head with every bubble that burst. Angelo. I was wishing he was there with me with every bubble that burst. Angelo. I hated him. I loved him. You know that.

I'd left the door very much on the latch.

It must have been gone ten o'clock when I heard this thumping on the door and a kick of a foot, even. Angelo. An angry Angelo by the sound of it, but still Angelo.

I hauled myself out of the bath, Radox bubbles everywhere, and into my towel, then dressing gown, and headed for the door. I was dying to see him there waiting for me.

I had to wait for ages before there was a chance to rush in behind some punky-looking girl with a key, blustering excuses as I pushed my way in. Anybody could blag their way into those flats, I thought, as I made my way up to Christina's. At last her door was in front of me. I was dying to see her, but I was also very angry, and not sure at all of what I was going to say. Why had I damaged the car? Couldn't I just feel *less* about people?

I couldn't. I never had been able to. And I never had been able to turn the voices, all of the different voices, away. Watch her. And watch yourself.

It was as if Angelo's jealousy had conjured a spirit out of the air and up to my door, as if he'd conjured a nightmare out of a day.

'Jonty!'

Jonty?

28. The Tower Block

'And you could do nothing to help?'

'This how the Italian Stallion fancies you then, is it, Teen? Casual? I was never that impressed, myself.' Jonty was in through my door before I could push it to or even shut my mouth. Amazed. And afraid – shaking with it. 'Long time no see. Just thought I'd pop around to have a chat with you,' he said. There was vodka and something else on his breath: he stank of it. Strong lager. Shit.

My hands went up to my face and Jonty's meaty hands came out to pull them down. He pushed me right back across the living room and into the bathroom again, invading me, pinning me against the window wall in there. Breathing on me: 'Nice and intimate in here, isn't it, Teen? No party walls to worry about. We can have our own little party in here, can't we? Because you shouldn't have dumped me like that, Teen. Girls like you don't do that to blokes like me. They just don't do it.' He was rubbing his dick the whole time he was talking to me, rubbing it with his fingers and shaking his head. 'Not to mention you lost me my job. There was no need for that, was there? Not over an accident like that.' Up and down. 'We had some good times in this flat, didn't we, Teen? We had some really good times here.'

He was that close that the lager on his breath was stinking in my face and I could see a bubble of slaver and a crumb at one corner of his mouth. Yet he smelled clean behind the booze. He was far too close to me and seemed bigger than ever in my tiny bathroom, squashing up against me like he was. I felt smaller than I ever had in my life before.

'We could have good times again.'

We could have some good times again, I knew we could. If we could only sort this out.

Wrong door. Panic. Remember. Remember the number. Remember.

If I could only find her flat.

'I never had good times, Jonty. Not with you, you know that.' My right arm was hurting where he'd scratched it against the wood of the doorframe. Jonty's eyes squeezed shut, as if he was trying to squeeze hurt out of them and failing. His hair looked really fair, which meant he'd just washed it, and I felt guilty, for some weird reason. Then his head came up and his hands squeezed my arms, tight.

That was what was bothering him: I could see it all over his face. It was why he couldn't leave me alone. He couldn't make me happy, ever, and he knew it. If he hadn't looked so furious, and he hadn't carried on rubbing his dick the whole time, I might have felt sorry for the nasty bastard. What I actually thought was: Is he going to rape me? And am I going to hold up this cardboard wall here while he makes up his mind?

I lifted my head, and could see myself in about three of the mirrors on the bathroom walls. I was backed up against a map of the States that I'd put on the bathroom wall, but I didn't look like I was in the States. I looked small.

I looked like I had never got out of Gateshead at all.

There was only one way I could think of to sort Jonty out and it was disgusting.

'Good times,' I said, smiling at him, hard. Acting my way out of it. Smiling. He leered back and relaxed a bit, pissed as he was. 'We always had good times, Jonty. You know that.' He smiled more.

I bent towards him and gently moved his hand away from his dick. I made myself not shudder. I rubbed him with my hand, up and down, and I put my other hand beneath his balls and started to squeeze. His trousers were thin and new. My fingers were on the seam between his legs. It was like being a prostitute, disgusting, humiliating, but it was all I could think of to get me out.

It didn't take long. What with the lust, the weakness and the drink, he was slumping against the wall opposite in seconds. Perfect. This drippy expression was smeared all over his face. My eyes were clear as far as he was concerned, always had been. Sex. That was the way to control men. Complete role reversal. I smiled at Jonty: he deserved it now. *I kept the one hand on his dick and the other beneath his balls, I looked right up at his face and squeezed as hard, as cruelly and as long as I possibly could.*

The noise he made was the most frightening thing of all.

I have never heard a scream like it, screams like it, not even that night she fell down the stairs.

One scream was Christina's and one scream was a bloke's.

Have you ever screamed as loud as you possibly could? Ever? You should try it.

It was a scream that freed me, a scream that connected me to the man in the painting and the voices in the church, but it was my *scream this time, filling me with oxygen and life, yet sounding as terrible as death. It filled the room and it made me big, bigger than Jonty, easily. It made me free.* Little Voice? *Chris Rae joined with Jane Horrocks, joined with Robbie Williams, joined with Judy Garland, joined with the air.* Big *voices. It was the complete opposite to that Christmas night when I let Angelo control my body like that.*

Christina Rae, the Queen of Screams, had found her voice at last.

The doors to either side of her were boarded up; it was dismal. It felt like I was stepping inside a Hitchcock film, but I felt such a surge of energy from hearing her scream like that, that I didn't think twice about what I was doing. *'And you could do nothing to help?'* I would do everything to help now.

I opened the door and walked inside.

Christina was standing in the middle of the living room in this poky little flat, even smaller than I'd imagined, staring at the corner of the room, wearing nothing but a thin dressing gown that was open at the front. I followed her eyes. Sticking out of the doorway of another room was a bloke's big foot. I had definitely heard a bloke's scream.

What the hell had happened?

'Angelo!' I didn't know what to say to him, didn't know what to think of him now. Because everything had changed at once. No, that's not it: I had changed at once, changed into me.

Christina turned around to me in slow motion, saying my name, her hair tangled and her mouth and eyes open very wide. Full of fear, I thought. Only it wasn't fear at all. It was a kind of energy, a magnetism, all of her own. Magical.

'I've done it!' she said. 'I've done it. You don't need to do anything.'

'What about him?' I wanted to know, waving at the foot. 'What did he do?'

The foot moved back into the bathroom, disappeared for a second, and then Jonty was in the doorway, looking bigger and uglier than ever in Christina's tiny flat.

I was across the room and banging his back against the wall before I could think and before he could move an inch away from me. I put my face right next to his and I snarled at him, practically, facing him down. I felt like tearing lumps out of his skin. I actually gritted my teeth, making it hard for me to talk.

'What the hell are you doing here?'

*   *   *

'Goin'!' Jonty said to him. 'I'm goin', Ango.' And he dropped his eyes down and shrugged himself out of Angelo's hands. It was as if it was between the two of them, somehow. 'Yours, like I said before.' There was no audience this time, so Jonty was that much quieter. Angelo went to open his mouth, he still looked pretty amazed, but I got in first. This was between Jonty and me.

'Except I never was yours, Jonty. You know that. You've got to leave me alone.'

'Don't worry, Teen, I wouldn't touch you.' He was that taken aback he wasn't even swaggering, or spiteful, any more. Shocked sober, for once.

It was a good job. Angelo looked like he was ready to kill him, dismember him and just about eat his insides raw. I put my hand on his arm and he didn't shrug it off or move towards Jonty, however much he obviously wanted to. He turned towards me instead.

'Did he hurt you?' he asked, with this real tension in his voice. But real caring too.

'No,' I said. Angelo and I were looking into each other's eyes now, ignoring Jonty altogether. 'He didn't hurt me.' Jonty couldn't hurt me because he'd never touched me in the first place. It was Angelo I had to worry about on that score. I rubbed my arm above the elbow. 'He tried to, but he couldn't.' I reckoned Jonty had had enough. He'd got the message all right.

'Leave it,' I said to Angelo.

'Leave it,' Christina repeated. Her eyes were so steady and so serious. I knew exactly what they were saying. How many times had I looked at Mic like that? I've dealt with it: you don't have to. It's my problem, my life, my father, my mother. And now, my Christina. There was no way she'd have let Jonty into the flat either: I'd seen her bruises, seen her tears. Leave it.

I felt like killing him.

'Get out!' I said, when I could finally contemplate moving

my eyes away from Christina's and towards his. Gripping the skin of my own arms was the only way I could stop myself from doing him some damage. But when I turned to Jonty, he was already heading for the door. I kicked it shut and the little flat shuddered. I put my hands on the door and locked it behind him, then I forgot about Jonty altogether.

I was much more worried about what Christina would have to say.

Angelo was actually tearing at the skin on his own arms in his efforts not to tear Jonty's face apart. But this was no time for sympathy. It was time to talk.

'I'll say this only once,' I said, and I meant it. 'There is nothing between me and Mr Gold. Never has been. He's a nice bloke, I like him, if I wasn't seeing you, I might like him more, but I've never been out with him, I've never touched him, I've never kissed him. I've only dealt him cards. He asked me out. I was just saying no when you walked across.' I was never normally that straight with Angelo, or that serious. It all came out in one breath, until the last bit. 'If you can't believe that, can't believe me, then we're finished.' I really meant it.

She meant it, the whole lot. She meant it.

'If I wasn't seeing you . . .' and *'He asked me out.'* Leave it. She'd said no. She'd come home with me, even though I'd acted like a complete arsehole. *'He's a nice bloke.'* Leave it. She was still with me. She'd put her hand on *my* arm, she'd touched *me*, even though I'd acted like an arsehole. Leave it. Watch yourself.

Mic wasn't there now and Christina was. I'd never thought I would think like that, ever. I didn't want to move away from Mic in stages, couldn't bear to lose the raw hurt, all that was left of the closeness we'd had. *'Raw life. Raw love.'* But I was losing it. And I was very close to losing her.

I sat down on her settee and turned my face away.

*   *   *

There was one really loud sniff, one big shake of the head and then Angelo lifted his face. He was trying not to cry. But as soon as he saw my face, his face got all red and worked up, his breath caught, his tongue touched the tip of his teeth and tears spilled down his cheeks before he could even cover his face. His mouth opened too wide then, like it was locked into a horrible death grin. He never *cried. He hadn't even cried when he'd told me about Mic. He started making a funny sort of huffing noise, as well, and rubbing his nose and face, not like when I cried at all. Trying* not *to cry was making it ten times worse. His skin looked all yellow and ill and oily, where it wasn't red and puffed up around his eyes and nose. I was half attracted and half put off by it, the crying, I mean. It was so extreme.*

It was so Angelo.

What the fuck am I doing? I thought. Mic was gone, my mother was gone, and university, and half of the friends I'd had there. All I had left was my job in the casino and the so-called new start with my father's family that I knew I would never take up. And now Christina was going. I hated myself.

And there were all these posters around the place – stills from films, photographs and advertising posters. Humphrey Bogart and Lauren Bacall were in a clinch right over her bed and another poster of Lauren Bacall told me where Christina's waterfall pose had come from. In the corner of her room, there was one of those cardboard models that they have in cinema foyers that even I recognised from *Titanic*. It made me realise all over again just how young Christina was. I could see her dream world all around me. I was what, who, she had wanted all along – most of the men in the photographs were dark and tall, exactly like me, but they hadn't just let her down completely, like I just had.

As soon as I was calmer, more normal-looking, I would go. I headed for the bathroom.

I kept my head down in there. When I'd got it together enough to look around me, the first thing I saw was that she had a map of America on the wall and the second thing I saw was a smear of blood, beside the sink. It was dripping down in the steam. Was it her blood, or Jonty's? I had to know.

I walked into the living room and said to her as softly as I could, 'Whose blood is that in there, Christina? Can you tell me what happened now?'

She lifted the cushion from the space beside her on the settee, making room for me, and I started to hope, just hope that there was a chance with her. Please God, I thought, give me one chance and that will be all I'll need from you. Ever. I remembered suddenly that I'd thought exactly the same thing the day Mic died.

So I sat Angelo down and I told him all about what had happened. Exactly what had happened. I even told him how I had touched Jonty, and why.

'It might not be what the self-defence experts recommend,' I said, 'but I had to get rid of him somehow – that's the only reason I could have for touching Jonty. Gave him the shock of his life. About time!' I laughed, but I had no idea how Angelo would take it.

Because little Chris Rae from Gateshead was taking life by the balls and grabbing it at last!

I laughed before any of the hundred other possible reactions could make their appearance; it was the perfect punishment for Jonty. Then I thought, He could have really hurt her while I was stewing away there in my car outside. That thought stopped me laughing as quickly as I'd started. If I got my one chance, then I would ask her to move into the church with me, I decided. But could Christina forgive me?

Maybe if Angelo could laugh like that, in his present state of

*mind, when I'd just told him about me touching another bloke's
bits, then maybe, just maybe, there was a chance for us. Back in
the celluloid business at last. I really loved him. I'd never loved
anybody like that before. Surely that was, is always, the most
important thing?*

*I smiled at him, dead steady. Some of what I felt must have
shown in my expression, because Angelo screwed up his eyes as
if he was thinking, 'Is that right, then?'*

*I nodded at him, one tiny nod, and took my last independent
breath for ten minutes.*

One chance, that's all that anybody can ask for and, this
time I'd got it. Thank you, God.

I held Christina to me until she couldn't breathe and had
to push me away to get some air, laughing. Then I picked
her up and carried her across the room to where her bed
was: I wanted to erase Jonty forever from her skin. And I
wanted to love her.

When I laid her on the bed, her dressing gown came open
over her breasts, and I kissed her neck, face and throat. Her
skin was full of light and almost transparent against the pale
blue of the dressing gown.

*Then Angelo turned into a dive-bomber, and my teddy was the
bomb, attacking my neck and stomach and face, making these dead
dramatic 'rat-a-tat-tat' noises as he went. And then Angelo turned
into a cheetah or something, and he scratched and bit and purred,
and generally made a whole load of fuss and fun and drama as
usual, until he pulled my dressing gown right off with his claws.
I was freezing cold, my hair was still damp, so I jumped inside
the quilt, pulling it back with my hand.*

And then I made love to her, with all of the feeling that I
had, until our love healed us and the new, pink skin was
formed. A new time for us. It was all that I wanted.

*   *   *

And Angelo was murmuring to me, murmuring that he loved me so much, that it was because he loved me so much that he was too protective, but he was sorry, he knew what a pain it was, what a pain he was, and I had a body like an angel, did I know that, and did I know how rare it was to be loved like I was loved by him, that he would do anything for me, that he'd never meant to hurt me. His voice and his touch and his love were all the same thing, and it built and built and built, as if we were walking up a ladder together to see this just fantastic view at the top, like the view from the flats, almost.

Just when I thought about that ladder, he started to talk again about Jacob's ladder, and men and women, merging into an angel's body, like the Angel of the North, and watching over people, like the Angel watched over my mam's house in Gateshead, and what a beautiful thing we made together, and had I thought about living with him, in the church? A magical thing. The magic stopped. *How did he know my mam lived near the Angel? I'd always told him she lived in Jesmond (although I'd been building up to a confession on that front, and even a meeting, maybe). And living with him? What should I say?*

I asked him a question instead. I couldn't risk letting him know that I'd listened to his phone messages – 'Don't worry about what happened in Mic's room' *– so I tried a sideways tack. 'Before you moved into the church, Angelo, was there some kind of a scene with your mam?' His body tensed up straightaway, letting me know that I was getting warm. I snuggled in to him. 'I mean, why not live at home for a while?'*

'We had a row.' The skin on his arm actually went cold as he lay there, remembering. 'It was stuff about maybe I could have done more to help Mic, or to help myself, amongst other things. She was always comparing me to him, when he was alive and afterwards.

'When she went to work one day, I took Mic's things from his room and got rid of them. I just couldn't stand her raking over the whole thing again and again. By the time she got home, the room

was practically empty and she told me to move out. I wanted to move out.'

No! *I turned away from him in the bed automatically, shocked. What exactly had he got rid of? Mic's bike jacket? The pointy shoes? Mic's degree certificate? Poor Mrs Logan must have felt as if she was losing Mic all over again. Was Angelo jealous of everybody, not just of me and Mr Gold, or whoever? Could I cope with that level of jealousy? Every day? Could I cope with Angelo, every day?*

When the talking and the touching was over, and Angelo seemed to be relaxing beside me, I had this ache in my chest. I knew it was rare and I knew it was beautiful, and I knew Angelo was both, but still I had this awful *sadness hanging over me that just wouldn't go away. This awful loneliness.*

I felt like I was loving Angelo goodbye.

There was no chance of sleep. Why had Christina turned her back on me after we had made love and talked so intimately? Why was she lying so stiffly, quietly, as if she was sad? I couldn't bear to ask. My throat ached. I know the church might seem weird to other people, but I was used to it, while I *wasn't* used to Christina's high, noisy flat.

And one thought, one burrowing, badgering, thought, kept coming back to me. Maybe the 'messages' that came from Mic, the messages that I depended on, didn't come from him at all? Maybe they were put into Irene's head from *my* head, *my* will? Maybe they came out of my need to hear from Mic, or my own distrust of Christina, or my fear of trusting her, if that's a different issue? Old Irene was one of the few people who knew exactly what had happened to Mic. She'd been at the inquest. We'd never talked about it, but she knew all right. How much did that affect the messages she passed on to me?

Those ideas took Mic further from me still, reduced him from a solid person to a liquid perfume to a vapour. Gas. I wished I could snatch the ideas back, swap them for the certainty that Mic's messages were 100 percent genuine, 100 per cent Mic. I couldn't.

But I could push the thoughts behind me, push myself back into the present and think again of Christina. So I lay in bed beside her and I held her in my arms until she fell asleep. I touched the skin beneath her eyes again, remembering how her eyelids were scented with flowers on Christmas night in the church. I bent to kiss her eyelids and this time they smelled of just skin, skin and Christina. In a way, I was relieved.

And I did sleep, eventually, in a lighter way than normal. It was permanently dawn in there, because of the lights from all the other flats around it, which was hard for me to cope with, the half-light. Those flats felt like they were swaying; it felt like you were out of control somehow. I know it was stupid, but I was sure that I could hear birds and bats and bees and wasps, flying in the air around the flat again and again in the night. And then there was the buzz of traffic, and the general electrical buzz of a city. Christina's voice was there too. *'He asked me out.'* And even, *'I had to get rid of him somehow.'* All night, I felt as if I was being pulled apart by the noises, and I kept half waking and half sleeping, until I wasn't sure of the difference between the two. Then my own voice was calling for Christina, questioning inside my head, my dream. My waking mind had no nails to grab my dream: my dream slipped through its clawless fingers and fell right into the back of my mind. The feelings stayed, though. They always stayed.

'Christina!' I heard the voice in my dream first. My dreams were full of insects, bats and questions, chants almost, and God knows what, and the image of the painting from Angelo's flat, with the dead-looking babies wound into its frame, kept appearing and disappearing, and I felt disorientated and strange. But as I woke up and remembered that Angelo was there, I wondered whether he had been shouting my name. Shouting it in my

dreams, or in my bed? I wasn't quite sure which world I was in for a while.

Then I thought that Angelo was having one of those awful, or fantastic, or whatever experiences again, his voice was so loud and strange. I was sure he was awake, but when I looked at his face, I could see in the light from the block opposite that his eyes were closed tight and he was still lying on his back in the bed. His mouth was going, though, as if he was questioning himself or somebody else. And he was tossing and turning around like he was in a fever or a fight, or both. I put my hand on his brow and it was as hot as if he was ill. What voices did he hear in his head, even when he was his normal self? And was it Angelo's voice that had woken me up, or had I sensed his feelings another way? Maybe our dreams were connected, I thought.

I put my arms around him and he relaxed all at once then. He really needed me, much more than other men need people. But I was worried that he found it so hard to manage in a different environment.

I slept last and woke first. My head was full of the same old questions. Did Christina fancy the guy from the casino? Did she actually want to touch Jonty, whatever she'd said? Would she like to start something up with Peter? I lay there, trying my hardest to wish them away, trying my hardest to wish a part of myself away – the jealous part. For over an hour, I tried my best to push the destructive thoughts, the questioning thoughts, away. And then Christina woke up, opened her eyes, turned her head and looked at me.

She smiled. I looked down towards her open, lovely, question-marked face. I touched her cheek. I had to ask her.

Angelo looked lovely. Even his funny half smile was there, the one I loved so much, and I shook away my sleepiness to focus on him, smiling back into his gorgeous, dark eyes as he leaned over me. Then he opened his mouth.

'There's just one thing that's bothering me, Christina,' he said, and he did that stupid little cough. Shit! 'How do you feel about that jeweller punter? Exactly, I mean? What is it you like about him?' I opened my mouth to get him to shut his, but he was on a roll, couldn't seem to stop himself. 'And Jonty? Was that the first time you'd seen him since that night of the accident?'

The ache came into my chest. I felt awful, but I knew I couldn't let myself be squashed by him any more. I thought again, How did Angelo know where my mam lived? He'd been following me. How many times? What was he hoping to find out? And would he ever be satisfied, however often he followed me, whatever secrets he dug up?

I thought of the girl on the pavement, that very first time I saw Angelo, and how she went back to the bloke after all he'd done to her. How many times had she done that? I made myself look at Angelo and his eyes were full of nightmares, just like I knew they would be. Even my mouth didn't want to say the words, nothing came out at first, but I had to make them heard. I owed it to myself.

'Go, Angelo. You'll have to go.'

One chance, my one last chance, and I had thrown it away.

29. Gold

'Angelo followed his brother. He'd always followed his brother.'
'Six jewellery shops. Pure gold.'

Even as I said it, I knew I didn't want him to go. Even as I said it, I knew he had to.

But where did that leave me? It left me about ten thousand feet above sea level, in a dingy flat, right beside Bengal, rocking in the sky, on my own. Typical. Angelo got up and left without a word, looking like death itself. It was hard not to call him back, he turned around at the door for a full five seconds, but his questions, his doubts, were just wearing me down. Happy New Year! Christina Rae, the Queen of Party Time.

And despite the fact that I had been so definite about turfing Angelo out, I was just as definite about wanting him back. Every day until New Year's Eve crawled by on crutches. Surely Angelo wouldn't let the New Year go by without getting in touch with me? But surely I owed it to myself not to go back to somebody who would spy on me, question me and mistrust me any chance they got? But I'd spied on him occasionally, when the need arose. Not constantly, though. There were no easy answers. And this was no easy time.

I still enjoyed my work at the casino: the clicking of chips into piles, the rustling of cash into boxes – it was reassuring. Felt like the only part of my life that was still the same. But I didn't know whether to look forward to working the same shift as Angelo or dread it, he looked so depressed.

One night he was off altogether, which meant I worried about him the whole night, whether he was all right in the church on his own or not. But perhaps that meant I had done the right thing. Did I really want to be with someone who found it hard to hold down a job? Exactly like my dad, even if for totally different reasons. But I felt so much for him. What should I do?

It was ruining my sleep. It was ruining my job. It was ruining my life.

Life in Bengal was rough. One night after work, I sat in my flat and I tapped, unwrapped and attacked a whole Terry's chocolate orange (which didn't help) and then drank a bottle of white wine (which really *didn't help) until the tears seeped out of my eyes and orange oil and alcohol seeped out of my pores. Only the inside of the loo bowl looked worse than I did the next day. My mother just said good riddance to bad rubbish, Italian men were that arrogant and would I perhaps think about Jonty in a new light now?* Good *advice.*

For days I did nothing but grieve.

For days I felt as if someone had died, it really was that bad. I was blunted by depression. What was the point of going to work? What was the point of staying in? What was the point of thinking about Christina when I'd blown it with her?

I turned to the last pages of the fragile notebook, without much hope that they'd be able to help. They were pages I had never read before and my mother's handwriting looked different, flatter.

Torn. A woman who gives birth is torn forever, changed forever. She sees her body split: the new life splits from the old and she sees the inseparable

---

separate. For me, Angelo's passage followed Michael's. Angelo followed his brother. When Angelo was pulled, with metal, from my body, my body tore and bled as if it had lost a limb. For Angelo, losing Michael was like losing a limb. He tore. How could he be the same afterwards?

When Michael left home for university first, Angelo got a part-time job to pay for a mobile and all the visits down to his brother. Then when Angelo travelled around Europe and America, between school and university, Michael would fly out in the holidays to stay with him.

And then they bought the bike, together, and Angelo saw Michael dragged from him, saw his blood, his brother, torn away from him through metal. Why did I expect Angelo to carry on with his degree afterwards as if the accident just hadn't happened, to carry on in his mind as if the accident hadn't happened? He just couldn't do it. Because what happens when you separate the inseparable? When the atom splits? When death separates off from life? It's either a start or an end. I'd just lost one son: I didn't want that to be the end for the other.

Michael's death was the biggest shock of my life. Everything about it was wrong, including, especially, my reaction to it. I would never have dreamed that I would react to it in the way I did, but how is a mother expected to react to the death of her child? Unthinkable. And I grieved alone.

Angelo followed his brother. He'd always followed his brother. I tried to drag him back to normal life, to university, to health, to sanity, as I put it. Put it too crudely. Too quickly. Too brutally. Angelo was torn between me and Michael, birth and death. And always listening for a message to tell him which way to go, just as he used to listen to Michael tapping messages through his bedroom wall to him when they were boys. As the months passed, I hoped that Angelo's life would pick itself up and that he could carry on as normal. But Angelo always followed his brother.

And now, my worst fear is the fear of something happening to Angelo. The fear of him following Michael. Because without Angelo, my life would be over too.

She'd understood some of it then, my mother; she'd understood that she'd hurt me, at least. She'd understood me better than I'd understood her. *'Because without Angelo, my life would be over too.'* How far did I want to follow Mic, alive or dead? What had Christina said about it? *'You're all that's left of Mic's energy, Mic's life.'* She was right.

There was one more entry, almost asking me to read it.

What does Angelo remember now? Does he remember how we used to meet up at weekends, when he was at university? How he would share his new friends, new ideas, with me, through his impersonations, his stories and books? Our laughter. Does he remember how happy he was? I used to love visiting him and his friends in his halls of residence and then in that disgraceful old farm they rented out later, with mice in the kitchen, beer in the fridge and no food in the cupboard.

And I wonder if he ever thinks about when he and I went down with Michael to Sheffield in the car when Michael started his course, Michael, singing away in the front, him laughing in the back, talking, me trying to drive and shut the pair of them up at the same time, and then the two of us going down there later for Michael's graduation? How we chatted away in the car and ate great bagfuls of kids' sweets, red licorice laces and shrimps, looking forward to seeing Michael and to celebrating the graduation together? Does he remember all of the Christmases, all of the birthdays and all of the clothes? The care?

Or does he remember just the stupid words that I blurted out both in shock and out of it, spilling like acid over him? Does he remember the times when I was tired, bad-tempered, depressed or just uninspired? Because I remember those times and those words, the very worst words, too. And I realise that those words moved down through layers and layers of Angelo's skin, right through to the centre of him. Angelo's thin skin. Because he is my son, in that as much as anything else.

And so now those words are moving their way down through the layers of my own skin. Burning. Burning both of us, because Angelo just can't forget them. And neither can I.

The next time my mother rang me, I would answer the phone.

When I went back to work the next day, when I was

right in the middle of handing out a cup of coffee to a punter, there was a voice. I had that lonely, dead tower block feeling again, jumping, looking around and knowing that no one else heard what I heard. It was the first time that it'd happened at work. *'He says the future is plastic,'* it said, *'He's got no future. The future is plastic.'* Everything seemed to be jingling, threatening, full of greed, from the dealers, the chips and the cash boxes, right up to England, America and the whole of the Western world when I thought about it later. Was this a future I could survive in? *'He's got no future.'* I didn't want to be plastic, a money machine.

There hadn't even been any more phone calls from home since Christmas Day; I was feeling guilty about that. Angels, the messengers of death. I was starting to realise that I would never be able to manage a long-term relationship.

You get the picture? Very much black and white.

It's a cliché but it's true: I was totally lost without Christina.

The only person I wanted was Angelo. Right? The only person in the world I couldn't have was Angelo. Also right. Impossible. What was I supposed to do, stay in the flat and weep? I'd tried that. Snarl at the punters and lose my job, so that I had nothing left? I wasn't going to try that.

One person I did think about, just a little bit, was . . . guess who? Six jewellery shops? Stop it! Mr Gold. Dead canny. And the nearer New Year's Eve got and the farther away Angelo seemed, the more I thought of Mr Gold. Remember what he'd said? 'Will you be working here at New Year then, Christina?' And do you remember my reply?

'I'll be here for you. As faithful as the North East snow.'

As faithful as Julia Roberts in Pretty Woman. *Six jewellery shops! As faithful and as loving as Demi Moore was to Robert Redford in* Indecent Proposal. *Six jewellery shops. Me and Mr Gold. Stop it. Honestly, all I wanted, really, was for Angelo to come back and somehow, for him to make it all right. But he didn't.*

Six jewellery shops. Pure gold.

Amazingly, it started to snow as I left my flat for work at eight on New Year's Eve.

I was almost, almost, doing a Jonty on New Year's Eve. I was following Christina. But I wasn't following her because I wanted to hassle her in any way; it was just that I knew she was on a late and I knew she'd be walking to the casino alone, from that area, just when the Town was most full of trouble. I also thought it was a good idea just to check that she was on her own, completely on her own.

Nothing much happened. I kept a good distance and apart from a couple of mouthy comments thrown at her (she volleyed pretty good returns), she was fine. It snowed on her hair and she hated that, of course, combing at the snowflakes with her hands before they could mess her up too much. If I had been with her, I'd have put my jacket over her head to keep her dry. If I had been with her.

It hurt like shit not to be with her.

I'd got a night off, so once I'd seen Christina to work, I dropped into Town to the Bigg Market where I'd arranged to meet Brett and a few of his mates for a few drinks.

I would have loved to have stood over Christina and watched her all night.

New Year's Eve and no Mr Gold. Even Shelley noticed.

'I'm sure he said he'd be in tonight,' she said. 'He's about the only punter you can have any fun with in this place.' Mind you, we still managed to have a bit of a laugh in the breaks, in the staffroom. And afterwards.

When I wasn't thinking about Angelo and what he would be up to that night, that is.

And finally, at about one o'clock, when I was on my break and feeling pretty tired of crouping, counting and smiling, Paula sent a message through that there was a phone call for me. Angelo, I

*thought. Angelo. I ran down to reception to pick up the phone. I
hardly dared lift the receiver.*

And then, at about one o'clock, something happened that
changed everything – or rather, put everything into focus.

Jonty. No surprises there.

Out on the town for the New Year, obviously. Pissed, also
obviously. And I wasn't, not as much as he looked, anyway,
so my first reaction was to avoid him. But he'd seen me, and
he gave his moronic-looking mates a wave goodbye before
heading across the bar in my direction. I had no idea what
he would say when he got to me.

'Ango,' he said, and kind of clapped me on the back. Not
going to start off the New Year with broken teeth then,
either of us. 'How're you doin'?'

'All right, Jonty,' I said. 'All right. What about yourself?'
Clubbed any baby seals lately? I thought. Battered any
women? Just as I thought that, this girl with huge brown
eyes, tiny, flappy hands and a little round face came across:
she looked about sixteen.

'Great man. Great.' Jonty was slurring like an alcoholic.
He slapped his arm around this girl's shoulders. Narrow
shoulders. 'This is Rachael, Ango. Rachael, this is Ango,
the bloke that Teen from the casino is with now.' She
nodded, rounding her eyes even more, curious, and I
wondered exactly what Jonty had said to this girl about
his heroic past with Christina. 'Did me a bit of a favour
there, Ango,' he said, putting his head close to mine, man
to man now. 'Bit of a handful like, isn't she?' I wasn't going
to bother explaining anything to Jonty, the state he was in,
and then he was away, slavering over baby 'Rache', the seal
pup, and her neck, which probably had bite marks all over
it already.

I ignored him until Brett was dragging my arm to go, half
an hour later. And then, after all the times he had deserved
it, Jonty finally pushed me too far.

He caught my eye as I was heading for the door with Brett. 'Happy New Year, Ango,' he shouted across, and then he walked over to me and put his mouth next to my ear. I had no idea what he was going to say. 'Like I say, Ango, you've done me a favour there.' He leaned nearer. 'She had an abortion, you know. Christina. There's only me knows: her ex told me. He telt her he'd never tell anybody, but he's a mate. Just between us, like. She was sixteen. Not on the pill.' Man to man. 'Like I say, I'm well rid.'

I floored him, pissed as he was, before I even thought about it, and then I headed for the door. In those seconds, I did think and I walked back to where he was staggering up, looking around for Rachael and probably wondering what had happened to him.

'Don't you ever tell anybody else what you just said to me! Ever.' I was whispering in *his* ear then. And then I left.

Was it true what he had said? Could it be true? And if so, what did it tell me about Christina? Those six words changed my whole idea of her in seconds. *'She had an abortion, you know.'* My Christina. *'She had an abortion.'* And she had never even told me.

She had killed a baby.

'Christina?' Not Angelo.

'Yes?' Who then?

'It's Mr Gold speaking. Richard Gold.' Richard? It took me a minute to take it in that he was ringing me. A silent minute. 'I just rang to wish you a Happy New Year,' he said. Tremendous. I slipped into my usual role, though.

'How nice of you, Mr Gold. And a Happy New Year to you. Everybody's been asking where you were tonight. Deserted us, have you?' My voice sounded plastic, even to me. Auto-croup.

'Not at all, Christina, not at all. It's just that I took our conversation to heart: I'm no longer a member of the Casino Club. Any time you feel like coming out for a drink with me,

you're free to do so.' He laughed, but he sounded a bit nervous. And most blokes would have been plastered by one o'clock on New Year's morning, but he didn't seem to be. 'Don't feel that you're under any pressure at all. Think about it. I'll be in touch. Or you could give me a ring. Have you got a pen there?'

I don't need a pen, I thought. It's Angelo I want to speak to. Still, there was a biro lazing around on its stand by the phone and a notepad. Pity to let a good man go to waste. Mr Gold rattled off his phone number before hanging up the phone and going back to whatever it was he'd been doing before. What did he do when he wasn't in the shop or the casino? I wondered. Richard, that is. In the shops or the casino. Six jewellery shops. Richard.

I wrote his number down. You knew I would, didn't you? But I didn't ring him.

30. Inside the Handbag

'Magical.'

It was days before I got in touch with Christina, long days for me to cool down and think in. Only at first I didn't think properly. I blamed her. I thought, Would she do the same to my child? To our child? How could she do that? She should have kept it.

And then I thought, But would you do the same to her? Get her pregnant in her teens, let her go through an abortion on her own, tell all your mates about it and let them spread it around half the pubs in Tyneside? And I thought of her house, imagined her room within it: the mother with the dry hair and the drier face, dreamless, and the father who wouldn't 'grow up'. What was she supposed to do? Put the baby up for adoption and then be dragged down by memories and regrets her whole life? She was sixteen, for God's sake. Where was she supposed to put a baby? Stick it in the corner of her bedroom in that house and watch it have exactly the kind of life that she had had, only worse? Watch it live through exactly the same kind of problems that she had lived through, with even less money and no father in sight? Watch it have the same sort of hopes and dreams when it hit its teens, and then watch the dreams drop to bits when some wanker like

Jonty, or his mate, came (briefly) on to the scene? Plenty of girls do the same, I thought, and manage somehow. For Christina, it would have been a kind of death. There are plenty of ways to die.

I *knew* what Christina wanted, I *knew*, and I was starting to understand why she wanted it so much. She dreamed of America and excitement and youth. Not babies. Not yet. And I knew how soft she was, inside.

I had a lot to come to terms with, just as she had had to three years before. It was a lot for me to cope with and coping wasn't my strong point just then. I didn't want to wreck it again. What exactly was I supposed to say to her if I did ring her up? Should I even let her know that I knew about her abortion? She obviously didn't want anybody to know – it coincided exactly with the time she'd moved in to her flat. So still I didn't ring her.

I watched her carefully enough, though. Very carefully. I watched her at work, when she wasn't looking; I watched her flat, you know, especially on the night when I knew she was on a late; I even followed her over to her mother's house, just once. And I walked past that jeweller bloke's shops, worked out where he'd be at different days of the week, that sort of thing. But I made certain that I wasn't seen and I didn't phone her. I wanted her to have some time to cool down as well. She certainly didn't look very happy.

I'd never seen her so quiet in the casino, both with the punters and the other dealers.

Mike Turner even had a word with me about it.

The time had come for one of our pay rises: that was how it worked in the Casino Club. Every couple of months or so after you got on to the tables, you would get a pay rise, until a dealer made nearly as much as an inspector, and then you would hope – I would hope – to train to become one. I'd already talked to Mike Turner about it before; he knew I was in a hurry to get on.

And I was a good dealer, dead efficient, dead friendly, quick, all that. The first pay rise, I'd been the one to be told first, out of the whole of our training school, graduates and all. Christina Rae, the Queen of Cash. It was the first time in my life I'd ever sort of won anything. I'd put every bit of my rise into my American fund that first week and since. But I knew that this time was going to be different: Peter had already told me earlier that week that he'd got his second pay rise. 'Got it afore ye this time, Chrissie,' he'd said, grabbing a handful of the Red Jersey off my back. 'Fuckin' Russell heed!' Shit! And then Mike Turner told me to see him in his office.

'Come in, Christina, and sit down,' he said. 'I want to talk to you about your pay rise.' I am getting one then, am I? I thought. Or is this the total kiss off? But I kept my mouth shut, I sat down and I smiled my croupy smile. 'I was just wondering whether everything was OK with you?' he continued. 'You've done very well with the Casino Club so far and I know you're an ambitious girl: you've got a real future here.' Amazing. But? 'But . . . you don't seem quite yourself lately.' Mike looked a bit embarrassed actually, but he carried on with the interrogation. 'You'll still get your pay rise, you're a good dealer, but you don't seem as happy with your work as you did?'

My silence was making it worse for him, but I wasn't going to help him out any. 'What exactly do you mean, Mike?' I asked.

'You've lost a bit of weight, lost a bit of your banter, your sparkle.' He sat back in his chair. 'Not quite so chatty with the punters, not quite so quick with the bets, that sort of thing.'

I didn't know how to reply to Mike, really. Dead depressing. It must have shown on my face.

'Look,' Mike said, 'I heard you had a bit of an upset . . . with Angelo, wasn't it?' I curled my lip. 'Don't take offence, Christina, it's just the casino's jungle drums at work as usual. But you've got to start thinking about yourself, getting out a bit. Like I say, you've got a pay rise to come. Have a couple of meals out, treat yourself, and don't forget to eat your meals here. Sermon over.'

I pinned a smile to my lips for the length of time it took to reach his door. I wondered if Angelo had noticed I'd been losing weight? I doubted it.

The day I noticed Christina was losing weight was the day I decided I'd have to try again with her, one more time. That awful dress was hanging off her. I'd never seen her look so low and I don't know if I'd ever felt so low myself. Enough. I got hold of the dealers' rota and I saw she had a day off coming up over the weekend, the same day as me.

I decided to surprise her. It would be harder to turn me away if I just turned up, wouldn't it? That was the best way.

Angelo still hadn't rung me. I almost rang Mr Gold up, but I didn't. I thought about it, though. And I thought about what Mike had said. 'Start thinking about yourself.' *That seemed the best advice of all.*

And if jealousy was Angelo's thing, and the casino's jungle drums were that powerful, then maybe, just maybe, being seen with the right person was exactly the way to get at him. 'You've got a real future.' *Why should I let Angelo, let anybody, walk all over me?*

So when Richard Gold rang me up one night and suggested a night out, we made a date for the following weekend.

I should have rung sooner. I nearly blew it completely.

I spent all day getting ready. I was quite excited considering I was going out with someone I didn't fancy massively, but he was nice enough, Mr Gold, very nice. We were meeting in the Town itself, near but not too near to the casino, so if I liked him, I wouldn't have the shame of him knowing where I lived, and if I didn't like him it would be easier to give him the slip and get back to the flat on my own in one piece. Not that I was expecting any trouble of the slippery sort with him, of course. Dead canny, Mr Gold.

And I'd told a couple of the more gossipy staff, old Porsche Lips included, that I was off out with somebody especially interesting, no names named, that weekend. I'd let it be known that he was a good bit older than I was and a good bit tastier than your usual run-of-the-mill date. Wouldn't take long for that to get around a few thousand dealers and then back to Angelo. And would that bring him back to me, or would it send him even further away? Served him right whatever, I reckoned. Dead hard.

When I went into my wardrobe to choose my clothes, though, I could have cried when I saw the black velvet Christmas dress hanging there. Angelo's present to me. Dead soft. And the dress I'd worn on my first date with him was definitely out as well. Still, even wearing my third-best dress and my second-best shoes, I looked reasonable: Mr Gold had only seen me in the old burn victim, so I didn't exactly have too much to live up to. I felt less sure about my feelings, half-excited and half-worried. Really worried. What would I call him for a start, Richard or Mr Gold? Either would sound pretty phoney on a date, if that's what this was. Was I doing the right thing? What do you think? Christina Rae, the Queen of Conclusions. Right thing or not, right man or not, right clothes or not, date or no date, by half-seven, I was finally ready to go.

As I went to shut my wardrobe door, I noticed the handbag that Angelo had bought me at Christmas lying at the bottom of the wardrobe, looking really lonely and neglected. He'd been so sweet that day, buying me all those things. I had to take one look at it. The red purse lay in the bottom of the bag. Magical! I turned it over and over in my hands, thinking of Angelo on Christmas Day. Remember what he'd said? 'You will get to America, Christina. Don't forget.' It was heavy for such a tiny rectangle of leather. I hadn't looked at it on Christmas Day, come to think of it.

I opened it up and there was a sheet of paper in it, wrapped around a fat wadge of new notes. I unravelled it. My jaw dropped. There was a fistful of money curling up in my palm. Surprise! It felt wrong seeing that kind of money in my hand, not some *punter's. I flexed my fingers around the notes. Wonderful. There was a note inside it too.*

Happy Christmas, Christina,
  Here's to a New Year in America and to you and all your dreams. Here's to both of us in America, together, living your dreams. I love you, darling,
  Angelo

Darling. I counted the £10 notes out, one by one, amazed. One thousand pounds! My own personal count, biggest drop ever! Darling. Would he still have loved me, I always wondered, if he had known the worst truth about me? What would he think of me, then? Spoiled? Soiled? Those voices in my head had always cracked a gap between us. I looked down.

The sheet of paper that had been holding the notes was on the floor and I picked it up. The rusty gold casket at the bottom of the sea, from the Skeleton Woman story, jumped into my mind, the one with the laminated map at the bottom. This version was a kind of computerised collage that Angelo had had made up, somehow, with a photo of the Luxor Hotel in the one corner and an image of the New York skyline in another, all misty in the background. Right in the centre was the Statue of Liberty. Christina Rae, the Queen of Freedom. Angelo Paulillo, the King of Hearts. Angelo's story-telling voice was whispering into my ear, my heart. 'That was the whole point of the story. She could take just everything that she needed from him and make herself all fat and happy and satisfied and warm, and he would be just fine too. That is what most people don't realise about being in love.'

'And are we in love?'

'Well, I am.'

He must have spent the last of his grandma's money on me and then some. But there was one last piece of paper in the bag, something that had cost him nothing. A poem.

Present

You give yourself to me, free

I take the arch of your foot in my hand
I touch the line of your brow when you smile
Feel your belly, warm, your wishbone ribs
The curved readiness of your body is waiting for me, always
A present

A showy gift at times, brightly wrapped, fun
But I can see inside the gold, see you
Small and plain and shy
And I prefer this

The woody warmth of your hair
The pine-needled wit
And the tree-ringed insight of your words
Are there for me

You give your laugh to me, without restraint
You push away the past and offer me the present
The biggest gift
And I take it

Unravelling the ribbons of my fear
You hold my secrets, safe, inside your hands
You open me
Then wrap me up in velvet and in smiles
And take nothing
I understand how hard you work, to package, to present
How often men have grabbed, without a smile

But you give yourself to me, free

Cost him nothing but time, understanding, and a life-sized piece of himself. 'And take nothing'. How could he say that? The velvet dress stared at me from its hanger, its shoulders slumped. He had always given me so much, always. It was so Angelo, *I could have cried. My Angelo. And how much had I given him? I read his poem again and I thought of the scrappy little one I had given him in the limo that night. All along the line, I had wanted to give, but how much had I really given? I had 'opened' him, yes, but when I'd found his secrets, his problems, his pain, all that I'd been able to do was, exactly like his poem said, wrap him back up again and smile. Useless. Did I have the maturity, the sense, to do anything more for him?*

I folded the collage and the poem up and I put them in my pocket, knowing that I would keep them forever and knowing that I would love them forever.

But what about Angelo?

Better not leave it too late, I reckoned. It was going to be hard enough to begin with. I spent ages getting ready: you know how important clothes are to Christina, appearances in general, really. I had decided not to mention what Jonty had told me, to let her have her silence, her privacy, if that was what helped her most. To hope that she could tell me in her own way. I felt better once I had decided that. I was still feeling pretty edgy, though, as I sat outside her flat, working my way up to knocking on her door.

Half-past seven on the dot and out she walks, all dressed up. Gave me a real shock. I jumped out of the car and ran across to her. She looked brilliant, thoughtful, but brilliant. Her head was down and she was in a hurry.

I kept my head down and my shoulders high as I left the flats; that's generally the best way to avoid trouble, I've found. It was hard not to look up, because my head was in the clouds and my eyes were full of pound signs, one thousand pound signs. And I was thinking about Mr Gold, working out how much it mattered that he was older than me. Just as I thought that, a middle-aged type walked past me – greasy grey hair down to his waist and not a shred on the top of his head – the Y2K+ version of the Bobby Charlton look. A bald mullet. There was my question answered clearly enough.

All in all, I was pretty well distracted. So I didn't see his car. Didn't see him at all.

'Christina.' And at last he was there, stepping out of the Fiat into my path, his face all creased and worried. I couldn't believe it! He took hold of my arm.

'Angelo!' Black eyes and the blonde. Back in business? Not that easy. Then there was the money. 'Listen, I just found the poem . . . and all that money, in the red purse. You must take it back. You shouldn't have given it to me. How could you afford it?'

'I have to talk to you,' he said, shaking my arm now, all energetic and upset. 'Forget about the money – it's not important. Keep it. Whatever happens, it's yours. Can you come back to the church with me?'

'Now?' I said. He must *have known about my date with Mr Gold: Paula couldn't keep her Porsche Reds shut for a minute, let alone a few days. 'I'm meeting somebody.'*

Was she meeting somebody, or was she just trying to save face? Impossible to know.

'Who are you meeting then?' I asked, making myself slow down, keeping my voice really gentle, keeping my temper, my jealousy, right out of my voice. Softly, softly. 'Although I know I've got no business to ask.'

This was a new Angelo altogether. But his voice sounded as gorgeous as ever, as gorgeous and as silky as the lovely dress that he'd bought me had felt against my body. As special as his rose petals had felt lying on my tongue. As smooth as the hundred £10 notes that I had just been counting out in the flat. I shrugged: now was not the time to melt: the spittle in my lap, the torn up tickets, the pee on the Jaguar.

What should I say to him? I had to decide quickly. 'A man,' I said, dead bold. 'Just a man.' I ignored his flinch, met his eyes, and I didn't even want to look away from the pain I could see. Revenge. A new Christina. I wanted to make him jealous, didn't I? Jealous enough to care about me that is, to make it up with me, not jealous enough to go for total control. He wouldn't get away with that one again, ever.

It worked. Angelo leaned closer. 'Ring him, Christina. I'm not telling you, but I am asking you.' I hesitated. His face was so close to my cheek: I could hear his soft voice, feel his words, his breath. Hypnotic. 'Make another date with him for later in the week then, if you have to. But hear me out tonight.' He must have seen me waver. 'You'll always regret it if you don't: you'll always wonder what I was going to say.'

'Not at the church, though,' I said. 'I don't want to go to the church.' It was too full of memories and his dark atmosphere.

'Fine,' he said. 'Whatever you want, Christina. We can just go for a drive or a drink, if you like. It's up to you. Obviously.'

Obviously. I went back into the flat to phone my excuses through to poor Mr Gold. Then I came back out of the flat, I got into Angelo's car, and he drove us right out of Newcastle to a pub in the countryside that he knew from when he was living in that farmhouse. He said it was a place where we could talk in peace.

And he was right. All night we talked, from half-eight or so until way after eleven, that is, and all night Angelo told me that things would change, that he would trust me. He would believe in me. He was sorry, he was really, really sorry. He loved me.

I believed him. I believed in him. And I loved him. Finding the money that he had planted for me just before meeting him again had to be more than a coincidence, don't you think, a message all of its own? But I didn't know whether anyone could change that much. So I still wouldn't go back to the church with him, but by the time he'd kissed me goodbye, we had a date for the next night.

I also, as somebody at the casino was bound to tell him, had a date with Mr Gold for the night after.

31. Angelo's (and the Ice Sculpture) ...

'You're an ambitious girl.'
'You've got a real future.'

That night, I pulled out all the stops for her. The minute Christina walked into the church, I wanted her to know she was special to me – she was everything to me. I wanted her to know that she was exceptional. So I'd racked my brains, emptied my pockets, and I'd prepared her a superb meal. The tarot had turned over the Ten of Cups – 'tender words', the message was, I knew that much by heart. I consulted my book for more information: 'Leave the answering machine on and let someone else answer the door,' it said. 'Talk.' Tender words. And I was sure that Christina would listen to them. I had great hopes for the night. Finally I picked up a surprise for the table from the casino.

I went around to her flat at eight o'clock to meet her.

We got back to the church at about quarter past eight.

The first thing I noticed was that Angelo had taken all the Christmas decorations and the tree down – well, I hadn't been feeling that festive myself lately. But it had started to look all strange again. One doorway was blocked off, badly, with hardboard and masking tape. Some of the furniture had gone, a couple of the old carved chairs, I think, and a big oak sideboard thing, and the pictures had changed. It all looked pretty dismal. Why did I get that awful feeling of going backwards in a train again? Really dismal. And although I'd known how much it would upset Angelo, I'd already stuck a cheque for £1000 in the post for him. Not that I would mention that to him now. No point in rubbing it in altogether.

Angelo had made a massive fuss over the meal. I could smell something soothing, savoury and herby, cooking slowly away in the oven, and the old table was all set with candles and flowers and a tablecloth, the lot. He had his eyes on me, he never missed a trick, as you know, and I was obviously doing a bit of an Ingmar Bergman impersonation, so he tried to cheer me up, handed me some wine and warm bread pieces with toppings on.

'You wait there for a minute, Christina – take your coat off and I'll just get the food sorted out.' I brought her a big glass of wine, to relax her. 'Thanks,' she said, reaching out for the glass and taking a long drink from it. The glass looked enormous in her hand, like a bowl, almost, and she looked down towards it as she drank it, avoiding my eyes. Sixteen, I thought. She seemed so young at nineteen. How had she coped with all that trauma, with the abortion, on her own? I handed her a couple of *bruschetta* with olives on and anchovy paste. I remembered that first night she came back to the church with me, wearing those big shoes; remembered how I'd stroked her feet, her legs. I would have washed her feet with my hands if she had wanted me to. Would now.

Everything was different now, though, I knew that. The church seemed to be making her feel uneasy all over again, but I was sure she would brighten up when she saw the food. I was almost sure. Not to mention the surprise from the casino.

So out he comes from the kitchen, one time after another, all arms and legs and nerves, with plates of chicken breast in a mushroomy sauce first, then a bowl of salad, a bottle of wine, and right at the end, a long china platter of bright, buttery vegetables. When he finally had the whole table ready, out he comes one last time (smiling his head off, but I could tell he was edgy underneath) with this ice sculpture, amazing, just like the ones they had in the casino restaurant when there was a big do on. He must have got one of the chefs there to make it for him. He set it right in the middle of the table. It was a sort of big cat, a lynx or whatever, and it was about eighteen inches long. I half smiled, remembering the magical chocolate shells from his story, and thought about the poem and the collage. Maps. And when I looked more closely, the salad even had petals on it, like the ones on our first date.

I wanted to love it all, to love the gestures Angelo was trying so hard to make for me, I tried to, but nothing *was lifting this heaviness from my chest and eyes. It was awful. I felt different. Everything looked different. He was trying far too hard, I thought, while I was swallowing hearts and flowers again. Swallowing them alive.*

I even saw desperation now in the way he'd left the money and the poem in the purse for me to find. It felt weird. Not weird and exciting. Just weird. The Old World and the New were suddenly too many miles apart. Angelo and I were suddenly too many miles apart. The church was full of his old memories and feelings: his notebook, his dead brother, his answer phone full of unheard messages, his visions, his fear and elation, his frightening extremes of feeling. His loneliness and bitterness. Angelo's needs, always Angelo's needs. What about his father's needs, his mother's needs? What about my *needs? I felt sorry for him, but that was making it worse again.*

I couldn't stand to look at how Angelo was doing. I didn't want to know.

Christina sat beside me at the table and started to eat her food. But she ate so slowly and smiled so rarely that I couldn't pretend to myself that the night was going well.

If she leaves me, I thought, I don't know if I can face carrying on. Maybe if I showed her that I understood the reddest place, the sorest secret – the abortion – maybe then I would stand a chance with her? Didn't I have a secret of my own that was sorer still than hers? I had to try. I had to get through to her somehow.

Losing Christina, I thought, would be the very worst thing that could happen to me.

I lifted my eyes from my plate. I looked into her open, question mark of a face, the curved cheek, and I cleared my throat. 'Christina,' I began. 'The abortion.' I dropped my eyes and then raised them to meet hers. '*Your* abortion. There's . . .'

And then the next worst thing that could happen to me did.

The phone rang.

Who the hell had told him about that? I had never told any-body. That fucking little cough! 'There's just one thing that's bothering me.' *Always just one thing. How many times had I heard that from him? Jonty, Mr Gold, the abortion, the past. No doubt he had a few little questions lined up now. Then, to top the lot, the phone rang.*

And Angelo, of course, didn't answer it. He looked at me and he looked at the phone. Rigid control kept his back glued to that old settee.

'Aren't you going to get that?' I hated *him right then. It took him a while to answer.*

'No,' he said, 'I'm not.' And he didn't move, not at all, unless you can count tensing up every single muscle and bone and feature he had in his body, that is, like he was about to fight somebody. Anybody.

As we sat there on the settee in silence, the phone was ringing and ringing away, making these sad little screams of its own, while 'The abortion. Your *abortion,' was screaming away in my own head, pulling me to pieces. I remembered his mother's*

description of Angelo's birth. Torn. How must all this be making
her feel? Torn. How would I feel if my son treated me like that?
Torn. Worst of all, how would I feel if Angelo treated me like
that? He looked pretty desolate himself.
    Torn.

That finished the meal altogether. I'd said to myself, I'd
been saying to myself for days on end, The next time she
rings, I'll talk to her. I've got to make some progress here.
Just because we've got death on both sides of us didn't
mean we can't fight it together. She hadn't even tried to
phone me over the New Year and guilt was eating me up.
Knowing about the baby only made it worse. Lost babies.
All parents make mistakes and everybody, every adult that
is, understands that, recognises the lost baby inside the
woman, even. But how could I talk to my mother about
those issues with Christina sitting there on the settee beside
me? And how could I talk to Christina about anything? She
looked colder and harder than the ice sculpture.
    It was too much, way too much. I couldn't even let any
of it show on my face, couldn't have Christina seeing me
look weak and upset again, whatever I was feeling.
    I sat there like stone, but everything inside me was
twisting and hot.
    And afterwards, when the chance had gone forever,
Christina looked at me as if I was a complete bastard,
which, of course, I was. I put down my knife and fork,
sat back on the settee and gave up on the food altogether.
Christina put down her knife and fork, got up from the
settee and she gave up on me altogether. Forever.
    She walked straight up the stairs and into the bathroom
without looking back.

The mirror was missing from the bathroom wall and there was
a painting in its place. I went all hot when I saw that and I was
filled up with anguish for Angelo. I knew *he must have been*

writing around it, or near it, but I really didn't want to look, now. Didn't want to see. But I was seeing anyway; his distress was all around me. I looked down from where the mirror had been and saw straightaway that his sink was really dirty. Grimy. Quarter-inch black hairs were stuck to the soap and scattered all around the rim of the sink. This was a new weirdness. However lacking he was in the interior design department, he was always immaculately clean and the church had always been clean too, give or take the odd bit of dust or mess. What on earth had he been going through here lately, all on his own? What had he seen late at night in the dark, and what had he felt? How low must he have been feeling not to notice, or not to care, that the sink was filthy? How could he stand it all? 'The abortion. Your abortion.' *My hands were shaking and wobbly as I washed them. How could I stand it all? I'd already ruined the life of one child, the voice that I pushed away all the time. I owed my children an exciting future. A clean future.*

But what would Angelo do without me?

I sat down on the side of the bath and started to really think. 'You've got a real future here.' *Did I want to be connected to all this terror? To this mess?* ('The mother's house is filthy, you know.') *I'd spent my whole life trying to get away from dirt and I was just about succeeding. And did I want to worry about Angelo forever? Or would I share his fears about mirrors and glass myself, in the end? I'd half shared in it all with him already. Would I share his fears about the future? Share his fascination with the past? Who would* choose *to be married to all that? Christina Rae, touched by the angels. A new idea altogether.*

How could *I stand it all?*

When I went to comb my hair, I looked up at the place where the mirror had been. The new picture, The Dance of Life, *was in the same old blacks and reds. Angelo's paintings, his memories, were so vivid; mine were pastel. There was a woman in this picture wearing a long red dress who looked exactly like me only with reddy-goldy hair, rather than my goldy-reddy hair, and a man with jet black hair, a waiterish suit on and a* very Italian-looking *nose. Sound familiar? They were dancing, the dance of life, I guess,* a pas de deux, *with the man leading. Or was it a* folie à deux, *with the woman following, always following? A woman wearing a white dress, her waist encircled with gold, was standing to their left, 'the wedding woman', I called her to myself, and a woman dressed all in black was standing to their right. It had to be death. The two waiting women looked exactly,* weirdly, *like me. Which version of me would the couple dance towards? I thought. Where would I go? Easy. I would go towards the wedding woman – the gold-ringed waist, the pretty dress, the pink and blue flowers of mine and Angelo's children. And Angelo? He would choose darkness – death, looking backwards. And all the time, the green grass of the painting would be growing beneath his feet. Beneath* our *feet. Beneath the feet of our new family, worst of all.*

I didn't want to stay with him because I felt sorry for him. And feeling sorry for him was starting to get in the way of fancying him. He needed me too much. How many nineteen-year-olds could cope with that, or am I just making excuses, do you think?

I had to leave the bathroom in the end, and I walked down the stairs towards the living room, gazing across at Angelo. The chicken was cold, the ice was warm and Angelo was both at once: cold, white and stiff outside; hot, red and liquid inside. He was still sitting there on the settee, totally poker-backed, and in front of him, the ice sculpture of the lynx was melting away, the lines of its jaws and teeth softening as water pooled into the platter below it like blood.

Angelo couldn't even look up at me.

And if, or when, Angelo's bones were to soften and recede, when his face was mapped and lined, how would I feel about him then? How would he feel about me when his suspicions had hardened to 'truths', some real, some not real? How many of his suspicions would I end up acting out, because his behaviour, or his goading, drove me to it? It would be 'the abortion' now. How many times did he intend to hark back to that! 'There's just one thing that's bothering me, Christina.' *Always just* one *little thing. Me. Could I manage that?*

It was Angelo's voice in my memory that answered my question: 'You mustn't try to "manage" situations like that, Christina . . . That's not what life is about at all.' *And then Mike Turner's voice chipped in:* 'You've got a real future.' *It was like hearing a prayer.*

I never did help Angelo to decorate his church. I had to leave him. I knew it. I had to leave him there and then.

I walked across to the settee to tell him.

32. ... and Mic's

'You wouldn't make me go on my own, would you?'
'Angelo, touched by the angels.'

I can't tell you about that conversation. I really can't. I'll never tell anybody.

Eventually it was over and Christina left. She wouldn't even let me drive her. She insisted. It had been the longest relationship with a woman I had ever had, the biggest relationship with a woman I had ever had, and I knew it would be my last.

My head hurt. My throat hurt. It felt like there was a cancer in me, black cells, hurting, dividing and spreading. Poisoning. There was nothing I could do to stop the blackness spreading, sticking, hardening into its bitter tumours now.

I stood at the bus stop, with all the other invisible people, and I cried. Nothing would stop the tears, not even embarrassment that I was crying in the street. What was embarrassment compared to how Angelo must have been feeling? Compared to how I was feeling myself? Nothing. And I was nothing. What, or who, could I believe in if I couldn't believe in myself? Nothing. No one.

I thought that nothing could make me feel any worse. I

went to bed at three in the morning, knowing I wouldn't sleep. I didn't.

And then it got worse.

The cheque for £1000 arrived in the post the next day.

My dreams were so strange and so vivid that night, I even wondered if I was beginning to be affected in the same way that Angelo was. I dreamed of him, of his intensity, his tenderness. He penetrated my dreams. It was as if he was trying to persuade me to go back to him in my sleep. And he would be so lonely. I woke up once in the dark, frightened, and realised how lonely I was going to be myself – worry over Angelo and just making a living had kept that hidden for too long.

But the next day, I dragged out my diary for the first time in ages and updated my dreams. When your impossible dreams turn into your realistic dreams, I reckon you need to update, don't you? Because La Vita E Bella. La Vita E Bella. *Still.* La Vita E Bella.

And like I've told you before, between me and Angelo, I was always the stronger one. Little Chris Rae from Gateshead was grabbing life by the balls and shaking it, again. Little Chris Rae from Gateshead would be packing her bags, climbing on a plane and heading for America for good before long. On her own. Leaving beautiful Angelo Paulillo behind.

'He's got no future.' After I opened my post, I slept. I hadn't slept all night, so I slept all day. *'He's got no future.'* I didn't eat. I didn't go to work. I didn't think, I just slept. I had to bottom out completely. It was like a death. *'He's got no future.'*

The next day was the fifth of January. Epiphany. The very last thing in the world I needed was to face my dad.

When I woke up at eight o'clock that night, I knew exactly what I had to do.

'Ango. Can we talk?' Mic's voice had been whispering to

me in my dreams, stirring me, disturbing me, and I knew exactly what he wanted me to do.

And what do you know? My date with Mr Gold was at nine o'clock.

I bet you think I'm the hard one now, not just the strong one? I bet you do. But I had to begin my life again and I'd already let him down the once, Mr Gold. It was all over with Angelo; there was no point in letting Mr Gold down as well, just for the sake of it. One problem was nagging away at the back of my mind, though, as I painted on my extra layer of make-up. I knew the casino's jungle drums, Paula's reliable Porsche Reds, would have told Angelo by now that I was seeing someone that night. Chaos and destiny. The words chanted themselves to me as I got dressed.

What on earth was going to happen to me next?

I spent a while getting ready to go out, but every now and then I had to stop, to try to cope with the floods of feelings. Cope with Christina. No one would ever understand me, accept me, love me the way that she had. And yet she loved her dreams as much, her plans to travel to America, to live the life of the films, whatever that turned out to be. She loved herself so much that she would meet other men, I knew she would, and she would move on without me. But I could never move on without her. *'He's got no future.'* It slowed me, exhausted me. I could never move on without her.

Because after the visions come the worst times, the dangerous times, when the fear, the dread, the excitement and the noises leave you. Grey dreaming of black. Dreaming of red. Screaming for red. Alone. And looking forward to death. My death, or hers?

That church felt almost like a womb to me – a place left to me and Mic, where we could be safe. It seemed part of our almost-twindom. *'Come with me, Ango!'* We were twins in life and in death. *'You wouldn't let me go on my own, would you?' 'Come with me!'* I couldn't let him go on his own. Could I?

By quarter to nine, I was hurrying towards the pub where I had arranged to meet Mr Gold. At least I could see to make my way across town on my own, with my contacts in.

I could see too well in one way, not well in another. Every shadow I saw on the way seemed to be Angelo; every dark and downcast head looked like his, until it lifted and showed me the face – the ordinary bones, the ordinary eyes. The ordinary mind. What I was doing, meeting Mr Gold, would burn the last bits of Angelo's heart out of his chest: I knew that. Think how angry Jonty was with me for hurting him far less.

It's wrong, but I almost felt as if I deserved to be attacked that night, to suffer. It had been the closest relationship I had ever had. And I had killed it. I couldn't imagine feeling that much for someone again. I couldn't imagine living with all those feelings again. I couldn't imagine living without them.

Maybe I did deserve to be attacked that night.

Still I breathed a sigh of relief when I got to Pink Lane and saw Mr Gold, Richard, waiting outside the pub for me and smiling. Safe.

Safe. I left it outside the church, underneath the seat in the porch. I knew that someone would find it there.

And I knew that the someone would probably be my mother. I left an extra letter in the box for her to read. I didn't want any blame to fall on her, especially now, when I had finally outgrown all of that.

There had been one more message from her on my answer phone. *'Angelo. I never thought I would say this, but I am glad to say that I have heard from your father. He's worried about you and so am I. If I haven't heard from you by nine o'clock tonight, then I'm coming round to the church to see you.'*

At twenty to nine, I put my jacket on, my head down, and made for the Quayside.

I had no idea where Mr Gold, Richard, was going to take me, but I wasn't surprised when he seemed to be heading in the direction of the Quayside: most of Newcastle's best pubs and restaurants are down there, as you know.

'I've booked us a table to eat at half-nine, Christina,' he was saying to me. 'Thought we could grab a quick drink on the way. Does that suit you?' I nodded at him, not very enthusiastically, I must admit. He took hold of my hand. He smiled. He smiled hard. His hand felt old, dry. His hand felt wrong. When he smiled, he smelled of toothpaste, aftershave and old people's teeth. Sour. I felt sorry for Mr Gold. I felt sorry for me. I felt stiff with sorrow for Angelo. What would happen if he were to see me now?

Just as I thought that, Richard Gold walked into the Stone Lion – and drew me after him by the hand. I nearly died.

Consummatum est. 'He's got no future.' I would cut the throat of our pain. *'A family problem.' 'A genetic thing.'* I had it all planned out before I even left the church.

I just wanted to be with him. It was the flatness, the greyness, the waiting I couldn't stand, the lack of present. Whatever I did, I knew there was no future for me now. I could feel it, right inside. Deadness. Nothingness. That was what I needed to burn away.

I took the oil lamp, a torch and some matches from the church.

By nine-fifteen, I was walking down the curving road to the river. It led me to the Stone Lion, and I looked up at the window to the seat where Christina had sat on Christmas Eve and she filled my mind. The wind was swirling, deafening, my ears were filled with a white-out noise and the buzzing of my feelings was loud. Massive.

There was a massive rumpus going on in the street down below the pub, the noise drew my eyes, and I knew before I looked down roughly what was going on. I knew that he was coming for me the minute I saw the dark head in the street and heard the noises bellowing out and up, above the yelling of the wind. I deserved it. I sat in silence.

The noise stilled.

Angelo lifted his dark, semi-curly head towards the window and his black, black eyes met mine . . .

And I understood at last. Epiphany. She was gone. She'd be getting on with her own life, just as she always had, as she had to, leaving me in the past where I belonged. Where I was stuck. The wind was disorientating me, drowning out the rest of the world, and the sky ran over me, vivid with violet and grey bruises, reminding me of Christina's skin the time that she was hurt. But why do we *always* have to be hurt? Munch's figure running in the redness across the bridge, screaming out his soul to the empty wind. Why does he have to scream? Why? No answers now. Just one more question.

'Ango. Can we talk?'

Mic's voice. At last. I took one last look at the empty window and then I turned away.

. . . and it wasn't him. It wasn't Angelo. It was just a Geordie man with a big dark head, a big open mouth and two big balled fists, reminding me of that first day and the man with the cross and the curled up girl on the pavement in the Bigg Market. Reminding me of Angelo. Why had I thought he would hurt me? I said to myself for the millionth time that the only person Angelo would ever hurt would be himself.

I turned away from the window, looked up at a picture on the wall, and I understood at once. Epiphany. For the second time in my life, The Lament for Icarus *was staring me in the face and this time, it was Angelo I saw there: just like Mic, but with curlier hair. How could I not have noticed that before? Angelo, just like*

*his brother Mic. Angelo, going just where Mic had gone. Cross
my heart and hope to die. Angelo's soft, dark voice whispered in
my ear as I stared at the print.* 'I'll be with him, with Mic,
again. He's not gone.' *My fingers scratched at the surround of
the fireplace that gave the pub its name, as I tried to take it all in.
The Stone Lion. I looked down at the sandy grains in my palms.
Real stone. Real terrors. Not plastic.* Real *lions.*

*I tried to shake the fear, the truth, out of my head, telling myself
that these were nothing but coincidences, and then I remembered
what Angelo had said the night he'd dreamed about Mic, about
not believing in coincidences. Chaos and destiny.*

The beautiful body of Icarus filled my mind.

*I grabbed my coat, garbled something stupid at poor, unlucky
Mr Gold, who was standing there at the bar, looking embarrassed,
with two dazzling cocktails in his hands, and I ran past him, down
the stairs and straight out into the street.*

*I was thinking as I ran, my breathing hard and frightened,
thinking of what Angelo might do and where he might go.
Freezing wind pulled two tears across my temples. A taxi stopped,
thank God, and I jumped inside, wiping hair and rain and
shadows away from my eyes.*

I knew exactly where to look for him.

I knew exactly where to look for Mic – I had always known,
but I had never been brave enough, or weak enough, to go
there before. The place itself was nothing new. It took me
just minutes to get to it, head down in the rainy wind. Not
all of Mic was gone. There was one last place to look. This
was the first time I'd had the courage to face what was left
of him.

My breathing was loud, my face wet, but at last the old
doorway was in front of me.

*My hands pushed at the door as I stepped through the little
porchway. I wasn't looking, I was just thinking, over and over
again: What is Angelo going to do to himself? What might he*

already have tried? Only after I had been knocking at the door, hard, for five full minutes did I step back and see what lay below the seat in the porchway.

I couldn't believe it. The red notebook stared at me from its dark new home, peeping out of the old wooden box where Angelo always kept it. I picked up the box and touched the corner of the book with my hands. Even now, raw curiosity moved me to turn the pages. Who had he left it outside for? What was he trying to say?

And where was he now?

The sound of footsteps coming up the street towards me made me push the book and the horrible old box back into its hiding place. I turned around and walked a few steps away from the church, half expecting to see Angelo standing there and working out what to say to him, when I looked again at a face that had Angelo's eyes. And at the dark man's side was a smart, stiff-looking woman, her face destroyed by stress. Shock, relief and sadness hit me as I realised that neither of his parents would have a clue who I was. It was as if I had made no impression on Angelo's life at all.

But this was how it had to be. With his parents there, he would be safe. I could do nothing more for him now. I never could share in his experiences, not really. I'd just shared in the frills around the edges, but madness doesn't have frills, only holes – holes that I couldn't, wouldn't, fall into.

So I put my head down and I carried on walking. I leaned right into the wind and I walked away from the door of the church and out of Angelo's life. For good.

I was totally alone; I'd always known I would be in the end. My mother or my father would have got to the candle box by then, but I couldn't think about that. If I had been able to stand it all, I would have. I couldn't. I couldn't even feel sorry for them. I felt absent, beyond pain, and the future felt absent too. Pointless. I had always known it was pointless.

My stomach was turning and twisting like my fingers, twisting the key in my hand.

'The key's in your hands, Jeanine. Use it. We're both worried about him.'

'But it's *his* house, Tony. His privacy has always been important to him. He's not exactly the best of friends with me to start with, is he, or with you? You've no idea how moody, how *awkward*, he can be if you cross him. He'll never forgive us if we burst our way in there now.'

'Will *we* ever forgive *our*selves if we walk away now?'

'Let's just have a look through the letterbox. Can you see anything in there?'

'I can see the whole of the living room and right up the stairs. There are no lights on, but the light from the street lamp helps . . . It doesn't look like he's at home. *God*, this wind. The house is empty. Have a look inside now – Angelo will never know you've been. There's no sign of him.'

'What a mess it is in there. We might as well leave it for now. He knew we were coming round to see him. I've never known anybody like him for pushing people away.'

'He's probably still celebrating the New Year – out in town with his friends.'

'And he hasn't even left a message for us.'

My last message from Mic.

The rusty door of the old tin wreck screeched open. It looked black in the darkness, but I knew it was the brownish-red of old blood in daylight. How many times had Mic and I kicked at the fragile metal door that stared at me now, as we shoved the bike in, laughing and elbowing each other on the way? Mic's arms. The metal of the door was peeling like diseased skin where one of my cold hands reached out to touch it.

Walking inside the rusty old garage was like crawling inside the oldest, darkest, reddest tunnel of them all. I thought of Hell and the womb, of dying and life, of beautiful, stinking, decaying Venice, and the thin metal shivered as I thought this. But I put my head down and dipped my way inside anyway.

My torch flashed over a black plastic bag, making the things inside it seem to move. Mic's last things from the hospital were in there; I remembered taking them away from my mum's house and laying them down in the garage. The bike lay right beside them. Touching the Duke was like touching a woman you used to love, years before, the bony angles and the curves.

I sat on the floor and rested my back against the bike. Its mangled, torn fairing was a face, nerves and meat exposed like the poster of the baby in Newcastle with its paper face ripped off. The glossy, red fibreglass to the side of the passenger seat was badly scuffed and torn. I pulled the objects from the black bag, pointing my torch at them one at a time, making a soft pyramid as I went. One shoe, just one pointed, stupid shoe. One black leather jacket. A T-shirt and some torn jeans. A pair of wraparound sunglasses that Mic had loved. A watch. A wallet, open, with an old photo of Katy suddenly laughing out at me from inside it. All of the things that he loved most were there in the grimy garage, which was lit only by the light of my torch now. I rubbed my back against the Ducati and smiled at Mic in the semi-darkness. I picked his leather jacket from the pile, I was so cold, and I pulled the leather, I pulled Mic's skin, around my shoulders. I could smell him, clearly, and I smiled again.

Then I opened up his wallet, delved right inside, and shone my torch on the fistful of contents that I found. There were four tickets to a friend's party that we had been going to go to the night after Mic's accident; I had forgotten about that altogether. There was a receipt for petrol, date-stamped with the day of his death, a bit of money, and one final photograph, of Mic and me in Italy, pulling faces at the camera outside the Sistine Chapel when we were in our early teens.

I turned the photo over in my fingers, put it on top of the pile like a shiny piece of coal on top of a fire, and my mother's face shone out at me in the torchlight, grimacing behind the camera as her finger clicked down automatically, right in front of my eyes.

'I wish I could have seen him with my own eyes though, Tony.'

'There's plenty of time. I'm here for over a week. What if we come back tomorrow?'

'You're right. Neither of us has seen him for months and he doesn't seem to have come to any harm. We'll have a quick look inside, just in case, and then we'll try again in the morning when he's not expecting us.

'It will wait.'

I touch his things, and I wait and I wait and I wait for a message from Mic. I try to make sense of the beautiful Turkish rug, of the story I am telling you. My dark red love story. The wind pours its nothingness through the cracks. There is no message. Is that a message in itself? I get up, creaky with the cold, and open the smooth, secret circles of the petrol cap, smiling at the tiny elephant there, despite myself. I grab Mic's T-shirt, dip it into the tank, pull it out, dripping, and splash petrol onto the pile of clothes and photographs. The garage reminds me of a Romany caravan, and I dip and dip again, until the last of its petrol has dribbled out on to the floor. I smell the sharp, volatile stench soaking into the old carpet and the clothes, and then I add some of the fuel from the lamp, leaving just an inch of oil at the bottom. The old garage is like a rusting iron stove, ready to light – there's even a hole at the top, like a vent – and Mic's belongings form the kindling. Mic paid for the petrol. The wind, myself and the matches are the other ingredients.

I finger Mic's last things, light the oil lamp, and wait.

I didn't even wait to see his parents walk into the church, I couldn't, I had my own future to walk towards. I'm leaving chaos behind, exhausted by it, emptied by it, but am I also leaving my destiny behind? It's a question bigger than myself.

And soon, I know that I will carry on towards my life in America, just like in the films – wide screens, big, big diary entries, bigger dreams. But alone: Kate without DiCaprio. I grew out of that film. Alone, except for a note, a poem, an ancient tortoiseshell hair clasp and a scrap of paper with the Statue of Liberty at its centre. Alone.

And I dread to think what will happen to Angelo now.

What will happen to me without Christina and Mic? Could I ever love anyone else like that? I hear Christina's words again, winding into my mind like the strands of her soft hair used to wind around my fingers. *'You're all that's left here of Mic's energy, Mic's life.'* What would Christina think of me if she knew? If she really knew?

I pull Mic's jacket sleeves around my arms. I smell the leather, squeeze it until it creaks, and I am back there, on the Ducati.

'Mic!' My voice battles with the Duke's. 'It's killing me riding back here. I need to swap around.'

'Awkward bastard! Can't you hang on a bit longer?'

'I've had enough. Stop the bike.'

We're in the centre of Tynemouth now, up a side street. I'm stationary, stuck behind a lorry, have been for minutes. And Mic's behind me, talking. He's taken off his helmet and he's jabbing me in the side with it, to get his main arguments across.

'Think about it! Do you really want to look back in ten years' time when you're an old git with a gut, an exercise bike, three kids and a mortgage, and wish you'd travelled more when you had the chance? Lived more when you had the chance?' He laughs, and I feel his helmet against my ribs. 'Come on, Ango. Think of all those open American roads, not to mention the women. What have you got to lose?' He hums a few bars of Springsteen.

I'm half-listening to Mic and I'm looking in the window of a chemist's shop. My hands are on the handlebars, my fingers are aching, and one of Mic's arms is around my waist. Suddenly, the back of the lorry is in my face. Cornered.

I throw myself sideways without for one second thinking.

Hitting the pavement jolts and bruises me badly and my head, inside my helmet, is banged so hard it rings. I sit up just in time to see the lorry mash the front of the bike. In time to see the lorry move back towards Mic, to see him fall sideways, heavily, slowly and awkwardly, his legs entangled in the Duke. His head hits the concrete, one blow. His helmet rolls like a bowling ball down the street and one scraped shoe lies in the road, next to a piece of torn fairing. The arm that was around my waist is outstretched, the fingers curling in. His eyes are open. Purplish, startling blood pools slowly between his lower teeth and his bottom lip, then drools out. My head aches. Seconds ago Mic was singing. Sunshine bounces off the creases in his leather jacket.

Can we go back? Please? Please? Just by a minute? Is there any way to go back?

No.

Mic's death was my fault.

I need to know what you think, Mic? About Christina, about me and you? Could anyone share your death with me? And what, *why*, is madness? Rage, revelation, regeneration? Can anybody share it with me? Why did I see the things I saw, hear the messages I heard, straight after your death, just when I was so certain that there was no God? What did that prove? Can regrowth follow the Death Card? What do you think?

Nothing. No voices, no lights. Darkness, apart from the torchlight and a circle of light from the lamp. Does that mean that I'm better, sane, or does it mean that I'm dead, like half the rest of the world? Is blankness better than burning? My fingers scrape the side of the matchbox. My fingers are numbing as I fumble at the matches in my pocket. Tiny flakes of scabbed rust shower me like rain.

A white square of paper moves in the breeze and catches the torchlight, inviting me to pick it out from the pyramid. It's folded into four, it's soft, and it smells of petrol. I jump when I see my name, 'Ango', scrawled on the paper in Mic's handwriting, and turn the creased sheet over and shine the torch directly on to it.

There's a colour photograph of the Ducati superimposed upon a map of the world, so that the bike is curving its way around the States on the globe, snarling, eating them up. Caricatures of Mic and myself are running after the bike and waving our arms, chasing it. Mic's done something digital to the photo, so that the bike has a wild, hungry face and big shoulders. I remember him then, patting his pocket and laughing. *'I've got the route planned out and everything. I'll show you it later. Come with me, Ango.'* There's a list of names down the right-hand side of the sheet: Boston, New York, Philadelphia, Baltimore, Washington DC, and more. *'Ango. Can we talk?'*

I smile as I imagine Mic sitting at his computer, compiling this list and grinning at the image of the Duke on the screen, working out how to persuade me to go with him. My smile fades. Mic would be furious if he could see me here. He'd tell me to pick up the map, put down the past and go, I know he would. Is this my answer?

But what about the other questions?

I question Mic more, breathing in the petrol, the leather and his smell. The Ducati digs into my back, as if it's trying to make a point of its own. I question myself more.

What do you do if death is forever? What do you do if you're totally alone, now and after death? What matters then? Is this what I have to understand? That the hope at the bottom of Pandora's box, the map in the rusting casket at the bottom of the sea, are only there to provide for the most immediate, mundane future? That magic and messages don't exist? They are huge, huge questions.

What do *you* think? I would *love* to know what you think.

I sit here in the silent, flaking blackness, finger the oily square of paper in my pocket, and wait for my answers.

Nights later, I see her. A different city, a different girl. Mene. The writing on the wall. I just catch a shot of blonde hair in the street, reminding me of that day with the bloke with the cross, reminding me of Christina, like everything else reminds me of Christina and has done for such a long time. But when she turns her head to me and I see her dark brown eyes, she reminds me of me. Me and Mic.

Still, she has something of the spirit of Christina, sitting in the back of the limo, smiling, sipping her wine, with her vision of the future lighting up her face. She has, too, the spirit of *Beata Beatrix*, with the Ponte Vecchio melting behind her. She is the red-gold girls from the dances of life, the dances of death, the dances of dreams. Moving at last towards me. I'd thought that some of me was dying, that all of me was dying, even, but it was God stretching me and making me grow. I finally understand why there was no last chance with Christina.

Chaos and destiny. Mene. A love story.

Now.